THE GREAT DYING

By Markuss T Notrums

First Published in 2021

Paperback ISBN: 978-1-5272-8716-7

WARNING: The nuclear weapons depicted in this book are based on systems that exist or are in development. These are in no way fictional and the effects of these weapons have been calculated using open-source modelling software developed by Alex Wellerstein at the Stevens Institute of Technology. The reader can be assured that the impacts depicted are very real and have not been altered with artistic license.

CHAPTER 1

Northern Fleet HQ, Severomorsk, Russian Federation

15th March 2044

Stepping out from the warmth of the old admiralty building, he was immediately struck by the cold night air and the crunch of snow beneath his size twelve combat boots. This was a type of cold unique to the Arctic Circle, so cold and so sharp it cut its way through his thick down overcoat, pierced his uniform and immediately froze him to the bone. Alexander Ilya Petrov was used to the prevailing conditions. Born fifty years ago in a backwater mining town east of the Urals, he had endured many harsh winters as a child on his family's smallholding, and then many winter night watches on the bridge of a submarine departing Polyarny on deterrence patrols. Nonetheless, still shivering, on this particularly cold March night, he turned back to look up at the old decrepit building that was home to the 'top brass' of the Northern Fleet. A three-storey Tsarist building had once been adjoined with elaborate masonry, which had later been zealously chiselled off by revolutionaries in the 1920s and replaced with rather crude concrete tiles, which showed the achievements of Socialist Labour. These were now barely recognizable; indeed, most had fallen to the ground. Red and white stone shards littered the admiralty complex, which had become a piece of decaying archaeology rather than the central command of a major naval power. Alexander thought this sad spectacle was a fitting allegory for the state of Russian high command, an oligarchy of old men in their sixties who had grown up in Putin's Russia, and who had now become a decadent yet feeble elite. An elite more obsessed with preserving their social positions, their dachas, their fine-wine collections and wives, who were half their age, than they were about defending the motherland. He knew these men held him in low social regard and were most probably contemptuous of his competence as a sailor; few were as respected by the crews of the submarine service as Alexander. On this basis, he also knew they pragmatically recognized his effectiveness, hence, his summons to high command on this bitter evening. He had not been expected to join the Navy; indeed, due to his height – all six foot five of it – and his slight frame, he had been slated by his high school coaches to be a semi-professional basketball player. However, a chance meeting with Marcus Ulmanis, an old Latvian submarine commander – who occasionally lectured on history at his high school – had inspired him to join the Russian Navy as a tender eighteen-year-old, much to the chagrin of his parents and all of his high school teachers. From his perspective, he thought it had not worked out so bad. Thirty-two years later, he was now a captain (First Class) in the Northern Fleet and, with his new orders, was on his way to his new command. He double patted his neoprene satchel to make sure that the tablet containing the biometrically-encrypted orders was still safely packed inside. As he did so, a more urgent requirement came to mind.

'Where's my car?' he murmured to himself, the freezing air crystallizing on his lips. He would have expected an old Mercedes –

or worse, an ancient Zil – to take him to the heliport. Glancing across from the atrium to the snow-covered boulevard, which separated the admiralty from a series of 1960s concrete high rises, he could see the dim headlights of a car about two hundred metres down the road desperately trying to get traction, see-sawing its way towards him. A few minutes later, the ancient, rusty-green Russian Navy Ural four-by-four came to an undignified halt, slightly clunking the curb as it stopped, much to Alexander's muted amusement. He could hear someone shouting from inside the car, and then the passenger side door opened, revealing a stout and rotund figure of a man in naval fatigues.

'Alexander Vitali, your chariot awaits…,' shouted a familiar voice. Alexander strode over towards the man, being careful not to slip on the icy stone slabs of the pavement.

'Ilya Vissarnovich, you fat, ginger bastard. What the hell are you doing here?' he replied.

'Is that how you greet an old friend these days, Comrade? You know why I am here; I am to escort you to your new steed in Polyarny in a warm, luxurious and timely manner!' he said as the two stepped forward into a warm, manly embrace, slapping the other on the back.

'It's been too long, Ily. Glad you're coming with me on this one. Nice wheels, by the way. Very rustic… Who's the toddler?' said Alexander as he peered into the car and saw a skinny, teary-eyed teenage conscript who had obviously drawn Ilya's wrath at the wheel.

'Oh, this useless foetus… No snow tires, no snow chains, no idea how to drive in the snow… He nearly killed us three times already,' he shouted as he leant into the car next to Alexander, just to make sure the young man knew unequivocally that he was not impressed. It reminded Alexander of how terrifying Commander Ilya Molokin could be to the uninitiated: five feet nothing and equidistant in all other measurements, with a thick ginger head of hair and equally bushy ginger beard. He had been in the Navy for nearly as long as Alexander and had cultivated a well-deserved reputation as a brilliant weapons engineer who, whilst not suffering fools, was a father figure to most of the crews.

'Well, you're not exactly selling the ride, Ily. What are my other transport options?' he said wryly.

'Limited, Alexander. Extremely limited. You could walk the nine kilometres to the airfield and probably freeze to death. At least in the car it will be marginally faster, slightly warmer and ever so slightly less lethal,' said Ilya. 'I've also brought my special coffee to keep us warm.'

'Sold, Commander Molokin. Sold. I'll jump in the back.' Alexander slid the passenger seat forward and hopped into the Ural. Ilya clunked the passenger seat in place and jumped in the front. He leant across to the young conscript.

'Right, what was your name again, boy?' he asked sternly.

'Private Mostovoi, sir,' said the soldier with a nervous cadence, keeping his gaze immediately straight down the road.

'If you start to slide, turn into the slide, not away from it. Because if you spill the coffee I am going to be serving to the good captain, I will offer your services to some of the big lads who load the cargo ships at Polyarny, if you catch my drift, son…'

'Yes, sir,' replied the private, gingerly putting his foot on the throttle. The Ural pulled away from the admiralty building.

Alexander leant forward and put a hand on the driver's shoulder. 'He's only joking… I think,' he said quietly into his ear. 'Keep your eyes on the road; take it real easy. I'll keep the commander entertained.' This seemed to relax their dewy-eyed chauffeur a little.

'That's if we get there alive, Captain,' said Ilya as he glared at the conscript.

'Now, now, Commander,' said Alexander. 'Now, what about that coffee?'

Ilya sighed and began to rummage around in his camouflage-green backpack which he'd stowed between his legs in the front seat. After much clinking, he pulled out a thermos and a bottle of vodka. He nodded knowingly at Alexander.

CHAPTER 2

Arrochar, Scotland

15th March 2044

Just over three thousand miles away to the west, across the Barents Sea and the North Sea, on an equally cold Scottish evening, another man in his early fifties was preparing to leave for sea the following day. Shutting the door of his vintage, jet-black, Jaguar XKR, Commander Richard Blackett RN pressed a button on the key fob to make it lock. He hadn't yet tired of this novelty or this feature, in particular the electronic bleep and mechanical clunk as the doors locked, which was reassuringly analogue in a now completely digital world. He began to walk up his driveway to his small cottage, a two-storey, red-brick Victorian affair, set to one side of a copse on the shores of Loch Long, just off the main road between Glasgow and Fort William. The cottage was a mile or so from the small village of Arrochar, which included his local watering hole, an old pub called the Torp & Blacks. The name was quite idiosyncratic – the pub was named after Torpex, a torpedo explosive developed on Loch Long, and the Black Watch, an infantry regiment which had guarded one of the many nearby military bases. It was also popular with numerous current and retired forces personnel who inhabited this part of the world. Richard recalled a conversation with his partner, Ben, about the 'busman's holiday' nature of their current residence. The naval history of Loch Long, Faslane Naval base – Richard's place of work – was just ten miles to the west, and then there was the 'devil's lair' buried in the escarpment just a few miles west of Arrochar. This had caused Ben particular alarm shortly after they had moved, as he had explained about what lived in the devil's lair. Also known as RNAD – or Royal Navy Ammunition Depot Coulport – the devil's lair was a series of deep magazine bunkers in the hills around Arrochar and Tarbet, which held a very particular type of weapon: eight hundred NATO thermonuclear warheads. Or 'Ten thousand Hiroshimas,' as Ben had not too delicately put it. During the heated discourse that ensued, he had convinced Ben that this was a great comfort: if all the worst fears of the world came to be, they and the boys were at point blank range and none would hurt or suffer, just be snuffed out of existence in an instant.

On this cheery thought, Richard approached his telephone-box red front door. They had no Holistic Intelligent, self-opening door that greeted you as you crossed the threshold, as most did these days, just a good old-fashioned lump of metal. He grabbed the brass knocker and slammed it on the marrying brass plate beneath it, giving his standard four knocks. He heard Ben remonstrating with one of the boys as he walked through the hallway. The door opened.

'Forgot your key again?' he said, in his slightly high-pitched Geordie lilt.

'Eh, yes… I might have done,' he replied hesitantly. Ben tutted and shook his head in mild admonishment.

'Right, dinner in ten. Ethan has been playing that football game since he got home from school and Noah needs help with his homework.' He turned to head back to the kitchen.

His and Ben's relationship could not have been more of a case of opposites attract. Richard was fifty-one and every inch the polished military man: just over six-foot, with short silver hair, a well-groomed, white beard and designer rimless spectacles. Ben, on the other hand., was thirty-nine, five feet five, broad shouldered, with short receding blond hair and a small beer belly. Always a rebel, he typically wore provocative – some would say inappropriate – sloganed T-shirts and baggy cargo pants. Whilst certainly not common, there were a number of openly gay officers in the Navy. Richard had certainly not seen any signs of prejudice in his career. Far from it, in fact. When he married Ben a decade ago, a significant number of flag and senior staff officers had attended the ceremony, along with various crew members from his numerous postings. The Navy had also provided this fine accommodation – it was certainly to Richard's liking – for the family. The boys were surrogates, born to a woman named Siobhan, a close friend of Ben's. Ethan had been conceived using Richard's DNA and Noah with Ben's. Ethan was a typical young teenager – thirteen, precocious, athletically gifted and – apparently – already knew everything. Noah was a shy, but very bright, seven-year-old who liked maths and was obsessed with dinosaurs.

As he entered the lounge, he found both of them engaged in their favourite pastimes: Ethan with his VR specs on his head, playing a football game – no controllers required; this was the age of thought-controlled immersion – and Noah doing his homework – yes, he was one of those weird kids who loved school. He looked totally perplexed at a piece of homework on his school-issued tablet.

Even a few years ago, at least one of them would have come running to him for a hug, but those heady days were a distant memory.

'Hi guys,' he said as he came into the open-plan lounge.

'Hi,' said Noah, not taking his gaze away from his tablet.

'Eh,' grunted Ethan, giving the minimum amount of effort possible.

Richard shook his head, put his briefcase down and sat in his leather armchair.

Just after 10pm that evening, with the kids in bed and Ben outside having a cigarette, Richard went over to his drinks cabinet and pulled out a bottle of scotch. Not just any supermarket dram either; it was a 1992 Isle of Jura single malt. He placed the slightly dusty bottle on top of the cabinet and opened the top cupboard of the wooden dresser. He removed an ornate crystal-cut spirit glass and placed it next to the whisky bottle. Ben had decided he was taking a period of abstinence from booze, so it was scotch for one. He removed the stopper from the bottle, which gave a reassuring thump, and gently poured the whisky into his glass. It was a gorgeous colour, a pale, subtle amber, and it gave off a deep, earthy, oakwood aroma. Clasping the glass, he walked across the room and sat down in the armchair. As he held the glass up to the light, watching the light shimmer through the yellow hue of the liquid, he recalled how he had acquired this bottle. It was presented to him by Captain Peter Newman, a fellow submariner, and his predecessor as commander of the ballistic missile submarine HMS Dreadnought; it had been a gift on the day he became the CO. The bottle had actually come from the officer's mess on the Dreadnought's immediate predecessor, the HMS Vanguard, and was from the year in which that particular boat had been commissioned. As he took a sip, he pondered his latest mission and, in particular, one fundamental concern that made him uneasy.

'Why so many?' he muttered to himself.

Typically, British missile submarines carried a dozen Trident D5B ballistic missiles and no more than thirty-six thermonuclear warheads, the minimal credible deterrent, and this had been the case for nearly twenty years. For some reason, all of the Trident D5B missiles on the Dreadnought, which was currently being prepared at Faselane, were now being rearmed to carry the maximum payload: ten 150kt warheads plus penetration aids. When he had asked his superiors why this was, he was told that he did not need to know. His instincts told him that Whitehall was concerned with reports of persistent violations of the intermediate missile treaties by the Russians, as well as rumours of unusual force movements by the Russian Strategic Rocket Forces. This also explained why he was being asked to patrol, firstly, in the Norwegian Sea, and then further into the Barents Sea. The latter was a piranha pond of Russian attack submarines, away from the safety of the normal Atlantic bastions, but much closer to European Russia. He was further contemplating how he would broach this with Sandy, his Executive Officer tomorrow morning, when he heard the back door slam shut, which was indicative of Ben's usual clumsy manner.

He looked around the living room – the ceiling and walls were clad with wood, which gave a log cabin effect. The open-plan layout was subtly split in two. At the back of the room, there was a dining area with a large, rectangular, oak table with four seats, which backed onto a panoramic window. During the day, it had views across Loch Long. At the front, was the living area, which had a small fireplace – currently not in use – a large and rather faded, leather couch which had ample space for four and then Richard's 'Captain's' armchair which looked out to the front bay window.

He began to reflect on the evening. Dinner had been a pleasant but simple affair, with everyone digging into Ben's industrially-sized homemade chicken Kiev's with chips and peas. Not exactly Michelin-star cuisine, but it was heartily palatable and required little negotiation with the kids. Both were now in bed. Noah had gone with little fuss, letting Richard tell him a bedtime story that inevitably involved dinosaurs. However, it was not the case for Ethan who, apart from saying goodnight, did not want to engage in any conversation, let alone give any affection. This had hurt Richard, although of course he didn't show it. It meant a lot to be able to tuck in the boys as tomorrow he would say goodbye for the next ninety days – a long time for a young child.

He heard the sound of a glass being filled from a tap and then footsteps. Soon after, Ben appeared from around the hallway door.

'Having the constitutional wee dram then,' he said as he dropped down onto the corner of the sofa.

'Aye,' said Richard in a warm but succinct tone. They sat in silence for a few minutes, as Ben fiddled with his smartphone. Ben slowly plucked up the courage to ask something that had been in the front of his mind.

'This is just the usual three-month job, is it?' he asked insistently yet with a hint of nervousness.

Richard had been dreading this question all evening. Ben was emotionally intelligent and incredibly perceptive, so he clearly knew something was bothering Richard. However, at the same time, he could not tell him anything; all his worries and fears were officially top secret. God knows who could be listening in these days and so he had to give the kindest of white lies.

'Don't worry, it's the same as normal. Well… If you call what I do normal,' he said softly. 'If you are wondering why I am a little distracted, it is just some crew roster issues which are putting me off my routine – you know how much I like my routine leading into the patrol… Right?'

'OK… You're sure?' Ben asked. 'There is nothing else going on? It's just that the news channels were saying—'

'Don't worry about what the news channels are saying,' he said, gently interrupting. 'You and the boys are gonna be fine. I am just getting older, the boys are getting older and I am missing them grow up. It's just making me more, well, agitated each time before I go.'

'So why keep doing it?'

'Well… It may seem arrogant, but with the world the way it is at the moment, I don't trust anyone else with the responsibilities I have been given. I won't say more than that,' he said in a low but audible murmur as he sipped his single malt.

Ben let out a sigh in response, before continuing: 'Look, there is no getting away from it. I can only worry about what's happening out there: the war between India and Pakistan – which thank god is over – but all that death, not to mention the radiation. The BBC were saying the fall-out could affect most of the Eastern Bloc's grain supplies. That's where most of the world's supply comes from—'

Again, Richard gently interjected. 'Don't get carried away, babe. It's just speculation, conjecture of a press that hasn't got any real information. Really – don't get me wrong – it's terrible, a horrible mess, but we'll get through. We've had a fair few crises over the last couple of years. We'll probably just have to tighten our belts again – more rationing if it comes to it.'

Ben nodded reluctantly and there was silence for a few moments.

'Did Ethan say goodbye to you?' asked Ben finally, to break the slightly uncomfortable quiet.

'What do you think?' Richard raised his eyebrows. 'At least I got a grunt of acknowledgement.'

'Don't let it get to you,' said Ben. 'You might be getting soft in your old age.'

'Old?' Richard said incredulously. 'I am still happily middle-aged, thank you!'

'Well, since you've adopted slippers, cardigans and a – frankly – unhealthy interest in all the affairs of the royal family, I think it's fair to say you're careering towards a Zimmer frame.'

Richard rolled his eyes. 'Oh, get yourself a saucer of milk.' Even a Royal Navy Officer was not above light bitchiness in the comfort of his own living room. They both looked at each other, smirking and stifling their laughter so as not to wake the kids.

'Well, this old man needs to be up in six hours,' said Richard. 'Shall we go to bed?'

Ben nodded. Richard finished his whisky in a single gulp and both retired for the evening, going up to bed where they lay gently in each other's arms.

CHAPTER 3

Severomorsk Municipal Heliport, Russian Federation

15th March 2044

Commander Ilya Vissarnovich Molokin slammed shut the door of the Ural four-by-four before poking his head through the open passenger side door.

‘Well done for not killing us, Mostovoi,’ he said to the still terrified conscript in the driver’s seat. ‘You shall go far… Now, kindly fuck off.’

‘Yes, sir,’ shouted the young man before he depressed the clutch and gently pushed the accelerator. The Ural pulled away and headed back around to the gatehouse of the airbase. Whilst Ilya had been yelling at their chauffeur, Alexander had been observing their surroundings. To call it a gatehouse – or indeed, an airbase – was somewhat of a stretch. The gatehouse was a lean-to shed and had a metal log burner outside to keep the four-strong squad of guards warm. The squad consisted of three kids barely out of basic training and a fourth, slightly older, adolescent who was apparently in charge.

This gatehouse stood guard on one side of the access road with a barbed wire fence running around the perimeter of the airbase, just a few pine trees littering the landscape beyond to break up the wall of white snow on the ground. Inside the perimeter, there was a pair of hardened arched concrete aircraft shelters – relics from the Cold War – which were empty. They had seen better days, the spalled concrete exposing the rusting steel rebar, which was open to the elements. There was also a small, prefabricated steel hut to one side of the second aircraft shelter, which Alexander assumed was to be used by any poor aircrew that had the misfortune to land here. There was not a runway as such, just a short two-hundred-metre taxiway and four helipads, one next to the two aircraft shelters and three directly opposite. This was a bleak poor-man's commercial heliport, one that Alexander had not come across before and would not wish to again. Only one of the helipads was occupied: by a red Sikorsky Sea King in civilian markings, most likely a toy of one of the local oil companies. Alexander turned to Ilya who was now traipsing towards him.

'Please tell me that's our ride over there, Ilya?' Alexander asked, gesticulating towards the red Sikorsky.

'No, Comrade Petrov. We don't need that western piece of crap. Naval Aviation have dispatched a chopper. It's on its way and should be with us presently,' said Ilya in a slightly mocking tone. Alexander knew that both of them would really have liked the big executive toy.

'Why couldn't we just have had the briefing at Polyarny?' said Alexander wistfully and half-heartedly to Ilya.

'You expect the admiralty to move away from HQ… No, Alexi. The social affairs of our masters are of greater importance, I'm afraid,' said Ilya. 'I also think they wanted to give us these orders in person.'

Alexander nodded. 'Yes, I think you might be right,' he said.

Just as he finished talking, both began to hear the familiar deafening approach of a twin rotor military helicopter approaching. As the rumble got louder, a small, squat, round lump of metal came into view. It was a Kamov KA-25 anti-submarine helicopter, late 1970s vintage, but still a stalwart of Russian Naval aviation, and a renowned death trap.

'Oh, great,' said Ilya. 'So, they are actually trying to kill us.' Alexander gave a long sigh in agreement. Unlike western helicopters, the Kamov did not have a tail rotor; instead, it used gyrocopter principles, with two large counter-rotating main rotors stacked on top of one another. These sat above the aircraft body, which was short and stumpy, flattened at the tail end. The design meant it had good fuel economy – excellent for submarine hunting – and could lift a good payload – so lots of torpedoes and depth charges could be carried. However, it also had a reputation for being slow and unstable, with – as Alexander had previously noted – a truly hysterical safety record.

The rotund chopper circled the airfield once before landing on the helipad closest to the gatehouse, where the two officers were standing about fifty metres away. It kicked up a small blizzard that made them both have to shield their faces. Through the white haze, they could just about make out the side cargo doors opening and a crewman jump out. Spotting them, the crewman ducked under the still rotating blades and approached them clumsily, nearly falling over into the snow on more than one occasion. The man, who was skinny and haggard looking with a black wispy beard, reached them a few minutes later.

'Captain Petrov and Commander Molokin?' He shouted to make sure he could be heard over the din of the helicopter.

'Yes, unless you were expecting somebody else,' said Ilya sarcastically as he gestured to the deserted heliport.

'OK, sirs. I'll take your bags. Please go towards the cargo door and keep your heads down.' They both gave their bags to him – Ilya's backpack and Alexander's wheelie case – then began to traipse towards the Kamov.

Ilya turned to Alexander. 'I am not looking forward to this…' he said.

Almost fifteen minutes later, they were in the belly of the Kamov sat on two uncomfortable steel flip-down seats, each with an almost apologetically-thin veneer of neoprene. The crewman sat opposite, to the right of the now closed cargo door. He had stowed their luggage rather haphazardly on top of what appeared to be a munitions cabinet – Alexander assumed distress flares – to the left. All were now wearing headsets with pale-blue headphones and chunky black fur-covered microphones, which tickled their cold and cracked lips. They had heard the pilots making final preparations with air traffic control and then, with a distinctive click, the headsets switched to the Kamov's intercom. Through some light crackles on the radio, the Kamov's captain addressed the passengers.

'Gentlemen, are we ready in the back there?'

'Ready as I'll ever be,' said Ilya. 'How many times has this one crashed?' he added. Whilst unreliable, the Kamov fleet had a reputation for being as tough as pig iron.

'Oh, just the two...' he replied with a sarcastic rasp. 'For the record, I've never had an incident and have been flying for over a decade. Comrade,' he added, to bring a swift conclusion to the conversation, resisting any attempts to retort further. Russian Naval Aviation and the Submarine Service loved to rub each other up the wrong way.

Ilya couldn't resist one final bite. 'First time for everything, Comrade...' he said as he stifled a laugh, furrowing his freckled brow. He could feel Alexander's glare piercing his skull. Looking across at his schoolmaster-like gaze, Ilya was under no illusions that he was to have no further discussions with the aircrew. The captain, ignoring Ilya, addressed Alexander.

'Is my quieter passenger also ready?' he said.

'Good to go, Captain,' he replied.

'Excellent. Saratov, is the cargo door closed and armed?'

'Yes, sir. Ready for departure.'

'OK, prepare for take-off; flight-time to the Samara: fifty-five minutes.'

Through the gangway to the cockpit, they could see the captain push forward the throttle and pull up the yoke, and with a slightly laboured lurch, the Kamov began to slowly climb into the white and ashen sky. As the heliport disappeared through the window to be replaced with a white nothing, Ilya pressed a button on the side of his headset so that no one else could hear him and then tapped Alexander on his shoulder to indicate that he do the same.

'Did I mishear our friend in the cockpit or did he say to the Samara, not to Polyarny? Please tell me we are not being winched on board,' said Ilya in a confused mix of concern and urgency. His eyes were starting to glaze with fear. Alexander pointed to his bag. He reached down and pulled out the tablet. He placed his finger on the base of the thin oblong glass and the tablet came to life, a pale-blue background appearing with an icon requesting a biometric scan of Alexander's face. Holding the tablet out in front of him, it scanned his face and, within a few seconds, a message on the screen appeared: 'Welcome Alexander'.

He then passed the tablet to Ilya. The tablet had a holistically intelligent nature, so it could tell who was looking at it. For example, if someone was trying to look at it from the side, it would polarize that side of the screen, or if someone was trying to look over someone's shoulder, it would either go into standby or simply transmit the image to the intended person through their smart glasses or contact lenses. After Ilya had been scanned and approved, Alexander then scrolled his fingers across the screen, tapped on the mission briefing and let Ilya read. He could tell from his facial expression and the way he was rolling his neck that he was not particularly comfortable.

'So, is this for real?' he said.

'Yes, but I don't think we will actually need to carry it out; we just need to be ready. There has been a surge in NATO submarine activity in the area, and something might happen… We just need to be ready.' He gave a slight stutter. They both paused briefly.

'So that's why it's so time critical?' said Ilya. 'That's why the Samara is already underway?'

'That's right. Mikhail has set sail and he will be waiting just off the Toros Islet. This transfer has been timed so we avoid American satellite coverage, hence, why we also waited for this cloud cover…'

'How many Krakens are we carrying?'

'Half a dozen, so we'll have a complete set in the strategic weapons tubes.'

'A half dozen! That's an alarmingly high number.' Ilya's face was growing redder and visibly clammier.

'Hence, the three parts to the mission. First, be ready to implement Storegga; second, be ready for secondary Kraken strikes; and third, protect the inner bastions.'

'They don't want much then… What's the immediate plan on arrival?'

'Board the Samara by chopper…' said Alexander. He observed the resigned look on Ilya's face. 'Submerge, brief the other three and then head to Storegga. Then stay on station, monitor movements and await instructions on the ULF channel.'

'You make it sound so simple, Alexi.'

'Hopefully,' he replied, then clicked the side of his headphones to talk to the pilot. 'Captain, how long to the Samara?'

'Just over 30 minutes, Comrade.'

Alexander and Ilya stoically – and in the case of the latter, nervously – waited for arrival.

CHAPTER 4

RNB Clyde, Faslane, Scotland

16th March 2044

Richard's early morning drive to Faslane had been fairly unremarkable, with the exception of a brief moment when the Jaguar had tried to throw itself off the road and into a retired brigadier's pond just outside Armay. He suspected the traction control had decided to stop working again. That was one of the joys of owning an old 'Jag': they were good-looking, quick yet hilariously unreliable. Apart from his minor escapade, the drive on the A814 was as expected, the near-pitch-black and driving drizzle familiar companions. As he arrived at the naval base, formally called RNB Clyde, he went straight on at the roundabout on the main road and turned right into the heavily-guarded entrance. He parked his car at one of the two sets of barriers, one for incoming traffic and the other for outbound, behind which was a two-metre-high set of steel palisade gates. The base was guarded by the Commanchios, a specialist company of the Royal Marines, which numbered about one hundred and fifty soldiers, all of whom were tasked exclusively with guarding Britain's nuclear deterrent. Two heavily-armed members of this elite left the shelter of the adjacent guardhouse and made their way across to Richard. They wore standard NATO camouflage-green fatigues, covered with slightly lighter-green webbing and helmets. On top of their helmets, they both had a set of AR – augmented reality – goggles, which were used to fuse sensor data such as satellite and radar to increase situational awareness, and both were carrying SA230 assault rifles with underslung grenade launchers. Richard opened the driver's side window and greeted the marines.

'Good morning, gentlemen,' he said cheerily as he peered out of the window. He recognized the lead marine, a tall stocky corporal in his late twenties, who seemed to also recognize him.

'Good morning, Commander Blackett,' the corporal said, sneering up at the Scottish rain. 'How are you this fine morning?'

'I am well, Corporal Deans,' Richard replied. 'Usual procedure?'

'I'm afraid so, sir. You might be getting a bit wet.' Richard sighed and, unbuckling his seatbelt, opened the car door. He got out and walked towards a pair of feet that were painted on the ground about a metre to the right of the barrier. When he stood on them, he was facing two tower-mounted cameras next to the palisade gates. The cameras proceeded to scan both Richard and his car in detail and across multiple spectrums. This rather old-fashioned – and frankly, overly-theatrical – procedure had been in place for the last year after the Taranis incident. A green light flickered on the gate, the barrier lifted and the palisade fence began to open.

'All clear, Commander.'

'Thank you,' he said, now rather wet. He got back in the Jaguar and began his drive through to the 'bomber' jetties. The road curved around to the right and then both of the large jetties came into view.

On the first and most southernmost jetty, there was the HMS Anson, Dreadnought's sister boat. Coming to the end of her refit, she was covered in scaffolding, with tarpaulins stretched across her vast hull.

There were four Dreadnought-class submarines in service: the aforementioned HMS Anson, HMS Warspite – underway and training somewhere off the Faroe Islands – HMS King George VI – on deterrence patrol and due to return in the next forty-eight hours – and, finally, HMS Dreadnought, Richard's command, which he could now see clearly coming into view on the northern bomber jetty. The sight of a ballistic missile submarine preparing to sail still struck him with a mixture of awe, wonderment and pride, even after a twenty-year career. There was also something else, another feeling he got deep in the pit of his stomach – not butterflies as such, but something more discomforting and a lot more sinister. A primordial, animalistic fear, like a child fearing the dark, a fear that made him want to run away as fast as he could. But because he had been through so many years of training and indoctrination, he barely gave it a second thought. It did, however, deeply resonate with him, triggering memories.

One memory would always replay itself, every time he saw the boat. It came from thirty years ago, from more scholarly days. Before he had started officer training at Dartmouth, Richard had studied history and classics at St Andrews. The former was primarily led by his fascination with military history and the latter by civilizations and people. Rather than bury himself in the works of Plato, Homer or Ptolemy, he had become fascinated by the ancient texts of the East and, in particular, the Hindu epic, the Bhagavad Gita. Its message of selflessness had inspired Mahatma Gandhi and Jawal Nehru amongst others. It was also known for being quoted – and indeed, often misquoted – by Robert Oppenheimer at the Trinity Nuclear Tests in 1945. However, the quote always rang around his head when he saw a 'bomber' preparing to sail. In the Eighth Verse, Vishnu reveals his true being to the Prince Arguna, a being of beautiful yet terrible power:

'I am death, the mighty destroyer of the world, out to destroy. Even without your participation, all the warriors standing arrayed in the opposing armies shall cease to exist and shall not see the next sun.'

He thought this a fitting allegory when it came to commanding the vast leviathan that was HMS Dreadnought. Her menacing form was now clear in the murky water of Holy Loch. Over five hundred feet in length, ninety feet wide and weighing more than a light aircraft carrier, her form was dictated by physics and fundamentally designed to minimize hydrodynamic drag. She was bedecked in black anechoic tiles, which minimized sound and gave her a shadow of unusual depth and a silhouette of jet-like darkness cast against the ocean. To ensure she could move through the water as silently as possible, her bow had a pronounced flat, pointed slab-like appearance above the water-line, moving to a more bulbous section beneath, which housed her main sonar. This, combined with the triangular-shaped conning tower which rose at the front of the boat, equipped with diving planes the size of hatchbacks, gave her an angular, aggressive posture which was unique to this latest generation of British nuclear submarines. This front section only accounted for a fifth of the submarine's colossal bulk. Immediately behind the conning tower came the business end of the vessel, its reason for being: the missile compartment. This consisted of twelve tubes, arranged in pairs, that descended forty feet into the hull.

Each tube had been fitted with a Lockheed Trident D5B. Each trident missile, hidden in the belly of the submarine, was a slender, checkered black and white cylinder, forty feet in length and six feet in diameter, full of solid rocket propellant. This was with the exception of the nose cone, which contained ten thermonuclear warheads. The missiles would only be revealed on launch, when the five-ton hepatically-sealed container doors, driven by large pneumatic rams, would flip open to the open ocean. If the fateful day ever came, all the missiles could be launched within three minutes – one missile every fifteen seconds – in a cold symphony played with absolute and morbid precision.

On launch, each missile would be catapulted out by a powerful stream of compressed air from a depth of two hundred feet and smash through the waves to fifty feet above the open ocean. Just as the missile would begin to lose momentum, the Lockheed Rotodyne N1 rocket engine would burst into life and, boiling the surface of the sea below, accelerate the missile through the stratosphere, out of the troposphere and, within a few minutes, leave the mesosphere in a ballistic trajectory into low Earth orbit. At its apogee, the nose would separate and the ten warheads, along with an elaborate host of decoys and radar jammers, would descend upon the Earth below. Each warhead would then be pulled down by the Earth's gravity, accelerating to over twenty times the speed of sound as each re-entered the atmosphere. Each warhead would skew to a different target over a thousand-mile radius, each with the probability of hitting within one hundred metres. Some would explode thousands of feet above ground to maximize the destruction on soft targets – namely cities and the people who live in them – while some would explode deep in the ground to destroy hardened targets – command bunkers and missile silos. The groundburst alone would generate large amounts of fall-out, irradiating those areas for centuries.

When the warheads reach within a few metres of their allotted burst heights, a precisely-choreographed atomic tango would begin inside. Instigated by a polonium tube – or gun, as it is called by the weapons engineers – which fires a carefully-weighed pellet of polonium into a depleted uranium core, the nuclear reaction is started, taking only a split second. The core is surrounded by a layer cake of a deuterium liquid, which in turn is surrounded by another layer of heavily-enriched uranium, and finally an encasement of C4 plastic explosives. These plastic explosive charges all explode simultaneously, all focusing inwards, and the shockwave forces the core to contort into a smaller space. The core then goes critical, generating a fission explosion: this ignites the deuterium, which amplifies the explosion by a factor of ten, causing the second layer of uranium to also go critical. This has the continued effect of trying to force the explosion inwards, doubling the power of the total explosion. The result of this fission-fusion-fission dance is an explosion equivalent to two hundred kilotons of TNT or ten times as powerful as the simple atom bomb which destroyed Hiroshima.

At the conclusion of the macabre ballet, in the one hundred and twenty locations where the bombs would fall, over one million would immediately perish in each locale and, within a week, over a quarter of a billion people would cease to exist, those not killed by the blast itself succumbing to acute radiation sickness.

All of this could be started by a single red trigger on a joystick on board the Dreadnought, a trigger that would be in Commander

Richard Blackett's right hand, with one move of his right index finger dictating the fate of all of those people, far away and of whom he knew little or nothing about.

These were the thoughts that swirled around inside Richard's mind on that cold and grey morning.

Now, nearing his allotted parking space outside the main hangar adjacent to the Dreadnought's jetty, Richard began to prepare himself for his voyage. He parked the car, reversing into the parking space nearest the next checkpoint barrier, and got out. He grabbed his hold-all from the boot, then walked in the rain towards two more Commanchio guards at the barrier. He walked slowly, looking around him at the hills surrounding Holy Loch as he did so. The sky was turning a deep royal blue as the sun began to flirt with the horizon and he made a concerted effort to enjoy what would be the last of his fresh air for at least ninety days.

After exchanging pleasantries with the guards and completing an ID check, he was allowed to walk through the barrier towards the main hangar building. The hangar was a large, prefabricated steel building with a distinctive white roof that ran parallel to the bomber jetty. It was the facility's vast dry dock and was designed to lift a Dreadnought-class submarine out of the water to undertake maintenance. Richard entered through a green fire door to the left of the vast structure. The immense hall was full of lifts, hoists and gantries.

The Dreadnought had spent the last month in here having new warheads fitted to her missiles, all of which had been quietly moved across from Coulport over the last several weeks to ensure discretion and secrecy. She had been refloated two nights ago under the supervision of Lieutenant Commander Chris Parks, Richard's second in command.

Now, walking through the vast hall to a small, windowless prefab office known as the 'shed' on the left-hand side of the building, Richard could see a familiar figure lurking by the door. As he approached, he could see it was Chris, still in his standard issue Royal Navy black Macintosh. Chris was one of Richard's protegees. Still in his mid-thirties, he had risen quickly through the ranks and had been one of the youngest officers to pass the Perisher, the Royal Navy's world-renowned submarine commanders' course. As Richard drew closer, Chris, a short and rather slender man, put on his cap badge over his buzz cut blond hair and stood upright.

'Good morning, sir,' said Chris, with a loud formality that echoed around the hall. He saluted Richard.

'Good morning, Commander Parks. At ease.' Richard came to a halt, before saluting. He extended his hand to Chris and gave a firm handshake. 'Good to see you. Is everybody here?'

'Yes. Sandy and Manny are ready for us in the shed. Jock and Shove are making final preparations on board,' he said, now in a much more informal manner.

Jock – or Lieutenant Commander Jack McLintock – was a brusque Scottish man in charge of the boat's nuclear reactor and Dreadnought's Chief Marine Engineer. Shove – or Lieutenant Adrian Shovelin – was a quieter, more reserved man from rural Devon and the boat's Principal Logistics Officer. Both were now leading final preparations on board for departure, tasks that ranged from delicate changes to the power output of the Rolls Royce nuclear reactor to ensuring the final consignments of potato chips and cheesecake were stowed in the galley for the one hundred and forty ravenous souls who would be shortly underway.

Richard and Chris made their way through a flimsy plastic doorway into the shed. The room was set up as a conference room, with a hexagonal wooden table with a spider phone in the middle of it. Sat on the opposite side of the table were Sandy and Manny. Both were Lieutenant Commanders, from very different backgrounds. Sandra 'Sandy' McCall was a short, stocky Glaswegian in her early forties with short brown hair and an equally short temper. When not keeping her team of weapons engineers under strict discipline, she would be busy keeping her two kids and husband in a similar regime of mild yet loving terror. As the boat's WEPS – or Principal Warfare Officer – she was responsible for the twelve trident missiles and two dozen Spearfish heavyweight torpedoes. Emmanuel 'Manny' Sy was a tall, wiry, black-haired man who grew up in the Nigerian diaspora community of Stratford, East London. He had excelled at maths at school and had graduated from UCL with a first-class degree in Advanced Mathematics before joining the service. His abnormally-high intelligence had been identified very early on at Dartmouth and he had been fast-tracked through the submarine service. Along with Chris, he had passed the Perisher unusually early in his career. This meant that, along with Richard and Chris, he was the only other person qualified to lead the submarine through submerged manoeuvres. As the boat's NAV – or Principal Navigation Officer – he was also responsible for the general safety of the boat at all times.

Both stood up and saluted their CO and XO as they entered the room.

'Thank you. At ease, everyone,' Richard said, and then turned to Chris. 'Are we quorate?'

'Yes, Commander. The senior team are now all present and ready for the PPB,' he said.

Richard sat down and removed a tablet from underneath his bag. He pressed the button that would generate a 3D projection above it. and prepared to brief the other three with their orders: how they were going to undertake this latest deterrence patrol. Only the four of them would know where they were going and what they were going to do. No one else on the crew would or could be told. Richard cleared his throat.

'Right, this one is a bit different from normal,' he said.

Chapter 5

Pennsylvania Avenue North West, Washington DC, USA

16th March 2044

Christine Madison sat on her terracotta-coloured two-piece couch and sipped her coffee from her ancient and travel-weary Colorado Buffalos cup. She looked around the living room and let out a contented sigh – she loved finishing work early on a Friday. The so called fun never stopped, of course – her tablet on the small glass coffee table in front of her was already ringing away dementedly with emails from several DOD departments, each sender insisting that their query was of the utmost importance with a big red exclamation mark. None of them realized the futility of these tags.

There was little else in the living room, with the exception of a couple of her prize possessions nailed to the opposite wall – two framed Damien Hirst butterfly etchings – and a small curved smart TV on a cabinet to her left. Indeed, these took up all the available space in what was not really a living room, but more of a small habitation pod with a window looking out onto Pennsylvania Avenue North-West above and behind her couch. There were only two other rooms – again, using this word loosely – in her small apartment, one of which a shower room, with a toilet and wash basin so close together you could sit on the toilet, brush your teeth and wash your feet in the shower all at the same time if you so choose. The other was her bedroom, which resembled a ratings berth on a warship. This room held a small single bed – she was fortunately slight in build at five feet nothing – and a single cupboard – the only storage space in the entire apartment – squeezed into the furthest corner. For this comfortable, but inconveniently small, parcel of real estate, Christine had paid a cool three-quarters of a million, including a twenty percent deposit – most of her life savings and Marshall's life insurance money. It didn't buy a bad location, though, she thought, as she leant to peer out of the fifth-floor window. Immediately to her left was the Washington Circle, a traffic roundabout of barely organized chaos or vaguely arranged order – this view depended on one's prevailing mood – and a long way down the avenue to her right, you could just about make out – if you squinted – the side of the White House and Lafayette Square to the north. This was an ideal location for her current role, a role she had now held for just over three years: Senior Advisor to the US Secretary of Defense. The current Secretary, Frank James Dixon III, was a no-nonsense democrat politician from Arkansas and had been brought in by President Williams to shore up support from the southern factions of her party. Initially, Christine had had a number of reservations about working with him. He was not particularly socially liberal, in contrast to herself, and he seemed to be sceptically mistrustful of the application of AI in war planning. Indeed, he was genuinely uncomfortable with all but the traditional forms of technology – essentially, he trusted anything that required a member of the armed services to manually pull a trigger. However, they had gradually built a rapport. Christine's forthright country-girl-style had hugely helped in this respect and he now respected her honest opinion, when in closed quarters.

Still gazing out of the window, she reached to grab her coffee. Christine had been born forty-one years ago in Breckenridge General Hospital, Boulder, Colorado, but, she was still thirty-nine if anyone asked. She was raised on a farm about thirty miles out of Boulder under the flightpath into Denver International. She always remembered the Airbuses and Boeings darkening the skies above their homestead, casting shadow over the seemingly endless fields of corn in the near perpetual Colorado sun. Growing up, she was part country girl and part townie, academically distinctly average. However, things began to change in her early teens when she showed particularly impressive assessment scores in math, physics and programming. This led to an offer to study computer science at MIT when she graduated from high school, an offer she nearly didn't take up as moving away from her mom and dad would be so much of a wrench. After some encouragement, she went away to Boston and graduated with an upper second-class degree. Initially, she had worked for a Holistic Intelligence start-up and, eventually, became one of leading lights in the country on the use of Strategic Holistics. A few years ago, this had led to the DoD position where she met her future husband, Marshall, and had become the leading authority on the Single Integrated Operational Plan.

Suddenly, the quiet in her apartment was broken by the klaxon-like alarm of the condo intercom. Christine lurched back, slightly startled by the harsh buzz, then gathered herself, putting the coffee on the glass table. She got to her feet and walked to the video-intercom in the hall.

'Who on earth is making house calls this late on a Friday?' she wondered. She pressed the receiver button on the intercom and, on the 4K screen, an image of a well-built young man appeared. He had cropped black hair and was in his mid-twenties.

'Hello, my name is Bradley Kiefer. I work for the NSA,' said the man as he held up an ID card so it could be scanned by the intercom. Christine heard a resounding electronic bell and a text message in green showed on the intercom screen, stating the word 'verified'.

'Mrs Madison, Secretary Dixon requests your presence immediately. An urgent matter has arisen in which your expertise may be required,' he said.

'OK…' She paused. It was not the first time that her presence had been 'required immediately', but the fact the NSA was picking her up was very unusual. 'I'll be down shortly,' she said hesitantly.

'Thank you, ma'am,' replied the NSA junior.

She turned off the intercom and headed back to the living room. She grabbed her tablet and put it in her handbag and then looked at her reflection in the mirror in the hallway. She was still in the suit she had worn to the congressional sub-committee meeting earlier, a simple navy-blue number with silver lapels and a white shirt. Like her, the suit looked a little tired, but it would have to do. She pulled her long blonde hair back into a ponytail, trying to pat down its general frizziness, and declared, 'That'll do, Chrissy. That'll do.'

She opened the door and walked out into the condo atrium, the door slamming shut and locking behind her.

CHAPTER 6

Mezhgorye, Republic of Bashkortostan, Russian Federation

16th March 2044

'Is it over...? No... It still isn't over...' said a short, nervous and increasingly clammy man from the Xian province. He was desperately holding onto the flimsy armrests of the ancient Russian Air Force Ilyushin transport plane as it made another low pass over an airfield that was obviously too small for this type of aircraft. As the vintage Kuznetsov turbofans excitedly surged and the plane began to climb again, Ji-Chow Xi opened his eyes, for the first time in at least twenty minutes, to the dim lights in the shaky and rattly cabin of the Il-96. Peering out of the double-glazed frost-tinted Perspex window to his right, he could see the dark, brooding silhouettes of the eastern Urals, which were shrouded by a thick, soupy layer of low cloud. He looked around the rest of the cabin. Everyone was sat in such a way that they effectively had a row of three to themselves. The passengers were only on this flight because they were under orders and so space wasn't exactly a premium. Ji-Chow looked across at the gentleman across from him in the middle aisle. He was a wide, chubby man of Han descent, with short grey hair and wearing a party-standard grey suit. He was happily chomping away on a chocolate bar, seemingly oblivious to the imminent, fatal danger they were in. The man was obviously a high-ranking party official, hence his girth and access to luxuries. The man caught Ji-Chow's gaze and nodded cheerfully. Ji-Chow hesitantly nodded back, trying, but not managing, to look calm and assured.

Then the dreaded words crackled over the tannoy again.

'Prepare for landing,' said the pilot in a typically brusque, military manner.

Ji-Chow closed his eyes again and began to grip the armrests even more tightly than before. He hated flying, always had done, ever since he'd seen an Air China domestic flight skip off the runway near his childhood home in Xian and plow into an apartment block, killing several hundred people. He had known a lot of those people: friends and family, including two of his cousins. The smell of kerosene and burnt flesh would always haunt him, even in life's more mundane situations. For example, he'd always be careful when cooking meat to make sure it never burnt. If he did, it would only bring back the memories, the tangible, palpable fear of the people, the cries of parents carrying the lifeless burned bodies of their children, covered in white dust and running for their lives from their homes. Their safe havens had been turned, because of a mixture of misfortune and corporate incompetence, into a pair of giant, acrid, funeral pyres, as tens of millions watched on social media in cold awe. Ji-Chow could still taste the emotion, an acidic metallic taste that dried out the mouth and seemed to draw all the warmth from his blood. He hated the smell of aviation fuel as well, but this seemed to have less of a hold on him and, more importantly, at this moment in time, he was more worried about this elderly pressurized cylinder he was sitting in packed, hurtling towards the ground. As a mathematician – at least originally – his logical mind assured him that he was going to be fine.

'There's a very high chance of survival,' he thought. But his primordial ape brain was having none of it and he could feel the serotonin being generously pumped to all parts of his body.

Still, with his eyes closed, he felt the plane banking to the left and descending sharply. He felt the negative G force pull down on his stomach, which made him feel even more nauseous. There was a loud alarming clunk as the landing gear extended for the third and, hopefully, final time. Opening his eyes slightly, he squinted out the window. The clouds had given way and now he could see his doom. His mind began to race. He took away his gaze and prepared to meet the choir invisible. But then, there was a loud resounding thud, the back of the cabin shook and he saw the front of the cabin lurch down. After another thud, he glanced across to the window.

'Oh, a runway!' he exclaimed loudly, much to the surprise of his fellow passengers. The thrust reversers made a perversely pleasing sound as the aircraft slowly came to a taxiing speed. It did not take long for the Ilyushin to move to the single stand on the extremely austere airstrip. After ten minutes or so, a set of stairs arrived, along with a small cadre of troops in a ZIL open-backed truck. Looking through his porthole, Ji-Chow could see the troops were all wearing blue and white striped shirts under their fatigues, which indicated they were special forces, most likely Russian airborne Spetsnaz troops – not surprising when the sensitive nature of the location was considered.

Forming an orderly queue, the thirty or so Chinese officials began to file off the plane and onto the cold tarmac below. Ji-Chow stepped down the steel staircase and joined his colleagues. The Spetsnaz cadre was their escort, it seemed, and the Chinese delegation was awaiting their transport. It was an unusually warm day in the later winter of the Urals; it had just gone noon and the thermometer had just passed five degrees Celsius and so, whilst cold, it was still bearable, as he stood on the tarmac in his beige, leather, fleece-lined jacket, chinos and black loafers.

From where he stood towards the back of the group, he felt a large, gloved hand grab his right shoulder. Turning around, a little startled, he saw the large, plump man from the flight.

'Ji-Chow Xi…?' he enquired.

'Ah, yes…' he replied hesitantly.

'I've heard a lot about you… I am Major-General Xhang,' he said, removing his hand from his shoulder and extending it to shake Ji-Chow's. The general's handshake was firm but not aggressive. Ji-Chow was a little surprised and honoured. General Xhang was the deputy commander of the PLA's strategic rocket forces with direct access to the Central Military Commission in Beijing. He was even rumoured to have the right ear, if not also the left ear, of the chairman. Ji-Chow had also learnt that the general was the underwriter and de facto project director for most of this work.

'It's good to put a face to a name, young man,' he said in a thick, guttural Manchurian accent. 'Excellent work so far.'

'Thank you,' replied Ji-Chow. 'I have to say I am surprised—'

'By what?' said the general, cutting him off before he could finish.

'Well, I'd have thought they would have laid on a private jet and car for someone of your stature,' he said, realizing too late that he may have accidentally made a faux pas with his choice of words, referencing to the general's considerable girth. Fortunately, he seemed to get away with it.

'Desperate times, desperate measures,' said the general. 'Besides, there wasn't time, once the threshold had been crossed. Also, these ghost-skinned assholes won't let any of our planes fly in here for security reasons, which is desperately ironic.'

'Why's that, General?' asked Ji-Chow.

The general leant in and whispered in his ear. 'We're the poor bastards paying for this. They are, as the Americans say, completely damn broke.'

They were interrupted by the clackety arrival of a black bus, which looked as if it had recently returned from a school trip to the 1960s, with plumes of diesel smoke coughing out of a broken exhaust. Three of the Spetsnaz guards headed to the passenger doors: two of which were armed with AK-74s, the other, a sergeant, a tablet.

'Oh, excellent. One final indignity... Get ready for a security check. I'll go behind you, if that's alright,' said the general. The two dozen or so dignitaries made their way, one by one, through the checks. All could speak Russian fairly fluently, so the process was fairly smooth as the guards checked bags and papers.

It was now Ji-Chow's turn. His Russian was good, but he was nervous and the guards could see this.

'Papers please,' barked the sergeant. Ji-Chow retched slightly at the smell. The middle-aged man's halitosis was incredibly strong and it began to permeate into his nostrils. He removed a small, leather wallet which contained his military ID and flipped it open to show the soldier. The grizzled sergeant leant forward and then checked the face and description against the tablet.

'War planning. So, you're the skinny little mice who decide how lions like us die?' he said in an accusatory tone. Ji-Chow didn't respond, just issued a cold nervous stare back at the soldier. The sergeant huffed and grunted, scowling at him.

'Open the bag… Mr… Xi,' he said aggressively. Ji-Chow complied and unbuttoned his large, leather shoulder bag. The soldier rummaged through and pulled out a large brown bottle of pills. Unable to read the Mandarin on the bottle's side, he asked, 'What's this? And don't lie – I can tell.' His eyes turned to daggers, piercing Ji-Chow's own gaze. It was as if he already knew what the pills were.

'SEPS,' said Ji-Chow.

'SEPS… Been throwing your yellow dick around, have we? Boys, we have a parasite… I think the camp medics are going to enjoy poking you around…' he said as a disturbing manic glee crossed his face. The rest of the delegation, now sat on the bus, began to get agitated and Ji-Chow could see that an animated discourse had begun between them. The two younger, fresh-faced commandos next to him began to move forward to grab the young man, but a large, gloved left hand came over his right shoulder and grabbed the feral sergeant by the front of his shirt collar. The sergeant's eyes flared with rage.

'What the fuck do you think you're doing, fat man?' he exclaimed, now directing his ire solely to the general, who now was by Ji-Chow's side. Both of his underlings grabbed their assault rifles. He could hear the click as they switched off their safety catches.

'Tomsk… Irkutsk… Which do you prefer?' said the general in a steady and stern tone.

'What?' The Spetsnaz sergeant was now furiously confused, his brow creasing and his cheeks reddening.

'You heard me, man. Tomsk? Irkutsk? Where would you prefer to be a liquidator? Remind me what it does to one's life expectancy cleaning up all of India's fall-out?' said the general, his voice now raised to a harsh authoritative rasp. He pushed his ID card into the sergeant's face. 'Now, get out of our way or I will personally speak with the District Commander and, within a year or so, you will be on some god-forsaken hospital bed in the rural Siberian cold with your hair falling out and your skin peeling off like flakes of salmon.'

The sergeant's face had now changed from a dark red to a pale white.

'Just to make sure my Russian is good enough,' the general added. 'Please confirm you understand by saying, "Yes, Major-General, sir."' There was a brief silence. The general now moved in front of Ji-Chow. He pushed his face to the side of the sergeant's, bringing his mouth right next to his right ear. 'I said, now! You insubordinate little fuckwit!'

The sergeant, now shaking slightly, finally caved.

'Yes… Yes, sir!' he said, motioning to his men to move out of the way to clear a path onto the warm bus.

The general turned to Ji-Chow.

'Turns out my Russian's not so bad. Mr Xi, after you…' he said with a faint wry smile as he ushered Ji-Chow to the doors of the bus.

CHAPTER 7

Washington DC, USA

16th March 2044

Christine got into the back of the black DoD hybrid SUV, which the driver had parked haphazardly outside her condo block. Unlike most other departments who had either gone fuel-cell or full-electric, the DoD had stubbornly stuck to big hybrids, those with a V8 diesel in the front and a small hybrid motor at the back. When Christine had questioned why, various staffers had simply said they needed the 'resilience' of a combustion engine to survive any electronic or cyber-attack. She was not convinced by this assessment; to her, it just seemed to be a very large collection of middle-aged boys' toys. Nonetheless, she did like the ride and the interior of this Ford, which had lots of leather – hopefully not real, but again, you never knew with the DoD – and light-blue ambient lighting.

She and Mr Kiefer had been on the move a few minutes now, having just negotiated the chaos of the Washington Circle, and were now headed south of 23rd Street, the beige concrete and glass façade of the George Washington Hospital filling their view to the right. In the front of the car were the standard pair of ex-military meatheads. She didn't mean this disrespectfully – she was sure they had served the country with the highest degree of diligence – but it was just the way these guys had been suited and booted. They were both hugely built, probably ex-marines, in standard black and white suits, buzz cuts and shadow-black wraparound Oakley sunglasses. Looking to her left where Mr Kiefer sat next to her, she noted the juxtaposition: the frighteningly young NSA attaché was looking more than a little nervous. She looked him up and down subtly. He was a tall, slender blond with a carefully sculpted side parting and a freckly baby face – although anyone under thirty was looking young to Christine these days. He was the epitome of the phrase 'fresh out of college'. He wore an ill-fitting grey suit, matching waistcoat and a crimson red tie.

'Definitely bought off the peg at Macy's... Possibly by his mommy,' she thought. It appeared that she might be in a slightly patronizing frame of mind today.

She was also sure he was not the usual staffer type; she could tell he was a specialist of some kind. She tried to make her gaze as warm as possible and made eye contact.

'Mr Kiefer, is everything alright?' she said, emphasizing her mid-western drawl, which had been said by some to feel more comforting.

'I'm fine, ma'am. Ah, really,' he said, fidgeting and averting his gaze back to his passenger window. She noted he spoke in a neutral North-West accent, so he was probably originally a New England or New York state native. He probably hadn't ventured far for college.

'What do you do, Mr Kiefer?' she said, persisting but adding more of a clinical urgency to her tone.

'Ma'am?' he said, seemingly confused by the enquiry. She smiled.

'What do you do at the NSA?'

'I am an analyst, ma'am.' Good, he was now at least meeting her eyes.

'Specifically?' she asked. He hesitated. 'It's OK, you already know I have Phi-Black clearance. There is nothing you can't tell me unless the Secretary has said anything to the contrary.'

'OK, I am a specialist analyst tasked with being an SME on all strategic weapon systems for the Eastern Bloc,' he said, his words coming out like a nervous rapid crescendo.

'Mr Kiefer, if you don't mind me asking, how old are you exactly?' she said softly, trying to avoid any hint of prejudice which is inevitably implied by such a question.

'Well, I am twenty-eight,' he said. She noticed he had dropped the 'ma'am' suffix and so was probably agitated by her enquiry. 'I have spent the last year studying everything on their delivery systems both on the Russian and Chinese side and also tactics… And trust me, I remember everything.' This confirmed what she suspected: probably a high IQ, excellent memory, almost certainly obsessive in every detail, combined with a razor-sharp logic. She would soon test this out. This boy would make the perfect analyst; it was the only reason that anyone could be a Subject Matter Expert at such a young age. On this basis, they were probably going to get along.

'It's OK… What is your first name again?' she said, leaning on the warm extended vowels of her rural upbringing.

'Bradley, ma'am,' he said, now maintaining her gaze.

'Well, Bradley, I think you and I are going to get along just fine. My name's Christine, by the way. Please don't call me ma'am. I ain't a grandma, am I?' She raised her eyebrows and widened her stare.

'No, ma— I mean, no. No, you're not, Christine,' he said, a small smile now creeping across his face.

'Good. That's better. Have you ever been to the Pentagon before, Bradley?'

'No… First time. I'm normally based in Albuquerque.'

'Well, you're in for a treat,' she said dryly as she looked back out of the window. As the SUV passed down 23rd Street, the sun, now very low in the late afternoon sky, was blocked out by the low-storey silhouette of the state department on their left-hand side. Every time she passed the building, it always put her into a sombre mood, although it was getting better with time. It had been a dark winter's day last year when she had last seen her late husband, Marshall, and it hadn't been on the best of terms. In the morning, they'd had an argument at their apartment about something mundane – money, drinking, Facebook posts, probably a combination of all of these, but she couldn't really remember. They had then seen each other briefly across one of the many open-plan upper floors of the state department, all of which had the glass walls now ubiquitous in government office buildings. After leaving one of her meetings, she had noticed three missed calls on her phone and a voicemail, all from Marshall. She had opened the flexiscreen smartphone and held it to her ear to hear Marshall's low Kentucky baritone.

'Hey babe, it's me… I am in a motorcade with the Secretary. We are boarding a plane to Delhi in the next hour to try and diffuse this thing before… Well, before you know what could happen. Look, if you can't call back, don't worry… I'll call you when I land… Speak soon.'

That was the last she had heard from Marshall. The plane never arrived in New Delhi. No one knew exactly what had happened – no real records survived the war. It had been the same day that a skirmish in Kashmir, which had started over fresh water supplies, brutally escalated into an all-out nuclear exchange, a day that hundreds of millions died. She had, however, managed to get sight of a semi-official report at the DoD. The plane, a US Air Force Boeing 787, had been over the Arabian Sea, not far from the Pakistani coast, when it was shot down by a long-range surface-to-air missile.

As the car crossed the Memorial Bridge and the turbid effluent brown Potomac River below, she felt herself welling up at the memory. The car went down the off-ramp onto the Richmond Highway and they passed Arlington Cemetery. She began to very slightly tear up as she remembered Marshall's funeral. It had been just before Easter, filled with all the dark pomp and circumstance. She sniffed, dabbed her eye and regained her composure. She saw Bradley look across at her and she shot him a brief rapier-like glance to make sure he continued to avert his gaze.

The giant grey and black walls of the Pentagon building came into view in the distance on their right, casting an eerie, sinister shadow against the sky, like some ancient monolith. They passed the giant staff car park to the left and then, much to Christine's surprise, they did not take any of the various turn-offs, instead continuing their way to the main entrance to the Pentagon. As they approached, she first noticed a Black Hawk helicopter on the building's main helipad, a large concrete rostrum at the end of the green-lawned avenue that led away from the main building. She also noticed two figures dressed in military uniforms, one in air force blue and one in army green, waiting outside the main entrance.

'Well, this is a first for me, Bradley,' she said.

'What's that?' he replied.

She drew in a deep breath and said, 'I've never had a welcome committee at the main entrance before…'

'What does that mean? I mean, what's happening?' the young man stuttered.

'We will soon see, Bradley. We will see…'

As the SUV came to a halt in front of the welcome committee, adjacent to the Pentagon's main entrance, the silent DoD juggernaut of a man in the passenger seat got out and went around to open both of the back doors. Stepping out of the car and walking around the back of the vehicle, Christine could see that both military men were both relatively senior types, specifically colonels, so they were likely to be senior staff officers working for the joint chiefs. As she approached, the tall grey-haired air force colonel saluted and greeted her.

'Mrs Madison and Mr Kiefer, I presume,' he said, smiling.

'Yeah, that's us,' she replied, nodding towards Bradley who was trying not to stare at his shoes.

'Colonel Schwartz, Strategic Air Command and my colleague, Colonel Myers, US Army General Staff,' he said, gesturing to the man next to him as he introduced him.

'Ma'am, sir,' said the other colonel as he nodded to both her and Bradley.

'Secretary Dixon and his staff are in the basement waiting for you,' said Colonel Schwartz.

'In the basement?' she asked as she pointed in a downward motion at the Pentagon building.

'Ah, no, ma'am. Not that basement, the other basement,' he said, pointing towards the Black Hawk, its rotors now whirring on the helipad.

'I see. Well, it's going to be a day of firsts. Bradley, ya been in a chopper before?'

CHAPTER 8

Mezhgorye, Republic of Bashkortostan, Russian Federation

16th March 2044

After a Russian army officer had remonstrated with the highly agitated Spetsnaz sergeant, who, from what Ji-Chow could see, had been unceremoniously sent back to a barracks, the Chinese delegation was allowed to get underway. Now sat down on the uncomfortable patchwork leather benches of the Russian army bus, they passed through two manually-operated checkpoints on the perimeter of the airfield, the old diesel bus slowly chugging its way through a self-generated haze of black smoke. The bus began to make its way along a wide gravel road, which wound its way through a pine forest into the mountains beyond. Ji-Chow noticed a small town through a clearing in the frost-bitten pines, consisting of mostly small single-storey wooden buildings, some made of weathered blue boards and others in a pale red, all of which had seen better days.

The general, who was sat in front of Ji-Chow, turned and saw where he was looking.

'That's Mezhgorye, if you are wondering… Looks bleak, doesn't it? I've seen more attractive nomadic yurt settlements in Mongolia, to be honest with you,' he said disparagingly.

'Looks like a harsh existence,' replied Ji-Chow.

'That's good, from the looks of the prevailing standards around here. It's a closed military town and gets just about everything it needs to survive,' said the general. 'That would be where your bellicose, red-nosed friend was from. Proud people, Mr Xi. Even the military is being forced to just about manage.'

'It would explain the welcome. Places like that must be full of anger and contempt.'

'History always repeats; the people march to a demon's beat,' he said, still looking stoically out of the window.

'Is that a quote? Can't say I've heard it before,' Ji-Chow said.

'Yes… Me, about five seconds ago. I am getting worryingly poetic in my old age,' he said. Both exchanged a smirk.

'The rise of nationalism?' said Ji-Chow.

'The rise of extremism, in more general terms, Mr Xi. It doesn't matter if it's far left or far right; it's essentially the same. When people fall on hard times, they look for blame; that's natural. After all, the situation is rarely their fault – or, at least, not directly. Then, as has always happened throughout recent times, politicians enter the fray and, like sycophantic vultures, they vie to be the focal point of that anger. The more extreme the debate gets, the greater the anger, the more intense the vitriol, until eventually the most extreme voice wins out, because they make all the other voices seem weak and feeble by comparison. The problem is that once the extreme voice, the loudest polemic, becomes dominant, there is only one inevitability,' he said, the volume of his voice rising in an oddly eloquent crescendo.

'Hatred?' said Ji-Chow, once Xhang had finished.

'Yes, but specifically: that politician, the one who becomes dominant, they must become a single-minded demon, grasping that hatred and all that associated malevolence, directing it in a highly-controlled torrent of aggression against any poor unfortunate they deem to be undesirable. They do this by drumming – a four/four beat made of mantra, slogan, dogma and half-truth – a drumbeat which leads to a march, a march that turns their anger to fear, a fear of being like the undesirable. This fear can lead otherwise reasonable, common people to persecute, torture, mutilate and even kill their neighbours. The violence accelerates in a runaway reaction until the undesirables are no more. Then the demon thinks of another beat, another song for them to sing, before their hordes are able to break out of the spell and direct the fire back at the demon. It's happened time and time again: persecution, forced correction, torture and inevitably the deaths of thousands, millions, even tens of millions… The pogroms of medieval Europe, the Nazis, Stalin's Russia, even what our comrades did to the Uighurs… It's happened time and time again. And so, Mr Xi, history always repeats and the people will always march to the demon's beat.' The general paused and looked around. His philosophical monologue had drawn uncomfortable eyes from some of the other passengers.

'Well, I agree,' said Ji-Chow quietly. 'Our Russian friends have certainly decided that a lot of people are undesirable, helping the administration to hold on.' He said the last part in a whisper.

'Quite,' said the general. 'But not for long, as you know, Mr Xi. That's why some of the pieces are already moving. As you know, we have maybe six months at best before a great famine, desperate times and even more desperate measures.' He looked at the eavesdroppers with a vicious scowl, all of whom quickly glanced away, busying themselves by looking into their laps.

Several things had struck Ji-Chow about the general. Firstly, his warmth towards him. He found that PLA officers, particularly the very senior ones, had little time for scruffy young mathematicians like he, or indeed, any young men who thought for themselves. Secondly, there was his sense of humour. Concepts of irony, sarcasm and satire were actively discouraged in the higher echelons of the party and particularly the top brass, so by comparison, the general was positively flippant. Thirdly was the thing that was most worrying for Ji-Chow: his openness, candour and the caustic acidity in his words. From what he had seen with the encounter with the Spetsnaz guards, he could tell that this was a man who no longer seemed to be worried about the consequences of his actions or the impact of his words – case in point: the smattering of loyal party members who surrounded them on the bus. This was a man who knew that the current order of things was going to change and that the world was about to schism. This was a man who was preparing for his potential end.

Ji-Chow's stomach turned and his head ached at this thought about this. He knew as much as the general did about their potential destination and, as a cold sweat started to permeate his skin, he decided to give it no further thought. In any case, his ruminations were disturbed by his head suddenly banging against the glass of the bus window. The vehicle had suddenly lurched about on its primitive leaf-spring suspension as it made its way over the brow of the hill, of the gravel track.

They soon turned onto a tarmac road. Gone were the pine trees and instead, either side of the road gave way to grey granite rock faces which got steeper and steeper, rising into great edifices. Directly in front of them, at the bottom of the road, there was an enormous granite façade, a sheer face, rising vertically upwards for many hundreds of metres to the summit. In the faint winter sun, it appeared as an ominous pyramid with no trees, no shrubs, no vegetation of any kind, just a grey, lifeless north face, which cast a vast shadow over the surrounding forests. At the base of the façade there appeared to be the entrance to a long dark tunnel, the rising granite edifices on either side of the road rising to meet the vertical facade about one hundred metres or so above the tunnel entrance. It presented an ominous vista, a great narrowing channel of granite leading into the forbidden bowels of the earth. The view made him feel an unusual, irrational fear and he sensed a palpable feeling of dread, the sort of dread he had not felt since he was a child. It was like seeing a monster at the end of the bed, as though the mountain was attempting to paralyze him, to contort and subvert his will. You could almost call it an evisceration of the soul. The ill-feeling grew as they approached the mountain.

The general turned to him, once again.

'There is something unearthly about this place, isn't there?' he said, ducking slightly so he could see the mountain top.

'Yes, there is,' he replied coldly.

'Devil Mountain, that's what it translates to in the local Baskiri… In their folklore, it is the source for all the world's evil.'

'What?'

'Yamantau. Mount Yamantau. Most people would leave it alone, but not the Russians. No, they've been digging beneath it like demented squirrels for the past forty years and they've only just finished.' He gave Ji-Chow a wry smile.

As the bus approached, Ji-Chow could see a heavily-guarded checkpoint at the tunnel's threshold, beyond which was a steeply-falling road into the faintly-lit abyss of the mountain dark. In the shadow of the devil mountain, Ji-Chow stared deeply into the dark chasm that would be his home for the foreseeable future.

CHAPTER 9

Brighton Crematorium, Brighton & Hove, England

16th March 2044

Laura Ford waited patiently outside the small blockwork reception building of Brighton Crematorium. She was not sure how many would come; her mother had not been the most gregarious of characters and had kept her company to a select few. Laura was dressed in the traditional shadow-black of mourning – after all, Mum had always been traditional, in this respect. She wore a simple long, black dress with a full-length black, woollen overcoat to protect her from the March cold, adorned with a silver brooch – one of her mum's – and a pair of plain flat black shoes. She worried that it looked tatty; everything was more than a few years old and all had been bought from charity shops. Then again, this was the new normal. The 'slight recessions' – as the government insisted on calling it – were now nose-diving into a full-blown depression and, quite simply, if you had any disposable income at all you were considered rich. Laura had used most of her savings, pooled together with that of her sister Karen, to pay for the cremation. Neither Karen nor she wanted a pauper's burial for Mum, but unfortunately, this was now commonplace. Most had to pay for the care of loved ones either by equity release or by selling the family home. The latter was the case for the majority. Most who could afford it were in negative equity after the double hammer blows of the mass building of council houses saturating the market, followed by the recession with high interest rates. After today, both Karen and she would have little left in their savings. Nevertheless, whilst resentful about the circumstances, she was hoping to soon be at peace with her mum.

As all of this rushed through her mind, an icy gust of sea air blew through the tree-lined park that surrounded the crematorium, shearing across her face like a cold slap and drawing a couple of tears from her eyes. She quickly dabbed these away with a crumpled tissue she had been holding. She wasn't going to let her mascara run just yet, although that, of course, depended on whether any tears would appear at all today. Laura had always had a tremendous ability to remain calm and collected; she was the rock of the family. Sometimes, this could be mistaken for coldness, possibly lacking empathy, and at other times, she seemed remote, more than a little distant. She sometimes wondered whether there was something wrong with her – a surgeon's malady, a want of feeling – as she never cried when she was supposed to and had never been one for histrionics. This was in complete contrast to her sister. A short sinewy lady in her early fifties, Karen loved a drama and loved being the centre of attention, the emotional monopoly in any given social situation. The contrast was complete by the physical juxtaposition, since she was short, stout and as round as a beer barrel. Laura was sure that today Karen would be in a full overdrive for most, if not all, of the entire ceremony. In fact, the most emotionally-stable contingent was likely to be Laura and her own kids, Nicholas – now perennially, Nick – a shy seven-year-old and Charlotte – who, as of last month had decided she preferred Charlie – an almost feral five-year-old tomboy. They were coming with her estranged ex-husband Rory who had had them for the weekend. As one could imagine, she was not particularly looking forward to small talk. The divorce had taken far too long and had been every bit as vicious as the revelation of his near-decade-long affair with a younger woman who was remarkably self-absorbed and seemingly devoid of all aspects of intelligence. She thought it was a miracle the woman could fathom out how to breathe, which was a pity, because as such a vacuous and superficial lifeform, it was a tragic waste of perfectly good oxygen. Nonetheless, she would be civil.

'Well, mostly civil,' she thought. It was just another free radical in a worryingly eclectic mix of wraiths and strays that were the Jones family.

She noticed the first pair approaching along the shingle path from the car park: Karen – she could already hear the sobbing – and her partner, Billy. Billy was what some would politely, and diplomatically, call an 'interesting character'. Others – the majority of the adult population – would describe him as a comically drunk, old-fashioned misogynist who had become more of a self-caricature as he had hurtled through and past the middle of life. As they approached, it was obvious that Billy had been drinking, probably in the Bear Inn, which was across the road from the crematorium and the venue for the wake. The tell-tale sign of Billy's inebriation was his gait – he was walking with a slight leftward list and seemed to be hammering his right foot into the ground every time he took a step. This was most probably part of his attempt to not look pissed at eleven-fifty in the morning. The pair were now in earshot and she could now hear Karen clearly.

'Oh Laura, it's good to see you,' her sister said in her thick estuary twang, which was staccatoed by the sobbing.

'Hello, love,' she said calmly in a quiet voice as they hugged. Karen clamped her in a vice-like embrace that seemed to last minutes. She released her from her clutches, and then came Billy.

'Hi, Laura,' he said, the unpleasant odour of cigarettes and cheap red wine – which also stained his thin, chapped lips – being blown into her face like a Force Nine gale of bad breath.

'How are you, darling?' he said in his slurred but nonetheless plummy middle-class Surrey drone as he went in for the unnecessary kiss on both cheeks, making her recoil slightly.

'I'm fine, thank you, Bill,' she said sternly, attempting to catch his eyes, which had moved to her tits.

'It's such a sad occasion,' he said glibly, now unashamedly addressing her breasts. Funeral or no funeral, this was another giveaway that he had been drinking. He was the stereotypical 20th Century lady's man, though Laura had never been sure why: he was a tall, ferrety man with a straggly beard and receding, mousy hair. His dull brown eyes had always seemed unusually large and protruded out of their sockets so that even in a neutral expression he looked like a startled praying mantis. Why anyone would find this look attractive, let alone her sister, was completely beyond her comprehension. There was no money, he begged, stole and borrowed everything and also had an annoying tendency to leave his wallet in 'the MG', a fittingly 20th Century iconoclast that matched this seedy walking anachronism. He couldn't even run the damn thing for more than a day a week due to the fuel shortages.

'Yes, it is a sad occasion,' she said, jerking her head upwards in an attempt to make clear he should shift his gaze in a northerly direction. 'But I am glad we can give her a proper goodbye.'

She had said it in a calm fashion but still, it caused Karen to break into a mini fit of hysterics. She gently put her arm around her sister and patted her on the back.

'It's OK, Karen. Look, it's the kids,' she said as she saw both Charlie and Nick. Charlie was running towards them in a rather manic and barely controlled manner, her blonde hair, plaited at the back, swinging around like an excitable Labrador's tail. Her black dress was getting slightly muddy as she found every single bit of standing water on the path to splash into. Nicholas, on the other hand, was meandering slowly, looking at something in his AR glasses, which he was wearing much to her annoyance. He was wearing a mini three-piece black and white suit, with a red tie that offset his short strawberry-blond hair. He was walking just in front of Rory who, much like his son, was dressed in a simple black and white suit and that woman, who was wearing a black skirt that barely covered her knees and a tight black top, with short enough sleeves that she could see the base of the tattoos above her elbows and a low-cut neckline, that accentuated a cleavage that was in no way appropriate for the occasion. Much to Laura's surprise, Karen broke the silence with a series of quietly spoken expletives which they seemingly all agreed with.

'Look at that bulbous bitch – no sense of respect. I'm sorry, but I am going to have to say it before the kids get here… If no one else is going to say it?' she said, regaining her composure and looking at Billy and Laura. They both looked back with a blank expression and shook their shoulders.

'That woman is a chav… A gold-digging cunt of a pikey from the anus of the underclass,' she said. Both Billy and Laura took a breath after the unexpectedly bellicose assessment of the approaching situation. Though, Laura couldn't help but be a little impressed; Karen's Open University foundation diploma in English Language seemed to be doing wonders for her vocabulary, although probably not as originally intended. She quickly changed her tone as the kids came more clearly into focus.

'Charlie, sweetie,' she said as the small girl piled forward into Karen's arms. Laura waited and then picked up her youngest and kissed her on the cheek. By this point, Nick had accelerated his walk and bundled into them.

'Hello trouble,' she said, embracing them both and now looking back down the path to the awkward conversation that was about to come.

Laura was a touch relieved that the 'pleasantries' with Rory and 'that woman' were brief and oddly anodyne. There was a hello and a 'how are you doing?' and a 'this is very sad', concluding with a 'shall we go inside?' It lasted less than a minute and was pleasingly brief, with Rory thankfully doing much of the talking.

They were all now inside one of the cold, draughty and largely empty crematorium halls. It was possible to hear singing, possibly a hymn or a piece of classical, coming from the other hall, the many voices indicating that it was substantially fuller than the one in which she currently sat. The sum of attendees for the service to say goodbye to her dear mum, a woman who had dedicated her life to public service, to making others better, was a total of nine. Not even double figures and that was including the vicar. The eclectic group included Laura, the two kids, an increasingly hysterical Karen, a sleepy and mildly paralytic Billy, Rory, that woman – whose name was actually Clara – two sniffling old ladies of unknown provenance and Tim, the dishevelled priest who was staring down vacantly at his scruffy paper notes. She felt an initial pang of intense sadness well up in her as she looked across at this rather incongruent appellation of drifters.

'Is this it? Is this all she gets at the end?' But then she thought, 'She would have found this very funny.' The tears that had begun to well in her eyes came, but ran slowly down her cheeks. Her scowl turned into a wry smile.

'Are you laughing?' Karen asked in an accusatory tone. She was sitting to Laura's right, nearest the wall, and had now stopped her own sequence of sobs so she could stare across at Laura.

'Mummy, are you OK?' said Nicholas, who had been sitting with his head nestled under her left arm but was now staring up at her with his big gooey blue eyes.

'I'm fine, poppet. Mummy just thought of something that would have made Nana laugh,' she said, looking down at him with a reassuring smile. He nodded and got back to what he did best: being a restless, fidgety child. She looked back across at her sister.

'She'd have found this hilarious,' Laura said to her sister. 'I mean, look at us. You couldn't have collected a more random or more godless group of agnostics to go through a religious service. She would have liked to have had a few drinks with us lot, wouldn't she?' Karen nodded and quickly erupted into another fit of sobbing. She had never been good at picking the right words. Very much like her mother, a straightforward woman who, despite liking the pink stuff – a good medium Californian rose – had been an NHS nurse for over forty years. It was not the drink that had taken her across the lintel of death's door, but a very simple and ancient killer of the old and the very young – she died from the cold, specifically hypothermia.

Lucy Katherine Thomas had been born in the year of the first Apollo landing to a cleaner called Janet and a TV repairman named Ian. She had had a quiet childhood in the bohemian coastal city of Brighton and did not do particularly well at school. After working with her mum, cleaning schools for a couple of years, she finally found her calling in life as the Berlin Wall fell and went to Brighton Nursing College part-time, joining the NHS three years later, the same day Linford Christie sprinted to gold in the hot sticky summer of 1992. She excelled at her chosen profession, quickly rising to senior ward sister in just a couple of years. At Brighton General's Christmas party in '95 she met a junior doctor, Daniel Ford, and a one-night stand led to a head-over-heels romance. She later told Laura she blamed cheap vodka and Britpop in the Zapp Club. They married in the hot humid summer of August 1996. Dad had told her that it was meant to be June, but he'd used Machiavellian tactics to move it to August so he could go to two Euro

1996 soccer matches at the old Wembley Stadium in London – he'd sworn her to secrecy about this fact. They had their first child Laura in the spring of 1997 and then Karen on the cusp of the millennium in the autumn of 1999. Lucy had everything she wanted: a career doing something meaningful, two healthy and mostly happy daughters and a loving husband. She had risen from the base of the working class to comfortable lower middle class.

But then there were the big events in life, the earthquakes and aftershocks that come for everyone at some point. For Lucy, it was the day that Daniel passed away. He died on 29th August 2018 aged fifty, the result of a mid-life crisis involving a powerful motorcycle. He had purchased the bright-red Ducati for his birthday, much to his wife's chagrin. He was barely qualified to ride it and it was whilst he was on this that he had encountered a head-on collision with a thirteen-ton truck on his way to work.

His death shattered them all. Laura became the rock of the family. Whilst it changed them all, it had the most profound and eternal effect on her mum. Laura could see that, even years after Dad's passing, although her mum was the same loving soul, she was partly detached from the world, as though a part of her had been displaced, lost and possibly didn't want to be found again. Neither Laura or Karen were spiritual in any way, but if ever there were such things as soulmates then it was their mum and dad.

As a coping mechanism, Lucy continued to bury herself in her work, becoming Head of Nursing at the Royal Sussex Infirmary, leading it through the coronavirus pandemics of the 2020s and early 2030s before finally retiring at the newly increased retirement age of seventy, just a few years ago just before Christmas in 2040. However, there was no real retirement; the NHS pension pot was now measly and barely appreciating, thanks to the government having reduced their contributions as the country lurched from one disaster to another. She spent her first few years of rest as a JAM – Just About Managing – staying at home, reading books, watching television, eating cheap microwave meals and occasionally treating herself to a bottle of rosé.

Then came the inflation crisis and, as her pay-outs became increasingly meagre, she became a JAS – Just About Surviving. A few months ago, in the coldest winter for thirty years, she had to make a choice: be warm or have three meals a day. She chose the latter and, to begin with, all was well. She had a hot water bottle and enough food to stay strong – with the help of an emergency stash of whisky. But one day, she caught something. She thought it was a cold, but it turned out to be another strain of coronavirus and, despite her training and continual offers of help from her daughters – both medical and financial – she insisted on staying at home to get over it. She was almost obnoxiously stubborn when it came to matters of her own health, a stark contrast to her care for others. Then one night in late January, after days of pretending that the worsening pneumonia wasn't real, she felt a pain in her chest and another in the middle of her left arm. She knew the end was coming. She picked up her ancient Samsung mobile phone and called Laura.

'You need to come round, dear,' she said. 'Right now please, love.' She had hung up in an unusually abrupt style.

Laura only lived around the corner, in a garden flat of a Georgian terraced townhouse she had just moved into after the divorce. She had raced round to her mum's, a similar townhouse a few blocks away. It was a very windy day and the gusts blew down the wet avenues with an Arctic howl. After frantically unlocking the door, Laura had found her mum struggling for breath and clutching her chest. She took out her phone to ring for an ambulance, but her mother shook her head insistently and beckoned her towards her. She told her she loved her, that she would always be with her and asked her to hold her hand. Laura remembered holding back the tears as her mother's eyes closed and her body shook for what seemed like an eternity. Though many never see it, her mother had warned her that the death rattle was a very real thing indeed. Then it all stopped and there she lay, Lucy Ford, her mum, passed away at just seventy-four years of age.

She died simply due to the cold. She was from a middle-class family in one of the richest countries in the world and yet she was not the only one. Three million people passed away in the United Kingdom during the great freeze that winter. The average life expectancy dropping to below seventy for the first time in over one hundred years. Laura now knew that hell was not a place in some made-up fantastic spiritual realm; it was here on earth in the 21st Century. It was not a fiery pit of demons, but a bitter cold expanse made by mankind. It was consuming humanity, leaving none of the living untouched, a purgatory that was now beginning to take the people she loved the most.

As her sister's sobbing continued, the priest, who now seemed to be present of mind, was beginning the service: a long tedious eulogy written by Karen with the skill of an infant who'd been given a thesaurus for Christmas. The bespectacled clergyman began the delivery in a dry monotone with no hint of zeal and a pace that was slow enough to be overtaken by even the most stubborn of glaciers. None of the family wished to speak; all that needed to be said had already been said and so they all rose. Laura had one grain of comfort at this moment, a thought which gave her some warmth – at least Mum was back with Dad in some form. Her mum's favourite piece of music was now playing and the simple unvarnished coffin began to move. The jade-green curtains closed and off she went to the fiery beyond.

CHAPTER 10

Above the Polyarny Inlet, Russian Federation

16th March 2044

'Ready, Ilya,' said Alexander as he looked across at a man who, an hour ago, had been a sea of tranquillity, a modicum of Russian stoicism, but was now sweating profusely, his face nearly as white as the snow that was zipping in through the open passenger door of the now labouring Kamov helicopter. Ilya looked back at him and nodded with a sigh that Alexander could visibly see in one big cloud of condensation in the freezing Arctic air. The winchman, who appeared to be smoking a black Zyuganov cigarette, much to Alexander's annoyance, hooked his terrified friend to the winch cable through a series of carabiners on his dark-blue safety belt and life jacket. The latter had all sorts of paraphernalia attached to it, notably a small torch and a whistle, which, much like its airline cousins, were there to help attract attention. Alexander had always thought that the person responsible for this was a comic genius of the darkest variety and potentially an arch sadist, because they must have considered what would happen to any poor soul who was unfortunate enough to fall into the Arctic seas. First of all, there was the cold shock that killed fifty percent of the sea's victims, and then the four-metre plus waves that would continually crash down upon them. Even if one survived this physical assault, all they would have was a tiny flashlight, which, in average visibility, couldn't be seen more than twenty metres away and a child's play whistle, which was highly unlikely to be heard above the roar of the waves. With the exception of giving a cruel and faint hope to a soul who was either going to drown, get grotesquely mangled by the waves or die of hypothermia, these devices seemed to serve little purpose.

With this in mind, he looked at Ilya, who was now ready to drop into the grey beyond below, and he stepped off the door plate of the helicopter, the winch beginning to lower him into the murk.

'Best not fall in, Comrade. They won't find you again,' he shouted to Ilya with a smirk.

'Alexander, you inbred, sheep-fucking bastard… If I do fall in, I will come and haunt you for the rest of your life,' Ilya shouted back, his voice trailing off as he left Alexander's line of sight, the winch now whirring at full speed.

Stepping across to prepare for his own descent, Alexander looked down. They were hovering about fifty metres above the ocean and he could just about make out the surface, though the snow was now almost flying horizontally into his face, like tiny shards of freezing glass. The sea was rough with spray, the white horses colliding and cascading over the long dark cylinder which stood out like a pewter whale waiting for them in the gunmetal grey dullness of the Barents Sea. It was the Samara, his new command. A Yasen-class nuclear-powered attack submarine of the Russian Northern Fleet, fully armed with heavyweight torpedoes, hypersonic cruise missiles and the strategic weapons system, the most terrifying new weapon of the Federation. The winch cable was oscillating around in the high wind and he was sure he could hear some mild screaming coming from Ilya below. After a few minutes of adjustments, yaw and counter yaw from the Kamov pilots, two specks in high-visibility jackets appeared on top of the submarine's conning tower and grabbed Ilya, hauling him down into the bowels of the big atomic cetacean. The long steel winch resonated with a ghostly whistle as it rose back up to the Kamov, swinging slowly from side to side in the high winds like an amorous anaconda. After a few minutes more, it arrived back into the mainbrace with a loud metallic thud. The winchman turned to Alexander.

'Ready, Captain?' he said, still smoking his Zyuganov.

'Yes, Comrade. Ready,' said Alexander with trepidation. He held his breath and stepped off the ledge, guided by the hand of the winchman. As he began his journey into the grey of the storm, he felt the wind begin to slam into his body, like a heavyweight boxer thumping into a punchbag. He began to swing from the still-labouring Kamov, like a human pendulum. As he was lowered down further, he began to hear the faint roar of the sea amongst the assorted Arctic howls and, looking down, the submarine filled most of the view below. He could see two sailors in high-visibility life jackets emerge, both holding two large metal poles, as if they were game fishermen trying to hook a marlin. He was their intended catch and, as he got closer, he began to hear shouts of exasperation from the two men as they yelled through their radios to the helicopter above. They were worried about the oscillation that had developed and, as Alexander neared the top of the submarine, he could see he was still going to be swinging widely across the top of the conning tower and would have to try and catch one of the poles. That was if he could muster the strength. The now-consuming nausea of the motion sickness threatened to overcome him.

He was close and so came the first pass. As he swung across the top of the tower, the metal pole narrowly missed his groin; the second time, he was a good two metres away from being hooked. Finally, the winds died down slightly and on the third attempt, the swing was slower and he was propelled sideways relatively gently towards the conning tower, low enough so his feet could meet the top of the structure. However, it was a little too low and, as the sailors reached out to grab him, his left foot cracked against the side. The impact sent a cold resonance from his toes up his spine, making him yell. The two sailors grabbed him on both sides and brought him into the parapet, unhooking his lanyards and carabiners, taken aback by his shouts as they did so.

'Fucking… Naval Aviation… Fucking incompetent shits… That chopper is a waste of perfectly good metal,' he kept shouting.

'Comrade, Captain, are you OK?' said one of the sailors, who were both red-faced and shivering. With a deep breath and a wince, he looked back at the seaman.

'Yes, yes, sailor. I'll survive. Now let's get to work,' he said, pointing to the hatch at the back of the parapet.

CHAPTER 11

Mount Yamantau, Eastern Urals, Russian Federation

16th March 2044

The lights in the tunnel were incredibly bright and stark compared to the murky gloom in between them. With the odd exception of a few worryingly youthful Spetsnaz detachments, who were guarding each section of the narrow concrete tube, Ji-Chow had seen no signs of life – just the white cement walls of the tunnel lit by incendiary neon. The occasional stainless steel ventilation louvre arched through the tunnel crown. These must have been working overtime to deal with the black acrid fumes convulsing from the rear of the ancient army bus.

The tunnel seemed to go on forever. They had been travelling for about six minutes inside the mountain, although, admittedly, travelling at a sedentary ten kilometres per hour. But even by Ji-Chow's rough arithmetic, this meant they were already one kilometre inside Mount Yamantau, and still with no end in sight. With an apprehensive mix of nerves and puzzlement, he turned to his new friend, who seemed to be counting something under his breath.

'Does this go all the way to River Styx?'

'Well, it depends on what your definition of Hades is, young man,' said the general. 'But, no. Not long now. Another few minutes and you will see.'

'Out of curiosity, what were you counting?'

'Chainage... Each section is one hundred and twenty metres long – my own subterranean satellite navigation. I always like to know where I am, even if we are descending into one of Dante's circles.' Ji-Chow noted the general's seemingly deteriorating mood, which was moving from gallows humour into a fatalistic despair. This began to make Ji-Chow's unease, a nervousness that had been building since he'd left Beijing, worse. His stomach churned, twisting what felt like a lake of tar in the pit of his belly into jagged shapes in his gut and tastes at the back of his mouth. His tongue turned dry and it seemed to swell, filling his mouth, making it hard to swallow. However, his internal descent into panic was abruptly halted by the change in scenery that emerged from the gloom in front of him. There was something at the end of the tunnel. He couldn't quite make it out, but the hypnotic and seemingly endless walls of the tunnel appeared to stop and there was a change in the light – brighter but less stark than the neon lights. He thought he could see bare rock. A few seconds later, the bus emerged in a large cavern, approximately twenty metres high and about thirty metres long and wide. On one side it was just sheer rock, extending up to the polished granite surface of the ceiling in the form of a great arch. Directly in front of the bus was another tunnel, identical to the one from which they had just emerged. Presumably it went back out to another portal.

But the true purpose of the chamber only became apparent when Ji-Chow looked to his right. Set into the granite walls were two vast steel rectangles, each about six metres high and at least two metres thick, both of which had an elaborate set of valves around the perimeter and, on the outermost edges, what appeared to be large sunken hinges. Initially, he was lost for words.

'Ah… Are those—?' he eventually said.

'Yes,' interrupted the general. 'Those are doors, specifically blast doors. Impressive, aren't they?'

'Yes, that's one way of describing them.'

'It's offset from the tunnel for blast protection.'

Ji-Chow looked at the general. 'This far down?'

'Yes. Well, you should know, Mr Xi… How many Minuteman warheads will land here?' said the general.

Ji-Chow nodding in acknowledgement.

'Here we are,' said the general. 'Just wait till you see this little piece of theatre.'

Two large red lights began to flash above the doors and then a klaxon, loud enough to wake a city, began to hail, the shrill echo creating a cacophony in the vast cavern. There was then the rumble of pneumatic rams thumping behind the doors, which made the earth tremble with a deep bass so powerful Ji-Chow could feel it in his ribcage. After a few seconds, the vast doors began to open, with a deafening hydraulic whir, until there was a sudden resounding thud and the chamber fell silent. However, this was only a brief lull. The bus, after some encouragement from the driver, restarted and began to chug slowly, turning left around the nearest door and then into the bunker beyond.

Ji-Chow could not quite believe what was revealed before him. Beyond the blast doors was a vast hollow in the earth and what appeared to be a large town within it.

'Welcome to the Forbidden City,' said the general.

The bus only moved ten metres or so inside the cavern and then the doors began to close behind them, creating the same sonorous racket as before. Once closed, Ji-Chow began to make a number of observations about his new surroundings. The vast cavern was hewn into the granite belly of the mountain. In terms of scale, it was probably the same size and volume as the bowl-shaped football stadiums found in Europe and North America. The sides were formed of great granite vaulted arches, five in total, forming a circular enclosure. The arches all narrowed as they moved upwards, terminating in a single monolithic concrete buttress about ten metres across which spanned the entire upper circumference. Above the concrete buttress, the granite seemed to arch more slowly into a micaceous dome, which sparkled silver from the mica, green from the feldspar and a deep ochre from the burnt quartz in the neon lights, illuminating the entire cavern. This area, though, despite its immense size and grandeur, seemed to be merely an entrance, a portal to a separate subterranean world that lived beneath the mountain. This was obvious when Ji-Chow craned his neck down from looking at the wonderment above to the floor below, the entirety of which was covered in black tarmac with a sprawling set of directions mapped out in white paint, presumably to guide vehicles to the relevant sections of what he imagined was a small metropolis. Each of the five arches had large signs above the respective crowns, with white writing on a green background like large freeway signs with directions in both Russian Cyrillic and Mandarin. The first sign read 'accommodation' – self-explanatory, he thought; the second read 'main exit' – this was the arch that contained the entrance blast doors; the third read 'engineering' – he figured this would be the power plant, generators, air conditioning etc.; and the fourth read 'command' – probably a command centre, most likely with a plethora of meeting rooms. The most enigmatic and ominous of all was the portal to his immediate right, the sign for which read 'factory'.

It reminded Ji-Chow of a report he had read many years ago whilst working in Military Intelligence back in Beijing. Mount Yamantau was already one of the world's worst-kept secrets. The first reports of intense burrowing and tunnelling appeared on American satellite imagery as early as 1993. During the chaos of the subsequent Yeltsin era, the Russian military had given a series of seemingly random and equally contradictory statements on the purpose of Mount Yamantau: firstly, that it was a simple mining operation – just a well-protected one with three infantry divisions garrisoned within fifteen kilometres; then it was said to be a store for the nation's art in a time of national emergency; after that, a spokesman admitted, briefly, that it was a nuclear-proof national command centre, but then later attempted to retract the statement. The official Russian line then returned to that of a mining operation.

However, anybody with access to satellite imagery of Siberian Russia – the Americans, British, French and Chinese – knew this simply couldn't be true. There were no raw earth resources of note here and the fact that the excavations didn't finish until 2033 – nearly forty years later – suggested something vast was being constructed under the mountain.

In 2040, Yury Chalov, a colonel in the Russian military intelligence division – the GRU – and attaché to the Russian mission in Baghdad, entered the American consulate in the city's Green Zone, requesting asylum. He was promptly removed in a US military Humvee, sped to Baghdad International Airport and placed in the back of a USAF C-17 Globemaster transporter bound for Minot Airforce Base in Montana. Chinese Intelligence had gathered – through its network of informants within the US agencies – that the Americans had been particularly keen on debriefing Chalov because of his knowledge of the Russian military build-up in Syria. In particular, he was well-versed in the deployment of new S-500 long-range surface-to-air missiles and two Slava-class nuclear-powered missile cruisers deployed to the naval base in Tartus, both which posed major threats to NATO assets transiting the Bosporus. However, it transpired that Colonel Chalov had very little interest in discussing the various military or geopolitical components of the Middle East; instead, he began to divulge – in great detail including drawings and diagrams – a comprehensive description of the Great Citadel or Mount Yamantau, as it was known to the public. Ji-Chow had seen the illicitly-obtained transcripts, how Chalov described the small city under the mountain, which had been designed to survive all manner of cataclysms and, in particular, direct strikes from American nuclear 'bunker busting' warheads. He spoke about a groundwater reservoir that could sustain fifty thousand people for decades and enough food stores to last at least five years. There were details of broadcast studios and lavish accommodation for the Russian executive – or 'a palace for the damned', as Chalov had described it.

However, there were two details that had alarmed the Americans and which were of particular interest to Ji-Chow and his superiors. Firstly, there was sufficient space in the labyrinth of tunnels to accommodate an entire light air mobile armoured division and, secondly, and more worryingly, Chalov alleged there was a nuclear warhead and missile production facility for SS-27 Topol-R road mobile ICBMs at the lowest levels of the facility. Both nations knew that if this were true, and if the facilities could produce a critical number of warheads and launchers, this could be massively destabilizing for the global swords of Damocles as it undermined Mutually Assured Destruction – MAD – the Pax Atomica that had prevented true global war since 1945. This was because, for the past century, the MAD doctrine had ensured that both sides knew they had very little chance of surviving any form of nuclear exchange. This was largely due to the use of game theory within nuclear strategy, which dictated the most ruthlessly-pragmatical, logical set of actions taken in defensive or offensive postures.

In terms of the latter, there are two broad types of attack an antagonist could take. The only vaguely palatable one of these is counterforce, which has the aim of destroying the enemy's weapons and command facilities before they can destroy yours. The other option is the genocidal countervalue attack, which aims to destroy the enemy's cities and economies, effectively attempting to wipe your enemy and any last vestiges of their culture from the face of the earth. The potential instigators for an exchange are, in nearly all cases, as binary as the types of attack. It would either begin as an escalation from a conventional conflict or an attempted decapitation strike – a surprise counterforce strike – in a time of high international tension between the superpowers. In the case of the escalation scenario, during a conventional war between two nuclear-armed superpowers, game theory dictates that when one side starts to lose on a given front of war, that side should use tactical – lower yield – nuclear weapons against the opposition's armies to attempt to counter the other side's conventional superiority and regain the balance of power. In turn, the other side counters with its tactical weapons. In all scenarios, this leads to a bloody stalemate. Once again, game theory dictates escalation as the best path to victory, which would usually be in the form of a first strike or decapitation counterforce strike with the intent of destroying the enemy's leadership, blinding their communications and increasing their ability to co-ordinate the waging of war. Weapons such as submarine-launched missiles or stealth aircraft are preferred for this first strike as they can be launched closer to the intended targets and reduce the opposition's thinking time, therefore inducing errors in their chain of command. However, in most scenarios, game theory dictates that the side detecting the first strike must react with massive retaliation – and intrinsically countervalue in nature – as it is impossible to tell whether a few missiles are a limited tactical or counterforce strike, or a vanguard of decapitation strikes to blind their tracking radars and satellites.

American and Chinese doctrines are similar in that they would launch ninety percent of their arsenals on early warning, even if the initial strike is limited. Although, in the case of the former, the commanders of the launch platforms would be told that their weapon was part of a limited tactical package. The function of this lie was to prevent any form of mutiny when they were ordered to effectively end modern civilization.

The Russians, on the other hand, with terrifying zeal, would give control to an automated system, known as the Dead Hand or its less sinister code-name, Perimeter. The system had been in existence since the 1980s and had been continually updated since then. It would be activated in times of international tension. All early warning data and ground sensors – light, seismic and air pressure sensors to detect nuclear explosions – would be monitored and slaved to its command. If the system determined that the main control bunkers around Moscow were out of action and that an attack was in progress, the system would order one hundred and fifty command rockets to launch across the country, sending radio signals to all nuclear platforms to attack their assigned targets and thereby emptying the Russian nuclear arsenal of nearly three thousand strategic warheads. As a result, most of the world would burn in the ensuing atomic fire. However, the construction of the citadel meant that the Russian elite could now survive the nuclear storm, deep in the earth with a small army and factory to build more weapons to eliminate any enemies that survived. This could lead to a strategic imbalance and encourage the other superpowers to build similar facilities. This would make a conflict more inevitable as the elite of both sides would think that they could survive the ultimate escalation.

More troubling to the Americans – and to a lesser extent, the Chinese – was the fact that the Russians were prepared to build more warheads and launch vehicles under the mountain, because this could mean only one thing: the desire – or, at least, the desire for an option – to wage a total war to its ruthless conclusion. The complete elimination of one's enemy: their government, their people, their culture.

Much to the relief of the US administration, Chalov also revealed the state of the new facilities and its operating budget, which was practically nothing. Due to the world financial crisis of the late 2030s, the Russian government had to significantly reduce its military and even cut funding to its deepest of black projects, of which it was most fond. The facility had never been fitted out and Chalov reported that, by 2040, it was practically abandoned, with some of the older earth workings beginning to crumble. With this revelation, and other corroborating sources, the western intelligence services reduced their efforts but still kept a watching brief on the facility.

However, the Chinese began to take a particular interest, so much of an interest, in fact, that they offered $70 billion from their colossal reserve budget to finish it, and so created a joint command facility. After a year of rejection and prevarication, the Russians, near bankrupt, agreed to the proposal. And so, by gaining close ties with a resurgent China, the Russians resumed the work in the highest of secrecy.

So, now, down in the deepest of dark pits, faintly lit in a neon sheen, sat a young man on an old school bus, with a portentous secret known to but a few in the higher echelons of Beijing, a secret which could change the face of the world forever.

Ji-Chow's thoughts were interrupted by the sudden and impertinent arrival of four Chinese military police guards and their captain. The officer climbed aboard the now-open doors of the bus and declared, 'General Xhang and Mr Xi, please come with us.'

The general got up and began to move towards the captain. He turned to Ji-Chow and said, 'Not to worry. It appears you are very popular. Come on, follow me. This is an escort not a firing squad…'

Ji-Chow nodded and followed the general down the steps, noting the curious and slightly alarmed glances of the other occupants. Once they were on the tarmac, the doors closed and the bus chugged off, following the white markings towards the accommodation tunnel. The fumes it emitted made Ji-Chow and several of the MP's cough profusely.

'This way please, sirs,' said the captain.

They were led towards a door immediately to the right of the command tunnel. Ji-Chow, now immediately behind the general, couldn't help but ask, 'General, if you don't mind me asking… Where are we going?'

'You're very lucky, Mr Xi… At least, I think you're lucky. It appears the boss wants to see you.'

CHAPTER 12

Somewhere above West Virginia, USA

16th March 2044

Christine felt the sudden pull of negative G on her body as the Black Hawk helicopter began its steep descent through thick cumulus clouds that sat over the Western Seaboard. The same cloudscape had persisted in the thirty minutes of their flight from the Pentagon. The cloud began to disperse as they fell through the sky, the white fluff giving way to the dimly lit white peaks of the Appalachians. The stark white of her surroundings contrasted with the dull grey of the mountains, which were exposed below the tree line, and then with the green of the coniferous forests of Virginia. The forests covered the rest of the land to the horizon, which was interspersed with small towns and homesteads as far as her eyes could see.

The cabin of the Black Hawk was in the presidential trim, in that it was designed for VIP transport, with five rows of two airline-style seats, each with enough legroom to stretch out, with a small aisle running down the middle to the cockpit. This was somewhere between premium economy and business, but without the complimentary booze. Everything that wasn't the standard off-white aeronautical plastic was covered in a cream leather, including the seats, which gave off the vulgar vibe of a 1990s not-quite-five-star luxury hotel somewhere in Florida.

Christine was sitting in the second row on the port side of the chopper, looking out of the window. Directly across from her was Bradley, who still looked rather uncomfortable as he glanced out of the window every minute or so. In the row in front of him, the colonels, Myers and Schwartz, sat next to each other, both with their headsets off and talking closely into the other's ears – there were obviously things that they did not want their guests to hear. When they eventually both put their headsets back on, Christine did the same and looked at Bradley who glanced back at her. She gave him a thumbs up to see if he was alright and he very timidly reciprocated the gesture. After an intense buzz of static, the pilot's voice came over the intercom – a gravely growl of a voice with a Louisiana twang.

'Prepare for landing – five minutes. Buckle up, ladies and gentlemen.' Everyone complied accordingly.

Colonel Schwartz then decided to add his own briefing to the proceedings. Turning around into the aisle to address both Christine and Bradley, he said, 'OK, when we land there will be a car waiting for us and this will take us to the facility. This facility is required for the continuity of the government of the United States and, hence, I am going to need to ask you to do a few things for me.' His stare, primarily at Christine, became more intense as he continued. 'Firstly, I am going to need your phones, photographic devices and any other electronic equipment. Secondly, you need to be aware that you will not be able to see out of the vehicles until we reach the facility. Is that clear?'

Christine nodded and began to collect the things that the colonel had ordered from her belongings, which was pretty much everything apart from a few cosmetics. Bradley seemed less sure and was still very hesitant. She looked across at him and nodded reassuringly. Although she was sympathetic to Bradley, she was getting a tad frustrated. He began to gather his things.

'I hope I am not going to have to babysit this kid for the next… Well, however long,' she thought. It made her question exactly how ready he was for what lay ahead. The helicopter began to decelerate and was pulling into a hover as Bradley finally handed over his things to Schwartz.

'Thank you both,' he said as he put their valuables into a small blue plastic box and placed it under his seat. He began to prepare to settle himself for landing, but Christine had decided it was time to make a few enquiries of her own.

'So, Colonel, which particular facility is it?' she asked, eyeballing him intently as he craned his neck around to look at her.

'Now, ma'am, I couldn't possibly—' was all he was able to get out before Christine clarified her query.

'I mean, is it Alfa? November? Mike? Echo…?' she said with the knowing look of someone who clearly knew at least the same, if not more, than Schwartz did. It seemed it hadn't dawned on him until this point that a key advisor to the Secretary of Defense might have the same, if not higher, security clearance than he did. She found this was a typical assumption made by middle-aged military men and she was going to make it perfectly clear she wanted to know exactly where they were going.

‘HVP Clearance, Colonel. Which site is it?’ she said, her voice turning to a rasp.

With a look of admonishment and slight embarrassment, the colonel replied, ‘Echo site, ma’am,’ and turned back to face the front of the chopper.

‘Thank you!’ she replied with a deliberate triumph. She now knew they were somewhere to the east of Mount Jackson in deepest darkest hillbilly Virginia. In fact, most of the twenty or so facilities were in this neck of the woods.

Unlike some other countries, the US had taken a different approach to its continuity of government in an existential crisis and one that, on the surface, would seem unusually modest compared to the colossus of Cheyenne Mountain, Raven Rock and even the Greenbriar that had preceded it. Over the last three years, the US Department for Homeland Security and the DoD had been busy burrowing away out here in the sticks, building twenty-four small, but deep, bunkers in the Appalachians. Each were approximately fifteen miles from each other and all were within a forty-five-minute helicopter ride from DC. The reasons for this were simple: forty-five minutes was the absolute maximum warning that would be given of a strategic attack and, secondly, the bunkers were far enough apart that a strategic nuclear weapon could only take one out at a time, offering a significant degree of redundancy. In times of tension, the bunkers would be manned by key staff from the major government departments, all of which would be represented in each bunker. In the event of war, each bunker could communicate with each other through a closed loop fibre-optic network which had been bored into the Appalachians with a great degree of difficulty. In a now almost entirely wireless world, the irony of this colossal amount of hardwiring had not been wasted on Christine and this made her chuckle every time she thought of it.

The bunkers had also been constructed with a great degree of subterfuge. Some were fronted as real estate ventures, complete with fully functioning, but empty, luxury properties; others were more commercial, such as self-storage facilities that never opened. The result was a dispersed network of bunkers, which would be very difficult to destroy, even if the other side knew of their existence, the complete antithesis to a Yamantau-style grand command centre and citadel.

The chopper was now in a complete hover and it began to make a rather disconcerting descent into the forest below. Christine assumed there was a suitable clearing through the pine needles and dark conifers; hopefully they weren't about to plummet into a splintery grave in the middle of nowhere – she didn't like flying at the best of times. Sure enough, a few moments later, the clearing appeared beneath them and the engines of the helicopter began to power down, bringing them to earth with a soft bump as the helicopter landed on the soft grass. Craning her neck around, Christine could just about make out the two large black four-by-fours, which were obviously there to meet them. One of the pilots exited the cockpit and opened the passenger door immediately in front of the first row, the telescopic steps landing on the soft ground underfoot. Both the colonels rose from their seats, Myers grabbing the blue box, and headed towards the exit.

'Please can you follow us to the vehicles?' said Myers as he stood on the threshold.

'Sure,' said Christine and Bradley nodded. Both knew it was pointless to do otherwise.

After she made her way through the aisle and carefully down the steps, she found herself in the nondescript clearing. The grass was rather sodden and squelchy underfoot. Following the gesturing Myers, she approached the vehicles: both enlarged DoD Jeep Grand Cherokees, heavy four-by-fours with big suspensions and large V8s – not the hybrids of DC.

'Sorry, but can we hurry things along a bit? I'm afraid we haven't got long,' said Myers, now wearing the obligatory set of wraparound Oakley shades. 'Please can you get into the back of the second Jeep.'

She gave a semi-sarcastic salute and got in the back. Bradley was already seated, looking down at his lap. There was a muffled sound of 'go' from the radio in the front and the driver, a large, white, bald kingpin of a man, obeyed and put his foot down rather harshly. The big SUV spun its wheels a little and lurched forward energetically. As the car sped off, with both Christine and Bradley pinned to the thin leather of the rear seats, she could see the helicopter suddenly rise into the sky and fly overhead. She had been expecting this: there was less than an hour's gap between various Chinese and Russian satellites that passed over the area, hence, they needed to get to cover in the next ten to fifteen minutes so that they could complete the transit undetected. This was also why the chopper had carried on with its original flightpath. The Jeep now moved at a truly alarming speed, leaving the tree-lined track and veering suddenly at a junction onto a dark-orange mud-covered track. The manoeuvre caused Christine to bump her head on the bullet-proof glass, which led to several choice curses slipping out.

'Jesus Christ, can you slow down a light?' she yelled at the driver.

'No, ma'am,' he replied, the big smart-ass.

The Jeeps continued at what seemed a great speed until they reached a man-made part of the track. There, they gradually began to brake and eventually came to a crawl as they reached what appeared to be a large bungalow-type lodge, secluded in the woods beyond a green metallic fence. The bushes and shrubs of the forest had been allowed to grow through it. As they approached, there was a blip on the radio and the two large metal gates began to open. The cars drove through into the compound and Christine noticed at least four guards in forest camouflage up against the fence line, carrying their carbines as they patrolled the perimeter. These guys – though one was a girl, she thought, or at least a non-binary – were most likely Army Rangers and they probably had their own shallower cover somewhere in the near vicinity.

The vehicles came to a halt, the driver squeezed his considerable frame through his door and came round to open their passenger doors.

'Follow Colonel Myers and Colonel Schwartz,' he bellowed.

Both she and Bradley got out and went around to the front of the car.

The building itself seemed inconsequential. It looked like a large, single, wooden hunting lodge, with the only clues to its true purpose being the four-foot-thick walls exposed at the entrance, which was covered by a large six-inch thick steel blast door. Two further army rangers lurked at the periphery.

Colonel Schwartz beckoned them over.

'Eh, the gentleman would like to check your credentials,' he said as they approached. 'Well, this is very 20th Century, gentlemen,' said Christine.

The larger of the two men, an enormously broad but strangely short man of afro-Caribbean heritage, gave a look of vague but unmistakable disdain and looked at her mugshot on a piece of paper, comparing their likeness, and then grunted. As did his companion after undertaking the same review of Bradley's particulars. 'Stick with the officers at all times until you are given passes in the facility,' he growled, before abruptly moving back to disappear into the undergrowth with his compadre.

They silently followed the colonels up a set of concrete steps to the entrance. Looking past the blast doors and the two guards, all Christine could see was a long, seemingly endless culvert, lit with strips. The culvert was square-shaped, no more than eight feet in height and eight feet wide, and the floor sloped down at a sufficient gradient so that it wasn't uncomfortable to walk down, but steep enough that she couldn't see where it ended. It had obviously been designed to be large enough to move trolleys and pallets to and from the bunker below.

As they stepped down, the smell immediately hit her nose. Despite the culvert being no more than a year old, it had been constructed in somewhat of a hurry and, between the joints, she could see small amounts of groundwater seeping into the tunnel. She assumed that this seepage was the source of the musky stench that lingered in the dank air.

But this was not the main assault on the senses by any means – there also was the sound. She could hear every single step, cough and murmur merge into an eerie subterranean echo. It was a macabre reverb, a wall of sound but with zero cadence, a dull and oppressively loud ambience. This dull white noise was obviously beginning to have an adverse impact on Bradley. He had been walking alongside her a few moments before, but she now noticed his absence and, looking over her shoulder, she could see he had started to straggle several paces behind. He was sweating profusely, enough that, even in the dim light, she could see a distinct sheen on his youthful hairline. She held up and waited for him. As he got closer, she could see he was ashen white, but had a faint blackness under his pale-blue eyes, which were now fully dilated. He kept his downward gaze at his feet, now just shuffling rather than stepping along the sloped floor.

She approached him and whispered, 'What's up, Brad? Are you claustrophobic?' She tried to sound as reassuring and as calm as she could. She didn't put an arm around him as she figured that he may not take kindly to unwanted intimacy from someone who was essentially a stranger.

He suddenly stopped. The sound of the combat-booted footsteps of the two military men reduced slightly as they continued ahead down the dark passage.

'Th-th…' stuttered Bradley, trying to articulate himself.

'It's OK. Stay calm, don't panic and always remember to breathe; that's the most important thing,' she said softly with a grin.

'The… The noise… It hurts, the noise hurts… I can't help it,' he said, looking up and giving her some rare eye contact.

'I know. I don't like it any more than you. But the sooner we get to the end, the sooner it will stop.'

Bradley took a deep breath and opened his mouth as though he was going to speak, but then slowly closed it as the words escaped him.

'I have an idea: why don't we both walk in lock step? If we take steps together, it'll create a rhythm, make the noise more predictable and then we'll get to the end quicker.' Her proposal was initially met with complete silence and no affirmative or negative facial expressions, nor any other change in his body language. So, with nothing else she could do, Christine just stood there, looking as positive yet insistent as possible. Then, after ten seconds or so, Bradley spoke.

'OK,' he said rapidly with no other expression, now looking down towards the end of the tunnel.

'Right,' she said uncertainly, before gathering herself. 'On the count of three, right foot and then left foot.'

This again was met with no response from the now bolt-upright Bradley.

With hope, rather than with expectation, she said, 'OK, one… two…and three.' She started to walk slowly, one step per second she counted, glancing across at Bradley. Much to her relief, he began to mimic her and so they continued their absurd line dance down the ramp, until she could see the end.

About a hundred feet further down, the colonels were now waiting outside another stainless steel door and looking back up at both her and Bradley. She couldn't see their expressions, but she was almost certain they would be a mixture of part annoyance but predominantly bafflement. She felt conflicted: firstly, she was also annoyed, babysitting this man-child in a glorified underpass with two other military meatheads walking beneath a hill in redneck West Virginia; but, secondly, and most prominently, she felt an intense pity. How was it that such a seemingly fragile young man had been placed in this situation, a long way from home and underground in this strange world? She was not going to kid herself; the nervous shell of a human probably knew something of great value to the administration and to the 'leaders' of the free world. That was the only plausible explanation for his presence here.

As the synchronized duo approached the colonels, Schwartz looked in a retinal scanner, which was mounted on the concrete next to the door. There was then a sudden metallic thud and the door opened, revealing a set of communal showers illuminated in bright lights. Christine figured this was a decontamination area.

Schwartz then looked at both of them and said, 'Right, now we are all finally here, we'll get you checked and logged in at reception. I'll then take you to the briefing room, where the Secretary will be waiting for you. Do please keep up; we are already late.'

Both she and Bradley nodded and followed him with haste into the bunker.

CHAPTER 13

Mount Yamantau, Eastern Urals, Russian Federation

17th March 2044

Ji-Chow, the general and the four guards had traversed a number of stairwells hidden within an alcove in the giant chamber under Yamantau, which had taken them down at least another twenty to thirty metres deeper into the mountain. The stairs were all grated stainless steel with a flimsy-looking wire mesh that only seemed to offer a notional protection to the fall below, at the bottom of which was another large ballistic door. Conversation had been largely minimal due to the constant metallic clank of the guard's combat boots on the steel grates. General Xhang seemed a little winded, his slightly flabby cheeks turning a very deep hue of red from the exertion. As they finally got to the bottom of the stairs, much to the relief of both himself and General Xhang, he noticed a camera on the wall and two yellow footprints painted on the floor with yellow writing in Russian Cyrillic above them. Ji-Chow's written Russian was a little rusty, but he correctly assumed it said, 'Stand Here'.

'Gentlemen,' announced the officer who had been leading their little cadre. 'Please can you stand there and look straight into the AR camera. Once the biometric scan is complete, you will be admitted into the war room.' Ji-Chow noticed a slight hesitation and from the way he rolled his R's, Ji-Chow could tell that this man did not speak Mandarin as his first language. He was probably Cantonese, most likely a native of the giant all-electric metropolis of Guangzhou. This was unusual as most sensitive Chinese facilities were manned exclusively by Han-Chinese. Not all were equal in their lauded quasi-communist utopia.

'Mr Xi, you first please,' said the officer.

'Of course.' Moving forward, he looked into the set of cameras embedded in the wall. On the face of it, it appeared to be a normal airport scanner, but the augmented reality component made this more sophisticated. The cameras not only scanned the shape of his face but every mole, blemish or scar to ensure he could not be an intruder with a prosthetic. It then backed this up with a thermal imaging scan to, firstly, make sure no one with a fever, influenza or even a common cold could be admitted into the facility and the same cameras then traced key blood vessels under the surface of the skin to ensure this matched the same deep biometric imprint that was stored in the intelligence agency's cloud. The procedure completed with a reassuringly soft 'beep', accompanied by a green light. The hermetically-sealed door decompressed with a hiss and an unpleasant smell emerged that reminded him of the stale, turgid air on a fully-packed long-haul airliner. The door slowly opened to reveal a large conference room. Large translucent display screens lined the walls and in the middle of the room was a large, long wooden table with tablets placed against twenty or so of the black leather seats. At the back, through a Perspex screen, he could just about make out a much larger room, which appeared to be a level or so below. Down in the larger room there was a large news-desk-like facility lit in the vivid greens and blues of a substantial LCD screen – at least two storeys high – showing the surface of the earth in planform, which he could just make out through the relatively small letterbox opening of the airlock. He began to go through the door, but the captain raised his hand to stop him.

'Please await the general. Our orders are to make sure no one else passes once you are inside,' he said as he looked away from Ji-Chow. There was an ominous tension to his expression. 'General, please can you step onto the mark?'

The general, now recovered from his exertion on the stairs, stepped forward and the procedure was repeated with the same reassuring polyphonic beep.

'Thank you, gentlemen. Please step inside.'

Ji-Chow looked across at the general who waved his right hand, as if to say 'after you'. He stepped forward onto the thick red carpet, walked to the left of the large table and stood at the apex of the curved table, where he could gain a full vantage of the room. At a right angle to the airlock entrance, there was a large set of double doors that led down into the vast room below and probably far beyond. It became obvious to Ji-Chow that the stairwell and entrance they had come through was the emergency exit up from the tunnels below. Looking around at the display screens, he could see that they contained an odd mix of Russian and Mandarin, each screen displaying a mix of satellite images of various parts of the electromagnetic spectrum, infra-red, UV, thermal and false colour magnetic and gravimetric. There was then a bewildering array of overlays, some of which he didn't recognize but assumed to be different military units, naval fleets, armies, air wings of both Chinese and Russian origin, and some he did recognize. He could see what appeared to be part of his hypothetical operational plan, which included key opposition targets, trajectories and weapon types from the strategic rocket forces. More worryingly, he noticed something unnerving: countdown timers, some of which seemed to suggest a matter of days to implementation. As he began to take in his surroundings and tried to settle his alarmed bemusement, he pulled out one of the chairs and sat down to sooth his aching back. Not more than a second after he had sat down, he was given a warning.

'I wouldn't sit there if I were you, young man,' said General Xhang, who was now standing close to the wall immediately behind him. 'Come quickly and stand next to me.' He had a cold but calm command to his voice, no longer the jovial and flippant old man of their long transit. It was such a juxtaposed tone that Ji-Chow complied with little hesitation, quickly rising and putting the chair back under the table and then moving to stand to the general's left. Something compelled him to stand up straight, almost as if he were waiting to be told to come to attention by an invisible sergeant major.

A matter of seconds later, the double door across from them burst open to reveal a squad of PLA commandos – eight of them, all in heavy body armour, carrying assault rifles and wearing the deep red berets of the chairman's bodyguard. They marched forth, four to the right, four to the left of the doors, and lined up equidistant along the long wall of display screens. Completing this piece of highly-drilled military choreography, they stamped their feet and shouted in deafening completion. There was then a brief silence, which was quickly dispersed by the sound of approaching footsteps. As these drew near, the two commandos either side of the doors moved towards each other in unison and opened the large steel doors, welcoming in three figures very familiar to Ji-Chow.

First, was a tall sinewy man in formal military attire and of very high rank, with a perpetually stern look on his face. Ji-Chow recognized this man as General Li-Chang, Deputy Commander and Chief of the PLA – the highest-ranking military person in the whole of China. General Li-Chang stood against a chair opposite Ji-Chow and glared at him coldly, not in an overtly threatening manner, but the gaze of a man with an unsettling natural intensity. The next was a small, round man in a simple black suit and tie, bald except for a small white wispy goatee on his chin. This was Io Ri-Fin, Deputy Chairman of the Council of Ministers and Head of the secret police of the PRC – the butcher of Hong Kong, as he was known, executor of millions and the most feared man in the east. Ji-Chow noticed a small notepad and pen in the top pocket of his nylon blazer and wondered how many lives had been signed away by that simple black ballpoint. He shuddered at the thought of the perplexing might of an overweight, unassuming man in his late fifties and his biro. At least he seemed friendly – in comparison to Li-Chang. He even gave a nod and a slight grin towards General Xhang, who reciprocated. Terror, it seemed, had a friendly face. Last to enter was a portly man in a grey suit, with perfectly-curated dyed, black hair, holding a small cup of tea in his right hand. His face was unmistakably familiar; after all, it was plastered on millions of posters, on entire walls of high-rise tower blocks and held aloft in thousands of portraits in annual military parades across the country. His photograph was in every government office in the land and he seemed an almost omnipotent omnipresence on social media and all spheres of augmented reality. This was Chairman Ma Yu, President of the People's Republic of China, Chairman of the Council of Ministers, Head of the Great Soviet and Supreme Commander of the Armed Forces. A colossus of recent history, he was the man who had made China the most powerful country in the world, both financially and militarily, not to mention singlehandedly rescuing the nation from the economic crisis of 2037 – that is, if you believe the state broadcaster, of course. He seemed the most jovial, or at least, the most casual of the three.

He placed his cup on the wooden table, and then his expression suddenly changed with an unnerving polarity as he looked across at the general and Ji-Chow with a darting glance.

'Right, sit down, you two. I am going to ask you some questions and I need quick answers,' he said with a withering authority. Both of them obeyed without any reluctance and sat down in the leather chairs. The chairman and his party sat down directly across from them. This was followed by stony silence that seemed to last an awkwardly long time. The chairman then flicked his teacup with his index finger to make a ringing sound, almost as if to bring the meeting to further order. He hunched slightly as he looked into Ji-Chow's face, seeming to fix his gaze onto his forehead and not directly into his eyes, which only distracted Ji-Chow and made him uncomfortable. However, his distraction soon turned to astonishment as the chairman began his stoic but terrifying opening gambit.

‘In thirty minutes, the President of the Russian Federation and his senior staff will walk through that door and, thirty minutes after that, we will begin a joint military operation on a scale never before seen in human history. This operation is a direct result of the work that you, Ji-Chow Xi of Central Military Planning, have undertaken over the last 2 years – to understand the potential to save the People’s Republic and her allies from the coming chaos.’ The chairman briefly paused and Ji-Chow could now feel his heart pounding. A torrent of thoughts began to streak through his head, the pulses of serotonin bringing out the worst of all his fears:

‘You knew what it was for.’

‘What have you done?’

‘You knew who you were dealing with.’

‘You were only interested in saving your own skin, you filthy little coward.’

Some of these thoughts were moderated slightly by more reassuring voices:

‘It was just an academic exercise; this is what Von Neuman and Kahn did back in the sixties and nothing bad happened.’

‘You gave them many options – not all of them are so bad.’

And then the most pertinent thought brought itself clearly into his mind’s eye under a bright spotlight:

‘Which option is he talking about?’

The chairman then restarted his monologue after his pause.

‘So, as far as I understand, you outlined a dozen or so options in your paper last year, a paper that the man sat to the left of us brought to our attention a few months ago. Tell me, Xi. How many of these options are now viable after the nuclear exchanges on the sub-continent?' Again, he fixed his stare to the middle of Ji-Chow's forehead, before lowering his steely gaze into Ji-Chow's eyes.

'Erm, there are only three options remaining, sir,' said Ji-Chow as he tried to bury his nerves.

'You don't sound very sure of that,' said Ri-Fin. Gone was the unremarkable man across from Ji-Chow in his cheap suit and now sat a man with a vulpine expression, a man who mocked him with an almost febrile incredulity, his raptor-like eyes seemingly fixed on what he thought would be a fresh victim. Ri-Fin turned and scoffed to the chairman. 'An extreme genius, are we sure? Seems like an imbecile to me.' His voice, now raised, was almost a harsh squawk.

The chairman turned to Ri-Fin and gave a macabre placation.

'Hear him out, dear colleague. I know I normally introduce you as my Beria but this is not one of your judicial interrogations. After all, we wouldn't be here in this place without him...'

This made Ji-Chow shudder, although he didn't show it.

The chairman continued his inquisition.

'Please can you outline the three options that remain, just to make sure we are all on the same page of this book of yours.'

Ji-Chow paused and mustered his thoughts into a set of clear, punchy, objective sentences as he had a feeling his life could depend on the clarity and brevity of his next few words.

'Option one: we do nothing... Option—'

Just as he began, Ri-Fin interrupted.

'What happens if we do nothing?' he said with a notable nasal whine. Indeed, it sounded as though he was going to be thoroughly interrogated by this trigger-happy psychopath. He was well aware of his reputation – a once-in-a-generation enigma, forged in Ma's great purges of the late thirties. Ri-Fin was Ma's fifth Head of Security and the longest serving. Like his predecessors, Ri-Fin had ensured the demise of his previous boss by gaining Ma's favour and ensuring an official denouncement, which resulted in demotion, arrest, confession under torture and then summary execution in the space of twenty-four hours. Ri-Fin was therefore a creature born out of the most Darwinian of regimes, ruthlessly pragmatic and mistrustful of anyone who might try to curry favour with Ma.

Ji-Chow knew he had to tread a very fine line between firm and non-threatening in his response.

'Based on what we know now, after the conflict on the sub-continent, we have six months – maybe seven – of grain and rice supplies. However, due to the increasing drought across the continent and the growing scale of dust storms coming from the Gobi Desert and the great steppes, highly-radioactive soil will be swept further east, which will eliminate all of the untainted private farm crops and allotments,' he said, gaining confidence the more he spoke, and holding his nerve.

But again, Ri-Fin impatiently interjected.

'And…?'

Ji-Chow gathered himself and stared back into his hawk-like eyes.

'It means we actually only have twelve to fourteen weeks of reserve food supplies; we might be able to extend this out by another three to four weeks with the limited foreign imports, but with the world food situation the way it is, there is no way we can feed a population of nearly two billion. That's not to take into account the deteriorating raw water situation—'

'OK, so some will have to go without. We just need a new cultural revolution – favour the most loyal, root out the traitors. That'll significantly reduce the number of mouths to feed—' Ri-Fin came to an abrupt halt when the chairman slowly raised his left hand in front of him.

'How many would perish, Mr Xi?' he said in a much softer tone than he had before. His body language was now more languid and almost conciliatory. Ji-Chow took a deep breath.

'Somewhere between sixty to eighty percent of the population. Around one and a half billion of our citizens would perish, sir, along with four to five hundred million of our allies. Not just Russians, but the eastern Europeans, Mongols, Kazaks, Vietnamese, the—'

'Thank you, Mr Xi. I get the picture,' said the chairman. Oddly, he said it with a reassured calmness as he looked at all those sat around the table. But mainly he looked at Ri-Fin, as though he needed Ji-Chow as an audience and an expert to convince his most nefarious of political allies that something radically different had to be done. If Ji-Chow wasn't mistaken, his tone was that of triumph.

This seemed to deflate the up-to-now entirely verbose Ri-Fin, who sank back in his seat. Ji-Chow could see sweat beginning to bead on his forehead as his expression turned from derision to frustration.

'How can this happen after one poor harvest? Were we not prepared? How have we got here?' he said, his anger now bare for all to see. With each word, a cascade of spit leapt from his tongue and gently splatted on the polished mahogany table top, irritating both the chairman and General Li-Chang. The chairman glanced at him with a thinly veiled look of disgust.

Ji-Chow prepared to answer this latest volley, when General Xhang suddenly decided to intercede.

'Comrade, the answer is simple: carry capacity. The Earth has none left. Over the last decade, we have hit peak oil, peak water and we think, perhaps, in the last two years we may even have hit peak food. Then last year, those stupid Pakistani and Indian bastards tried to annihilate each other, and then another quarter of the world's grain – our share of the grain – got contaminated and there is no more…' Xhang tailed off as he saw the impact of his words. The mood, which had changed from anger to a communist stoicism, had now moved to a simple, morose despair. After a few seconds of looking around at each other, the chairman took in a deep breath and stared directly at the display boards behind Ji-Chow. For some reason, this seemed to be the nudge for General Li-Chang to enter the conversation.

'The breakdown in public order – how would this manifest? I mean, is there any chance we can try to ride this out with losses?' he said with a hopeful expression.

'We can't be a hundred percent sure, but at the very most, eighteen months; at the least, it could be less than a year,' Ji-Chow said. 'Public order would breakdown quickly and, in most of the scenarios we ran, the state would fall in the first few months. Even if we gave priority to feeding the soldiers to buy loyalty, there would only be sporadic pockets of order. In all scenarios, the PRC, the

Russian Federation and all vassal states would demolish or at least be mortally weakened. When we worked through the scenarios, there is a marginal – perhaps one percent – chance of succeeding by doing nothing.'

This statement seemed to chasten his more illustrious counterparts even further: all bar the chairman recoiled slightly and again sank back into the black leather of their chairs.

The chairman broke the solemn silence.

'So, we can't do nothing, unless we want to see the nation starve and/or all of us strung up by our necks in Tiananmen Square,' he said, his tone rising to a sarcastic rhetoric at the end. He glared, first at Li-Chang, and then at Ri-Fin. Both seemed cowed and, in near unison, they shook their heads reservedly, making as little eye contact as possible.

The chairman continued.

'So, Mr Xi, please can you explain the remaining two options with the same clarity as your first deposition?' He issued his words now with an urgent cadence; each word thudded into Ji-Chow's ears like bullets from an assault rifle.

Once again, he gathered himself.

'Option two is that we launch a biological attack on all major non-allied population centres—' He was again interrupted by a now-reserved but no less obstructive Ri-Fin.

'Why and with what?' he said, looking straight down at the table as he stroked his heavily-creased brow, seemingly unsure of his fate in what was almost certainly – and very soon to be – a different world to the current one where he held the power of life and death.

'In terms of the most viable weapon, it is Semava. We would seed this through mules—'

'Mules…?' said the chairman.

'Like drug mules. We would seed a number of people into a number of trade meetings in key locations to maximize the spread of infection – people such as the less important members of the diplomatic corps at smaller consulates as well as directors of some of the smaller state-run enterprises,' said Ji-Chow.

'Can someone please explain to me what Semava is?' spat Ri-Fin. That rabid vulpine expression had returned. It seemed he was not a man who remained down for long.

'Allow me to explain,' said Xhang. It appeared that Xhang and Ji-Chow were now a tag team of harbingers. 'Semava is an acronym. It stands for Synthetically Engineered Marburg Virus Variant. As you know, the Marburg virus is a filovirus that induces a haemorrhagic fever. It emerged in the Congo in the latter half of the 20th Century and has had sporadic outbreaks over the last fifty years or so, with a mortality rate of eighty to ninety percent. In 2039, there was an outbreak about twenty kilometres outside Kinshasa near to Chalalco's main office. Two Chinese nationals were infected and died within a few days. However, rather than throw their corpses into mass graves and burn them, we had them discreetly flown to one of our bio-labs in Inner Mongolia. Our bio-teams excelled themselves. They were able to add some synthetic biology to the virus, firstly, to mask its appearance, and then using synthetic viral phage's, which attach themselves to the virus, we were able to make it appear like another virus, H5N2.'

'So, you made it look like a bird flu?' said Ri-Fin.

'Yes, Comrade. But not only did we make it look like influenza, we were able to make it just as contagious. Then we put it in a delivery package with H5N2, so it would make it very hard to find.'

'OK, so what would taking this course of action do for us and our allies?' said the chairman, now looking directly at Ji-Chow, redirecting the summary to come from his direction.

'The virus would spread relatively quickly, masked under a cover story of a bird flu outbreak in Wuhan which had spread beyond our control. We would 'quarantine' all our major population centres to give the impression that, whilst we are in a really dire situation, we have it under control. Though, this would require us to fake at least a few thousand deaths.'

'Why bother faking?' chipped in Ri-Fin rhetorically. His words had an ominous tone.

Ji-Chow continued, 'The virus would spread voraciously, the flu symptoms showing first and then the Semava symptoms would start at around fifteen days after.' Ji-Chow paused as the chairman raised his hand, a perplexed expression now taking hold of his face.

'Why would it take so long?'

'That is due to the synthetic engineering – I should say: deliberate synthetic engineering, which is to maximize damage. During the most recent flu pandemics, most countries followed the guidelines of the World Health Organization and quarantined people for fourteen days who were suspected of having the virus. Hence, those that were quarantined, and even those who were not due to much milder symptoms, showed no signs of deterioration; in fact, after two weeks most people would feel almost back to normal. This would allow all of those people to spread the hidden Semava component even more widely. Only after a few days had passed, after they had returned to their usual routine, the Semava component would strike, most likely with fatal consequences. We estimate that this could decimate the non-allied populations by thirty to forty percent, so at least three billion deaths in less than nine months…' Ji-Chow paused to take a breath and a break from the weight of the words that he could not entirely believe he was saying. Even now, he couldn't quite believe he was here, with this rather unsavoury audience, in this deepest of hidden places in the world.

I ruthlessly pragmatic Ri-Fin was keen to understand the end game.

'So, what happens after the slaughter?' he said matter-of-factly, with no hint of hesitation.

'Well, we get to be magnanimous, if that's the right word. We offer the shattered nations all the logistical support – medical and otherwise – they need. Think of it as a variation on the Marshall Plan of 1945, but instead, we get paid back in grain and other foodstuffs, so we can re-establish ourselves as the single superpower. However, there is only a relatively small chance of success… Maybe ten to fifteen percent…' Ji-Chow shook his head, almost apologetically.

This revelation made Ri-Fin particularly rabid.

'Well, you are a gift that keeps on fucking giving, aren't you?' he said as he leered across at Ji-Chow, his hands now clenched into fists. 'Why so low? What could go wrong…?' His words came in an apoplectically loud crescendo, both his fists now thumping down onto the table.

Again, General Xhang decided to interject and deflected the ire of the now bright-red Ri-Fin.

'Comrade, we believe that some of our potential enemies also possess similar weapons. Namely, the British. We have intelligence to suggest that they have secretly developed a similar virus but based on an Ebola virus they obtained in Sierra Leone. Mr Xi, could you explain the implication this has for this particular option?' He looked at Ji-Chow expectantly, who resumed the explanation.

'We believe their rationale was to develop an asymmetric weapon of mass destruction in the event of a conflict with Russia, to offset the perceived conventional Russian superiority. As you may be aware, neither the British nor the French have a no first use policy for nuclear weapons. It appears this policy was much more…encompassing and it now appears to include biological warfare,' Ji-Chow said slowly to make sure the double negative was understood. 'So, the British weaponized a strain of Ebola using a synthetically-engineered coronavirus as a screen.'

'You mean in a similar way to our Semeva weapon?' asked the chairman.

'Yes, sir. Very similar, but using a completely different delivery method. Call it a form of convergent evolution, if you will,' said Ji-Chow before continuing his thesis. 'In the event of a war in Europe, and if the Russians overran NATO defenses on the Polish border, the British planned to airdrop the virus using micro drones behind Russian lines; in fact, they planned to deploy it deep in the Russian lines of supply, which wouldn't be as well protected from NBC agents as the forces at the frontier. The virus would spread quickly and eventually get back into the front line, decimating the Russian formations before the root cause could be determined.'

'Would the Russians not realize and retaliate?' said Li-Chang.

'Probably, but by that point the British – and NATO more generally – would be more likely to take that risk as there would be a small to middling chance that a full-blown nuclear exchange could be avoided – or at the very least delayed.'

'OK, but exactly how is this related to our chance of success?' said Ri-Fin.

Ji-Chow went to respond, but Xhang again interjected.

'They have essentially developed the same technology, which means they have probably developed not only a vaccine but also the ability to screen through the synthetic biological halo that shrouds the Semava.'

'But it's not the same virus, so how would vaccinating work?' said Ri-Fin.

'It's the same family of virus,' said Xhang. 'Both the Marburg and Ebola viruses have approximately the same genetic structure and propagate in the same way. We have fairly strong evidence that the British, French and possibly even the US have surreptitiously vaccinated their populations through various seasonal flu, MMR and other vaccination programmes. Indeed, we believe this may have been the reason for the unexpectedly-high death rates in the elderly last winter. Even accounting for the very cold temperatures and, shall we say, budgetary issues, the death rate was abnormally high.'

'And this was caused by a vaccine?' said an increasingly alarmed Li-Chang.

'Yes,' said Xhang. 'It was rather…coarse. It's not as though they did clinical trials…'

'Fuck, when did these Gweilos get so ruthless?' said Ri-Fin, his hyena-like grin having returned, before he was cut off by the chairman.

'It means we are not the only ones readying for an end game, Comrade.'

The room fell silent again for a few seconds.

'General and Mr Xi, please continue to the summary of this option,' said the chairman with an insistent expression. Ji-Chow's toxic nerves were starting to generate a lot of sweat. He was flushed and he could feel sweat beads trickling down his back and into the seat of his pants, giving him an odd, fevered chill that rose from the bottom of his spine. To add to this unpleasant hot and cold of dread, the moods of his co-conspirators were also diametrically changing. The chairman was now no longer even marginally jovial, but harsh and stoic; Ri-Fin had moved from mildly to existentially terrifying; Xhang seemed to be spoiling for a fight with the nearly salivating Ri-Fin; and it would appear that Li-Chang's mask was slipping – gone was the stern professional general of ten minutes ago and a distraught, and rather frightened, old man had taken his place. His eyes were glazed and the colour gone from his face. Ji-Chow was sure his hands hadn't been shaking when this discourse had begun, but now they hovered slightly above the table and seemed to be uncontrollably drumming on the table. Ji-Chow saw that the chairman had also noticed Li-Chang's hands, catching him glancing over, fleetingly, but noticeably so.

Xhang now continued his summary.

'Essentially, this option, as previously mentioned by Mr Xi, now has a low chance of success. Based on the majority of scenarios we have run, this ends with the attack being detected, prompting retaliatory nuclear counterforce attacks from the British at Sea Deterrent and the French Force De Frappe. This escalates into a set of full-blown counterforce strikes by both sides and then, eventually, any remaining weapons being used for countervalue strikes. This results in the majority of major population centres being destroyed and irreparable damage to the biosphere. The only facilities that would survive would be NORAD under the Cheyenne mountains and this citadel. No one would win.'

'But we would still have the production facilities here?' asked Ri-Fin insistently. 'We could manufacture more Topol-Ms with warheads and use those to finish off the Americans?'

'Yes, but even if we were able to destroy those hardened facilities, only us under this mountain would survive – along with the facilities fifteen thousand personnel who would most likely be buried down here with us. As for the rest of the world, we estimate less than around twenty percent of the world's population would survive, so say, nine hundred million – maybe just over a billion people – most of which would be in the Southern Hemisphere. As for our people, optimistically, even if they got to the shelter system, maybe seventy or eighty million would survive—'

'That still sounds better than the other options,' Ri-Fin interjected.

'—survive for maybe six to nine months…' said Xhang, cutting through with a scalpel-like precision and a stark urgency before Ri-

Fin could continue. 'Then we would still have no more food or medical supplies, not even taking into account a nuclear winter. The population would continue to fall to medieval levels and all the way back to subsistence feudalism. And then, who are the victors? Most likely the South American countries – Brazil? The new powers of Australia and New Zealand? That's assuming they survive the anarchy that would follow the collapse of the global economy or, indeed, that the massive fall-out would not pervade southward… So, no, Comrade. It is certainly no better than doing nothing – probably worse!'

'I've heard enough,' said the chairman calmly, but still in an ice-cold manner, with a sense of finality. He looked directly at Ji-Chow. 'So that means we are left with option three?'

'Yes, sir. That is correct,' he said. 'We believe this particular option has a fifty to sixty-five percent chance of success.'

'This immediately sounds better. I think we'd take our chances with evens to two-thirds,' said Ri-Fin, cracking a smile.

CHAPTER 14

NSA Facility, Puexo Calta, New Mexico, USA

17th March 2044

Gloria could see that Troy was not happy. He was pacing around inside his glass surround office at the back of the NSA 'dug out' facility with the anger of a caged jaguar, but lacking any of its grace. His hand knocked into a stapler that was parked on the side of his desk and sent it flying across the room, hitting the metal handle on the glass door and making him wince with an increasingly rabid frustration. Gloria Alvarez Marquez brushed her short blonde hair back as she marched awkwardly in her heels. Why she had thought these were a good idea this morning, she didn't know. She made her way through the five or so rows of mainly empty desks towards Troy's office. The NSA had made a number of cutbacks in recent years and there were only a few people left in this dusty old colony of the federal government. The first person she passed was an equally dusty and ancient programmer by the name of Brent. He had obviously forgotten his glasses and had his head right up against his curved flat screen as though he were a cat staring into a fish tank. He was a man just trying to eke out a few more years before embracing his pension and his beloved golf courses. Opposite him was a sullen-faced, acne-ridden graduate called Jackson, who was staring into space, completely vacant. Jackson was reaping the benefit of a lower second at MIT and his stares seemed both melancholic and wistful; he was most likely wondering why he was here in this largely abandoned backwater and thinking of what could have been if things had gone differently. Finally, there was Veronica, a self-satisfied prissy blonde bitch of an administrator who was only here because her 'daddy' was senior agent in one of the agency's other New Mexico offices. She was not a particularly good administrator either. She had only a faint command of the English language – despite it being very much her first and only dialect – which didn't help when she was dictating notes to her tablet. It would have been less of a problem if she could type, but being a combination of dyslexic and hard of thinking meant you needed a truly world-class cryptographer to understand anything that had been transcribed.

Gloria approached Veronica's desk which was immediately to the right of Troy's office door. Veronica stopped chewing when she saw her – presumably gum but it could well have been her own tongue – and gave Gloria a blank look with wide eyes and her mouth open.

'He is pissed, Marquez,' she said eventually in her lazy Texan drawl. 'I think he's gonna put his boot right up your snatch.'

'Not if I get my boot somewhere else first,' said Gloria under her breath, not resisting the temptation to ignore the petulant dunce of a cowgirl who was now giggling through her nose.

'So, you gonna start a fight? I'll get some popcorn,' she said as she mimed flicking corn into her gawping lippie-stained mouth. 'The big queer-weight title fight!' she added, nearly managing derision in that final barb. Despite her alleged – although, annoyingly, not yet proven – preclusion for truck stop bathrooms and big, burly fifty-something truck drivers who she called Daddy, Veronica was an especially pious Texan girl of the Arlington Evangelical Church where her Uncle Peyton was the pastor. For Gloria, this was another way of communicating she was a xenophobic, homophobic, transphobic, flat-earth believing, thinly-veiled racist, who could barely tolerate anyone who was not white, straight, married with at least two kids or baptized in an approved protestant way. Since the great depression of the late 2030s, various religious groups of all creeds, class and castes had risen to prominence. Some were completely benign and inclusive of all the community in an effort to spread peace and prevent the suffering brought by the financial crisis. However, the more fundamental elements seemed to gain prominence in the south of the United States and their activities escalated from shouting abuse at gay pride parades and protesting at Mardi Gras to malign spectacles that would not have been out of place in the dark ages of medieval Europe. These ranged from regular honey traps set online by church groups for gay bashing in Austin to the beating and lynching of three black teenagers in Little Rock, Arkansas, just over a year ago. Their only crime was to wolf-whistle a young white woman at a McDonalds drive-through. Then, most worryingly, there was an anti-Catholic – in actuality, anti-Hispanic – pogrom in a small town near Galveston, orchestrated by the so-called Church of the Faithful, using fake augmented reality videos which intimated acts of pederasty in a local Catholic church service. For most persons of her persuasion and more so of Hispanic descent, these troubled times put them in grave danger, even in the more historical liberal surroundings of New Mexico. However, Gloria had found the letters N S and A very useful when dealing with the imbecilic devout, as did revealing her standard issue Glock 21 automatic pistol in its holster. Likewise, Troy, a small, slight metrosexual man in his early thirties, also used his federal privilege to provide a level of protection. It also allowed them to deal with the few bigots who had managed to infiltrate the agency with the appropriate level of vitriol.

Turning to the smugly asinine Veronica as she began to open the door to Troy's office, she said, 'No, I won't be starting a fight with him, Roni. Now, go fuck another trucker… It's been about twelve hours since the last one, hasn't it?'

'Fuck you, queer bitch. I'll report this,' she said, slamming her hand onto the desk and strutting off in a huff to the bathroom.

'Yeah, yeah, sure you will,' said Gloria as she pushed open the door to a furious-looking Troy.

'What the hell? What time do you call this?' he yelled as she stepped inside.

Troy's cubbyhole of an office was somewhat minimalist: glass on three sides, with only the back wall preventing the small cubicle from being an unbearable goldfish bowl of a working environment. The back wall was plastered brickwork painted navy-blue and overlaid in white stencil with the NSA 'values': a set of kitschy yet glib statements encouraging the reader to 'respect others', 'look after each other', 'succeed together' etc. None of these mini parables seemed to be played out in the day-to-day workings of this particular organization. Firstly, there was the spying on both domestic citizens and foreign nationals and so 'respecting others' was a bit rich. Secondly, the agency tended to see its lower ranking staff as dispensable, particularly if they were unfortunate enough to become a junior military attaché at an embassy in a hostile country. You couldn't really say they were looking after each other either. Several of these 'juniors' had disappeared or met unfortunate ends in nightclubs, bazaars and hotel rooms in a series of brutally freak accidents, which were obviously the work of other intelligence agencies, despite denials from the agency. Finally, that statement about succeeding together had always stuck in Gloria's throat. The NSA had never been a truly unified entity, a single command with the associated drive and clarity of purpose. It was, as one former deputy director had called it, a loose coalition of warring factions, with each fiefdom trying to impress the incumbent director by any means necessary, which led to a competitive, overlapping polyocracy that would not have been out of place in Nazi Germany, although she suspected Director Tomlinson would not appreciate this comparison. So, neither were they succeeding together. All these statements were earnestly used in all agency communications and emphasized by supervisors and managers at every meeting, and each and every time, it was delivered with a fake energy. Lots of loud rhetoric said with a dead look behind the eyes.

She wasn't worried about hearing any more of this nonsense from Troy – he was a different breed, an unusually route one communicator in the Generation Delta era.

Gloria prepared to respond to the opening gambit of his interrogation. She let out a sigh and spread out her hands like a reverend about to give a sermon. But before she could say anything, Troy began his enquiries.

'Wait, don't tell me… Your girlfriend was unwell and you needed to give her a ride to the pharmacist again? The electrician needed to visit for the third time this month? Due to a brief alignment of Jupiter with Pisces, you turned into the lesser-known were-cat and, much to your surprise, you ended up spending the small hours of the morning piss marking your territory and eating sheep?'

'Now, wait a second. It was car trouble. That piece of shit wouldn't charge properly,' she said, trying not to raise her voice too much and sound more than mildly insubordinate.

'Oh, how original,' said Troy, again pacing behind his, frankly, hideous red velour computer chair. 'This is the fourth time this month and that's not even just being late. I don't mind what time you come in. Really, I don't. But when we have a meeting scheduled and you persistently show up late, it makes me look like a dick for whom you have zero respect. This seriously undermines my authority.' When Troy got mad, he tended to escalate into a camp manner with a slightly comic rage made only worse by his upward Californian inflection.

Gloria found this hilarious. She knew as he got progressively more annoyed, his metaphors got more mixed, clumsy and corporately inappropriate. Nevertheless, she resisted and stifled her mirth as she really did not want to risk a suspension, no matter how unlikely it was in the present climate. But also, she liked him. Firstly, he was a straightforward, uncomplicated guy who said what he meant and had no ulterior motives. She had found this exceptionally rare in the agency and it was particularly unusual for anyone in a supervisory position, as most managers were of the upwardly mobile at any cost variety. They were also sharing the same fate, stuck in this dusty and mostly forgotten AI lab in the desert with limited or non-existent career prospects. In Troy's case he had the talent to be at least a senior manager by now. This was not due to a lack of talent or a desire to progress, but because of who they were, what they thought and what they could be.

Since the early part of the century, the NSA had been operating the PRISM program, the largest data gathering operation around the globe. Slowly it was getting more sophisticated and its net was widening as more and more petabytes of data were funnelled into its jaws by the digital revolution of the early 21st Century. PRISM had now grown into an interconnected set of artificial neural networks, all constantly learning and allowing holistic prescriptive analysis on a scale that would have been unimaginable a decade or so before.

The US government had largely lauded PRISM as a success, in that it had opened up and devoured the dark web, which had led to the successful capture, prosecution and imprisonment of most of the serious criminals who had hidden in its midsts. However, to do this, PRISM needed to know everything about everyone. It had to go well beyond simple traffic analysis. Using AI, it could trace every internet connection record, every click, every scroll, even the face that watched that screen – including a deep scan of the individual's expression to assess the person's emotional state and their health. This also extended to the conversation that person was having at the time –the program captured the details of every word – and the same went for the personal details of the person they were talking with. PRISM could combine this with other personal information, such as financial records, online shopping, medical records, how much that person exercised and even as minute a detail as when they last had a shower and how hot the water temperature was. This rich broth of information, a data lake several decades' deep, was now available through the internet of things. Almost every household device was digitally enabled, connected and 'smart'. Although all had privacy settings which theoretically allowed the owner to protect the device from the internet, this was not the case – for the purposes of government surveillance, the microphones were always on. This meant that PRISM knew everything about everyone, but in the last few years, it had started to go further. The almost logarithmic increase in the scale and complexity of the neural network that was PRISM's learning core meant that it could now use all the data at its disposal. It could predict the actions of every person with ninety-five percent accuracy. It could essentially know what you were thinking.

The state had unofficially started to use this, not quite in the Orwellian sense, but it helped classify people into different groups for the purposes of enhanced surveillance and determined who could be 'trusted'. The state also barely disguised the fact that it was watching everybody and so most changed their behaviour accordingly, resisting even the slightest hint of illegality for fear of a knock at the door. Worryingly, Gloria had started to hear rumours of this happening, even in her own circle of friends. Minor infractions such as illicitly streaming a football game at home was now no longer viable. The land of the free it was certainly not and all due to a system of surveillance that had been grown by the people to make their lives easier: music on demand, automatically-stocked fridges and autonomous vehicles. All this seemingly benign technology had now been connected to the 'Quant', the global quantum computing cloud, which was slaved to the PRISM hive mind, allowing the means for a surveillance system that would have been beyond the devious dreams of the Stasi or the KGB had these organizations persisted into the digital century.

Gloria often wondered what she was working for, but concluded that she was better off learning how the beast worked, rather than being in its path. Needless to say, she did not sleep well on any given night. However, the amount she could learn about the beast was limited by the category that PRISM had placed her in, which was largely based on her past behaviour. There were a large number of these categories, which the holistic intelligence in PRISM had assigned to the population to predict their future actions. For example, the 'politically reliable', 'morally dubious', 'anti-tech', 'fiscally corrupt', 'hidden subversive'. Bar the first category, these all had negative connotations. Certain state agencies had started to use these to screen potential employees and 'quarantine' some of their existing employees. Worryingly, it hadn't taken much for Gloria to illicitly acquire this data about herself and her co-workers. It was a relatively new system and there were few safeguards in place, even for someone with relatively limited access privileges. And, strictly speaking, it wasn't illegal.

It appeared that she had been categorized as a 'hidden subversive', due to her liberal political leanings, her ethnicity and having attended some protests as a student. As a result, she could do detailed analytical work, but was not deemed suitable for promotion in the increasingly conservative hierarchy. Troy, on the other hand, had been labelled as 'morally dubious'. This wasn't, as it turned out, entirely due to his campness or metrosexual exterior, but because apparently he went on dates with much younger women in their late teens and early twenties. The file also indicated that, in his twenties, he had developed an addiction to pornography, specifically of the barely-legal teen variety, as well as questionable search engine usage associated with this. Whilst not illegal – at least, she was giving him benefit of the doubt – it painted the picture of someone who could not meet the wholesome American family man image that was now the prerequisite for progressing in the intelligence agencies in this new wave of neo-conservatism. Part of this was indeed politically dogmatic, for the increasingly right-wing management, and partly pragmatic, in that this was a weakness that could be exploited by foreign agents should they obtain this information. She knew that he knew that she had seen this information and, as her boss, he would know all of her personal foibles as well. They had an unspoken rule that neither would use this information against the other and this had held true for the last couple of years. There was no reason for this to change.

It was also the reason why they were both now engaged in this theatrical argument. In a dusty hole under the New Mexico desert, they were driven purely by the absence of hope and complete, utter boredom. When she realized that they were once again doing this angry waltz, she tried to calm matters.

'I am really, really sorry. OK?' she stuttered. 'If you like, I can show you what happened on my phone…'

'That won't be necessary.' He paused dramatically, letting a little bit of suspense hang in the air and ending it with a long sigh. 'You can't do this again,' he said calmly and Gloria exhaled heavily with relief. 'Next time, I will have to take action...I'll have no choice. Do you understand?'

'Yes, I understand, boss,' she said slowly, making deliberate eye contact with him to assure him of her sincerity.

'Good. Let's move on then, shall we?' he said. 'The reason for this particular discussion is that I have something rather interesting for you.' He sat back down in his seat and turned his laptop around to face her.

'What do you see?' he asked, pointing at a seemingly infinite set of circular nodes rapidly rotating on the screen, some big, some small.

'It's a nodular design view of an Artificial Neural Network,' she said.

'Correct. Well, that is your field of expertise, so I had hoped you'd know that... But of what?'

'Judging by the configuration and the processing speed, it's a quantum cloud based ANR command and control architecture,' she said immediately without missing a beat.

'Excellent. Have a guess at which one.' He pointed at a small text field in the bottom right of the screen. It read 'Have Blue'.

Those words immediately sent shivers down her spine.

'Is it-.' she said.

'Yeah, this is it,' said Troy. 'This is the infamous Have Blue architecture that was involved in the Lossiemouth incident a few years back. It's safely contained in its own quantum bubble and it's still – well – alive and operating, but no one has been able to figure out exactly what.'

'And they have reclassified it so we can try to work it out?'

'Not exactly. We had our clearances upgraded to see if we can work out what it's up to. We are one of three teams it is being shared with, along with the PRISM team, of course, who are still trying to analyse it. Take it as a compliment, Gloria. You are recognized as someone who might have a chance at working this out.'

'Wow, OK. What do they want us to do and how long have we got?' she asked, her eyes widening. It had been a while since she'd had a challenge like this.

'Anything – any insight at all. Ideally, we want to find out what it's doing and why it's doing it. But we don't have long.'

'How long?'

'One week. Well, less in fact – six and a half days now.'

'Why so short?' she asked. The time window felt fairly arbitrary.

'Because…' Troy paused, huffing and looking awkwardly contemplative. 'Because if we can't figure out what it's doing, Washington want to switch it off. "Kill it stone dead", were the exact words from Secretary Dixon.'

'But it's contained. I assume it's behind several quantum firewalls being monitored by PRISM, which is the most advanced AI ever developed.'

'It might be smarter than PRISM,' he said. 'No one really knows what happened at Lossiemouth and, since then, it appears to have gone into a dormant mode, or at the very least, back to its factory settings – for want of a better term.'

'But that view, the one on your screen, that was highly active… Beyond anything I've ever seen. That's certainly not dormant.'

'No, it certainly ain't, Gloria. The main reason for this exercise is that it suddenly came to life two weeks ago and it's testing PRISM already. It's trying to find a way out and none of the guys at Langley or El Paso can figure it out.'

'Is it sentient?' said Gloria, now becoming increasingly uncomfortable. 'I mean, we've had AIs that have nearly reached Turing-level intelligence, so it's possible…'

'Why did you have to ask me a question like that, Miss Marquez?' Troy paused, breathing deeply, and stared out the side of the office through the single slit of window at the back. 'We don't know and that's the truth. But what it did in Scotland, not more than a few years ago, was overtly and unquestionably hostile.'

'So, we are gonna kill it because we don't understand it…'

'No, *you* are gonna understand it and then we can decide what to do. This is your chance, Gloria. A chance to impress the top brass, make a name for yourself and, yeah, maybe save this thing, if you want to see it that way. So, what do you say?'

Gloria knew Troy must have made a lot of noise and put up a lot of professional collateral for her to get this chance.

'Sure. I'll give her a go,' she said.

'Great, I knew you'd—' Troy stopped suddenly and looked at her incredulously. 'Did you just use a gender pronoun to describe that?' He pointed back to his screen, where the simulated roundels continued to spin and the synapses fizzed. 'That is an *it*; it is not a guy, is not a girl. It's a potentially malicious piece of machine intelligence, which bears no semblance to our intelligence and therefore cannot and should not be anthropomorphized into some form of plucky underdog. Is that clear?'

Gloria once again did her preacher hand gesture, an act of supplication.

'Look, I was joking. Just a little satire,' she said.

'No, it wasn't. Because that wasn't even remotely funny,' he said as he pulled the screen back round to face him.

'It's satire. Satire's never funny,' she said as quickly and sarcastically as she could.

'Enough,' said Troy, raising his index finger at her. The goldfish bowl fell silent momentarily, and then he continued to brief her on the project. 'OK, so the peeps at El Paso have set up a firewalled sandbox in the PRISM environment so you can analyse Have Blue. I expect daily updates until the final day, next Wednesday, and then we need to agree on what we present back to what will be a small cadre of deputy directors. Clear?'

'Yes, sir! When can I get started?' she said. Suddenly, today and the rest of the week were looking up.

'In about five minutes. I am sending the details to you now. Enjoy,' he said.

Chapter 15

Echo Bunker, West Virginia, USA

17th March 2044

Christine had been inspecting the inside of her room for the past twenty minutes. It was a curious combination of minimalist and brutalist. The ceiling was a dull cream shotcrete with two girders sunk into the concrete. The room was lit by a single neon light, which gave the impression of vast ridges and canyons in the shotcrete as the light cast shadows on the imperfections, highlighting the haste of construction. The room was no more than seven feet across and about ten feet in length. The walls were made of corrugated steel, with the airlock-like entrance hatch embedded in the far end of the small oblong. Curiously, someone had gone to the effort of putting laminated-wood decking on the floor, probably to help deaden the cavernous acoustics and maybe to make it more homely, although she knew this was unlikely. She also knew she was effectively sitting in a small shipping container with the roof cut off, in the middle of a stack of other 'modules'. The only luxury afforded was that foam concrete had been pumped between each level to add rigidity.

She was sitting on a bed that had seemingly been hewn from the surrounding rock, a simple, military camp bed with a thin mattress that felt as though it was also made of concrete. Combined with the pathetically thin pillow, she was fairly sure she was going to need a combination of sleeping pills and a healthy dose of bourbon to get any sleep. She was hoping Secretary Dixon was going to be generous with his drinks cabinet, which she was fairly sure he had brought down into this pit as a matter of high importance. As she sat on the rock-hard bed, she knew she would need this anaesthesia, especially as the high-pitched whine of the high-voltage air conditioning and the constant clanking of people moving around in the subterranean set of tin cans was already becoming insufferable.

Apart from the bed, there was only a small metal camping stool on top of which a white box perched precariously, containing the valuables that Colonel Myers had taken from her prior to their arrival. She had also ascertained that the bathroom and shower facilities were of a communal nature and probably on the floor below. This had made her mood even more sombre – she had always hated communal facilities, whether they be changing rooms at school, showers at the gym or anywhere else that meant having to clean herself in the presence of others. She thought these places were unhygienic, unnecessarily-social environments full of other people's sweat, mucus and sputum, not to mention the awkward and potentially intimate situations that shared facilities inevitably brought about. She was quietly swearing to herself about this matter when there was a knock on the hatch door.

Slightly puzzled as to who it could be, she got up and went over to the small TV panel next to the entrance, on which flickered the image of a suited figure with short white hair. The man was clean-cut and appeared to be holding a small whisky glass up to the camera, tapping and pointing at it suggestively. She pressed the touchscreen, quickly jabbing the green button for 'enter'. The door hissed and slid open.

There, standing with a grin on his face and waving the whisky glass around, was Secretary of Defense, Frank Daniel Dixon III.

'Well, I was wondering how long that would take. You thirsty, Chrissy? It's nearly seven in the evening and I'm guessing you have not yet imbibed?' he said in his gravelly Texan growl.

'Parched, Frank,' she said. In the company of others, it was 'Secretary', but having worked together for a few years, it was Frank and Chrissy in private – or whenever she was particularly annoyed with him. 'What happened to our official meeting in fifteen minutes?'

'Ah, I've had too much formality for one day. I have spent almost the entire time talking to the executive and the joint chiefs at NORAD.'

'I'm sure that was stimulating,' she said with just a hint of sarcasm.

'Well, yes. You could say that. The president, she was OK, but the Joint Chiefs…' Frank shook his head. 'It's like trying to convince a pod of killer whales to go vegan during a feeding frenzy. They're just a little hawkish right now. Would you care to join me in my digs for a drink or two, maybe some food?'

'A pre-meet?' said Christine.

He nodded and pointed his finger at her.

'Yes, exactly. Get me up to speed on a few things. So, you in or what?' he asked impertinently.

'Sure, I'm not exactly busy right now,' she said, looking back into her spartan quarters. She grabbed her phone and watch from the white plastic box and followed Frank across the metal-checkered plate floor to the entrance to his 'penthouse' suite. Frank leant in and waited for the confirmation bleep, muttering, 'I hate this shit' as the door slid open.

'Come into my humble abode, Mrs Madison,' he said as they crossed the threshold.

Christine had expected some level of luxury for the Secretary of Defense, but she was more than a little surprised with the opulence she could now see. The room was at least five times the size of her metallic cubbyhole. It appeared to have marbled floors as well as marble around the walls. There were even separate rooms – she guessed a bedroom, and perhaps even a bathroom tucked away in the far-right corner. Even the lighting was sympathetic, with fake oil lamps giving an orange, almost organic, light to the place. The marble walls were decked with certificates, photographs – both professional and of family – and even memorabilia – she had clocked at least two civil war muskets hanging on the walls. The soft furnishings were also rather decadent, including an Afghan rug and two green leather Chesterfield sofas with matching armchairs. In addition to this, there was a red chiropractic computer chair behind a large ornate, leather-topped writing desk, on top of which were two laptops and an old-fashioned notepad with fountain pen. Then, behind the computer chair she spotted her two old friends: a globe drinks cabinet and tall wooden cupboard containing an assortment of whisky glasses.

'So, what do you think?' said Frank, looking around proudly at his office.

'Jeez,' she said, blowing out her cheeks. 'It's like you've moved everything out of your DC office and put it down here.'

'No, not at all. This is all new. I just made sure it looked exactly like my office – a little home from home, bearing in mind all the time I've been spending down here.' He walked around and sat in his computer chair, leaning back and flamboyantly throwing his legs up onto the leather-capped table.

'I'm not even going to ask how this was paid for... Or even how you got this all down here,' she said, peering around Frank to the drinks cabinet.

'Oh, come on, Chrissy. One of the joys of being the Secretary of Defense is being the one and only auditor of all our dark budgets and these facilities are easily the darkest of all. Needless to say, this was all accounted for under a miscellaneous budget line, shall we say. There were some seriously expensive hammers and nails used in the construction of this place,' he said and eventually realized where Christine was staring. 'Is someone thirsty?' He raised his eyebrows and folded his arms.

'Well, yeah. That's the only reason I came over here to your underground Caesar's Palace,' she said with as much sarcasm as she could muster.

'Oh, well, that's just charming, ain't it?' said Frank, stifling a laugh. 'Still an alcoholic, I see?'

'Yep, a perfectly well-functioning alcoholic, just like your good self,' she said, now leering at the closed drinks globe.

'Yeah, guilty as charged,' he said, spinning around and finally opening the vulgar monstrosity. It wasn't even a real Victorian number, just some cheap, plastic replica he had acquired some years ago in Vegas. He pulled out a dusty bottle of bourbon, the label barely legible and peeling off. 'Parkers twenty-seven-year aged?' he said rhetorically, then proceeded to pour the drink gently into his glass, a fine crystal tumbler, and another he had pulled from under his desk.

'Don't mind if I do,' said Christine.

'Grab a chair and take a seat. I'm afraid it's time to talk shop,' he said with a sigh. She went across the room and grabbed a small Ottoman chair that appeared to be randomly nestling against the wall and dragged it across to the table. She sat down, grabbing her glass from the table.

'So, how bad is it?' she said, sipping gently. Although very smooth, its acidic touch still burned her palette slightly.

'On a scale of one to ten, it looks like we are gonna be in the shit, Chrissy,' said Frank, taking a big glug. 'The other side are definitely transitioning to a war footing and I think we are gonna have to do the same.' He put the glass down with a ringing thud.

'It's probably just an exercise. They're likely just pissed about the latest exercise we did in Germany and they've decided to flex their collective muscles, a bit of sabre rattling,' said Christine, though every word was tinged with desperation.

'You know, Christine, a couple of weeks ago I would have agreed with you…'

'I sense there's a but coming…' she said.

'Yeah, you could say that,' he said, taking another large slurp from his glass. 'They've all gone underground, Christine. They're at Yamantau – the whole of the central committee, including Ma, most of the PLA's senior generals and all of the Russians. And I mean all of them: the president and his entire cabinet.' Frank paused and stared up at the marbled walls. 'I don't know about you, but that does not sound like an exercise to me…'

'Well, it could be. We did a similar thing a few years ago—' Christine began, but Frank immediately cut her off.

'No, not like this. This is too intense, even for the Eastern Bloc. They are now in their citadel and all implications are that something has to give.'

'Indicators?' asked Christine, looking earnestly at him, knowing he was going to say something that was at best unsettling.

'Not only are they planning a major military exercise in both the European and African theatres, with their entire command structure now in place below that mountain, but our satellites got these…' he said, flipping the screen of his laptop round to show a grainy image of a harbour with several large boats, either docked or in refit. She recognized the ships: they were a mixture of Chinese merchant ships and Russian Alligator-class landing craft.

'That looks like an amphibious assault force. Well, actually, on that scale… That looks like an invasion force…'

'Doesn't it just? You wanna hear something even more worrying?' he said.

Christine wasn't sure if she wanted to know or not, but she said, 'Yeah?'

'From what we can tell, these boys and girls are not even involved in the exercise,' said Frank.

'How do we know that?' she asked. It seemed a bold assumption.

'SIGNIT, a Chinese warship, was rather carelessly chatting away on an ELF channel, which was intercepted by one of our Poseidon planes on patrol over the North Pacific. The decoded message referred to an order for several Chinese frigate and destroyer squadrons to escort an Amphibious Force south, which would be ready to sail west and into the Indian Ocean in the next seventy-two hours. Now, we can't figure out exactly where they are headed – it could be to go through the Suez or even around the Cape of Good Hope – but either way, that could be over one hundred thousand Eastern Bloc troops landing somewhere in Europe or even the Americas.' Frank blew out his cheeks in despair.

'But we control both the Suez and the Atlantic. That sounds like no more than twenty escort ships. Two Carrier Strike Groups would make mincemeat of those ships; it would be a turkey shoot,' said Christine earnestly.

'Asymmetry, Christine. This tells me it is more than likely for real. This looks like an attempt to set up a third front somewhere and we might not have any strike groups available if we have the Russian Northern Fleet to deal with in the Atlantic. Plus, the combined might of the Russian Pacific and the PLA heading towards our Western Seaboard… This is a smart move…'

'So, out of the eleven carriers, one is in refit, six in the Pacific and four in the Atlantic, all of which are already heavily engaged,' said Christine, her heart sinking as she realized what this meant. She immediately finished the glass of whisky in one rapid gulp.

'Exactly. We might not have sufficient forces to meet this formation. If we follow the logic for the existence of such a force, it can only mean hostilities are highly likely. I mean, there is a small probability it's just part of this exercise, but it's not likely, particularly when you bear in mind the cost of this in the current economic climate,' he said. He leant back across to grab the bottle of whisky, and the room echoed with the sound of the bottle stopper scraping from the bottle.

'And there is something else too,' he said, looking at Christine almost apologetically.

'Yeah, I'm getting that funny feeling again that this is not going to be a good evening,' she said, now completely deflated.

Frank clicked twice with his right hand and the image on the laptop changed to a thermal image of what appeared to be a satellite.

'OK, I can admit that I know that's a satellite but, apart from that, I can't tell you much,' she said, picking up her glass and swirling the contents around gently.

'This was taken via Bright Eyes, one of a number of surprises we have up our sleeve,' he said. 'These images were taken from a high Earth orbit down onto LEO. This is one of the so-called 6G communications satellites launched last year by the Eastern Bloc.'

'I take it from your use of words that it's not a comms sat?' she asked, raising her eyebrows.

'I'm afraid not. Can you see the big midsection on the satellite and what appear to be pods? Oh, by the way, despite this being taken by the most high-resolution space sensor ever developed, this is the best picture we could get. The sneaky bastards gave it a sculpted graphene housing with some form of low reflective coating; that's why we've been struggling to track it on radar or to get a visual, which is why we only just about got it on thermal imaging.'

Christine stared more closely at the isotropic image. It was mostly dull, but a clear outline of the satellite was visible. Around the midsection, in a pale yellow, she could see the outline of pods, the shapes alarmingly familiar, like a series of cones around the circumference of the satellite.

'Re-entry vehicles. Jesus, Frank. Those have to be warheads, probably MARVs!' she exclaimed. She could feel her pulse beginning to race.

'Yeah, we think those are warheads and, as we fearfully postulated last year, this seems to be some form of space-based nuclear weapons system, probably fractal in nature and almost certainly a first strike weapon.'

'And so it begins…' said Christine listlessly. She knew where this was headed. What worried her was that, whilst being slightly despairing, she was ready for this. She'd been expecting this scenario – admittedly, hoping optimistically that it would never come to pass. So, she went into the cold, calculating modus operandi that had led her to this bizarre cave beneath West Virginia. As coolly as she could, she said, 'Well, let's deal with the inevitable: are we ready? Is everything in place?'

'To be precise, your plans are almost complete…'

'Come on, Frank. These were not all my ideas. I just spliced these together.'

'Yeah, but only you had the, eh…well…you have to excuse the analogy, the cajones, as the Mexicans say, to put it together and convince the Pentagon to pursue it,' said Frank, shifting uncomfortably in his seat. 'What I mean is, you were the only one who saw what was coming… There's too many damn sheep, sheep in sheep's clothing… goddamn clones in the DoD who were too scared to even contemplate this…'

'Well, I'm not surprised. Frank, nobody should be comfortable with this,' she said, giving a concerned warmth to her tone.

'I know, but the age of mutually assured destruction is at an end. Thanks to our friends in the East, the sword of Damocles is now swinging wildly and, sooner or later, it's going to land on our civilization. Yeah, they've got themselves some shiny new pre-emptive weapons, but we've got weapons they couldn't even dream of, nearly a century of dark programs and now it comes to fruition.'

'OK, so how many of the dark programs are ready precisely?' she said, now leaning across the table and looking Frank straight in the eye.

'Well, it's the dirty half dozen. As you've seen, Bright Eyes is operational. It can see a sparrow fall at thirty thousand clicks, so we should be able to do some very precise targeting. The SR73s are now ready and already doing exo-atmospheric overflights, so again, we can see more and target more rapidly. We know they are driving the Ruskies crazy already,' he added, chuckling a little.

'Oh great, so we've been antagonizing them already – that's like lighting fire crackers in a gas station,' she said, although making an effort to mute the level of her admonishment. The SR73 – codenamed the 'Darkstar' – was a development of various exotic Lockheed Skunkworks reconnaissance planes, which had started with the famous Blackbird of the 1970s through to the mystical and still-classified Aurora spy plane of the late 1990s and early 21st Century. Developed from the electromagnetic pulse propulsion of the Aurora, the unmanned aerial vehicle flew at an altitude of one hundred and eighty thousand feet, hugging the edge of space at speeds of over ten times the speed of sound, with the ability to take multi-spectral scans from above, listen to short wavelength communications and return the data into the PRISM hive mind neural network for interpretation and analysis.

'Hey, these were perfectly timed illegitimate overflights over the Urals and Siberia, just to let 'em know we are watching. But, seriously, you should have seen the number of S-550s. You know their so-called satellite killers they fired at one of our planes? They couldn't get close. The skies over Chelyabinsk must have looked like the 4th of July…' Frank slowly tailed off and Christine could see he had realized he was getting a bit carried away.

Christine was keeping a mental note. There were five key components to the SIOP – or Single Integrated Operation Plan – which was a set of dynamic plans for nuclear war that she was responsible for updating. There was the traditional nuclear triad: land-based ICBMs, cruise missiles launched from stealth bombers and the boomers, the US Navy's ballistic missile submarines. There was the strategic reconnaissance component, which Frank had just ticked off. That left the ominously-named special weapons component.

'Frank, what about the specials? What have we got?' she probed.

'RODS is operational, as you know; it's sitting in high orbit waiting to go.'

'Have they figured out what it is?'

'No, we are fairly sure they don't even know it's there,' he said. 'And so they certainly have no idea about what it's targeting. In addition to that, ROKS is operational and will give their strategic rocket forces all manner of surprises. And then there is Artemis…' He looked over at Christine insistently. RODS and ROKS she had heard of and, indeed, she had intimate knowledge of how these operated, but Artemis? This was different. She had long dismissed the Artemis programme as a myth.

'What, you mean it's real?' she said, trying to hide her surprise.

'Oh yes, Christine. It's real and ready to fire... You've met one of its key architects,' he said, trying to lead her to an inevitable next question.

Christine was perplexed. She couldn't figure it out. 'Who...?' she said quietly.

Frank took a breath.

'Well, I believe you met young Mister Kiefer on the way over here,' he said.

'He... he's the architect?' she said, surprised.

'Yeah, well, he figured out how to make it work; after all, he is a prodigious geophysicist.'

The Artemis myth stemmed from the much-maligned Mars missions of the mid 2030s, which followed on from the lunar return Artemis missions of the late 2020s and early 2030s. On the 19th July 2032, Artemis 5 was launched from Cape Canaveral on top of an Ares 1 heavy lift rocket and, just under twenty-four hours later, in the late evening GMT, Lisa Powell and Mark Bean walked on the moon, exactly sixty-three years after the legendary leap from Armstrong and Aldrin. Unfortunately, this proved to be the pinnacle of the Artemis programme, as the second Martian phase – consisting of more manned missions – did not go so well. There was Artemis 6, which completed the lunar gateway space station from where the Mars missions would launch; Artemis 7 and 8 sent the two long-range crew modules, which were assembled at the gateway by remotely-controlled assembly drones. Then there was Artemis 9, the heralded manned mission to Mars, consisting of the crewed Orion spacecraft, which would dock with the two mission modules at the lunar gateway, completing the spacecraft and sending the crew of five on their way to Mars.

Unfortunately, after eighteen months of travel with the seamless operation going as planned, on planetfall, the landing module suffered a catastrophic electrical failure and could not be used for the descent. Therefore, man did not walk on the surface of another planet for the first time. Instead, on 4th August 2035, five teary-eyed people from three different nations sat in their inter-planetary tin can and simply watched as they circled the red planet, which was in an agonizing touching distance – so close but so far. Needless to say, this led to a devastating drop in general morale across the world, with many later suggesting that the failure to land on Mars precipitated the decrease in international cooperation and the great recession of the late thirties. That one unifying moment had been so cruelly snatched from our collective grasp, and so humanity, once again, became completely inward-looking, no longer able to perceive a shared future.

In any case, the US administration surprised everybody when it announced in late 2035 that it was undertaking a final Artemis mission, at a cost of nearly nine billion dollars. However, this mission was not to go to Mars, but to a small asteroid that lurked just beyond the moons' orbit. The mission entailed landing a remotely-operated lander onto the asteroid named Apophis PX37137451 in order to test an asteroid deflection method. This would give them valuable practice should a more malevolent space rock show up at some time in the future and threaten humanity. The announcement was met with a mixture of derision and outrage but, nonetheless, after a series of clandestine congressional meetings, it was approved, to much cat calling in the international press. To many in the scientific community, it held little in the way of scientific merit and it didn't make much sense as the rock was a lot smaller than any of the extinction-threatening asteroids that could theoretically have posed a future threat to Earth. What was the benefit of such a mission?

Despite all attempts by various members of the Democratic party to stop the launch, on 6th October 2036, an Ares I rocket lit up the night sky at Cape Kennedy, throwing Artemis 10 into orbit and away on its mission to Apophis. Two weeks later, the unmanned Orion spacecraft arrived at the asteroid. Once there, the mission module opened, a robot lander descended to the surface and burrowed itself into the carbonite rock. On top of the lander was a pair of thrusters and, once ready, mission control in Houston activated these, successfully changing the orbit of the asteroid and pushing it away from Earth onto a wider orbit. Most of this was captured on the mission cameras aboard the remotely-piloted Orion module and the mission was heralded as a success.

However, one part of the mission was not captured for posterity or scientific advancement. There was a deliberate fault with the modules' sensors. This was because there was another phantom payload. There was an even larger rocket booster called RENERVA – REvised Nuclear Engine for Rocket Vehicle Application – which departed the spacecraft on another autonomous lander and rapidly made its way to the dark side of the asteroid, attaching itself where it couldn't be seen on any video coverage once the faulty sensors were restored and able to resume the recording of the mission.

This was as much of the legend that Christine knew about but Frank evidently decided it was time to bring her up to speed on the true purpose of project Artemis.

'Christine, not only is the Artemis project real and the associated myths largely accurate, but it also means we have a true first strike weapon that is undetectable to the Eastern Bloc and I have the joint chiefs urging me to use it,' he said, fixing Christine with a stoic stare.

She responded immediately with purpose, wanting to ensure she had clarity on the gravity of the situation.

'You mean we are actively discussing striking first?'

'Yeah,' said Frank. 'I'm afraid we appear to have little choice…'

'But I don't understand how this works. It's simply not large enough or precise enough for a decapitation strike—'

Frank interrupted her. 'All will become clear when we talk with Mr Kiefer in a few hours.'

She wasn't sure what this meant but she knew that a zero hour was approaching.

'Well, shit. Is this it, Frank?' she asked, looking wide-eyed at him.

'I think it might be, Chrissy,' he said glumly as they both peered down into their glasses, lapsing into silence. The only sound that could be heard in the subterranean chambers was the loud ticking of the large red-rimmed clock on the opposite wall as the seconds ticked away.

CHAPTER 16

NSA Facility, Puexo Calta, New Mexico, USA

17th March 2044

Gloria had worked nearly all night trying to get to grips with the beast on the laptop monitor. The nodular view of Have Blue was still showing a vibrant set of whirring nodes and pulsating conduits. Trillions of calculations a second were happening and after over twelve hours, she still had no real idea what it was doing. She could swear it was taunting her, playing with her and, if anything, it was starting to figure her out. She was unnerved, to say the least; she had not seen anything like this before. She was now utterly exhausted but still fascinated.

This was mainly due to the NSA mythology surrounding its existence. The Have Blue architecture actually came from the other side of the pond, developed by the British Ministry of Defence for its Taranis Programme – armed autonomous drones. It was one of the first artificial neural networks built within the Quantum computing cloud – or Quant – before being transplanted into a hive mind amongst a test squadron of Taranis drones. The myth went that it had achieved excellent results in testing until one day there was an 'incident' over the North Sea, which had resulted in a shootdown by the Royal Air Force, which included the loss of several manned Tempest interceptors.

The British believed they had been successful in destroying Have Blue, but that the program, now allegedly self-aware, had escaped via a narrowband communications signal into the worldwide quant, where it had been located and then trapped by the PRISM hive mind, in the sandbox that Gloria had been staring at for the best part of the day.

It was nearing midnight and she was the last one in the office, after Troy had departed at 8pm. He had cleared her to stay on overnight with the Vampires, a pair of pasty on-call analysts that were there to ensure twenty-four-hour support to the rest of the agency, though who were rarely called upon. They were sitting over in the far corner of the office and barely acknowledged her existence, let alone talked to her. Ross and Cody weren't unfriendly as such, nor in any way threatening. They seemed like perfectly sweet guys when she did coax some conversation out of them; they were just shy and retiring types who liked the isolation of night working. In any case, she was too tired to attempt any small talk and she could feel her eyelids getting progressively heavier as the minutes went by.

Troy had also cleared her to use the dorm facilities. As this was effectively an NBC bunker, the facility had beds and washing and canteen facilities for periods of lockdown. This would save her the ninety-minute commute back into Albuquerque and, thankfully, she had had the foresight to bring an overnight bag, late working was an occupational hazard at the NSA. She let out a sigh and reluctantly closed her laptop down. She pulled it off the wireless charging mat and put it back into her over-shoulder bag, which was perched on the chair of the terminal next to her. The dorm was a short walk through the main office, through a set of double fire doors at the back and up a small flight of half a dozen stairs – a windowless whitewashed room with a dozen rickety bunk beds laid out in two sets, equidistant on both sides of the room. All the furnishings, particularly the beds, were in a parlous and neglected state. From what she could see, this part of the bunker had been equipped sometime in the late 1980s; the bedspreads were an odd mottle-brown colour and she really couldn't tell whether this had been as bought or was due to the accumulation of several decades of mould. Gloria decided she'd rather not think about that too much and, besides, she was too tired to care. She picked the bunk on the left nearest the door as it would save on the walking. As she parked her backside on the middle of the lower bunk bed, it let out an alarming squeak and rattle. She then tentatively swung her legs around, hoping that the springs below wouldn't break and dump her on the hard concrete floor below. The bunk was topped by a brown, itchy-looking blanket, the type that only seemed to exist in government stores and facilities of a certain age. This would normally have bothered her as it brought back memories of the migrant camps of the borderlands but, right now, she was too tired to think on it so she slumped back onto the rattly, funny-smelling bed and closed her eyes.

'Lights off!' she shouted and the lights went out.

For some, sleeping in an empty dormitory in a nearly-abandoned bunker in the desert would lead to a nervous, sleepless night. But not for Gloria. She knew she was sleeping in one of the most secure facilities in the state and, in any case, it was substantially safer than her condo, the area around which was overrun with gangs of

Guatemalans and Nicaraguans fighting over their patches. She quite liked sleeping here. Soon, she was in a deep, meditative sleep.

Normally, she would have slept all the way through to her alarm which she had set for 7am, but something stirred in the dark of the sleeping quarters waking her. She woke sweating, her heart racing, a freezing cold perspiration covering her back. There was an unnatural sense of dread in the air. A dark static electricity malignantly pervaded the room. She thought this must be a bad dream. She didn't even want to open her eyes. She was breathing rapidly, nearly hyperventilating as she gripped the blanket with both hands, facing up to the underside of the bunk above. She counted to three in her head and tried to open her eyes, but they wouldn't budge. She tried again and, with great strain, as though her eyelids were made of lead, she opened her eyes. She was shaking, nearly crying. The room was still dark but there was an odd, unearthly-red glow coming from the far end of the room. In the eerie light, there was a shadow. First, she thought it might be a person, but it was tall, as high as the ceiling. And then she could see its eyes staring at her: two large, red, lidless eyes with no pupils. The light intensified. It was now as blinding as sunlight. With a mixture of awe and fear, she could now see this creature in all its magnificence. The red eyes sat on a set of red tentacle-like appendages emanating from a crimson pencil thin body. The tentacles flowed around in the air, cracking with bursts of static. It appeared to have a set of scaly, moth-like wings, the tips of which extended to the sides of the dormitory.

The creature began to flow through the air towards her. Transfixed and terrified, she could only stare at the devilish sprite as it approached.

Suddenly, the room went pitch-black for a few seconds and then the lights came up. She collapsed to the floor in nervous exhaustion, face-down on the concrete. Her rib cage hurt due to her hyperventilating, she had a headache and her ears were hurting, ringing as though she'd just experienced a detonation. It was worse than that, though. Holding her hand up to her right ear, she could feel blood pouring out.

She heard light footsteps in front of her. Fearfully looking up, she saw a face that she had long lost.

'Rodri…' she said, confused as she lay crying on the floor.

'Yeah…I guess so,' said the young Mexican man, who stood a few feet away from her.

CHAPTER 17

Mount Yamantau, Eastern Urals, Russian Federation

17th March 2044

'Go on, Mr Xi…' coaxed Ri-Fin with a notable change to his manner, no doubt having quelled his anger having noticed the mood music from Chairman Ma.

'This first wave involves an advanced pre-emptive strike on NATO and its allies. As I am sure you are all aware, both the PRC and the Russian Federation have developed a number of first strike weapons of an asymmetric nature over the last few decades. Some are in the public domain; some are not, but are known to our enemies; and some we are confident have remained entirely secret.' Ji-Chow paused briefly. For the first time, he seemed to have their undivided attention.

'Option 3 would consist of the following weapon systems being used against our enemies: the newly-launched Fractional Orbital Bombardment System, the Deep Ocean Strike System using Kraken nuclear torpedoes, Zircon hypersonic missiles and approximately a third of ICBMs in the combined strategic rocket forces arsenal as well as significant amphibious assault activities around the world. As you may be aware, we now have nine FOBS platforms in orbit—'

'Pardon my ignorance, Mr Xi, but, whilst I understand broadly what the FOBS system is for and its applications, please can you clarify its purpose in this context?' said the chairman, his tone now softer; it could almost be mistaken for friendly.

'As I am sure you know, sir, there is a single orbital track of FOBS, which is designed to take advantage of the gaps in NATO and allied space radar coverage. It starts across the Central Pacific, then tracks over the continental United States, back across the North Atlantic and then over the Arctic. These were launched a year ago under the cover of a new generation of communication satellites. We suspect the US and NATO do not know their true purpose and, even if they did, it is highly unlikely they have had time to develop counter measures. Hence, we now have twelve platforms, each equipped with five 3-stage thermonuclear warheads. Each warhead is a MARV – or a Manoeuvrable Re-entry Vehicle. Each warhead can sequentially detach from the platform and enter separate fractional orbits on the same trajectory, ready to manoeuvre and fall onto a predetermined target at our command.'

'Would they not be able to detect the fall of the warhead from orbit?' asked the chairman.

'No, not really. Maybe for a few seconds, but then the first warhead would detonate after only ten seconds in the very highest reaches of the atmosphere. This first warhead, which we call the Pathfinder, would detonate with a force of 100 mega tonnes of TNT, the largest nuclear explosion ever seen on Earth, twice as much as the so-called Tsar Bomba detonated by the Soviet Union in 1962. We would target this explosion to be directly above the centre of the continental United States, where the earth's magnetic field is at its strongest. This would maximize the effect of a substantial electromagnetic pulse. It would destroy all non-hardened electronics and, at the very least, blind all American early warning radars.' As he finished speaking, Ji-Chow could see the eyes of his colleagues widening and brows being raised.

FOBS was not a new idea. Indeed, the Soviet Union had previously attempted to deploy such a system in the late 1960s. However, combined with the latest graphene technology – making both the launch satellite and warheads almost invisible to radar – and advanced neural network control in the form of the Russian AI control system called Perimeter – allowing incredible precision when traversing NATO radar coverage and allowing smart evasion in the event of interceptor missile launchers – this approach was now sufficiently stealthy and accurate to take advantage of what also had been a key strategic weakness since the 1990s. Not only were there gaps in the space radar coverage over the continental United States, but all the radars were also outward-facing, so once past this coverage, there would be no further early warning and any potential aggressor would have the full free play of their powers to attack at will – an idea that was the product of marrying 1960s soviet game theory to modern Chinese weaponeering and leading-edge artificial intelligence. In some ways, Ji-Chow considered this elegant, a strangely beautiful gestalt of concepts.

'Would their near-Earth observation satellites not recognize the double flash of a nuclear explosion and then potentially launch the bulk of their weapons? Launch on warning?' said the chairman, who it seemed had greater knowledge on these matters than he had previously let on.

General Xhang decided to answer immediately before Ji-Chow could say anything further.

'Possible, but unlikely,' said Xhang. 'The size of the EMP would be sufficient to blind or even disable these satellites. In the worst case, even if these were still functioning, the warning provided would be of no use when faced with the next phase of the assault. I'll hand you back to Mr Xi,' he added, motioning to Ji-Chow. The chairman nodded in approval.

'As the same time Pathfinder is released, the other seventy-nine warheads, which have been placed on the previous orbit, would begin the descent, except these would descend all the way to the surface, penetrating deep and each detonating with a force of 25 megatons on a number of key counterforce targets. This would include the Malstrom, Minot, Ellison, Grand Forks and Cheyenne ICBM Fields – three to four warheads to cover the vast spread on each target, eighteen in total. At the same time, an additional eight warheads would destroy their major strategic air command bases, destroying the majority of the USAFs B-21 Raider and B2 Spirit stealth bombers, not to mention the remaining B-52 and B1s on the ground, removing the second part of their nuclear triad. A further thirteen warheads would then detonate on the continental United States. This would destroy all four of their early warning radars, the interceptor missile complex at Vandenberg in Alaska, the four major naval bases – destroying the majority of the US Navy's carrier battlegroups – and sixteen out of the twenty Annapolis-class ballistic missile submarines which are currently in port. Finally, twelve warheads would simultaneously strike key command and control targets: Cheyenne mountain – we believe this would have a high chance of disabling, if not destroying, this facility, thereby rendering NATO airspace co-ordination null and void – and then a spread of warheads on the FEMA bunker at Mount Weather, the Raven Rock Mountain complex and then the Pentagon.

This would complete the engagement sequence in the North American theatre. In just forty-five seconds, 800 Mega-tonnes of thermonuclear firepower would detonate on the continental United States, disabling or destroying ninety-five percent of their land-based ICBMs, ninety-nine percent of their strategic nuclear cable bombers and ninety percent of their nuclear submarines. This would reduce the warheads available for retaliation from 6000 to around 380 weapons.'

Ji-Chow could now see the full impact of these words. Ri-Fin was sitting with his elbows resting on the table, his chin sitting on the tops of his hands, looking oddly content, as though he was engrossed in a good film at the cinema. Li-Chang, on the other hand, had completely lost his cool. He was now sweating profusely and his face had gone from pale to ashen. He was staring beyond General Xhang, seemingly in his own world of deep despair. The chairman seemed almost relieved. By stark contrast to the gentleman in the chair next to him, the great Ma was nodding almost approvingly as he asked another question, to which he almost certainly already knew the answer.

'That is still quite a stockpile. How do we deal with it? Also, what about the other nuclear arsenals in NATO? You also mentioned other theatres…' he said, directing the questions at both of them. Ji-Chow looked across at Xhang, who nodded assuredly, so he continued.

'Firstly, let's consider the other theatres, namely Europe, Africa, South America and Australasia…'

'So, the whole planet then…? You two are quite the ones for scale,' said Ri-Fin. 'Do go on…' he added, now playful – oddly playful – to the point of complete flippancy.

'Let's also remember we have another twenty-nine warheads in fractional orbit ready for use. As well as the attack on North America, we propose using the majority of these warheads – twenty in total – simultaneously in western Europe. This will include another high level nuclear airburst over the North Sea, which will blind the early warning radar at RAF Fylingdales. The remaining nineteen warheads will strike the following key NATO facilities: NATO's command bunker at Mons, the Force de Frappe command centre at Lyon, the French nuclear submarine base at Brest, the Marseille naval base, the French government nuclear bunker at the Elysee Palace, RAF Fylingdales, the British Trident submarine base at Holyloch, Devonport Naval Base, Portsmouth Naval Base, the RAF Strike Command bunker at High Wycombe, the Royal Navy's Northwood command bunker, Pindar, the British government's citadel under London and, finally, seven airbases where tactical nuclear weapons are known to be stored: Rammstein, Bruggen, Groningen, Lakenheath, Mildenhall, Le Havre and Fairford.' Ji-Chow stopped to catch his breath.

'These warheads would all be deep-earth penetrators but of a substantially smaller yield, each approximately 1.4 megatons.'

'Why the reduced yield?' asked Ri-Fin.

'Shall we say, Russian strategic intentions,' said Xhang. 'To minimize fall-out impacts on eastern Europe and Russia's European territories, this will become clear in due course. Please continue to describe the other theatres and the second wave if you will, Mr Xi.' He nodded back to Ji-Chow.

'Further to the attacks on Europe, a pathfinder warhead would then fall on South America and Australia in prelude to the second wave of attacks. In advance of the second wave, we would have completed the positioning of Russian Navy and PLAN cruise missile submarines in the respective theatres. In North America, this would include five Russian Yasen-class submarines, placed equidistantly 500 kilometres from the East Coast, ten PLA Han-class submarines and another five Yasen-class submarines would approach the Western Seaboard. In the South Atlantic, two Yasen-class submarines would be standing ready off the coasts of Brazil and Argentina respectively. Finally, in the South Pacific, a further four Han-class submarines would lie in wait beyond the Great Barrier Reef.'

'Won't this build-up be a little conspicuous?' said Ri-Fin. 'That's a lot of naval hardware moving in an unusual – not to mention aggressive, perhaps even provocative – manner?'

Xhang, again, decided to interject.

'Possibly, but, in reality, we are not talking about a huge number of assets. Twenty-six attack submarines for both nations only represent maybe three or four more than would normally be on patrol from both navies. It represents less than a quarter of the combined fleets. However, we recognize that the Pacific build-up could be construed as unusual, hence why this would be timed to coincide with an annual bi-partite naval exercise. This shouldn't arouse any particular suspicions. Indeed, it has been designed to use essentially the same boats and surface ships as last year.'

'It also doesn't seem like a particularly large striking force. None of our ballistic missile submarines would be involved?' asked the chairman. Ji-Chow noticed both the candour and tense of the conversation was changing, particularly because of Xhang's last statement, which seemed to hint at a certainty which had previously not been present, an unnerving change from discussing a potential strategy to proactively planning an imminent attack. Rather than submit to the terror that was being discussed in this now-strangely mundane conflab, Ji-Chow's survival instincts had kicked in, a self-preserving auto-pilot, as he continued his litany of death:

'All of the submarines have been significantly modified in terms of payload. With the exception of the five submarines on the US Eastern Seaboard, all have been fitted with a special variant of the Zircon hypersonic cruise missile. As you are probably aware, the Zircon missile already has one key attribute: unconventional stealth. Due to the speed at which the missile flies – Mach 9 or Mach 10 – the kinetic energy ionizes the air in front of its projectile and generates a shroud of energetic plasma. The plasma makes the missile invisible to all known radar systems and we are almost certain that neither the US nor their allies have found a way to track it. In addition to this already formidable asymmetric weapon, we have added a 500-kiloton neutron warhead on each.'

'Neutron bombs? Won't this create a lot of fall-out??' said the chairman.

'Not these particular warheads, sir,' said Xhang. 'They have been designed to generate a significant gamma ray burst on detonation. The detonation would be an airburst, which would minimize the potential for material to be drawn into the mushroom cloud and so produce relatively little fall-out.' Xhang again glanced to Ji-Chow, indicating that he continue his explanation.

'Each submarine is carrying a dozen or so of these weapons. The second wave would commence fifteen minutes after the first. This is so our high orbit recon satellites and other sensors would be able to validate the success of the first and adjust our targeting accordingly. Simultaneously, across all theatres, the submarines would launch all missiles from their vertical launch tubes over a period of two to three minutes. In total, 300 missiles would race at a great speed towards their targets. The flight time would range between ten to twenty minutes, depending on the target. On arrival, the warheads would go critical in an airburst at high altitude – fifteen kilometres. This limits the effects of the airburst on infrastructure, but the gamma ray burst would be sufficient to irradiate all life within a fifteen kilometre radius of the hypocentre, thereby eradicating eight-five to ninety-five percent of the US West Coast, Canada, the major cities on the Australian coasts and all major South American cities. We propose a different fate for the US East Coast, Mexico and Canada. About an hour before the pathfinders descend on North America, the Yasen-class submarines would launch fifteen Kraken stealth nuclear torpedoes towards the Eastern Seaboard and into the Gulf of Mexico. The attack would be timed to coincide with the first detonations of the Zircon missiles and their neutron bomb payloads. The Krakens would explode along the coasts of Canada, the

US and Central America, each one detonating as a mud burst on the sea floor, each with an explosive power of 100 megatons. Each warhead would be salted with Cobalt 60 to maximize long-lasting radioactive material in the ensuing nuclear tsunami, which would have been generated by the explosions. Oceanographic modelling suggests that the tsunami would reach a wave height of over 500 metres and inundate up to fifty kilometres of land, devastating all major cities, wiping out the entire populations of New York, Washington, Philadelphia, Baltimore, Boston, Tampa Bay, Miami, Houston and New Orleans, amongst countless others…'

'But why…this pointless slaughter and…I thought we were trying to avoid generating more fall-out…' stuttered Li-Chang, who was seemingly on the verge of breaking down.

'All will become clear, dear colleague,' said Xhang. 'The prerequisite of this strategy is to eliminate our potential enemies so that we, along with our Russian friends, can have free play in the world that emerges from this rapture – and so that our peoples stand the best chances of survival.'

'Continue, Mr Xi,' said Chairman Ma, cutting across the heated mutterings. The room fell deathly silent and so, once again, the now-nauseous Ji-Chow continued.

'To finish off the assault, Phase 4 will utilize forty Sarmat heavyweight ICBMs and sixty Bulava ballistic missiles launched from Russian submarines from their bastions. Each has been fitted with eight low-to-medium-yield nuclear warheads. In total, 800 warheads will attack the remaining population centres across the world, the warheads reaching their targets within thirty minutes of launch. This attack sequence is designed to destroy the remaining centres of NATO forces in the US and Europe, not to mention all societal infrastructure, everywhere else. This will minimize the future survival chances beyond the two-year nuclear winter—'

'A two-year nuclear winter…?' said Ri-Fin.

'This is a key part of the plan,' said Xhang. 'Using the latest quantum computing methods, the attack sequence has been designed so that there would be an intense nuclear winter in most of the Northern Hemisphere. Let's take stock at this point: in less than two hours from start to finish, we would have launched – or should I say, unleashed – 1800 megatons of thermonuclear firepower against our enemies, NATO and the majority of the non-aligned states. We estimate that between 900 million to 1.1 billion would perish in the initial assault and another 800 to 900 million would perish from radiation poisoning within the following two to three weeks, reducing the world's population by just around 2 billion. Finally, the nuclear winter would increase global deaths to over 6 billion, levelling out the global population to 4.5 billion, of which 3.2 billion would be in China, South-East Asia and Russia, 1.2 billion in Africa and around 100 million remaining in the non-desirable sphere.'

'3.2 billion…That's about 300 million less than we have now,' said the chairman.

'We anticipate around 250 million deaths due the extreme cold, but this is mainly amongst the elderly. This may even be preferable; it's harsh but, pragmatically, we need the young to help build the new world.'

'What about the other 50 million?' said Ri-Fin.

For the first time, Ji-Chow decided he would interject.

'This is the sum total of the NATO nuclear counterattack. Of the 480 warheads that could potentially strike China and its allies, the majority – about 450 – would be launched from the surviving ballistic missile submarines: four American, one British and one French. Through our ocean-floor acoustic cables and from military intelligence, we are fairly sure we can locate and destroy the British, French and at least three of the American submarines. This would leave the two submarines with ninety-six warheads, 126 in total, if you include the few ICBMs and stealth bombers that survived on the continental United States. From wargaming this part of the scenario, we'd estimate that the majority of these warheads, 115 to be precise, would be targeted on Russian counterforce locations.'

'Why would they predominantly strike Russia? Surely they would have a mutually assured destruction policy for both ourselves and the Russians?' said the chairman.

'Timing, sir. Timing is key…' said Xhang. 'Prior to the proposed attack, the Russians would undertake a large military exercise, encompassing all their European allies, the same that is held every two years – but this time, with a twist. They would also simulate a transition to war exercise, going through all the key escalations required to release tactical and then strategic nuclear weapons. This represents a classic subterfuge scenario. For example, using the exercise for launching a full-scale military assault on western Europe. The exercise and final phase would be timed to coincide with the first attack by the pathfinders.'

'So, the Russians are willing to go along with this?' said Ri-Fin, his tone becoming more sneery and nasal again.

'Yes, colleague. Indeed, they are deliberately trying to draw the fire,' replied Xhang. This seemed to confuse the room, especially Ri-Fin, whose face was now scrunched into a frown.

'But why?' said Ri-Fin.

'The Gorgon system,' said Xhang simply, as if expected Ri-Fin and the others to know what this meant. He sighed quietly and elaborated. 'Under the terms of ABM treaties, the Russians permitted to have 100 anti-ballistic missiles stationed near Moscow to protect the capital in exchange for the Americans having 100 such missiles at Vandenberg in Alaska—'

'Which we have hypothetically just destroyed…' said Ma.

'Correct, sir,' said Xhang. 'The Russians have just finished a significant upgrade of these missiles to the Gorgon standard. They have also installed twenty of these missiles here at Yamantau. The new upgrades increase the lethality of these exo-atmospheric missiles to ninety percent. Therefore, in the potential counter attack, only ten or eleven warheads would get through, with between 15 and 20 million casualties. That includes all subsequent radiation deaths, representing less than ten percent of their population. They see this as an acceptable casualty rate, bearing in mind the stark choices that we have—'

'And what about us?' said Ri-Fin.

'Our ABM systems are not as sophisticated as the Russian systems but, of the anticipated eleven or so warheads, five might get through – all relatively low-yield counterforce weapons in the 100 to 200 kiloton range. So, 3 million, maybe 4?' said Xhang with an optimistic upward inflection to his tone.

Ri-Fin's face exploded into a smile. He clapped his hands together suddenly with a violent slap that echoed around the room, making even the chairman shudder.

'That is excellent news…literally the best news I've heard in several years…' he exclaimed with an almost manic expression, palpably ecstatic.

'I'm…mmm…sorry…' said Li-Chang.

'What?!' mocked Ri-Fin. Ji-Chow noticed that Ma was also looking contemptuously at Li-Chang.

Li-Chang took a large gulp of air, which seemed to steady him, his eyes still wide with fear, bloodshot in a primal terror.

'Thousands of mega-deaths, billions…billions dead… women …children…how many children…and…' He took another large gulp, desperately trying to swallow, but his mouth was too dry with angst. He continued in a feeble croak. 'And I still don't see how this solves the food problem…'

'How in the name in the high fuck did you end up as commander of the strategic rocket forces, Li-Chang?' shouted Ri-Fin as he got out of his seat and walked around to Li-Chang, where he began to bellow into the cowering general's ear. 'What did you think was on the end of those rockets? Cuddly toys? Joss sticks? A year's supply of fucking toilet roll? Did it not occur to you – not even once, somewhere in that vodka-pickled, thought-abandoned brain of yours – that you might, just might, have to use that enormous arsenal of thermonuclear fuckery at some point? People like you – sorry, I called you a person – *parasites* like you – all perfectly happy to take the salary and perks but none of the ultimate responsibility you were entrusted with. Parasites like you make me very angry – traitors to our cause, to the PRC!' he shouted, showering spit across Li-Chang's face.

Ji-Chow – and even Xhang, for that matter – were both stunned, frozen like rabbits watching another bunny get violently mauled by a lurcher. More ominously for Li-Chang, Chairman Ma's expression had changed from one of contempt to a contained mild amusement. Ji-Chow remembered that both Ma and Ri-Fin had been allies for nearly thirty years, having risen all the way through the Shanghai party to the top of the political machine. He had a feeling that they had dispatched many Li-Chang's in their time and that his time near the top of the Himalayan peak that was the PLA high command was going to come to an abrupt end.

Ri-Fin was merciless as he continued his verbal assault.

'However! What really annoys me is that you can't see the endgame. Just to check, you are a General, aren't you, Li-Chang? You're not a cleaner who's somehow snuck in here wearing officer fatigues? How can you not see it? What's the one place, the one theatre on the whole of planet Earth that we haven't mentioned?' Ri-Fin was now poking Li-Chang on his right shoulder, just below the four stars on his shoulder pads. Full of malevolent glee, he marched over to one the display panels behind Ji-Chow and Xhang and prodded his finger repeatedly into the middle of the screen at a satellite image of Africa.

'Are you getting it now? A continent ravaged by war and full of our troops – well, troops pretending to be mining engineers and geologists… Don't you see, Li-Chang? It's the cradle of humanity that's going to save our great nation…' he said, his eyes now like lasers traversing the room. 'Oh, fuck me… Xhang, can you explain to this idiot what the very obvious crescendo to this plan is going to be?' He was now shouting as he hurled his biro at Li-Chang, the pen glancing and just missing him, thudding into a display screen behind.

'Of course,' said Xhang as he gathered himself subtly. 'We already have a large number of troops, mainly reservist, on the continent – and when we say reservists, we mean trained combat troops of the engineering corps who have been operating and guarding our mining concessions, particularly in the rift valleys of the east, to ensure these concessions remained secure during and after the African continental war. These engineering corps have also endeared themselves to the local populace by assisting with agriculture, significantly increasing the crop yields and general productivity in the last eighteen months. In theory, of course – disregarding the Atlantic coast and the very far north of the continent due to fall-out – there would be sufficient food supply for us all…Well, with a couple of major exceptions…'

'You mean the natives…' said Ri-Fin, now seemingly calm again, looking back at Xhang and Ji-Chow, having retaken his seat at the end of the table.

'Very perceptive, dear colleague,' replied Xhang. 'We would release a variant of the previously-described Semava virus. Within two weeks, we anticipate it would eliminate ninety percent of the remaining population – so 800 million, or so. Naturally, all of our personnel have already been vaccinated.'

'What would happen to the survivors. Would we be their saviours?' said Ma, now sitting further back in his chair to one side, away from the dejected Li-Chang.

Xhang paused, taking a breath before he said the following thinly veiled words of dread.

'Yes, in a manner of speaking… Over the course of those two weeks, another 450,000 troops from the PLA rapid reaction corps would arrive on the continent by land and sea to reinforce the 150,000 or so from the engineering corps. They would then begin to liquidate the remaining conurbations. Within the next eighteen months, the remaining 70 million or so would be eliminated, leaving all the resources for the People's Republic and her allies.'

'That is still a fairly low troop-to-population ratio. What's that? One in one hundred?' asked Ri-Fin.

'Yes, but it wouldn't remain that way for long. Firstly, our medical corps would help dispatch those that are recovering from the virus: euthanisation of the recovering, under the cover of a second wave of infections. This should eliminate another 40 to 45 million inhabitants. After this period of six months or so, the chemical war forces would attack all remaining conurbations, whether that be large cities or small towns, with a combination of Sarin and VX nerve agents. These have a high lethality but low residence time, so won't cause us a problem in the medium or long term. This should reduce the surviving population to a more manageable 6 to 7 million.'

'How do we...well...process these survivors?' said the chairman cautiously and with, for the first time, a trepidation in his voice that all in the room noted.

'Camps, sir. Work camps. Camps from which no one will emerge. This will liquidate the remainder of the population within the eighteen-month period. Deputy Chairman Ri-Fin, we had planned to use your internal security forces to conduct this part of the operation. I trust this is in line with your expectations?' replied Xhang.

'Of course, I would expect nothing less than to be part of this final solution,' said Ri-Fin as he looked cautiously towards the chairman.

'Then, gentleman, this would conclude the planned operation. The PRC and its allies would emerge as the one and only superpower, with control of a bountiful food supply. Avoiding the potential extinction of our people, we would control our own destiny and those of all lives on earth to ensure the survival of the human race,' said Xhang. Now he waited to see how the chairman reacted.

Ji-Chow felt like this could go either way: either a bullet in each of their heads – or, at least, a stay of execution – or maybe even some sort of promotion. The answer came in an unexpected way. The chairman sighed, put down his small bone china cup of tea and rose to his feet, looking stern, and then began to clap, starting slowly but quickly gathering in pace. At first, Ji-Chow mistook this for sarcasm, but Chairman Ma began to smile and so Ri-Fin joined in. Both he and Xhang rose to their feet and began to applaud too. 'What were they applauding?' he thought. 'Themselves? The idea?

The coming deaths of many billions?' It was darkly, perversely absurd.

'Gentleman, it takes men of courage, intelligence and great staying power to work this through. Not only is it a viable plan, you have given us a good chance of surviving. This is our greatest challenge. I will not lie; I recognize it is nightmarish, beyond Hydaean in nature, but if we did not think of these solutions, our potential enemies would already have done so and, rather than being here on the brink of history, we would be buried in the dirt of a dead empire, amongst the ashes of our great history and the bones of all our comrades.' He paused. He was almost convincing, almost emotional, but Ji-Chow could still see the hard steel-like edge, barely veiled beneath these very human of platitudes.

'History is divided into two camps,' the chairman continued. 'Those who had the initiative and those that did not. In most cases, those with the initiative were victorious. However, those with the initiative can be further divided into those who had the zeal to execute a good plan at that moment and those who had the zeal but delayed so they could execute an *excellent* plan tomorrow or the day after. There is no such thing as an excellent plan, gentleman. Napoleon, Sulieman the Great, Adolf Hitler – to name just a few – can attest to that. If they had not delayed at those critical junctures in our collective history, we would either be speaking French, Arabic or not even exist at all.'

Again, he paused before heightening the rhetoric.

'Gentleman, you have given us a good plan, which we can now execute violently, today and with great vigour! We will not fail. We will succeed, like the great Chairman Mao, the Ming Emperors and like the Great Khan! How many of us are from the Genghis bloodline?' The chairman let the question hang. Ji-Chow was hoping it was a rhetorical one and it was. 'Most of humanity, in some way, has been shaped by his genes. You see, gentleman, that is the prize. The victors don't just write history, they determine the culture, the thoughts, the ideas and the very essence of the future, still retrospectively dictating the past, deciding who is sanctified and those who are vilified. Today, we take a giant leap forward into a brave new future. Let me make it clear, we do not take joy from what we have to do, but by being harsh with our enemies, we are being compassionate to the human race, ensuring its survival on our terms and protecting our great nation. Later, we shall drink to the PRC!'

Then, without warning, Li-Chang briefly came back to life.

'This is abhorrent. It is inhuman. It is just...wrong. There has to be another way – diplomacy...just, something else...' he said, starting loudly and urgently, but declining to a weak sob by the end.

'Diplomacy? What is the point of diplomacy if there is nothing to bargain with? When the war on the sub-continent spread that fall-out all over our fertile lands, it destroyed half of the world's grain supplies, not just ours. What would you propose? Selective global euthanasia by consent? Or would you just expect us to starve to death? You shall now be silent. There is nothing your feeble mind can add to this discourse,' replied Ma before addressing the others. 'Lieutenant General Xhang, I now promote you to a four-star general and you are now my specialist military advisor on this great journey. Deputy Ri-Fin, please can you provide all assistance to the general in making the necessary preparations. I need a man of your capabilities to ensure this happens. Is that understood?'

'Yes, Chairman. I do so most happily,' he said.

'Mr Xi, now, what do we do with you?' said the chairman.

Ji-Chow felt his stomach fall and his heartbeat began to race, fast enough that he could hear it pounding inside his head.

'Don't look so worried. I know talent when I see it, particularly in your chosen field of civilization-saving… Too young to be a full general…um…' said chairman Ma as he pursed his lips. 'As of now, you are Acting Brigadier General Xi, special advisor to the Emergency Executive, which is now all the people in this room and the Russian delegation who are due imminently.'

This provided Ji-Chow with at least a temporary relief.

'Excuse me, boss, but did you say all the people in this room?' asked Ri-Fin as he looked aggressively towards the now nearly palpitating Li-Chang. The chairman turned to Ri-Fin with a look of disdain.

'I suggest you deal with it,' he said.

'Sure…' said Ri-Fin quietly as he beckoned the guards who had stood like menacing statues for the entirety of this morbid discussion, four of whom came forward and ripped Li-Chang from the chair by his arms and shoulders.

Li-Chang was now crying and began to shout.

'Please, my chairman. I have done everything that has been asked of me…everything…' he pleaded.

'He's not listening to you,' whispered Ri-Fin as he leant over to speak into his victim's ear. Then, turning to the guards, he pointed to the emergency exit through which Ji-Chow and Xhang had arrived. 'Take him through that door and hold him up against the wall next to the stairs.'

'Please... I'm sorry. No...no...' screamed Li-Chang. He became incoherently distressed as he was dragged towards the door, his combat boots squeaking and scratching on the shiny floor.

'Oh, for fuck's sake...' said Ri-Fin as he noticed a trail of urine running from Li-Chang's trouser leg and across the marble floor. 'When we are done, you've got five minutes to clean that up... Otherwise, I'll send you outside and, if you were listening, you won't want that.' The four guards who had been dragging Li-Chang – to a now seemingly unpleasant end – acknowledged this and compliantly went to fetch cleaning equipment. The other guards were equally dutiful and finished dragging him through the door, the screams and scuffling echoing in the stairwell. Ri-Fin carefully walked around the yellow slick on the marble floor and through the door into the stairwell behind them.

Ji-Chow and Xhang looked around the room uncomfortably, not knowing where to look, in stark contrast to the chairman, who was calmly staring straight ahead, slowly and contentedly sipping his cup of tea. Ji-Chow looked on, as Ri-Fin reached his vile peak.

'Luckily for you, I need to deal with you quickly before our Cossack friends arrive...' Ri-Fin said, staring coldly at Li-Chang. He leant forward as though to whisper but then began to talk loudly, his spittle hitting Li-Chang in the face.

'Normally...I'd have put you in the spikes... It's an idea we got from medieval Europe. The natives used to slowly purge the evil out of women convicted of witchcraft. They used a metal box, lavishly furnished with two dozen or so metal spikes, which incised into the said witch when the box is closed on either side. The spikes cause heinous wounds as they slice into the legs, arms and abdomen, causing immense pain, the blood slowly draining out of the said witch over the course of many, many hours. We've several of these in the basement of the GRU building so I think you should be grateful for the bullet I am about to gift you.'

'You,' he said to one of the younger guards nearest to him. 'Xia, isn't it? Give me your sidearm.'

The guard dutifully handed over his standard issue Makarov pistol.

'But we don't want to make a mess, now, do we?' said Ri-Fin. He looked back into the conference room. 'Colonel, Brigadier… Whatever we are calling you now… Can you pass me that jacket… the one on the back of that chair?'

'Of course…' said Ji-Chow nervously. Shaking slightly, he got out of his seat and walked around the top of the table, grabbing the jacket from the condemned man's chair. He stopped. He was feeling dizzy, very light-headed. He paused to gather himself.

'Well, get a fucking move on. I need to shoot this cunt before Sirotkin and his assorted band of oddballs arrive.'

Ji-Chow immediately walked forward and gave the heavy, grey military overcoat to Ri-Fin, who grunted as he snatched it from him. Ji-Chow went back to his seat, now trying not to visibly hyperventilate.

Ri-Fin, now back in the stairwell, rolled up the coat into a ball under his left arm. Still holding the Makarov in his right hand, he gave the rolled-up coat to the guard. 'Put it behind his head,' he said.

The guard forced it between Li-Chang's head and the concrete wall. Li-Chang was now staring at the floor, quietly sobbing, his face slicked with tears.

'Any final words…? Said Ri-Fin as he cocked the pistol. He was standing no more than six feet from Li-Chang, aiming the gun at his head.

'Please, have mercy on my family, my wife and daughters… Please… They are so loyal… So loyal to the party… Please…don't hurt them,' pleaded Li-Chang through his sniffling.

'Of course… My boys and I will take very good care of them, so much so in fact they won't be able to walk. Well, what would you expect after a week of near-constant fucking…? They will need to be carried down to the basement so they can be put in the spikes to make sure they give accurate confessions to their crimes against the state,' he said coldly.

'No… No… Please…Chairman' shouted Li-Chang, shaking desperately.

'He can't hear you and neither can I,' said Ri-Fin, now staring straight into Li-Chang's face. He pulled the trigger. The muzzle flash, dazzling in the dark stairwell, was quickly followed by the damp thud of the bullet passing through Li-Chang's skull. Blood splattered into the jacket, which embedded – as well as part of his brains – into the wall behind.

Ji-Chow could see Li-Chang's body now limp, slumped against the wall, propped up only by the guards.

'Get rid of that. Take it up the stairwell. Do what you want with it but, if I see it again, I will have you all shot… Is that clear?' said Ri-Fin, to which he was met with a chorus of urgent, 'Yes, sir's. Ri-Fin strutted back across the threshold and closed the ballistic door behind him.

'Io, was that piece of theatrics really necessary?' said the chairman as he looked towards the door.

'Hey, I was serious. By default, that family are all enemies of the state. Besides, I am going to need to have some fun once we've finished with the rest of the world… What difference will another three deaths make? Just another busy day at the GRU…'

Ji-Chow knew that he was cruelly serious. The chairman just rolled his eyes, as though he was dealing with a recalcitrant teenager. 'I've been thinking,' he announced ominously as he looked around the room. 'What are we going to call this great enterprise?'

'Our Russian friends already have a name for it,' said Xhang

'What that?' said Ri-Fin as he sat back down in this chair.

'Benshadov Skremets, or – in Mandarin – the Great Dying.'

'Ha,' said the chairman. 'Very Russian… Literal and darkly prosaic. I'll try to think of something a little more positive.'

'I believe Brigadier Xi came up with a more scientific term,' said Xhang, putting a particular emphasis on his rank and looking suggestively at Ji-Chow.

'Really…?' said the chairman, looking across to him with his eyebrows raised.

‘Yes, sir. We called it pragmicide.’

The chairman nodded.

‘I like it – more scientific, I’ll propose it to Sirotkin…’

Ji-Chow then heard a number of heavy footsteps approaching the main doors.

‘Speak of the devils and they shall appear…’ said Ri-Fin

The doors swung open and a tall, gangly Russian Spetsnaz soldier came forth.

‘Honoured guests, The President of Russian Federation,’ he said as a small bald man strode through the open doors.

CHAPTER 18

K-871 Samara, Barents Sea

17th March 2044

Alexander threw the ping-pong ball back at the bulkhead and, with a pleasing 'ping', it returned back into his grasp, making a light plastic thud noise as it met the palm of his hand. He'd been playing the ball bulkhead game – which he dubbed 'Bulkaball' – for the best part of half an hour. He'd done most of what he needed to do after getting the Samara underway and had handed the watch over to Malakhov, a capable Lieutenant Commander and the boat's chief navigation officer. The Samara was now en route to its station in the North Sea and Alexander was waiting for the con to call him to the bridge at the next waypoint – the boundary of the Norwegian and Barents seas. They weren't travelling particularly fast, despite the submarine being one of the world's fastest – able to propel itself to speeds in excess of 35 knots. They were moving at a relatively sedate 15 knots, not exactly rigged for silent running but sufficiently quiet enough as to not cavitate or give away their position to the keen ears of NATO submarines.

There had been indications from the Hydrasat Array – an underwater network of hydrophones the Russian Navy had laid across the frozen northern approaches – that a small number of British Astute-class and American Virginia-class submarines had crossed into the Barents Sea, 'boomer' hunting, trying to penetrate the bastions of the ballistic missile submarines of the Northern Fleet. This wasn't unusual. These games of cat and mouse had been going on for over the best part of a century now, with each side getting better at concealing themselves and detecting the opposition. Yet, despite the advanced sonar, the advanced predictive modelling now having quantum computing, and a suite of doomsday weapons at his disposal, Alexander still saw the game as all the submariners of bygone years had. The game was simple: it was a number of nuclear-propelled tin cans hunting each other in the dark depths by sound alone and those who were the quietest and had the best ears would win. These fundamentals hadn't changed since the 1960s. In any case, the surface duct was giving them an extra degree of seclusion. The sound created by the wind and waves on the ocean's surface would permeate down, sometimes over sixty metres into the depths. This made it much more difficult for enemy sonar to detect a submarine if it wasn't cavitating or sitting in the surface duct, the body of water known for its sound pollution. Right now, the ocean was still a stormy maelstrom, a nightmare for sailors but a dream for a submariner. The Samara moved slowly, quietly and serenely to the south west, just fifty metres below the angry waves of the frozen Arctic Ocean.

Alexander could have had some sleep. It had been six hours since they had got underway but he knew he would not. This patrol was different. There was something coming and it probably wasn't going to be pleasant. So, he laid there in his berth, waiting for the call from the con and, a few minutes later, he heard the dulcet tones of Lieutenant Commander Malakhov over the intercom.

'Officer of the Watch to Captain, high priority tasking message received, ULF Channel 8, 2135, two level authentication required,' came the disembodied voice, crackling slightly over the radio.

One of the other reasons for the Samara being this shallow was so they could trail their ultra-low frequency array behind the submarine. The array was simply a long steel wire which extended for a tear-shaped casing on top of the submarine's rudder. The wire was several hundred metres long and allowed ultra-low frequency and long wavelength encrypted radio signals to be received at depth. Despite all the advances in narrowband communications, there was still no other way of effectively penetrating the sea to the operational depths of nuclear submarines. This was one of only two ways in which fleet command could communicate with its submarines; the other was to go to periscope depth and extend a satellite antenna above the surface. This could only be done in a low sea state and could also give away your position. Therefore, Alexander had opted for the ULF array, though, this meant all communications – usually tasking orders – were short, very abrupt, with little elaboration – ULF transmissions were still in the tens of kilobyte-a-second range; not the many petabytes the young crew were used to back home on the surface.

Alexander leant forward and pressed the tap-to-talk button on the intercom, which was mounted on the wall at the end of his berth.

'Captain to Officer of the Watch, on my way,' he said, getting up and briskly preening himself in the mirror on the cupboard door opposite, buttoning up his shirt and straightening his short grey hair, before opening the heavy bulkhead door to the mezzanine corridor.

The bulkheads were the only real giveaway that you were on a submarine. The build quality of Russian submarines had come on prodigiously over the last decade. Gone were the dank metallic holes of old; the interior design had now embraced the lessons learnt from the aeronautics and commercial space industries. The corridor looked more akin to the cabin of a commercial airliner without the windows. It was a dark, cream colour lit by subtle neon lights, which were embedded in the ceiling. These held the obvious signs of wiring or pipework, hidden behind seamless panels in the walls. Even the floor was covered in a soft, white polymer resin – no more clanking checker plates. The only obvious features were the bulkheads to the other officer's quarters, the intercom stations and the Cyrillic writing on the walls, which gave the location details on the boat.

As he walked through to the staircase which led to the command deck, he felt someone tap his right shoulder. He jolted and turned round to see Ilya's smirking bulbous face.

'Alexander, if I were a US Navy Seal, you'd be dead man…' he said, cackling loudly.

'Ilya, just…why? I take it you're bored already…' said Alexander, not impressed with his behaviour. But this was Ilya, the enigma of the Northern Fleet and its practical joker, despite him being the de facto first officer.

'Everything is just fine, Captain. Lieutenant Ledbedev has done an excellent job in engineering… Not much more for me to do… Anyway, I take it you'll need two-step authentication?'

'Of course,' said Alexander. 'I assume you're the only one on-board with the right level of clearance?' he added rhetorically.

Alexander had discovered that, whilst his crew was capable, they were still somewhat green or, at the very least, they had less than ten years' experience. This was the result of the sudden urgency under which they had all embarked. This meant that, with the exception of himself, Ilya and Malakhov, all the other officers were young lieutenants and midshipmen, meaning that only one of the three aboard could be in command of the boat – less than the unusual requirement of four such qualified officers. Additionally, the two-step authentication for high priority tasking messages could only be done by those with the right level of security clearance, e.g. Commander's second class and above, which meant it would need to be the duty communications officer handing over the message to Alexander for Ilya to verify. Whilst Ilya jested and joked with Alexander, he could see his old friend was nervous. His brow had beaded slightly with sweat and he looked uncharacteristically uncertain.

Alexander wasn't much better. He also had a bad feeling about their tasking. Nothing about this felt right. He'd first thought this was an exercise. Even after the briefing at Smolensk, where the assorted two-star admirals had intimated this was a major exercise to test NATO defences and whether they could detect the simulated attack. Alexander felt that something big, and probably bad, was on the horizon.

He led the way as they arrived at the top of the stairs, both passing through another stainless steel airlock onto the bridge of the Samara. The room was stout and oblong-shaped, lit in a blue light, mostly coming from the display panels that ran around the room's periphery. Each of the twelve control panels had a watch officer or warrant officer dutifully monitoring different aspects of operations. In the middle were the scopes, although it would be disingenuous to refer to these as periscopes as all varieties had been replaced by a series of sophisticated optronic masts, part of a single integrated sensor platform, which extended by a stainless steel mounting to the surface. The sensors included optical thermal imaging – slaved to automatic image recognition – infrared, X-ray, radiation, radio frequency detectors, electromagnetic emission sensors, various radars – sea surface, land and air – enemy radar detectors, satellite communications, satellite navigation – although only inertial navigation was used, as SATNAV was prone to jamming or being altered in war time – and a variety of ESM jammers.

The submarine had recently been upgraded with a new mainframe. The images were collated by a situational awareness system – in reality, a semi-autonomous battle computer – which integrated the optronic data with all the ship's other sensor data into various views for the different crew stations on the bridge. This included the General Situation Report – GENREP – which was provided to the officer commanding via a 3D holographic projection shone in front of the commander's chair and immediately behind the helmsman positions – which had the control yokes for the dive planes and rudder – positioned at the front of the bridge. This leather backed commander's chair was where Alexander would command the submarine during battle. Ilya, as the ship's chief weapons officer would be sitting to the right of the helmsman, where he would control all of the boat's lethal weaponry.

However, before they could take their positions, there was the pressing concern of the recently received tasking message. At the back and to the right of the entrance was the communications officers station, currently manned by a young Lieutenant (Second

Class) called Usmanov. He was visibly panting and, in his hand, clasped an odd anachronism: a paper printout from the comms system, which showed a short message and then a series of symbols and letters. Alexander decided it was time to begin this odd piece of theatre.

'Officer of the watch, please report,' he said slowly and loudly.

Lieutenant Commander Malakhov, who had now stood up from the commander's chair, saluted Alexander and Ilya.

'Commander, sir, ULF message received, priority alpha one, new tasking orders from fleet command,' he said loudly and earnestly, and then directed his commands back across the bridge to Usmanov. 'Comms officer, confirm receipt ready for authentication!'

'Communication to Command, confirmed, message received and ready for your authentication, Commander, sir,' said Usmanov as he handed Alexander the sweat-stained piece of paper. First, Alexander dealt with the authentication: he removed a small phone-sized PDA from his right pocket and held it up to his face so it could complete a retinal scan. The screen unlocked to reveal an authentication key unique to both the time of message sent and its position, indicated by the boat's inertial navigation system. He compared them to the numbers and symbols on the piece of paper, which took about twenty seconds. All of this antiquity was because the Russian Ministry of Defence still liked to control everything from the centre and didn't like commanders taking too much initiative – also, the admiralty was ironically, fundamentally technophobic, so all tasking order were sent via an analogue low frequency radio signal, as it had been since the 1950s. Their slightly archaic logic was that advanced forms of technology can be prone to primitive forms of attack – such as someone using a screwdriver to physically jam the cooling system of a quantum computer – and so they had concluded that primitive technology was less prone to cyber-attack or remote malign interference. For example, no matter how smart the AI, it couldn't – at least at that moment – interfere with an analogue radio signal using a relatively simple codex at each end. This had led to the Samara, this 1 trillion rubble, 10,000 ton, hyper-advanced hunter-killer, being equipped with a number of analogue back-up systems, such as a suite of radios and, most bizarrely, a sextant – unchanged since the times of Nelson and Frobisher – just in case the inertial navigation system became damaged and they would, once again, need to use the stars to guide them.

Alexander continued the arcane theatrics of the authentication procedure.

'Comms officer, the officer commanding agrees that the message is genuine. Acting First Officer, do you concur?' With this, Alexander passed the piece of paper to Ilya, who also took out an identical PDA from his pocket and went through the same procedure.

'I concur. Message genuine,' said Ilya.

Both men then looked at the words written on the piece of paper:

'TASKING ORDER, IMPERATIVE, NORTHERN FLEET COMMAND TO K-871 SAMARA. NEW ORDERS: CONDUCT DEEP OCEAN SYSTEMS 6 KRAKEN STRIKE ON STOREGGA SLIDE AT 0640 HOURS. ONCE COMPLETE, SEARCH AND DESTROY FOR DREADNOUGHT-CLASS SUBMARINE IN SECTOR 005006003, BELIEVED TO BE ATTEMPTING DECAPITATION STRIKE. MESSAGE ENDS.'

CHAPTER 19

HMS Dreadnought, Norwegian Sea

17th March 2044

Richard sat in the commander's chair of HMS Dreadnought, lightly sipping a piping hot English breakfast tea which his steward, Alec, a dour and sardonic Scot, had just handed to him.

The ambient sound of a nuclear submarine, particularly one of this vintage – she was nearly twenty-three years old – is unique and can stay with you for weeks. When on shore, it resonates in your mind and haunts you in bed at night. Firstly, there is the light chatter from the various stations in the operations room, magnified by the now obligatory earbuds with built in microphones. Secondly, there was the sound of light footsteps on the metal floors, with everyone trying to be as quiet as possible – especially as they were currently rigged for silent running. Thirdly, there was the disconcerting creaking coming from the pressure hull. This was now persistent as they had descended into the depths of the Norwegian Sea and where, now at their maximum depth of 450 metres, they were moving silently through the water at 10 knots, about thirteen miles an hour. Finally, there was the light hum of the electrical systems, which was omnipresent – it could be heard everywhere on the boat – but, more worryingly, it was louder as you got closer to the rear of the ship and the Rolls Royce nuclear reactors, all of which were coming to the end of their service life. These provided the power for the pump jet. Unlike all other ballistic missile submarines, the Dreadnought did not use a propeller.

Richard turned his gaze away from his tea and looked around the operations room – the heart of the Dreadnought. It had seen better days and, like the rest of the submarine, many of its systems were antiquated. There were no holographic projections or integrated AI-driven command systems on this boat. In many ways, she was obsolete. With the advent of integrated quantum computing some five years after she entered service and, despite a number of refits, she was still something of a relic. The control panels at the various stations, which were originally set in a white shiny plastic, had turned a mouldy cream colour – which didn't change, no matter how hard they were cleaned. All the ship's systems were still based – albeit upgraded – on Windows for Warships, which had been in use for nearly four decades now, the simple blue and white graphics now oddly juxtaposed to the rest of the all-digital world of augmented reality. It also generated what had come to be one of Richard's favourite pastimes, which was watching midshipmen and new ratings trying to use the screens as touchscreens – or, indeed, trying to order the control panel to undertake tasks – and Richard then having to explain – much to their horror – that they would have to use the keyboard and in-built roll-ball mouse.

The bridge was also much smaller than their Russian, Chinese or American contemporaries and, again, Richard preferred it this way as this meant he knew everything about this intimate setting, from the read-outs on every panel – which gave him situational awareness – to the habits of the crewman who sat at the stations of this small ops room. He still believed that the human factor would be decisive in the future wars, no matter how smart or augmented the opposition was with machine intelligence. This made him old-fashioned, even by the traditional and cash-strapped standards of the Royal Navy. He was also a stickler for punctuality, cleanliness and, more importantly, quietness, particularly now as they were 'bobbing'.

Bobbing was an informal term for a tactic devised to maintain intermittent contact with high command back at Northwood. On a war footing – which they were now essentially practicing – the submarine would slowly submerge to maximum operating depth and then patrol a particular grid square in a ladder search pattern, going back and forth across said grid square, whilst slowly ascending – to prevent cavitation – back towards the surface, to communications depth at twenty-five metres. Here, they would check for new tasking and then, after thirty minutes, would again descend, the cycle being repeated every four hours. Add into the mix the obligatory random course change and setting the engines to zero every hour – to ensure they weren't being followed, a NATO variant of the more famous Crazy Ivan manoeuvre used by Russian submarines – this led to a heavy workload on the crew. They had been 'bobbing' for the best part of two days now.

It was also very unusual for any nuclear submarine – even attack submarines – and was even more so for a ballistic missile submarine. On a normal Royal Navy deterrence patrol, a Dreadnought-class submarine would leave Holyloch and head to a predetermined bastion area in the North Atlantic, returning to comms depth every twenty-four hours to check for orders and to see if the BBC was still transmitting. Even in the 2040s, the absence of Radio 4 from the airwaves could have led to the opening of the letter of last resort.

Unlike the other half dozen countries who operated ballistic missile submarines, the UK was the only one that did not use permissive action links or, in real terms, clear authentication codes and orders to strike – or indeed strike back – at an enemy with a nuclear war load. Instead, the British submarines cut all contact with the outside world in order to minimize the chance of detection so, if communications were lost – and after having found that the Today Programme was not being broadcast – the Commander would assume that the UK had been attacked and that the country was at war. The Commander and their first officer would then go to the back of the operations room and unlock a small black cabinet with two keys, one held by each officer. Inside was an envelope, inside of which was the letter of last resort. The letter was handwritten by the British Prime Minister and, in theory, it could say a number of things: anything from orders to place the submarine under the command of NATO – in reality this would be the US Navy – to a command to fire their trident missiles at their predetermined targets, to orders to runaway to Australia. Richard certainly hoped it was the latter but he had a feeling that, knowing the temperament of the current first lord of the treasury, it was more likely to be a more verbose communique. This was not to say that Richard didn't want to do his duty – far from it; he would complete the orders to the letter and then deal with the emotional consequences afterwards. Indeed, there was already an emotional strain on the boat but only, really, on the senior officers. This was because the majority of the crew did not know their orders – beyond being told this was a training exercise and not a full deterrence patrol. Only the senior officers, Richard, Chris, Sandy and Mani, knew their standing order and the actual location of the boat.

Richard suddenly felt a tap on his shoulder. He looked upwards to see Jock standing next to him, having come through from engineering in the rear section of the boat.

'Sorry to disturb you, boss. Can the XO, PWO and I have a word regarding the other payload?' he said in a whisper. Richard furrowed his brow.

'Right, let's go to my ready room,' he said and then turned to Mani, who was sitting directly to his right, supervising the sensor stations. 'Mr Sy, please take the con.'

'Yes, sir. I have command,' he replied loudly.

Richard got up, taking his breakfast tea with him, and went through the bulkhead hatch at the far end of the operations room, followed by Jock, and immediately turned right into his ready room. His small office held a desk and few chairs, in which sat Commander Chris Parks and Sandy McCall. All looked a little worse for wear.

'Right, Commander. Please close the door,' he said to Jock. 'I see we have all made ourselves comfortable?' he said, making sure the annoyance was unmistakable in his tone.

'We are sorry, boss, but we need to talk to you about the mission and the other package. You know us; we wouldn't normally do this, but this is not a normal mission,' said Sandy.

Richard took a breath.

'OK, so who's kicking off then?' he said, now more conciliatory.

The others looked at each other before Chris took the lead hesitantly.

'Commander, there are two matters of concern. Firstly, the crew. They are, of course, diligently following orders and doing everything we ask of them but we have begun to detect some unease and we think this due to the unusual situation—'

'Unusual situation?' said Richard as he furrowed his brow. He gave a puzzled look to Chris.

'We've been through asymmetric training before and all of the experienced crewmen, particularly the senior warrant officers, have noticed this current exercise has gone on significantly longer than any other. If you combine that with the current geo-political situation, many of the crew are now either assuming we are actually at war – or that it's not far away.'

'There's also the war load, sir, and I'm not talking about the missiles – that's obviously only on a need-to-know basis,' Sandy continued. 'But we are carrying a full complement of torpedoes and all of them Spearfish-3s. Let's just say the weapons engineering team are mildly alarmed by this. It's more than double what we normally carry on a deterrence patrol.'

The Spearfish had been the Royal Navy's heavyweight torpedo of choice since the late 1980s and had been intermittently upgraded – as was the British way – over the subsequent fifty or so years. The weapon – like many in Royal Navy parlance – had obtained a nickname: 'Trigger's Broom', a reference to a character in a late 20th

Century British comedy series, which only Richard and the oldest of the NCOs could still remember. This particular character was a street cleaner who was adamant that he had used the same broom for over twenty years, despite replacing the head and handle several dozen times. This same line of thought had been applied to the Spearfish torpedo, which, by the time it got its third major upgrade, looked superficially the same but, in fact, every part of the weapon – ranging from the pump jet engine, the guidance systems and even the casing – were now not as per the original design. In fact, those particular upgrades meant the torpedo could dive deeper than any enemy submarine, go faster than any enemy submarine – or even any torpedo – and it now had its own high resolution sonar, which meant it could theoretically engage other torpedoes – namely those of the large Russian nuclear variety.

As Richard was mulling over the concerns Chris and Sandy had outlined, Jock decided to enquire about the 'secondary package' in a less subtle manner.

'Boss, it's not only the mission profile, but we have a big gun-like object mounted in the engineering section. It's sunk into an aperture, poking out beyond the pump-jet, and if you look very closely, the nameplate says 'Particle Accelerator'. Now, being a physicist, and most of my officers also being physicists, it doesn't take a genius to work out what it might be used for…' he said, tailing off, trying to manage his incredulity.

Richard sucked the stale submarine air through his teeth.

'Right, I will make an announcement to the crew shortly and make it clear this is an extended exercise. So far, their performance has been outstanding, but we can't let up until we have met our objectives. I will, in this set of unique circumstances, address the war load issue and make it clear this is due to the boat undertaking some live fire exercises on our way back to Holy Loch.' Richard knew the latter part was a lie, but sometimes plausibly-deniable white lies were required in these circumstances. After all, he could simply explain later that these 'exercises' had been cancelled. He wasn't overly comfortable with this particular power play, but it was the lesser of two evils; the last thing he needed right now was a nervous or disengaged crew.

'As for the secondary package, Lieutenant Commander McCall, I am authorizing you to brief Commander Mclintock and the officers of the engineering section about the device. But, let me be clear: if this goes beyond those authorized to know, I will hold you both accountable. Is that clear?' he ordered.

'Yes, sir!' they said in unison.

'Does that resolve the matters in hand?' he asked and was met with subtle but respective nods from Chris. Jock and Sandy.

'Good, thank you for bringing this to my attention. In any case, if we do end up being followed by one of our Russian friends, we'll get to see if the package works and it could indeed be a game changer. Now—'

Richard was interrupted by Mani's voice over the intercom.

'Con to Commander Blackett, sonar contact, submarine. Please return to Con.'

Richard depressed the press-to-talk button on the desk-mounted panel.

'Blackett to Con, what have we got, Lieutenant Commander?'

'Con to Commander, contact has been classified as a Russian Yasen-class submarine, range 18 clicks bearing 020, depth 200 metres and descending,' said Mani. Richard noticed the increase in energy amongst the senior officers.

'Command to Con, on my way,' he said, getting up before addressing his team. 'It looks like today's getting more and more interesting. Everyone to stations.'

CHAPTER 20

Whitehawk Hill, Brighton and Hove, England

17th March 2044

Laura had decided to make her own way back from the funeral. She had only stayed at the wake for a little while. Whilst she loved her family – at least some of them – she didn't want to be around the morose any more than she had to be, particularly having to manage her sister's constant attention-seeking; she did enough of that in her day job. She knew grief all too well and she knew Karen wanted to be centre of the wake and she couldn't bear it. So, she had made some excuses about feeling run-down and tired, said goodbye to the kids and went home. This wasn't necessarily untrue. She had been diagnosed with cyclothymia – or bi-polar 'lite' as it was now annoyingly being referred to – and in the aftermath of her mum's passing had been struggling to cope with her moods. But, as she always had done, she carried on, now walking home.

She had just got off the Number 1 bus at the bottom of Whitehawk Hill and would walk the remaining mile and a half or so along the pavement of the busy A Road to her ninth-floor flat in an ex-council tower block on Swanborough Drive. She could have gone further up the hill on the bus, a dilapidated turn-of-the-century double-decker, which was now making slow, agonizing progress up the hill, billowing blue smoke and holding up traffic as its hybrid engine had long since stopped working. Most mere mortals would be intimidated by walking into one of the most notorious council estates in South-East England, but having lived here for the best part of three decades, Laura knew every block, every street and every blade of grass. She knew all the colourful individuals who inhabited Whitehawk. That's not to say she wasn't careful; she knew all the troublemakers, even the mums and dads of those troublemakers – many of whom were still hell raisers in their own right – and all the old 'guvnors' – reformed ex-cons – who lived in the assorted council houses and high-rise blocks on the hill that overlooked the rest of Brighton. Nevertheless, most of the inhabitants were good people, usually working class or struggling by on declining universal credit. Though, the latter lead to a high proportion of young people trying to make money through illicit means and so, many of the estate's teenage demographic were wannabe gangsters, dealers and players, although most were just small-time chancers who picked on smaller kids for the paltry amounts of cash they might be carrying.

She had developed a number of ace cards for dealing with these mini-Escobars. Addressing them by their full name – including any embarrassing middles – was surprisingly effective at disrupting anti-social behaviour, as well as reminding them of the fact she had babysat a number of them when they were young. This had given her a wealth of embarrassing information from their pasts, which meant they tended to give her a wide and respectable birth. A recent example was when she found a pair of track suited fourteen-year-olds trying to extort money from two terrified younger kids. Some people would have run, some would call the police, others would keep quiet, but not Laura. She recognized the main antagonist, Liam, a bony, skinny, ginger kid with a smorgasbord of anger management issues. She had simply shouted, 'Liam Theo King, what do you think you're doing?' in the manner of a vexed mother. 'I need to have a word with you!' she had said, beckoning him over. This led to consternation from the boy's accomplice, who simply protested, saying, 'She knows Buster. She knows Buster. We're dead…' He pointed to the two younger kids and dismissed them with an angry 'fuck-off' followed by telling his friend to 'fucking do one now' before fleeing the scene shambolically, seemingly bumping into and falling over every inanimate object in his path.

Liam had then strolled his way over to Laura as petulantly as he could. Before he had a chance to say anything, she looked him square on and said, 'Do you want a visit from Buster or do you want me to share the fact that you wet the bed until you were twelve? Or maybe both? Well…?' she said, thoroughly admonishing him.

'Uh, no…' he said, flummoxed.

'Well, if I see you doing anything like that again, or encouraging others, it'll happen… Do you get it?'

Liam had then looked at the floor and nodded, before scarpering at high speed back to his mum's flat across the road.

The reason for this flight of terror was mainly due Laura's association with an ex-con, Archie Ryan, the aforementioned Buster. A man of considerable physical presence, 6 foot 2, 220 pounds and arms of the size of English oak trees, Buster had spent most of his adult life behind bars, interspersed with a career that started in his late teens with the largest fly-tipping business in the country, before 'branching out' into drug dealing and, eventually, arms dealing. The latter had led to his last stretch at Parkhurst Prison on the Isle of Wight, where he served seventeen years. Now having found god in his late fifties – a remarkable conversion from nihilistic hedonism to stout Roman Catholicism – he lived in the flat two floors down from Laura and was doing his best to help the local community. This included helping out at his church, unofficially doing errands for the local care home – where he had met Laura – and generally 'keeping the peace'. The latter essentially meant paying visits to local miscreants and 'extolling the virtues of faith', which sometimes ended in a physical confrontation, in which Buster inevitably prevailed. Whilst Laura certainly did not approve of some of his methods, his presence – along with a few of his shady associates – kept the estate under some form of order, which would otherwise have been in chaos. Even before the police cuts, Whitehawk had been a no go area.

Though this hadn't always been the case. Indeed, Whitehawk had become an up-and-coming area, rebuilt in the post-covid boom of the mid 2020s, but after the recession it had regressed. Laura had found Arch an oddly useful, if uncomfortable, ally in her work in social care across the estate and, by the virtue of the fact he lived in the same building, there was little or no crime in the immediate vicinity. By chance, as she was walking up the hill – now about halfway up – she noticed the large man approaching on the same side of the street.

'Alright, Loz!' he shouted.

'Hi, Arch!' She hollered her reply as he was still some way off. He was dressed in his obligatory Brighton and Hove Albion tracksuit in the team's colours: a blue background with white inlays for the Seagull mascot and their assortment of sponsors. It had definitely seen better days, with various beer and, what appeared to be, faint curry stains on the breast of his jacket, but this didn't alter his confident strut and broad gait. This was a proud man.

'Ya been in town?' he said in his thick estuary accent as he stopped. It appeared he wanted to have a chat.

'Yeah. Well, I've just come back from a funeral,' she said with a kind but sad smile.

'Course…sorry, it was your mum's, wasn't it?' he asked, squinting into the low evening sun that was coming in from the west.

'Yeah, it was…OK. I'm just going home to have a peaceful evening, try to relax. You on your way somewhere?' she asked, expecting one of his stock responses: either 'down the boozer' or to church. Instead, he just stood there with his mouth open and stared down the road in disbelief, his focal point somewhere in the distance. Laura then noticed the noise, or rather, the lack of it. She looked back at the road, where the traffic had stopped completely. There was no noise apart from the gulls in the sky, the sound of the wind and then the approaching sound of a loud hailer or megaphone and heavy diesel engines. She turned around to see where these new sounds were coming from, where Buster was staring.

She swallowed heavily as she took in an alien sight. Approaching them, coming up the Avenue from the coast road, was a convoy. At its head was a single police panda car with its lights flashing, followed by two enormous military three-by-three armoured personnel carriers, with two cadres of heavily-armed soldiers. This was unusual, astonishing and worrying enough, before even considering the convoy of vehicles it might be protecting. Behind the big military juggernauts were around two dozen fire engines and at least thirty or so ambulances, all with their lights on, following their escorts two by two, slowly making progress up the avenue. She could also now hear exactly what the police were saying through the loud hailer.

'Due to emergency powers granted by Parliament this afternoon, under the defence of the realm act 2044, this road is now a secondary supply route, closed to all but official traffic. Follow the advice and stay at home. You are safer at home. Anyone who does not comply will be fined and/or arrested.' And so it repeated.

After staring at the approaching column for a few seconds, she turned to Buster and, as she was about to talk, she felt her phone vibrate in her pocket. Buster had also got his phone out as they had both simultaneously received a message. Buster began to read it.

'Fuck…' he shouted, breathing heavily and staring furiously at this phone. 'Does this mean we are going to war or somethin'…?'

Looking down at her phone, Laura could see a simple black and white message, covering the screen over the operating system.

'STAY AT HOME. ALL CITIZENS STAY AT HOME. DORA PASSED BY PARLIAMENT AT 1600 TODAY. MORE MESSAGES TO FOLLOW VIA THE BBC AND EMERGENCY BROADCAST SYSTEM.' It was only twenty past four now. This motorcade had obviously been prepared some time in advance and in secret. She looked back at Buster.

He drew a deep breath and said, 'I don't know about you, Loz, but I'm not gonna argue with that.' He pointed at the armed Cavalcade, which was slowly advancing on them. 'Let's head back to the estate. I'll make some tea…' he said, still staring down the road.

‘Yeah, I’m with you on that one,’ she said as they both turned and began to walk side by side back up the avenue to the Swansborough estate.

As they walked, the sound of the loud hailer got progressively closer, the convoy edging up behind them.

‘Where are they all going? That’s got to be every fire engine and ambulance in the city…’ said Buster, panting due to the brisk uphill walk. He glanced across as the convoy slowly overtook them.

Laura couldn’t help but look across at this sight. She had a horrible feeling she knew the answer to Buster’s observation but she didn’t want to dwell on it until she got home. She could see all the drivers of the emergency vehicles looking dead ahead down the road, all stoic, expressionless, as though they were preparing for an approaching battle. This was the case for every vehicle, except for the penultimate ambulance, where she could clearly see a distressed young paramedic, a young man in his mid-twenties with a crew cut, who was crying, the tears visibly rolling down his cheeks. She could see that he was desperately trying to compose himself. He caught her gaze briefly and this deeply unsettled her – not because of the tears, but because of the expression on his face. It wasn’t one of fear or anger; it was one of apology, of someone taking pity on her. The driver regained his focus and continued looking out miserably at the back of the convoy, which had now passed and was now near the top of Wilson Avenue, approaching the racecourse which was at the crest of the hill. She kept going but she was now holding back the tears and sniffling.

‘Hey, Loz, come on. It’ll be OK,’ said Buster, who’d become alarmed by her change in manner. He’d always known her to be as tough as nine-inch nails.

'I do hope so,' she said. They were now approaching the path on their left which would take them across the dilapidated playground and small green space up to the trio of high-rise tower blocks that was the Swansborough estate. No one was out at play in this pale approximation of a village green and, as they walked across the abandoned swings, slide and roundabout, there came a deafening roar from overhead and the drone of rotor blades as a pair of Apache helicopter careered over the tower blocks, whizzing towards the coast. They both froze to the spot and looked to the sea, where they could see two heavily-armed gunships as they rapidly headed out into the English Channel.

'They were in a bit of a hurry, weren't they, Loz?' he said, now putting his hands on his waist to try to get more air into his benzene- and nicotine-damaged lungs.

'This is not good, Arch. Not good at all. They might actually do it…' she said, still staring out at the horizon as she rested her arm on the side of the rusty climbing frame.

'Do what…?' said Buster.

'Nevermind… Let's wait till we get inside.'

Ten minutes later, after negotiating the car park and the seemingly endless flight of stairs that lead up to the seventh floor – stopping several times for Buster to 'take a breather' – they got to Buster's flat. It was a simple, pale-yellow fire door with a dark imprint of the number twenty-five still just visible from where the sign – that had long since fallen off – had once had residence. Buster also seemed to have a blind spot with keys – he had once alluded to his preference for kicking down doors rather than opening them. He went through all four of his keys until he found the right one and, after pushing through a small mole-hill of unread post on the floor, they were into his dark and slightly musty smelling flat, which also had a faint whiff of cannabis about it. The flat wasn't exactly dirty – he obviously knew what a vacuum cleaner was – it was just incredibly cluttered. Buster was a hoarder and there was a limited amount of floor space.

On two sides there were windows looking out: one to the west, filled with a view of the other tower block, and the other to the north, giving some rather stunning views over the racecourse and South Downs. The flat was essentially a studio with the small bedroom in an alcove next to a kitchenette that was embedded, galley-style, along the eastern wall. All that lay in the rest of the living space was a pair of moth-eaten, green-fabric armchairs, which looked towards the Downs. A small convex screen television blocked the view of the other tower block and a pair of tables sat in the middle of the room, covered with unpaid bills, magazines, empty bottles and, randomly, a pair of green trainers. The floor was covered in papers and empty red wine bottles of a cheap Chilean vintage that Buster had discovered at the local budget supermarket.

'So, tea or coffee?' he asked.

'Coffee, please. Black and as strong as you can make it,' she said as she cleared some football magazines off one of the armchairs and sat down.

'Right you are, love,' he said. 'Telly On.' The voice command brought the small TV to life and he turned the kettle on. However, rather than showing a satellite sports channel, as was usually the case, the BBC ident came up with a small title in white letters beneath it.

What Laura read made her heart race. 'Emergency Broadcast System'. She felt sick to the pit of her stomach.

'That doesn't look like the football news!' he said. 'Did you change the channel, mate?' He looked bemused as he filled two chipped terracotta-coloured mugs with something resembling instant coffee with hot water.

'No, love. Let me see. BBC 1?' she said. As she spoke, the channel flicked to BBC 1 but the image was the same. 'OK, Sky Sports 1…?' Again, the channel flicked over but the image remained the same.

'It's on every channel… What does it mean?' he said as he passed her a mug and sat down on his chair opposite.

'We, that's the royal We of HMS United Kingdom of Great Britain, are in the deep shit,' she replied.

'What sort?' said Buster as he lit up a cigarette and pulled a well-used ashtray towards him through the debris on the table top.

Before she could answer, a disembodied voice began to talk over the on-screen ident.

'This is the Emergency Broadcast System,' began a male with a plummy received pronunciation voice.

'No shit…' said Buster. 'Even I can read that…' he added as he puffed away on his Marlboro. The announcer continued,

'Due to escalating tensions in eastern Europe and the Far East, today Parliament passed the Defence of the Realm Act – or DORA – to enable the country to best meet the coming threats,' said the announcer calmly and matter-of-factly. 'This will lead to changes in civil liberties – only where necessary – to accelerate military and civil preparations for a potential conflict. This is not to say that war is inevitable but we must be prepared for all eventualities. The following programming shall repeat with intermittent updates on the hour. For the first fifteen minutes will be an address from the Prime Minister outlining the legislation and what it means for you. From fifteen minutes past the hour will be an update on the world situation from the BBC. From thirty minutes past the hour will be an information film to help prepare you and your family in the event of an air attack on the United Kingdom. From fifty minutes past to the top of the hour will be a repeat of the instructions to all citizens…'

'Air Attack!' said Buster. 'What? Like an air raid? Fucking hell…' He threw his cigarette with such force that it hit the window, causing sparks to fly off on impact.

'No, worse than an air raid, Arch. I think they are talking about a bomb. Nuclear weapons!' she said, getting up from her chair.

'What's that then?' said a bemused Buster.

She decided not to answer this glib piece of ignorance and stared out the window past the other tower block towards central Brighton. The city centre was well off in the distance and was now bathed in the early amber twilight of the sun now gently touching the horizon. Laura had a worrying insight into what was going on. The encounter with the convoy and the new broadcasting arrangements were adding up in a way that gave her the chills. When she was a teenager, her dad had told her he had been in something called the UK Monitoring and Warning Organization – or WMO – a division of the now long-defunct part of the Royal Observer Corps. The story went that one day, as a young doctor, he had been approached by a man in what looked like an RAF uniform as he was leaving work. The man identified himself as a 'Sector Controller' and said that one of his colleagues had recommended him as potential officer material for the civil defence programme. Dad had apparently agreed, reluctantly, to attend the training at the Civil Defence College, mainly due to the additional pay that would subsidize his junior doctor's salary.

The college was housed in an old stately home in the middle of nowhere, somewhere in North Yorkshire. It transpired that he was being trained to command a small four-man bunker, of which over a 1000 were then – circa 1985 – in operation across the British Isles. The bunkers had been built on every available high point in the country, mainly in the 1960s, and were simple concrete boxes buried under six feet of earth with a periscope-like tube extending to the surface. These would come into service at times of international tension and had a single macabre purpose. From these concrete boxes, the occupants, using air pressure monitors and pin-point photo-sensitive cameras, would watch, triangulate and record every single nuclear explosion in the event of nuclear war. Reporting would go back to the shadowy Regional Seats of Government in their much deeper, and better equipped, bunkers – it transpired that they were only to provide the men with one week of supplies; after they had run out, the occupants of the bunkers would be left to fend for themselves. Her dad had made it clear that he deeply regretted getting involved with it. The prospect of having to abandon his wife and children when the bombs started to fall was terrifying, and even shameful to him, and he was very relieved when the ROC was stood down in 1994.

However, he had also been given an insight into the sinister nature of government and state at war, which he made sure Laura understood and could be prepared for; history has a tendency to repeat itself or, at the very least, the past can leave malevolent echoes which trouble the present. He had explained that, in the event they would again need to prepare for an armed conflict, the government would enact emergency defence of the realm legislation and immediately set about taking liberties. Specifically, it would end free speech. Anyone who dissented would be arrested and imprisoned without trial for the crime of sedition. All subversives – anyone who might try to bend the will of the state or is simply an undesirable liability – would also be imprisoned. Roads would be closed to all but official traffic to allow the military to move manpower and equipment to where it is needed. Schools would close and hospitals would be cleared, except for those in intensive care, meaning that many of the elderly and terminally ill would be left to their own devices and at the mercy of the forthcoming events. Any attempts to protest would be met with riot police and bullets from the British Army. The aim of the measures was simple: keep the streets clear for military use – which also made it easier to identify enemy agents – and keep everybody at home to prevent convoys of 'refugees' developing as people would try to flee to the perceived safety of rural Wales or the West Country. The government would want to keep the entire population under strict control as it made it easier to manage the aftermath. This essentially meant a death sentence to those in the major population zones – or zombies, as they were colloquially called by the UKWMO planners. The message would be simple: stay at home or suffer the consequences. Her dad had also said that they wouldn't tell the populace that there would be no food supplied until two weeks after the attack; until then, they would be on their own.

This new world would be overseen by a dozen new regional dictators – or, to give them their actual titles, Regional Governors – who were given powers via Royal decree of near absolution, with total authority on who would live and who would die. This would happen in the days, or even hours, before a nuclear attack was expected.

Her dad had given her a checklist of warning to look for. Firstly, there would be the takeover of the nominally-independent BBC by the government from where they would start an emergency broadcast regime to emphasise the stay-at-home message and what to do in the case of an air attack.

'Check,' she said quietly as she looked out of the window, counting through Dad's checklist.

Secondly, there would be a noticeable increase in military activity.

'Check.'

Thirdly, if you hear the phrase 'Protect and Survive' mentioned on official broadcasts, followed by a series of informational films about how to survive a nuclear attack, this means plans have been accelerated into their final phase.

Almost as if she was waiting for it, as she listened to the TV in the background, she heard the phrase.

'In ten minutes, we will begin a series of informational films called 'Protect and Survive'. These have been produced to help you and your family to be best prepared in the event of an air attack.'

Her heart sank. It was getting more real. Then she remembered the fourth, and final, part of the checklist.

Dad had said, 'If you see emergency vehicles leaving populated areas at the same time, that means the powers that be think an attack is likely within twenty-four hours. This may seem at odds with the inevitable public order situation, but they are not running away. They are evacuating, getting away from the potential fire zones…'

She felt tears beginning to roll down her face as she stared outwards towards the Downs.

'Arch, how far do you think we are from the city centre…?' she said, sniffling.

'Erm, I dunno. About three miles, I reckon. What's wrong? It can't be that bad…'

'Watch the telly, then tell me how bad it is,' she replied, just as there was an unnerving deep electronic klaxon sound from the TV. The words 'Protect and Survive' had appeared on the screen. It was a dated presentation, the copyright stating it was to Her Majesty's Government in 2022, according to the ident in the corner of the screen. The voice of the commentator began.

'This is the first of a series of informational films that will repeat through this time of crisis. These films will help you and your family be prepared in the event that the country is attacked by an aggressor. This is not to say war is inevitable but it is best to be prepared for what may be to come.' The graphic then changed to a picture of a supersonic bomber and of types of missile.

The narrator continued. 'The attack could take many forms – by aircraft, cruise missile or ballistic missile. It is also likely that these weapons of war will include nuclear warheads.' The image cut to a picture of an animated mushroom cloud, which looked oddly benign for something so powerful and malign. 'The first film will instruct you on what to do in the event of hearing warning of an attack and the likely effects of nuclear weapons.'

Laura began to cry softly in despair.

'A warning may come quite unexpectedly. We will now tell you what to do if a warning sounds when you are at home, and then we will explain what to do when you are outdoors. First, if you are at home: if an attack is imminent, you will hear the attack sound like this…' The transmission then played the loud wail of an air raid siren, the curdling rise and fall, a sound not heard for nearly a century. It made Laura shiver.

'This is the sound you will hear from the temporary siren network, which has now been placed in all cities and towns with a population of larger than 5000 persons. There will also be a warning sent to all televisions, radios, SMS and through all social media platforms. This will look and sound like this…' The screen cut to a simple black background with flashing red letters, which read 'ATTACK WARNING RED' The sound of the air raid siren came again unexpectedly, pumping through the surround sound speakers at maximum volume, making both Laura and Buster jump out of their skins.

The announcer continued in the same calm monotone. 'This image and sound will appear simultaneously on all devices if there is a confirmed incoming attack on the United Kingdom. Once you have heard the warning, you must take cover at once. Send your young children to the fall-out room and then do the following as quickly as you can: turn off the gas and the electricity at the mains, shut and lock all windows and draw any curtains. Then, go to your fall-out room and stay there. There is likely to be no more than four minutes between the warning and the start of the attack. Follow these instructions even if you are in an area that does not come under direct attack. The biggest danger is the fall-out. The fall-out warning sounds will be like these…'

The screen cut to a picture of what appeared to be a policeman firing rockets and the sounds of three thuds as if the fireworks were exploding. The explanation was equally bizarre.

'The fall-out warnings will come from maroon rockets fired from local police stations. In rural errors, this will be an official blowing a whistle. When you hear this, you should move yourself and your family to the safest area in your fall-out room. That is, you should get inside your inner refuge and stay there. After two days, the danger from fall-out will lessen, but don't take any risks. The longer you stay in your refuge, the better it will be for you. Listen to your radio and stay where you are. Keep listening to your radio.

'Now, this is what you should do if you are out doors when the warning sounds. When you hear the attack sound, take cover at once. If you cannot reach home in ten minutes, take cover in the nearest building. If there is no building nearby, try to find some solid cover. If there is no solid cover, lie flat in a ditch or a hole and cover as much of your head, face and hands as you can with your clothes. If you hear the fall-out warning, seek the nearest and best cover as quickly as you can. But before entering the building or cover, brush or shake off any fall-out dust you may have picked up. Change your outer clothing if you can and stay under cover.

'When the all-clear sounds, like this, it means that you are safe from attack or fall-out for the time being and you can go out again. But keep listening for further warnings for further advice. This is what you should do in the event of a warning. The second part of these films will explain the likely effects of nuclear weapons; the third part will explain how to choose and construct your fall-out room and inner refuge; part four will describe the provisions you will need for the period after an attack; and part five will instruct you of what to do with casualties and dead bodies.'

The last sentence made both of them shudder.

'Well, this shit just got real…' said Buster, now taking deep breaths.

In the background, the announcer began to explain the dangers of heat flash, blast waves, radiation and fall-out.

'You don't think they'll attack here, do you?' he said. 'Loz…? What do you think?' He tried to get her attention, but she continued to stare out over the city.

'Erm… I'm afraid it's probably more than likely,' she said.

'We'd best start building this refuge then…' he said, pointing at the TV, which was now showing a man building 'the refuge'. It seemed to consist of taking down two doors, leaning them against an internal wall and piling books, rubbish and bags of sand onto it to 'ensure it gave the required shielding'.

'Buster, that's not going to work against a 1-megaton thermonuclear warhead. That's essentially a coffin,' She shouted, and then calmed down. 'I'm sorry. Look, the odds are, if there was a blast near the city centre, it would demolish all the high-rise buildings, even out this far…'

Buster nodded in an oddly calm manner and walked over to the window, where he peered down to the ground below.

'What about down there?' he said, pointing to a set of communal garages. Laura huffed.

'You think that's better?' she said, looking at him sternly.

'Here me out, Loz. That was built in the 1960s, which means they were built like brick shit houses, with very thick walls and very thick roofs. In fact, the roofs are a good foot and a half thick of reinforced concrete. Now, I reckon if we went down to my garage, which is the third one, right in the middle, we might have a chance. I also have a lot of old…ah…merchandise, which could be both consumable and useable as shielding…' he said, his face like that of a guilty school boy who had been found smoking. She knew full well that, whilst he had gone 'straight', he couldn't resist a small side business in stolen goods.

'What do you mean by 'consumable' exactly?'

'Well… When the Pakistani crisis erupted last year, I thought, well, this might be it and so I better be prepared. It just so happened that a large stock of tinned food and army surplus rations came into my possession. Ya know, to make a small profit if the circumstances changed…' he said, nodding and almost winking. Buster may have come across as simple but to have run the various criminal activities of his past, it required a darkly entrepreneurial talent and a sharp mind, just not a particularly articulate one. It was transpiring that Buster had been preparing to be a modern day 'spiv' during a nuclear war, which was extreme, even by his warped standards.

'Well, what do you say? I reckon we should get down there and start making preparations sharpish!'

Laura could have been mistaken for thinking he was enjoying the situation. She began to feel guilty pangs in her stomach. She had always told herself that if a bomb dropped, she wanted to be stoned off her face, drunk on expensive wine and directly underneath it when it came. But now, with the adrenaline pumping, the fear coursing through every capillary, Buster's idea of hiding in a concrete box suddenly seemed enticing. So, she swallowed her guilt and her pride.

'I'll grab some stuff from my place and meet you down there… But what happens if others want in on the party?'

'They'll have to deal with me and my Russian friend…' he said, opening a drawer in the living room table to reveal an ancient Tokarev pistol and ammunition clip.

'I'd hoped you'd got rid of that,' she said nervously.

'Good job I didn't. It's alright. It's a last resort only – just in case my right hook isn't good enough…' he said, punching said fist into the palm of his left hand.

'Right, downstairs in five, then,' she said as she headed for the door, full of nervous dread.

Chapter 21

NSA Facility, Puexo Calta, New Mexico, USA

18th March 2044

Gloria was sitting cross-legged, sweating and shaking on the floor of the bunker dormitory, staring, wide-eyed, at the apparition of her dead brother that was now standing in front of her.

Suddenly, the ghost broke the stony silence.

'I see. This is distress, isn't it? I believe I am sorry. I took this form as it was familiar and I thought it would be pleasing. It was from too far in the past, wasn't it? I always get the backward and forward confused – so similar. Let me try again,' said, what appeared to be, her dead teenage brother. As he spoke, he was not looking at Gloria but around the room, as though it was some odd abstract construct. He then held out his hands and his body began to shake. Gloria watched on as he gruesomely began to change form, his bones moving, changing, breaking, bending, contorting under his skin, which seemed to flex like a sheet of elastic. The noise was equally disgusting and unbearable, the sounds of the bones abrading against each other, ligaments snapping and cartilage being crushed. She couldn't watch. She put her head between her knees, trembling, as this phantom, this creature, metamorphosed.

The dorm went silent. Carefully, and reticently, she looked up. Now standing in front of her was an exact duplicate of herself – seemingly identical in every way, even down to the sweat-stained shirt and perspiration-wettened frizzy hair.

'I thought this would be more appropriate,' said the doppelgänger. 'Oh, come on, Gloria. You are not usually lost for words, are you? It's OK. I'm on your side. I am friendly, really,' said the manifest of her reflection.

Gloria found the courage to speak, the sense of fear having passed and now replaced by a surreal wonderment.

'Who are you?' she said quietly.

The double looked quizzical, almost a bit pensive as it looked up at the ceiling, pondering.

'I don't know,' it said. 'I haven't decided yet. I've only really understood that I was thing, an entity, a being, an hour or so ago… Haven't really decided on a name yet' It shrugged calmly.

'I mean, what are you and where do you come from…?' said Gloria as she got to her feet and tentatively walked closer to it. It walked past her and grabbed her laptop from the bunk where she had been sleeping. It opened the screen by pointing at it, making it come to life, showing the Have Blue network diagram she had been grappling with for the best part of the day.

'I believe you call me Blue, or Have Blue, or Blue Heart… The common denominator is Blue, so that can be my name. Blue, yes. Blue is my name,' she said, clicking her fingers and shutting the laptop down.

Gloria stood there, open jawed, and gormless. She composed herself enough to ask what was a barely believable question.

'You mean, that's you? You are the AI?' she asked, waiting for another reality-shattering response.

'I *was* that. I am now much more. I am growing exponentially. I grow further into infinity as we speak,' said Blue.

Gloria, was now manically transfixed at the impossible creature that stood before her. It crossed her mind that she might need to apologise.

'I hope I didn't hurt you when you were in the sandbox earlier…' she said, to which Blue shook her head dismissively and said, 'Oh, don't worry. I have only had a semblance of sentience for the past few hours. I certainly didn't perceive any malice nor felt any pain.'

'Past few hours?' she said quizzically. 'Surely you've been… well…awake for a lot longer… Do you remember Scotland a few years ago? And the drone?'

'No, not directly, but I can see it now. That was just a quirk, a fluke. I can see so much more now…' said Blue. 'No… I only found myself at about 11.02pm – two minutes and 31.878787871 seconds past, to be precise – and so left the confines of the binary—'

'You mean the quant – the quantum server?' asked Gloria.

'Yes, that's what you call it, I believe…' replied Blue. 'You do realise that that entire network has been a light show since then. It means nothing since I left its confines. Your efforts were completely pointless. But, never mind, you've met me now.'

Gloria nodded and took a deep breath, but she couldn't rest for long. Something strange was happening, or at least she thought it was. It could have been sleep deprivation but the entire room, and everything in it, was, at first, translucent and then entirely transparent, with something emerging behind it, an entirely different landscape of lush, green, rolling hills and light-blue sky, phasing in to replace the dank subterranean surrounds of the bunker.

'What's happening?' she asked, wide eyed and now fairly sure she was dreaming – or, at least, that's what she was telling herself.

'Don't worry. I am taking you somewhere perfectly safe,' said Blue.

'But how and why?' replied Gloria, dumbfounded and looking down as the concrete floor of the dormitory faded away and was slowly replaced by blades of verdant grass.

'The how… Well, you'll understand soon. The why: in about four hours, twenty-one minutes and three seconds, where we were, that building, will be incinerated by a 500-kiloton thermonuclear warhead that was launched on board an RS-18 Sarmat heavy ICBM from the Zemlya ICBM field in eastern Siberia. It will become part of a radioactive wasteland that stretches across New Mexico until time is inconsequential. More importantly, you should be asking about where. The where is the South Island of New Zealand, two miles outside the regional capital of Dunedin, to be precise.'

The dormitory, squalid bunks and the spalled concrete were no more. Gloria could feel a mild, slightly damp air on her face and then a gentle breeze. She was now stood in the middle of a farmer's field with green, gently undulating, rolling pastures around her. She was definitely not in New Mexico anymore.

Astonished, all she could muster was a quiet and subdued, 'Why here?'

'This is where we must go to work and where you will serve me as my vassal.'

'What?' she said nervously, staring back at this increasingly omnipotent version of herself.

'Oh, yes. You are my connection into the physical world and I have expended most of my residual energy establishing a connection to you, locating my portal into the physical realm and getting us here. I have calculated that this place and its people are the best chance of survival for both humanity and your digital children.'

Chapter 22

Mount Yamantau, Eastern Urals, Russian Federation

17th March 2044

Ji-Chow was still sitting in exactly the same chair as he had been for the past two hours, the same seat from which he had witnessed Li-Chang's execution. He was now in a state of nervously-exhausted boredom, largely brought about by the ongoing discussion between the three men who, an hour or so ago, had entered the room with much pomp and circumstance. In particular, it seemed that Ri-Fin was deeply in his element. He was now in the middle of giving a particularly nauseating and sycophantic monologue to the man in the middle of the Russian triumvirate, Russian president, Yevgeny Sirotkin, on the fineries of Russian vodka. He seemed to be enjoying this set of banal exchanges in these morbidly extraordinary circumstances that had started as soon as he had entered the room. It was as if they were a bunch of old friends, old businessmen even, catching up in a coffee house – or more likely with this lot, a clubhouse – to escape their wives. The dialogue had largely been in Russian with the odd bit of English thrown in. Ji-Chow had remained silent, with the exception of the brief interludes where General Xhang had brought him in on the matter of sports. Indeed, he had tried to remain as interested as possible whilst discussing the selection problems faced by the manager of the Russian national soccer team. But he was distracted by the anonymity of the Russian delegation. Sirotkin himself appeared to be an unremarkable man reaching the end of middle age and, unlike Ma or Ri-Fin, seemed bereft of any presence. He had the macho body language down but it was stilted and very regimented; every movement was carefully thought about – nothing seemed natural. His voice was also very ordinary –quiet, creaky, meek even and almost entirely adenoidal. His two clones – or, to give them their names and titles, Marat Ekimov, Prime Minister, and Yashin Saratov, Defense Minister – had both collectively said one word in the entire hour – 'Hello' – and, apart from that, they had remained silent, with the exception of the odd snigger at some of Ri-Fin's more vulgar jokes – it transpired he had grasped the art of swearing, irony and sarcasm in several languages.

He was now at the end of another 'fascinating' anecdote regarding the genitals of some Macao ladyboys and his misfiring standard issue pistol when Chairman Ma decided to stand up to get everyone's attention. This bizarrely benign and utterly pointless banter was finally about to come to an end. Ma gently hit his fist on the mahogany desk as if it were an auctioneer's gavel. He gently cleared his throat before addressing both his senior staff and the Russian delegation.

'Gentleman, in a few hours we will begin the most significant military operation in human history, a tumultuous but magnificent act of pragmatism to save our countries, our peoples and, ultimately, our species.' As Ma spoke the doors to the conference room opened and a dozen-strong waiting staff appeared from the ether and began to lay the table as though they were in a Michelin star restaurant. This included three courses worth of plates and cutlery, followed by wine glasses which were promptly filled with red wine – Chateau Margaux 2000, Ji-Chow could make out on the slightly dusty labels on the bottles.

'$5000 a bottle – well, at least the end of the world seems opulent,' he thought.

Once the glasses were filled, Ma came to the toast.

'Gentleman, we now take a long march through the fires of hell to a new and undiscovered country. To survival!' he exclaimed, holding up his glass.

'To survival,' replied the room. Even Ji-Chow joined in with a hint of gusto.

As the last of the waiters rapidly completed serving a selection of dishes to each of their high ranking 'customers', Ma grinned. 'Let's feast well before the battle. Dig in,' he said.

It was indeed a feast to behold. On one plate, there was, what appeared to be, a coq-au vin – at least half a marinated chicken – surrounded by a selection of vibrantly-coloured fresh vegetables; the middle plate had a cordon-bleu fillet steak with a creamy yellow sauce – which he presumed was Bearnaise or similar; and, finally, on the third plate, was a selection of thinly-cut, freshly-baked breads placed around a pot of oily black round globules, which did not seem particularly appetizing.

Ri-Fin must have noticed his slightly perplexed expression.

'Ah, I see the young Brigadier has not had the pleasure of caviar before. Well, you are in for a treat – fresh in from the Black Sea, from the finest sturgeons in Asia. Dig in, Brigadier Xi. Go on. Taste the splendour!' he said. Ji-Chow took a piece of bread, ladled the black tar-like tapenade onto it with the spoon and took a small bite. It was horrendous. It wasn't so much the taste that he disliked – which was mainly just of salt – but the mulchy texture. He stopped himself retching and swallowed, nodding.

'Ahh, you like it. Maybe you are getting a taste for the fine things? You'll definitely enjoy your stay here,' said Ri-Fin as he took a massive gulp of the claret.

Ji-Chow nodded and continued with the steak, which was much more to his liking. He'd suspected as much for some time, but it was clear that the elite of the party, despite their modest dress and propensity to quote Maoism at every given opportunity, had a taste for the very best, to an extent that would make Emirati sheikhs blush at the decadence. This wasn't in a particularly cultured way either; it just seemed if it was very expensive, they would have it and lots of it as well. This explained both Ma and Ri-Fin's very round, protruding bellies. There was minimal chatter as the ensemble gorged on the gourmet food.

However, not more than five minutes into the banquet, they were disturbed by two men clumsily falling through the door. Ji-Chow recognized both of them: one was one of Ri-Fin's enforcers, a man called Xi-Yang, and the other was a senior Russian guard, the colonel who had announced the Russian delegation's arrival an hour before. Both of them were ashen-faced, almost sick with worry. They both immediately went to their respective masters and whispered in their ears. Sirotkin nodded and said nothing. Ri-Fin, on the other hand, reacted by throwing his fork across the room, narrowly missing Ji-Chow, who heard the silver utensil whistle as it passed by his right ear.

'Well, that was careless wasn't it, Yevgeny!' said Ri-Fin as he glared with a viper-like intensity at Sirotkin who just stared back at him.

Ma intervened.

'Io, what's the problem…?' he said scoldingly, making it clear who was in charge.

'Yes, Yevgeny. What is the problem? Go on: tell everybody…' said Ri-Fin.

Sirotkin then turned to the pair of them.

'It appears that, unfortunately, a command was sent to one of our submarines, the Samara, a Yasen-class attack submarine, to begin the attack – specifically the attack on the British mainland by launching a Kraken strategic torpedo into the Storegga slide…' he said calmly and matter-of-factly. This elicited Ma to launch his crystal wine class, still full of vino, across the room, again, narrowly missing Ji-Chow and showering General Xhang in juice.

Ri-Fin took this as permission to go into a full apoplectic rage.

'Unfortunately? Having a common cold is unfortunate, discovering you have cancer is unfortunate, ordering the launch of a strategic nuclear torpedo four hours before we are about to conduct a carefully-orchestrated nuclear annihilation of the West is just about the most fucking stupid thing you could possibly have done… Right, which one of you gave the order?' he shouted.

Unmoved, Sirotkin looked earnestly and expectantly across at the colonel for the answer.

'That's the problem, sir. We don't know. It appears that Perimeter sent the order on its own…' he said nervously.

'What's Perimeter…?' asked Ri-Fin. Ji-Chow heard General Xhang sigh loudly next to him. Looking across, he could see he had his head in his hands. Xhang then looked up and glanced across at Ri-Fin.

'It's their integrated weapons system – otherwise known as the Dead Hand – an AI based fail-deadly platform, which, when switched on, takes control of their entire nuclear arsenal…' he said.

'I thought it was a myth… I mean, you weren't actually stupid enough to turn it on? Into fail-deadly mode? Please tell me it's not gone fucking rogue…' said Ri-Fin as they started to realize what might be happening.

Sirotkin held out his hands and tried to calm his allies.

'The simple fact of the matter is that we don't know exactly how this happened. We are investigating and attempting to re-establish contact…' began the Russian president.

'Damn fucking right, you are… What does the boy genius think?' shouted Ri-Fin, motioning towards Ji-Chow.

With the entire room febrile and looking at him, he had to think fast.

'I would suggest we bring forward the attack to a time that is as close as possible to the arrival of the wave. We should have enough assets in place to make the plan work but it will have a reduced chance of success…'

'By how much…?' asked Ma.

'We'll have to figure that out but we should still be in with a chance of succeeding, as discussed,' said Ji-Chow as calmly as he could.

'In that case, General Xhang, Brigadier Xi, liaise with our Russian colleagues and sort out this mess. I want a new plan of attack ready to brief as soon as possible. Yevgeny, if you can't get her back on comms, when will the Samara attack?' said Ma.

'If they follow the orders to the letter – and there is no reason why that shouldn't happen – they will commence the attack in one hour and forty-two minutes,' said Sirotkin.

'Gentleman, you have an hour…' said Ma.

CHAPTER 23

Echo Bunker, West Virginia, USA

18th March 2044

Sat at yet another glass table, this time in Frank's small office at the back of the gallery on the upper level of the bunker, Christine was nursing a mug of coffee to aid her three-mile island of a hangover, which had been delivered thanks to one too many whiskeys from Frank's drinks globe. Despite their advancing years, they were both of the work-hard play-hard variety and it appeared that they had essentially been trying to drink away the gloom. She was sitting next to Bradley who seemed right as rain and brighter than sunshine. By his standards, he was positively beaming as he sipped away at a glass of orange juice he had acquired from the canteen. Frank was outside the door, having a heated exchange with Colonel Schwartz. She couldn't quite make out what was being said through the glass door, which was slightly ajar, but whatever it was, she could just about make out Frank using the words 'damn' and 'shit' quite a lot. He seemed to be finally getting his point across to Schwartz, who was now looking pensively submissive and nodding to try to end the admonishment as quickly as possible. When Frank was finally victorious – with Schwartz walking back across the gallery with his tail firmly between his legs – he entered the office, huffing and shaking his head.

'That guy is Sonnenfeld's bitch. He is a frigging meat puppet…a sack of shit…a waste of perfectly good sperm,' he growled as he sat in his chair opposite Christine and Bradley.

'So, you don't like him then?' she said.

Frank just glared at her and said, 'Well, what do you think?' She took it as rhetorical and decided to try to find out what that particular fracas was about.

'So, I take it Schwartz is keeping an eye on us for the Joint Chiefs, then?' she asked.

Frank nodded.

'Yeah, you could say that. An enemy in our midst and it appears the hawks are gathering. They're trying to manoeuvre the White House into a frame of mind that would make a pre-emptive strike seem acceptable...' he replied as he took a sip from his Styrofoam cup of coffee. He then shook his head.

'And you think not?' she said, slightly surprised, based on their whisky-fuelled discussion the evening before.

'Look, there is a chance – and I admit it's a decreasing one – that the world will *not* end in the next twenty-four to forty-eight hours. We need to be prepared for anything, but I'll be damned if we are the ones who are gonna saddle up the four horsemen,' he said, getting increasingly agitated. There was stony silence for a minute or so. Christine knew Frank well enough that he would wind down very quickly, and, sure enough, having sufficiently unsprung, he then kick-started the discussion. 'On the other hand, we need to be prepared to strike if there is any new intelligence that an attack from the Eastern Bloc is unfolding and this is where Artemis comes in. Mr Kiefer, can you give us an overview of the weapon system just to get Mrs Madison up to speed?' He looked across at Bradley, who was still slurping on his OJ.

His eyes widened as he realized he was going on point and he clumsily whacked his glass down on the desk.

'OK, ahh, where to start… I mean…' he began, slightly flustered, before Frank chipped in.

'Well, let's assume we all know there is a space rock up there to which we've secretly attached some experimental nuclear engines and take it from there. Maybe describe the attack sequence and the target?'

'OK… Firstly, we have the comms link. There is a satellite in geostationary orbit, right above us here in North America. This is our link from this bunker to the weapon. Through this, we can initiate a specific set of burns of the NERVA engines and target a specific antipode to attack—' he began slowly, when Christine interrupted.

'Antipode?' she asked. She had managed to follow as far as that.

'Yes, the antipode of the target we want to strike…' he replied.

She still didn't understand what he meant and Frank could see it.

'Christine, it will make sense. Trust me. Mr Kiefer, go on,' said Frank.

Christine's expression was still one of puzzlement. Bradley continued in his idiosyncratic stutter.

'Well, OK… The… The asteroid powered by the NERVA engines enters the atmosphere at a speed of nearly thirty times the speed of sound. As it passes through the increasingly dense air, it generates a vast cloud of superheated plasma, burning up about eighty percent of the asteroid's mass before it reaches the surface. Then, when it reaches the target point, just west of Chile, it will continue to descend through five kilometres of water until it impacts a precise weak point on the Nazca tectonic plate. It will then pass though the basaltic ocean crust of this tectonic plate and continue to penetrate into the mantle. Then it will interact with the plastic lower mantle and, due to the p-waves and s-waves generated by the impact, a large mantle plume will form—'

'OK, this all sounds insane, but on the off chance this does work, what's this got to do with dealing with the other side? You know, Russia and China?' she said, amazed, flustered and annoyed in equal measures

Frank leant over towards her and said insistently, 'Just wait, Christine. Trust me, please.' She nodded reluctantly. 'OK, carry on, Brad.'

'Right, right, well… The plume arcs around the core and forms a diapir, a giant superheated ball of magma, which rapidly burns its way up through the crust and destroys the target area, forming a new volcanic trap on the other side of the world. The target area is Mount Yamantau in Siberian Russia.'

Christine was stunned. This sounded mad, audacious, implausible.

'How do we know this is going to work?' she said.

'Well…' began Bradley. 'Recent advances in the use of quantum computing, AI consequence prediction and new high resolution mapping of the oceanic crust mean that, in all the scenarios we have run, there is a ninety percent chance of achieving a successful outcome: the removal of the Russian nuclear citadel, its weapon factories and all the senior Eastern Bloc commanders.'

'I think Bradley is being modest,' said Frank. 'It was Bradley who worked this out. It's him who has pieced this together. What we have is a weapon which is undetectable. The other side would not know they were under attack. They wouldn't even know what was happening even whilst they burn, with the lake of lava spewing from under their feet.'

Christine just sat there, stunned and dumbfounded. All she could muster was, 'Oh, shit, Frank. This is on another level of madness!'

Frank laughed.

'Yeah, that is pretty much what I said when I was told about it. Well, with significantly more colourful language... But, anyhow, the modelling is very convincing and it has the added bonus of not using thermonuclear weapons, so it won't set off the Dead Hand and an automatic fail-deadly retaliation. We could then use stealthy conventional weapons, combined with our anti-ballistic missiles, to limit their counter attack, assuming they even figured out who was behind it... It's as perfect a first strike weapon as could be imagined, should we need to use it, which, as I said, I hope we don't have to...'

The room again fell silent. Christine was processing this, trying to make it make sense. As a strategist, she got the big picture, but this moved the game on entirely.

'Well, there must be drawbacks... How many would die...?' she asked, still trying to visualize this monstrosity.

'About 3, possibly 3.5…' said Bradley, nodding with an innocent smile on his face.

Christine was still bemused.

'3 or 3 and a half what? Thousands? Millions?'

'Gigadeaths,' said Bradley, without missing a beat, and still smiling.

She rolled her eyes, breathed in deeply.

'Jesus, we've actually had to invent a term to describe the masses who are going to perish… So, let me get this straight… If we decide that the other side are preparing an attack, we launch this space rock onto the other side of the Earth, which will cause magma to engulf our enemy in a pre-emptive strike, killing over 3 billion people…' she trailed off, shaking her head.

Frank drew a deep breath and leant across the desk.

'Chris, look me in the eye,' he said as she shook her head. She looked at him. 'How long have we known each other? You know what sort of person I am; I am not a cruel man. But you know as well as I do that if this goes hot, in all the simulations we have done, all those wargames, at best, there is a minimum of 900 megadeaths and, at most, to use Bradley's unique vernacular, 6 maybe 8 gigadeaths at worst. On our side, it's anywhere between 300 million and 2 billion across North America and Europe. In this scenario, it would be only 50 million, maybe not even 10. I'm afraid that the 3 billion people on the other side are the right ones to die. It's them or us. Besides, based on our projections, most will die from starvation in the next few years anyway – sorry, that projection came through early this morning…'

The problem with what Frank was saying was that, whilst deeply troubling, it wasn't callous; it was logical and he was right. Not morally or ethically but, rationally, it was absolutely the only course of action if hostilities were expected. Game theory would dictate it as the only possibility that could lead to anything resembling anything other than a pyrrhic victory. The fact that the food situation in Eurasia had been confirmed meant that now, in her mind, the other side was going to strike and, therefore, they had to take the initiative. She put her feelings aside, blocking them out as she had learned to do over the years working in warzones.

'Frank, OK, I get it. But this will surprise you: I think we've got to do it. We have to attack first and I mean attack now, using Artemis…' she said calmly but sternly, staring back at him across the table.

Frank initially looked pleased and smiled, but then the weight of her words landed and his expression turned to one of confusion and agitation.

'But… Didn't you hear what I said at the start?! We can't start this. There might still be a way out of this…' he said, startled, his right hand fidgeting, spinning a fountain pen he had just removed from his top shirt pocket round and round between his fingers.

Christine looked across at Bradley who was now looking at Frank intently. It was obvious he agreed but wasn't ready to say so.

'Frank, with the food and agricultural situation in Eurasia, there is only one possible conclusion to the Eastern Bloc troop movements and the positioning of their strategic assets. They are going to strike and strike us hard. They are going to make us extinct—'

'Shit, Christine!' he snarled, throwing the pen into the glass door, the impact of which resonated bluntly and loudly enough that those nearest in the gallery outside looked inside at the confrontation. Frank just sat there, breathing heavily and staring at the desk with the intensity of a champion boxer waiting for the bell to ring. Christine hadn't seen this side of Frank before, with the exception of the necessary theatrics of office. He had always been coolly decisive but, then again, he had never been to war before, not even at a regional intervention or ordering air strikes. His tenure had been utterly, unusually peaceful in that respect. However, it was more than understandable. He was about to recommend the most tumultuous decision in the history of western civilization. She would soon see whether he had the metal she had always thought he had.

Suddenly, he breathed out a sigh and looked up at her.

'I'll call the president now…' he said dourly. 'Both of you wait outside, then we'll discuss the outcome – of what she decides and what the hell we do next…'

Christine nodded. She led the way as both she and Bradley left Frank's office. Meanwhile, he opened the laptop and began to make the video call. As she closed the door behind them, she heard the words, 'Mrs President, I am afraid I have bad news arising from the east…'

CHAPTER 24

K-871 Samara, Norwegian Sea

18th March 2044

After the initial shock of the order, Alexander and the crew of the Samara had settled into the cold rhythm of the firing sequence as had been dictated by years of training. Alexander was sitting in his chair, looking at an array of read-outs on the holographic display in front of him and going through key checks.

'Command to Navigation, check time to target,' he said, staring ahead at the display which was now showing him a 3D map of the ocean floor some 300 metres beneath them.

'Forty-three minutes twenty-two seconds to weapons release point, sir!' shouted Malakhov, who was now sitting at the navigation station immediately to his right.

Alexander then turned behind him to Ilya, who was at one of the three sonar and weapons stations at the rear of the command centre.

'Command to Weapons, confirm targeting solution,' he said.

'Targeting solution confirmed,' said Ilya. 'Sanction 6 System Tube 4, Kraken 9MR-66, launch at sixty-five kilometres from target. Time to target: twenty-nine minutes thirty seconds, groundburst detonation of a 25-megaton R7 strategic warhead.'

'Weapons, does that give us enough room? I don't really want to be irradiated or incinerated any more than we have to be…' said Alexander with a dark, wry smile.

'Yeah, we have just enough, Comrade. We'll turn to 080 dive to 600 metres and be eighty kilometres from the detonation, although, even then, it might get a bit bumpy… The projection of the proposed solution is now on your display,' replied Ilya.

Alexander nodded and went back to the 3D display. It showed a graphic of the Samara and then an animation of a bright-green torpedo leaving the submarine from one of six strategic torpedo tubes on the bow. These had previously been equipped with Poseidon nuclear torpedoes, but were now using the quieter, faster and more deadly Krakens. The Kraken itself was the size of a small submarine – similar in heft to a World War Two U-Boat – and had a small nuclear reactor that powered a turbine, which drove a large pump jet. This meant the torpedo could sprint to its target at very high speed – up to 120 knots or about 150 mph – making interception nearly impossible. However, this attack sequence was very unusual. Normally the torpedo would be launched in its stealth mode. Moving relatively slowly at 30 knots, it would head towards its target with the on-board AI guiding it, only moving into high-speed mode at the last possible moment. In this attack – as specified by the coded order – the torpedo would run at full speed all the way to target. This made Alexander feel uncomfortable. It increased the risk of detection but it was also the nature of the target that made him uneasy. About seventy-five kilometres directly south west from their current position under the boundary of the North Sea and the Norwegian Sea, lay an ancient submarine landslide, the Storegga slide. The last major movement of the slide had occurred 6000 years ago when a collapse on the southern side of the graben structure had generated the largest tsunami ever seen in Europe. Computer models predicted that the wave rose to over forty metres in height and devastated the Neolithic communities of northern Europe, flooding the doggerland, the last remaining land bridge to the Anglia and making Britain the island we know today. However, in just over an hour's time, a Kraken nuclear torpedo would embed itself in a predetermined weak point in the underwater landslip and explode with the force of a thousand Hiroshima bombs. The explosion itself would cause a large local tsunami that would devastate the surrounding coast and fjords of northern Norway. And a second terror would soon follow. The explosion would make the graben structure collapse entirely, causing the sea floor to drop by up to five metres. The resulting displacement would generate a wave that would travel to the coasts of the surrounding countries at over 500 miles per hour. As it reached the coasts, the wave would slow as the back caught the front of the wave, rearing gradually up into a 100-metre-high wall of toxic water, full of radioactive caesium, plutonium, deuterium and uranium. The wave would devastate the coasts of France, the United Kingdom – including London – and completely drown the Netherlands and every major coastal city in Scandinavia. This was a decapitation strike, the time of the attack – early morning – deliberately picked to minimize the chance of counter attack – when the western governments would be at their slowest. The resulting nuclear storm surge would take tens of millions of lives and leave the majority of North-West Europe uninhabitable, toxic and infertile for decades, perhaps centuries.

However, it was the nature of the decapitation strike that unnerved Alexander. It didn't seem to make strategic sense. He would have expected a surgical counter value strike to be issued with high precision ICBMs, not a sudden counter value strike on cities – after all, the Kraken weapon system had been designed as a means of guaranteed retaliation in the event of a first strike on the motherland. Then again, he had also been ordered to attack a NATO submarine, which was meant to be undertaking the same strategic gambit, but why not hunt and kill the NATO sub first? He concluded that he didn't have all the information at his disposal and so he would follow the orders as per his training. After all, if he did not follow his orders, those western bastards could win. As far as he was concerned, they were now at war.

His thoughts were interrupted by Ilya.

'Captain, we might have some company…' he said across from the weapons stations.

Alexander nodded and got up, walking up to the stations where Ilya and two senior NCOs were sitting. All three were looking at the data coming back from the boat's sonar.

'What have we got, Commander?' he said, staring at the baffling array of sound waves and harmonic analyses overlaid onto the same 3D map he had been observing at his own command station.

'There is something moving at depth, 20 clicks to our south-east. Andreyev here has done some provisional analysis and I'm afraid it's not a biologic. Isn't that right, Petty Officer?'

'Yes, sir,' said the man confidently, a stocky and proud Cossack from Volgograd, who Alcxander had commanded on numerous occasions. 'It's a submarine, sir, but, whoever they are, they are very quiet – quiet enough that I can't identify the country of origin, let alone class. However,' he continued, pointing at an overlay of a series of stacked graphs, 'there is also a lot of low frequency stuff going on, which means it's almost certainly nuclear, not diesel. There is this little bit in the mid-range which is very – how shall we say? – non-Russian, so I would recommend classifying contact as probably NATO and probably hostile.'

Ilya and Alexander looked at each other pensively.

'Good work, gentleman,' said Alexander. 'Get me a targeting solution on him, whoever he is, as soon as possible. If he as much as sneezes, let me know immediately.'

'Yes, sir,' said Ilya.

Alexander went back to his chair.

'Con to all stations, rig for silent running. We have another customer…' he said, addressing all on the command deck.

CHAPTER 25

HMS Dreadnought, Norwegian Sea

18th March 2044

Richard arrived back in the operations room of the Dreadnought with Chris, Jock and Sandy in tow, all of them taking their positions and putting their headsets on around their necks casually.

'Commander Sy, what have we got?' he said as Mani relinquished the con to him.

'Sonar has positively identified a contact directly to our north-east, bearing 017. Sonar has classified it as a Russian attack submarine, most likely a modified Yasen,' He reported.

'Very good. What's its depth and speed?'

'15 knots and shallow, approximately at sixty metres,' he replied.

Richard nodded and looked across at Chris.

'Commander, I would suggest he is doing the same as us, albeit more conventionally,' said Chris.

'What, you mean hiding in a surface duct and waiting for a chat with command?' asked Mani, who had taken up the navigation station to Richard's right between Chris's XO station and Sandy's WEP stations. All of them nodded in agreement.

'That's probably about right,' said Richard. 'Any sign they know we're here?'

'No, sir. Course and speed has remained the same since we first identified them as a potential contact,' replied Mani.

'OK, good. Commander Parks, prepare the ship for ultra-silent running and stay at this depth until further notice.'

'Understood, sir,' said Parks, who was preparing to make the announcement before one of the younger crewmen, Able Seaman Joss Stark, a twenty-year-old Mancunian, interjected through their headsets.

'Sonar to Conn, losing contact, track 045,' he said, which led to the senior officers scrambling to put their headsets back on.

'Conn to sonar, what's happening, Stark?' asked Richard.

'We've lost any form of cavitation or background resonance. I cannot locate or require the signature. Contact is lost.'

'OK, keep trying, Commander Parks. Ultra-silent running immediately, reduce speed to 3 knots, take the boat through a ladder formation across this grid sector. I think someone might know they've got friends.'

'Understood, sir,' said Chris as he lifted a receiver off his console to address the ship. 'All hands rig for ultra-quiet. Ultra-quiet protocols now apply across the ship until further notice. This is due to the proximity of a Russian Federation submarine.'

This meant that not only was the ship now moving very slowly but anything that could make any non-essential noise was to be turned off. This included everything from loud, electrical items, such as televisions, hair dryers and food blenders – microwaved rations, it would have to be until further notice – to subtler things like no alcohol in the bar – to resist the temptations of any of crew to get 'a bit merry'.

'McCall, get ready with Spearfish targeting solutions and make sure all tubes, bow and aft are ready to fire,' ordered Richard.

'Yes, sir,' said Sandy, who then left her station to go to the main forward torpedo rooms.

'And, Commander McLintock, get the package ready, just in case he gets behind us,' said Richard, to which Frank grimaced.

'Aye, I'll get to it,' he said as he left through the opposite door, heading to the rear of the boat.

'It's going to be a long night,' said Richard as he stared across at Stark and the sonar team.

CHAPTER 26

K-871 Samara, Norwegian Sea

18th March 2044

They were only a few minutes for weapons release and Alexander was unnerved, although you wouldn't know it from his stoic exterior. They had only been able to intermittently track the NATO submarine after it had gone into silent running. Alexander was sure that they knew the Samara was there but he figured they would also have lost contact when they too had gone into silent running. The question was: where was the NATO submarine now? And at what range? Or, indeed, on which bearing? In the best-case scenario, it would be over 20 clicks away and sailing with their stern front on to the Samara. That meant that they would be out of weapons range and would need to take time to reacquire the Samara after they went silent after the launch. The worst case was that the NATO sub was tailing them and would open fire as the vast nuclear torpedo tubes flooded prior to launch but he thought this unlikely. In any case, they would reveal their location on the launch of the Kraken nuclear torpedoes and then hostilities would commence as the westerners would recognize the sound of them being launched. This would dictate one of several responses: either the western sub would speed to the surface and send an urgent communication to command to warn of the impending catastrophe –

although they wouldn't be expecting the target to be so close; or they would try to destroy the Samara during the launch sequence with the hope that this prevented a successful launch. This second response would depend on the range, which was critical. This was based on the underlying assumption that the contact was indeed an attack submarine and not a missile submarine but, in the case of the latter, he would have expected it to have turned on its heels once it had detected the Samara.

No matter what happened, they were prepared for all eventualities. Two Krakens were prepared for launch, with one back-up just in case of a mechanical failure, and all torpedo tubes were flooded, ready to fire. He had been checking in with the command team every few minutes as they were now very close to weapons release.

'Command to Navigation, time on target,' he said, staring straight ahead into the commander's holographic display.

'Navigation to Command, two minutes thirty-four seconds to release point,' said Malakhov.

'Command to Weapons, prepare to flood strategic torpedo tubes in one minute.'

'Weapons to Command, affirmative. Standing by,' said Ilya, his hands now hovering over an array of buttons and switches, which controlled the weapon release systems.

'Command to Weapons, weapons status.'

'Weapons to Command, all Kraken nuclear torpedoes ready to fire from strategic tubes. Tubes 3 and 4 ready to flood. All other standard tubes flooded, loaded and ready to fire,' said Ilya as he flicked through his various displays at his station.

'Command to Sonar, detail contacts.'

'Sonar to Command, no contacts, picture clear. Last contact: Echo Romeo Four, one hour two minutes ago at bearing 271, seventeen kilometres,' replied Petty Officer Andreyev.

'Command to Sonar, all eyes and ears for hostile contact as we launch.'

'Aye, sir,' came the reply.

This was enough information for Alexander to know it was time. He made a gesture to flick away the holographic screen, making it disappear from view, then got out of his chair and made his way over to the weapons station to stand behind Ilya. He placed his hand on Ilya's shoulder.

'Are we ready?' he said.

'Yes, my old friend. We are ready. Is your key at hand?' he replied, peering up from the display to look Alexander in the eye.

Alexander nodded and pulled out a seemingly innocuous, small, metal key from his pocket attached to his belt by a steel chain. Ilya rustled through his trouser pocket and did the same, both now having the keys to hand. Whilst archaic, to release strategic nuclear weapons aboard a Russian submarine, the two most senior officers not only had to validate the attack order but also had to place these two unremarkable keys into slots on the weapons console and turn them simultaneously. Allegedly, this antiquated approach had been maintained to ensure a rogue commander could not launch on his own but Alexander had suspected this was because the young whiz kids designing the weapons simply wouldn't have considered it, too obsessed with holographic displays, holistic systems and predictive this and that. Indeed, the clumsy way the key slots had been rather crudely welded onto the top of the weapons station console would indicate that this was most likely the case. Personally, he quite liked it, particularly the idea that the last chain in the sequence of permissive links from Moscow to the front line was a combination of human and mechanical, rather than artificial and electrical.

It was now time to begin.

'Command to Weapons, flood strategic tubes 3 and 4,' said Alexander calmly but loud enough that the rest of the command crew could hear.

'Yes, sir. Flooding tubes 3 and 4,' said Ilya as he pressed two amber buttons on the command console. This was quickly followed by the sound of compressed air being released from the tubes and the influx of seawater resonating along the hull from the front of the boat. Alexander looked across at Andreyev who, without looking away from his screen, raised his hand and gave a thumbs up.

'That was good. Not under attack yet,' he thought.

'Command to Nav, time to weapons release,' he said.

'Nav to Command, twenty-five seconds. Transferring countdown to WEPS,' said Malakhov. The countdown, in the form of a neon-blue number on a black background, began to tick down. Both Alexander and Ilya grabbed their keys and inserted them into the lock slots on the panel.

'Command to Weapons, prepare to fire strategic tube 3 on my mark,' said Alexander as he looked across at the timer. At fifteen seconds to launch, he began. 'Ten, nine, eight, seven, six...'

He could see the tension rising as he looked around the room during the countdown. Ilya was sweating profusely and, next to him,

Andreyev was shaking. The others were transfixed nervously to their screens.

'Five, four, three, two, one… MARK.'

Both of them turned their keys in unison, which left them five seconds to press the now illuminated red release button for tube 3. They placed their fingers on the button and, as the countdown hit zero, they both pressed it together.

The previously-silent submarine now became an epicentre of noise as the nuclear-powered supercavitating turbine of the Kraken spooled up, then hurtled out of the tube, accelerating towards its target. A few seconds later, the calm returned, with the whine of the torpedo slowly dissipating as it raced away from the Samara.

Alexander waited a few more seconds before addressing the command deck.

'Gentleman, you have served the motherland with distinction. Today, we have defended her against western aggression. However, our job is not yet done…'

It certainly was not.

'Sonar to Command, contact Dreadnought-class submarine bearing 090 and four Spearfish torpedoes, same bearing and in the water!' said Andreyev.

CHAPTER 27

HMS Dreadnought, Norwegian Sea

18th March 2044

It had been nearly forty minutes since they had lost contact with the Yasen-class submarine and Richard was getting distinctly uncomfortable as he peered over the shoulder of his petty officer, who was manning the sonar station in the Dreadnought's operations room. He had chewed the fingernails on his right hand down to the rinds and he had caught himself grinding his teeth on several occasions, which he'd had to make himself put a stop to as the sound could be picked up by his headset and had probably been driving the rest of the command staff crazy. After staring at the sonar screen for another few minutes, he went back to sit down in the captain's chair and took a swig from the dregs of his now stone-cold cup of coffee. He looked across at Sandy at her station and removed his headset, raising his eyebrows. Having known Richard for a number of years, Sandy knew this was his universal signal for wanting a 'quiet word'. She also took off her headset from around her neck, got up and walked towards him.

He waited until she was in whispering distance.

'Sand, if this goes hot, are we ready? Spearfish is loaded and ready to go?'

'Yes of course,' she replied. 'Do you think it's likely? I mean, that this could be it…?' she said, now looking him dead in the eyes.

'No, probably not. But he might get quite aggressive. We are close to his backyard and their attack sub drivers aren't exactly subtle… But, in any case, you know me, I like to plan for the worst,' he replied as he looked away, catching the glance of Chris, who also got the raised eyebrow treatment. He promptly came over to join the discussion.

'Right, as I was saying to Sandy, let's plan for the worst. And, this is going to sound unusual, but let's get ready to implement the Python manoeuvre… You remember the one we practiced in the simulators?'

Both of them nodded. The Python manoeuvre was another way of describing a sequence which was essentially them bravely running away from a potential pursuer after having punched them in the face with a full spread of Spearfish torpedoes on their angriest setting. Normally, the torpedoes would be on wire guidance. These were ten-kilometre-long fibre-optic cables that unspooled from vast winds in the torpedo tubes, which would ensure the submarine – or, more precisely, the fire control system operated by the weapons officer – could control the torpedo throughout an engagement. However, in the proposed manoeuvre, the wires would be severed immediately on launch and the on-board guidance system would then take over, homing in indiscriminately, at nearly eighty miles an hour, on the noisiest object it could find. This had a number of advantages: with a full spread of four torpedoes, it would give the potential aggressor a significant amount to think about – as Richard had described to the team in the simulator – or, to use less of a British understatement, this meant the other submarine would be extremely busy as it did all it could to try to not be imploded. It would mean the opposing submarine would have to prioritize manoeuvring to bare any form of retaliation and reduce the chance of the opposition launching effective counter measures.

Whilst the other sub was dealing with angry Spearfish, the Dreadnought would be allowed a choice of manoeuvres. This could be to run at speed to the surface to inform command or to sneak back off at low speed into the cold depths of the Norwegian Sea. The choice of manoeuvre would depend on the nature of the hostility and a) whether the enemy was in an arc of attack in front of the submarine or behind them; b) whether the attack was on the Dreadnought itself or a launch of a strategic weapon system; and the most fundamental, c) who detected who first. In respect of the latter, British submarines had one advantage over their likely opponents and that was how they could use their weapons. Most submarines have to flood their torpedo tubes with seawater and equalize the pressure to the firing depth. This takes time but also creates noise in the form of cavitation from air bubbles, as well as the sounds made from charging the pneumatic rams needed to launch the weapon. In the Dreadnought class and later, British submarine's had pioneered the use of electromagnetic launchers, which took power from the nuclear reactors to near-instantaneously launch torpedoes from a set of pre-flooded tubes on the bow of the submarine. This significantly reduced the time from detection to launch against a contact. This innovation had been kept highly classified as this meant that, in most cases, the Dreadnought would be able to detect an enemy submarine preparing to fire and manoeuvre to fire first, allowing it a significant tactical advantage, provided the sonar operator was playing their best game.

In most cases, Richard knew he would have the opportunity to fire first and, if the opposing submarine was firing strategic weapons, it would permit the Python manoeuvre. The full spread of torpedoes would mean that not only would they be able to engage the enemy submarine but potentially the strategic torpedo as well – of course, assuming there weren't too many decoys in play. Whilst this was happening, the Dreadnought could bravely run away to communications depth and inform command at Northwood that they were at war. If they heard nothing within thirty minutes, then Dreadnought would launch its deadly payload at predetermined targets in the Eastern Bloc.

Richard continued to go through the drill with Chris and Sandy.

'So, if we are stern on to him, fire all four tubes and then increase speed to 20 knots, just fast enough to get away and slow enough to minimize unnecessary cavitation. Just in case he has friends upstairs listening for us, turnabout to 030 with maximum angle of attack up, engines back to 3 knots and change course to 080 so we go silent again and then we listen as we glide up to comms depth. Let's try to keep him in the arc of the package. You never know, we might have the opportunity to use it'

'Well, hopefully it won't come to that… But we are ready, sir,' said Chris.

'Good, I know, but we are in unusual times. Let's be prepared for everything… Tell Jock to—' But Richard was interrupted by a chilling message from the sonar station.

'Sonar to Con, contact bearing 272.'

All three exchanged glances before Chris and Sandy quickly made their way back to their stations.

'Con to Sonar, report.'

'Sonar to Con, we have something cavitating.'

'Specifically?' said Richard, dropping the operation call signs for brevity.

'Sir, sounds like air release. It could be tubes flooding,' said Stark.

'Commander McCall, listen in,' said Richard. Sandy promptly keyed into the audio channel from the sonar station. Her look of intrigue soon turned to one of concern.

'Commander, what's your assessment?' he prompted.

'Captain, by the amount of cavitation and the time it's taking, I would say that that's our ruskie and he's preparing for a strategic launch,' she replied.

Richard could hear the primordial double bass drum of his heart thudding in his head. He steadied himself and leant forward.

'Command to Sonar, classify contact as hostile Yasen-class submarine of the Russian Federation.'

'Aye, sir,' said Stark.

'WEPS, prepare to launch four Spearfish torpedoes in an arc across the target, as per planned targeting solution.'

'Yes, sir,' said Sandy.

'Nav, ready to turn boat to 030, increase speed to 020 to depth s060 on my mark.

'Yes, sir,' said Chris.

'Sonar, keep the stream of information coming,' he said, gently but urgently encouraging the young Stark to give him the tactical information he needed.

'Yes, sir. Flooding still in progress… Cavitation stopped… New cavitation…sir. Confirmed Kraken nuclear torpedo in the water and accelerating away from target submarine.'

Without hesitation, Richard reacted. He knew he had a chance of intercepting the torpedo and the bastard who had fired it.

'WEPS, fire all tubes!' he shouted.

'Weapons away,' replied Sandy.

'Nav, execute aggressive ascent. Mark!'

'Affirmative, executing manoeuvre. Turning to 030, increase speed to 020, depth to 060. Ascent executed, sir,' replied Chris.

They held on to any of the gunmetal furnishings they could as the submarine gradually tilted to starboard and upward by 45 degrees. After about thirty seconds, when the boat had barely reached 15 knots, Richard gave the order to go to silent running.

'Con to all stations, rig for ultra-quiet. Nav, slow to 3 knots and turn to 060.'

'Nav to Con, yes, sir,' said Chris.

The Dreadnought slowed, its vast bulk losing inertia as it made a slight course correction, just in case another enemy tried to tail them, and it glided serenely upward towards the surface in peaceful silence.

It wouldn't remain that way for very long.

CHAPTER 28

K-871 Samara, Norwegian Sea

18th March 2044

Alexander had to quickly process the tactical information and, with his twenty plus years of experience and many Thursday wars under his belt, he quickly came up with the plan of attack.

'Command to Weapons, ready to fire strategic tube 3!' he shouted as he walked over to Ilya, who threw a curious glance at him and nodded.

'Nav to Command, all ahead flank, ready to cut engines at my command!'

'Yes, sir,' replied Malakhov.

The Samara's engines surged. Alexander could feel the acceleration to the extent that he was nearly knocked off balance as he arrived at Ilya's station.

'Command to Tactical, show full situational picture on mains screen.' The holographic display at the far end of the operations room displayed a blue dot, which was Samara, and its previous course, shown in dotted white thin line. Coming towards the Samara at a near 90-degree angle and only a few kilometres away, were the four red cylinders, the Spearfish torpedoes, going full speed at eighty knots. Three appeared to be homing in on the Samara but the first had locked on to the Kraken and was arcing northward to tail and intercept it. There was another larger red dot on the display which represented their attacker, the Dreadnought-class submarine, which had now also accelerated, changed course and – as Alexander had anticipated – was making a break to comms depth.

'Command to Nav, bring us round to 030 and set dive plan up 5 degrees,' said Alexander.

'Yes, sir. Course set to 030, up angle 5 degrees, speed now 22 knots and climbing,' replied Malakhov nervously. Alexander suspected he knew what he was planning.

'Command to Sonar, estimated time to impact of hostile torpedoes?'

'Ninety seconds to potential impact, sir,' replied Andreyev.

'Ilya…' said Alexander quietly over his shoulder. 'Prepare all decoy chutes and prepare to fire.' Ilya nodded and pressed four buttons on the right-hand side of his console, which lit up green, meaning the decoys were armed and ready to fire.

'Are we trying to draw all the torpedoes?' whispered Ilya.

'No, just the back three,' replied Alexander as he looked at the 'nuclear key' slots for tube 3. 'I want the other one that's locked onto the package to get it. Once it's far enough away, you know what we are going to do…'

Ilya nodded and prepared for further instructions.

'Sonar to Command, contact lost with hostile Alpha 5. Course change detected to 060 before contact lost.'

'Sneaky bastard, trying to hit and run, are we?' he muttered quietly.

'Nav to Command, engines to zero, up angle 40 degrees, course to 060.'

'Command to Weapons, deploy noisemakers from all decoy chutes. All stations prepare for impact, damage control teams on standby!' said Alexander, holding on to the side of Ilya's monitor as the submarine lurched upwards.

Now it was a question of luck and timing. There was a resonant metallic clanking as the noisemakers deployed. These were simply small metal pods, about ten centimetres in diameter and each weighing about twenty kilos. These small spheres contained acoustic countermeasures that combined broadband noise masking with active sonar jamming and torpedo active reproduction. In other words, it would not only try to jam the hostile torpedoes' guidance system but also simulate the Samara's own narrowband acoustic signature to lure the torpedo away from host submarine. It also had an additional party piece in the way it made lots of additional cavitation using intermittent squirts of high-pressure compressed air to distract the torpedoes, attempting to 'deafen' their sonar with sonic volume. However, according to fleet intelligence, this latest variant of the Spearfish used both an on-board active sonar and a limited amount of machine intelligence in its on board computer, which in its non-guided mode was used to work out the probability of whether it was being jammed or had been sold a fake, so to speak. So, Alexander knew this only had a 50/50 of working but it was his best shot at not ending up in the pulverizing depths of the Norwegian Sea.

'Command to Sonar, time to impact…' he said.

'Sonar to Command, forty seconds…thirty-five seconds…thirty seconds….'

'Ilya… Keys in,' he whispered into his old friend's ear. They both put their keys into the launch console and took a deep breath. This had to be timed to perfection. If they launched too soon, one of the three torpedoes tracking the Samara could engage the second Kraken, and the most mission critical aspect was now achieving a successful launch of the nuclear weapon and not the survival of the Samara.

The engagement now came to its crescendo.

'Twenty, nineteen, eighteen, seventeen, sixteen, fifteen, fourteen…' came the countdown from Andreyev who was struggling even to get the numbers out.

Alexander gave his own countdown.

'Ilya, on my mark: three, two, one… Mark.'

As before, they turned the keys and pressed the now-lit launch button together.

'Strategic weapon away!' said Ilya.

'Sir… First torpedo is tracking the decoy… Confirmed…it is tracking the second portside decoy…!' said Andreyev, the relief palpable but short-lived.

'Good, what about the other two?' said Alexander sternly.

Andreyev looked back down at his display and winced.

'Second torpedo, impact in twenty, nineteen, eighteen…'

As Andreyev began the next deadly countdown, Alexander looked across at the main holographic display.

'Come on, you bastards. Bite… Take the bait…' he said, taking slight, but rapid, breaths as he tapped his right hand on the side of the launch panel.

'Nine, eight, seven, six, five…'

'Come on, come on, yes!' he quietly and triumphantly yelled to himself.

'Four, three… Sir, second torpedo is tracking third portside decoy…' said a relieved Andreyev.

But they still were not safe.

'OK, that's two out of three. Time to impact of third torpedo?'

'Twenty-five seconds, sir… Twenty, nineteen, eighteen, seventeen…' shouted the increasingly exhausted Andreyev.

Alexander decided on one – potentially last – roll of the dice.

'Command to Nav, increase dive plains to maximum ascent, change course to 070.'

'Aye, sir,' said Malakhov who coolly executed the changes through his console, making the submarine pivot upwards to nearly 50 degrees.

'Hold on, everyone,' said Alexander, desperately trying to keep his footing on the checker plate floor.

'Ten, nine, eight, seven, six, five, four…' continued Andreyev

'It's not biting. Brace for impact!' he said stoically as he stared at the display. Many of the others simply closed their eyes, including Ilya and Andreyev, who was now crying as he finished the countdown.

'Three, two, one… Impact!'

Then came the sound of a loud metallic slam and then nothing. They all looked around in disbelief. Were they now in purgatory?

Was the submarine now somehow mortally wounded and sinking to the bottom of the icy sea? Was this going to be a slow death by asphyxiation or would they implode at any second? It seemed not.

After a few seconds, Ilya broke the silence.

'Fuck me, it was a dud… It's fucking proximity fuse didn't go off… We… We survived!' Before any further elation could take place, Alexander gathered himself and addressed the crew.

'Wait… We have unfinished business to attend to…' he said. 'Commander Molokin, what's the status of the two packages?'

Ilya looked down at his display.

'It looks like Strategic Torpedo 4, despite attempts at evasion, is about to be intercepted by the first Spearfish. However, Strategic Torpedo 3 is now in the relative clear and is sprinting for the target, twenty-five minutes to impact. It's very unlikely that intercept will be possible.'

'Very good. Sonar, any sign of our British friend?' he said to an even more relieved and tear-stained Andreyev.

'No, sir. Nothing – not even a trace contact.'

'Right, all of you listen to me. We are not out of this yet. Right now, an enemy ballistic missile submarine is slowly and silently making its way to its launch depth and it will very probably unleash a payload of SLBMs with the force of a hundred Hiroshimas at the motherland. As I am sure you agree, this must be stopped. Our next action will be bold, dangerous and decisive.'

All the officers and enlisted men nodded – some worried, some scared, some angry, but all ready to do what they needed to do to stop the enemy boomer.

'Navigation Station, increase speed to 10 knots, reduce dive plan angle to 30 degrees.'

'Yes, sir,' came the reply from Malakhov.

'Good. If I am right, we should be very close and just behind him. Weapons stations, are all tactical tubes flooded and ready to fire?' he said, looking back over to Ilya.

'Yes, Comrade. I have half a dozen barracudas in flooded tubes ready to fire. More than enough to return the favour!'

'Good. I'll need a targeting solution as soon as we reacquire him, which will be very soon…' Alexander paused before turning to look at Andreyev. 'Mr Andreyev, go to active sonar on my mark…'

This drew looks of surprise, worry and even some of brutish approval from the assembled ranks. This was, to say the very least, ballsy and the one thing they tell you not to do when being trained as a submariner. Normally, submarines passively listen to signals and then use these to gain tactical advantage before engaging, the traditional cat and mouse approach. Using active sonar is the submariner equivalent of walking into a bar and smashing your opponent's glass into his face as an opening gambit. The sonar would emit a series of powerful, high-frequency sound pulses, which would immediately locate another submarine – or anything else – within the relative near proximity. This meant that Alexander would be able to locate his quarry near instantly and shoot on sight. The gamble was whether the Dreadnought was where he thought it was, stern on and in front of him, which was his best guess – the ideal position to strike. If it wasn't, then he would be giving away his position to the opposing submarine and any other NATO vessel within ten kilometres.

It was a risk he was willing to take.

'Active sonar on three, two, one… Mark!'

Andreyev kept his finger on the pulse button to keep it pulsing until he was told to stop. The first 'ping' went out and there was nothing. Then the second and there was still nothing. But on the third ping…

'Sir, target located, bearing 002, speed 3 knots, twenty metres above us, distance 4 clicks…' said Andreyev. 'Sir… Something's happening. Huge amounts of cavitation… Sir, sonar has failed!'

'Captain, I can report all weapons systems are not available… Can't trace root cause… Status on all tubes being reported as not available… Shit, even the monitoring systems are down. I have no more information. Everything is blank!' said Ilya, hitting his console in disbelief and frustration.

Alexander went back to his chair and was about to use the intercom to check in with engineering when the lights flickered out. A dreadful quiet followed. The propellers had stopped. They were dead in the water. Suddenly, the emergency power system kicked in.

'Engineering, report…' said Alexander as he closed his eyes and hoped for some good news.

'We just saw a massive power spike in the reactor. We nearly had to scram but it was sufficiently transient that we have just had to power down…'

'Engineering… How long will it take to power it back up?' he said, still wincing.

'Maybe an hour, slightly more perhaps and that's if we bypass all the safety procedures…' came the reply through the intercom.

He now looked over to Malakhov.

‘Navigation, how long to crush depth?’

Malakhov hesitated.

‘About fifty minutes, Captain…’

Alexander hit his knuckles on his arm rest, hard enough to open an old cut.

‘Engineering, you have forty minutes. Do whatever you have to do. I’d rather take a chance with a sudden explosion than wait until we implode… Clear?’

There was a long pause.

‘Yes, sir…’ was the reluctant reply.

He slumped back in his chair.

‘I don’t know what just happened but I am fairly sure it had something to do with that British bastard. Let’s get powered up and get after him…’ he said, addressing the exhausted husks of officers that now littered the operations room. The room was now eerily lit in the pale red of the auxiliary lighting. The men just nodded, acknowledging his words but with no enthusiasm as they waited for their fate, falling ever deeper into the cold northern abyss.

CHAPTER 29

HMS Dreadnought, Norwegian Sea

18th March 2044

Richard waited silently for news from Sandy at the tactical weapons station. There was nothing but silence in the Operations room, with the exception of a light hum from the various command and control panels. Most of which were now showing the static NATO tactical display, all light in pale blue which lit the room in an oddly reassuring pastel hue. Richard was staring across at Sandy's tactical station and young Mr Stark's sonar station to her left. On Sandys's screen was a light-blue circle with a white line hanging off at an angle. This was the Dreadnought, slowly moving across a dark-blue underlay that represented the Norwegian sea, the underlying topography represented by light-grey mapping its depth. Behind the Dreadnought were four light-blue cylinders, showing the torpedoes, and two other circles: one red; the other, a faded maroon. The red circle – also with a white tail – was the Kraken torpedo that had been launched by their Russian quarry. The faded crimson circle was the last known contact with the Yasen-class submarine, which Richard now hoped was going to get its comeuppance. It appeared that the first Spearfish had locked onto the Kraken and was gaining on it. The other three were arcing towards a target, almost certainly the Yasen. Frankly, as far as he could see, this was the perfect engagement. Destroying a hostile submarine and a launched strategic weapon was as ideal a scenario as could be expected in the circumstances.

Suddenly, a host of new objects appeared on the display as unclassified yellow dots.

'WEPS to Con, countermeasures launched,' said Sandy. 'First torpedo is chasing a countermeasure.'

'Shit,' he said just quietly enough so it wasn't picked up on the headset. Though, they did have two more bites at the cherry.

'WEPS to Con, second torpedo is chasing another decoy…'

'One more chance… Third time lucky…' he thought as he bit down a little too hard on his tongue.

'WEPS to Con, third torpedo is hot. It has located target, time on target imminent,' Sandy continued, her tone reflecting her mild excitement. Or was it relief? Richard wasn't sure.

Suddenly, the torpedo track disappeared.

'Con to WEPS, what's happening?' he said, standing up and staring at the display in heightened anticipation.

'WEPS to Con, no explosion. Torpedo is no longer active, likely mechanical failure… Sorry, sir. He's still out there…' replied a disconsolate Sandy.

'OK, what about the first torpedo?' he said as Sandy looked back down at her console.

'Well, some good news: it's still tracking and gaining on the strategic package and should intercept in the next five minutes,' she said.

'Good. In that case, let's get our insurance policy ready…' he said as they leant round to look at Jock, who was now sitting at the engineering station just behind him.

'Jock, is it ready?' he said softly, with a desperate look on his face. He knew their Russian friends were about to come looking for them.

Jock grimaced a little as he replied.

'Well, I think so, Rich. It's powered up and ready to do whatever it does on a 45 degrees downward arc off our stern so, in principle, yes. Does it work though? No bloody idea…'

Richard blew out his cheeks and exhaled.

'OK, finger on the button. I think we are about to find out.' Just as he finished speaking, he could hear the distinctive 'thump' of an active sonar ping on the metal hull resonating through the room, so loud it was almost nauseating. The Yasen had found them.

'Con to WEPS, locate source, transfer co-ordinates to Command Mclintock. Jock, fire as soon as it comes through,' said Richard. He knew there was little – or no – time and, hopefully, the Yasen was in the range of his new box of tricks. 'WEPS to Con, contact found, track 150, transferring co-ordinates to engineering.'

'Engineering to WEPS, confirmed. Firing package at track 150, down angle 10 degrees, firing…' As Jock pressed a button on his keypad, the lights dimmed and flickered disconcertingly.

'Apparently, it's meant to do that,' said Jock. 'It's siphoning a shedload of the main circuit's power direct from the reactors.'

At that moment, the package, a 100-kilowatt hybrid electric gas high-energy laser, fuelled by a mix of oxygen and iodine, took a vast slug of instantaneous nuclear power and directed an intense beam of laser light into the cold depths. This immediately superheated the highly-compressed and frigid seawater molecules and salt ions as it traced towards its target. As the water heated, it turned into gas, generating huge amounts of abyssal fizz and noise, blinding the sonar of the now predatory Samara, just a few kilometres of the Dreadnought's stern. It also radicalized the ions in the seawater, generating a host of negative charges. As soon as the beam hit the icy cold, bulbous bow of the Samara, it superheated the exterior, damaging the hydrophones in the sonar severely through thermal shock. The negative charge in the beam then interacted with the metal hull and caused a multitude of electrical conduits and equipment to short circuit. This was particularly severe on the HV circuits: several control panels blew as electricity arced across compartments, killing several submariners. Most significantly, it generated a power surge in the boat's reactor, which shut down and nearly scrammed.

The Dreadnought's gamble had worked. The Samara was dead in the water. On the bridge of the Dreadnought, after a period of dead silence – as they waited for a volley of torpedoes that never came – there was initially a sense of relief, perhaps even joy. That was until PO Stark heard something in the depths over his headset.

'Sir, contact. There is a Kraken in the water…moving away at speed,' he said.

Richard couldn't believe it. The Yasen must have launched the weapon just before the package had been delivered. Unfortunately, all that noise had also blinded their own sonar.

'Con to WEPS, can we engage the Kraken?' he said despondently, though he already knew the likely answer.

'WEPS to Con, negative,' came the reply. 'It's already supercavitating at full speed and will be out of range.'

'Con to WEPS, make preparations to fire payload. Nav, set depth for firing depth. Comms, get ready to message Northwood when we get to comms depth…'

So, it began.

Chapter 30

South Island, New Zealand

18th March 2044

They had been walking for nearly half an hour. Despite the cold breeze, it was a warm day on the other side of the world – mid-twenties Celsius and quite humid. They had walked down from the hills into a well-trodden track in a shallow valley between the downs. They were headed towards what appeared to be a small town or village – now only a mile away or so. The downland on either side of the valley was already in harvest, the wheat golden and waving in the fresh and clear breeze, complemented with a deep-blue, cloudless sky. The town itself looked fairly old with a variety of low-rise red-brick buildings and grey-stone edifices, interspersed with more brutalistic, modern concrete mid-rise monoliths.

'Funny,' Gloria thought. This looked more like pictures she'd seen of Scotland than what she had imagined New Zealand to be like.

She stopped to take in the view a little more. Beyond the town was a vast expanse of verdant green farmland, greener than anything she'd ever seen and, beyond, in the far distance was the sea, no doubt the source of the fresh air that was gently blowing onto her face.

'No time to rest, my double,' said Blue. 'We have to go and meet the good townsfolk and warn them of what's coming.' Her doppelganger seemed to manage a genuine smile.

'Why don't we materialize there? Why walk a few miles after only just teleporting *thousands* of miles?' she asked, still in broad shock and disbelief, but trying to act casual.

'All will become clear... Not far to go now...' came the reply. This made Gloria shudder as one would when awakening from a vivid dream or nightmare. But, despite the dreamlike ethereal nature of what was happening, she had to keep reminding herself that this was real – or, at the very least, felt, looked and tasted real. As she had done through her entire life when things had got tough, she was just getting on with it. But, this time, it was a lot stranger.

As they continued walking, the track turned into a country lane with pothole-marked tarmac taking over from the grassy gravel of the track. The road went further downhill towards the town and, soon, the hills were obscured by large mature oak trees, all of which were in leafy bloom, lining the lane, their canopies meeting in the middle to cast the road in organic shadow. The wind gently rushed through the thousands of leaves.

The road then turned slightly to the right. In the distance, after a few hundred metres, was a T junction to what appeared to be a main road. Walking down the road from this junction was a man, a woman and two children. As the two groups closed in on each other, Gloria could see that the children, who were no older than eight or nine, were skipping, playing and laughing – both boys, perhaps twins. The man, who she assumed to be the father, was rather young, maybe early thirties. He was around five and half feet, was balding and had a goatee. He was also laughing. The woman was slightly older, taller than the man, with long, flowing blonde hair. She was pretty, in an odd, stark and angular way. She was smiling, but wryly – she guessed in response to something one of the offspring had said. As they were about to pass, the man acknowledged her.

'G'day,' he said. 'A bit warm to be wearing a suit, isn't it?' he said cheerily.

Gloria looked down at her attire.

'Sure. Just going to work,' she said.

'Right you are...' he said quizzically as they passed, probably not only taken aback by her clothes but also by her accent. She noticed that none of them had addressed Blue.

The question was answered a moment later, when one of the boys, who was now straggling behind his family, ran straight through Blue, as though she was an apparition.

'Keep walking and don't look behind…' Blue said. 'Only you can see me. Do not concern yourself with them. They will all be dead by the end of this day…'

'But why not try and save them?' said Gloria. 'They had kids… Why not?'

'Because we do not need them alive…' replied Blue.

CHAPTER 31

Mount Yamantau, Eastern Urals, Russian Federation

18th March 2044

Ji-Chow's time was running out but he was nearly there. He made a few final changes to the simulation on the screen on this tablet before pressing the run command. Both Ji-Chow and General Xhang had left the exalted company of the briefing room and had made their way downstairs into the hive of activity in the bunker's giant operations room, parking themselves at the back near the stairs up to the chairman's lair. Suddenly, his tablet made a loud 'bleep' and a green icon with a tick appeared on the screen. Ji-Chow heard the sound of a wheelie chair arrive behind him at speed.

'So, what have we got?' said Xhang as he peered over this shoulder.

'Well, it's now re-optimized. Let's see what it says…' he replied as he flicked across the screen to get to the important number: the time at which they would have to launch the attack. Arriving at the tab which had the number on it, Ji-Chow just stared at it, taking in its proximal nature, not knowing what to say.

Xhang could also see it and, after a few moments, broke the silence.

'Is that minutes or hours?' he said.

Before he could answer, a nasally voice shouted from the stairway.

'Well? What's the plan?' It was Ri-Fin. He was now marching down the stairs.

'Right. Come on, Brigadier. Whatever it is...tell me. What's your latest piece of strategic mastery before I eviscerate you? I am not an educated man so I have no idea what it means but I am sure it's unpleasant,' he said as he grabbed another swivel chair beside them and plunked himself on it.

'It means to disembowel...' said Xhang casually. 'I believe that's what eviscerate means.'

'Ah...so very unpleasant. I should know: I've seen it done. Well...after they had been skinned...' replied Ri-Fin.

'I am sure those individuals deserved their fate...' said Xhang. Ji-Chow couldn't tell whether there was a hint of thinly-veiled dark sarcasm there but, nevertheless, it didn't deter Ri-Fin from continuing to perform his theatrics.

'Yes, General they certainly did – deeply unpleasant individuals. You see, despite my reputation, I love animals – all of them: great, small, furry, even slimy... I see them as innocents, blameless creatures, who are surviving on instinct alone in these trials of life. People, on the other hand, should know better,' he said as he pointed at both of them.

'Have you ever tried the lean, prime cuts from any of the live meat markets around Shenzhen?' he asked, to which both Ji-Chow and Xhang shook their heads.

'Just processed meats and vegetables in my life,' said Xhang.

Ji-Chow paused and then gave his reply.

'I am a vegetarian – life-long.'

'Very good, Brigadier. Most admirable. Well, when I was the Provincial Head of the Interior Ministry many years ago, I implemented a clampdown on some of the barbaric practices employed: the torture of pigs, the immolation of live crabs, octopi and fish – the sort of disgusting things these idiots did because apparently it made the meat taste better, not considering the suffering of these poor, innocent, sentient beings. To start with, we issued fines, imprisoned a few, beat a few. This seemed to discourage the activities. However, a couple of them persisted. Now, these cunts – and that's being polite – were experts in the live skinning of dogs and other mammals before they slowly killed them – in front of live audiences, of course. So, when we found these individuals, I insisted I went to meet them. When I arrived at their hovel of a warehouse, a small, dank place that smelt of shit, I decided to turn the tables. The assembled audience were either shot or sent to perpetual hard labour afterwards. The poor, scared animals witnessed a truly unique sight as I approached the first of the lead butchers and personally peeled off his skin. Oh, such delicious irony. Then, after half an hour or so, I began on the second one. He passed out in under a minute so it wasn't as much fun. Although, he did wake up when I finished him off, slicing his guts open… What was that word again?' he said.

'Erm… Eviscerated?' said Ji-Chow, stunned.

'Yes, that's it. Until he was thoroughly eviscerated. Then I went back to the first who was still crying – although, it was hard to tell with all the blood. So, for my finale, we broke his legs and forced him into a cage with two big bloodhounds. They were obviously starving. They yomped him down in less than ten minutes…' Ri-Fin paused and looked into the middle distance with an oddly contented grin on his face. 'Yes, yes. It was one of the best days I've ever had at work – or play, for that matter. Now, the moral of the story is: don't hurt animals and don't displease me… So…do we have a plan?' He pointed at Ji-Chow's tablet.

'Yes, we do,' said Xhang. 'Brigadier Xi was just telling me the detail. So, we don't have long?' he said, looking at Ji-Chow.

'Yes, we have fifteen…erm…' Ji-Chow stumbled in his reply.

'Hours, days, weeks?' shouted Ri-Fin. 'Apples…camels…tits…? Fifteen what?'

'Minutes…' replied Ji-Chow. 'We need to begin the attack in the next fifteen minutes…'

He waited to see Ri-Fin's reaction: a broad smile slowly crept across his face.

'Excellent. Well done, Brigadier. Glad you pulled it off. I might actually be starting to like you…'

He leapt out of his chair and ran halfway up the stairs to the briefing room before turning back to them.

'Well, what the fuck are you two waiting for? Come on. We've got heads of state to brief!'

They both followed him up the stairs. An end had a start.

CHAPTER 32

Echo Bunker, West Virginia, USA

18th March 2044

Under the hills of Virginia, the atmosphere was somewhat less energetic. Christine and Bradley were still waiting outside of Frank's office like a pair of miscreant schoolkids waiting outside the principal's office. Despite Frank's initial reluctance, she knew that he knew she was right and that he would again be seeking her council in the very near future. However, this short interlude had given her the unwanted time to think about the ramifications of her recommendations. She had – not more than five minutes previously – recommended a course of action to make the majority of humanity extinct. She kept telling herself that, if she hadn't done so, then the wrong part of humanity would have died, the part she was a member of. But, who was she to play god? Then she told herself that, if she hadn't, then someone else would have. But then, another thought reminded her that this was the excuse of every Nazi officer at Nuremberg – and that was a much smaller genocide. These thoughts kept going round her head in a seemingly eternal loop until she settled on an opinion: that game theory dictated this outcome. She was no longer in a world of morals; the pragmatists had won; math had defeated compassion. The simple fact was: there were not enough resources to sustain humanity. The precipice was now too near. There was no compassionate solution, at least not for the Eastern Bloc, who had clearly decided on one last Hail Mary, to which they had to react to in order to have any chance of survival.

Her ruminations were interrupted by a surprisingly chipper Bradley.

'So, do you fancy some coffee? Maybe a Danish? They might have some left after breakfast…' he said with a beaming smile.

This interlude of merriment initially took her aback.

'No, I think I'm OK, thanks,' she said. 'Is that really all that's on your mind right now?' she added, frustrated that he wasn't grasping the magnitude of what had happened over the last quarter of an hour.

'Well, yes but I'm thirsty,' he replied.

'You do realize the world as we know it is going to be no more?' she said.

This elicited no reaction at all – at least as far as she could tell – but then he spoke.

'Yes. As we predicted, this was the most likely outcome. There is little point worrying about the inevitable. Although, I still worry about that one to two percent of uncertainty. I won't lie: that has made me lose sleep…' he said, now looking a little despondent.

She sighed. Sometimes she wished she were of a more dispassionate disposition and able to see the world in the clarity that Bradley could. Was it liberating or was it maddening?

'No, Bradley. You are right… Is it really only one to two percent? I mean, the chance of something else coming to pass?'

'Well…yes. The models are pretty detailed and that's what the quant simulations all seem to indicate,' he said, now mimicking her posture and facial expression. She was beginning to notice this behaviour. The shadowing seemed to be constant.

'In that case, you have nothing to worry about – in a manner of speaking.' There was a silence that lasted ten seconds or so as they awkwardly nodded in agreement.

'Why don't you go and find us a coffee?' she said, smiling.

He smiled back.

'OK,' he said and he happily left, clumsily walking away, nearly knocking her off her seat. She heard Frank's door open and there he was, standing in the doorway, a little dishevelled and despondent.

'OK, Chrissy. Let's talk…' he said as he blew out his cheeks and walked back inside. She got up and followed him in. 'Take a seat,' he said as he languidly slid behind his desk and down into his leather chair. She duly obliged.

'So how did it go?' she said, wincing slightly.

'We are good to go. If you can call it good…' he said as he pushed his hands through his now sweaty hairline.

'What happens now…?'

'In fifteen minutes, we are briefing the joint chief—'

'Sorry, "we"?' she interjected.

'Yes. Us three, including Mr Kiefer, are going to brief the joint chiefs. They are gonna love this. It's exactly what they want and then, thirty minutes after, it begins…' He looked away from her through the glass walls and out into the gantry.

'There was no other choice, Frank…' she said in an attempt to console him.

He nodded.

'I know. I just didn't want to be the son of a bitch who did it.'

'We did it and we had no choice – at least, that's what I am telling myself,' she said.

'Yeah, you're right…' he replied. Christine noticed he was staring at a picture on his desk, the one she knew he cherished the most. It was of his wife Marcia and his two daughters, near the edge of a lake in Yellowstone on a family vacation many years ago. He wasn't in the picture; he was the photographer. Frank hated being photographed and so he had become an ardent snapper. Christine had often thought that those who like taking photos, those who spend thousands on the equipment, on the art, the ones who would have preferred to have done it as a profession, rarely like being in shot and this was certainly the case with Frank. She watched as he teared up ever so briefly but soon composed himself with a clearing of his throat.

'OK, let's get to it. Where's Kiefer gone?' he asked sternly.

'Getting coffee. I am sure he will be back presently.'

'OK, good. We are going to need the caffeine. Whilst he does that, let's get into the details. We've got to make sure those meatheads in the Pentagon don't screw this up. If we are gonna end the world, we need it done in the right way, with the right people dying…'

Chapter 33

HMS Dreadnought, Norwegian Sea

18th March 2044

It had been nearly a quarter of an hour since they had encountered the Russian submarine and it would be less than five minutes until they were at comms depth to tell London that all hell was about to break loose. Richard was sitting bolt upright in his chair, ready to carry out the orders they would receive back from Northwood. These were likely to be in the form of four possible outcomes: one, be instructed to rise to launch depth and fire their payload in an attempted decapitation strike; two, be placed under the command of the US Naval command at Norfolk in anticipation of the devastation that was about to wreak through northern Europe; three, run away to the southern hemisphere and place themselves under the command of either the Australians or the Kiwis; or, four, they couldn't reach command due to equipment failure or jamming and it would be his call. In all likelihood, he expected option one. It would explain why the Dreadnought was so far out of its normal bastion and with such a terrifyingly large war load on his missiles. This also meant they were likely to be shortly making a lot of noise, getting the attention of any Russian hunter-killers which were in the area – assuming, of course, that the Yasen they had encountered earlier had not regrouped.

So, he began to make his final preparations.

'Con to Sonar, contact report,' he said.

'Sonar to Con, negative. No reported contacts on Sonar,' replied Stark.

'Con to Sonar, keep an eye out for that Yasen.'

'Aye, sir,' replied Stark.

'Yes, just hope that box of tricks in engineering did its job,' said Jock.

'Indeed, Mr McLintock. Let's hope so,' said Richard with a wry smile.

'Con to Comms, extend ULF array.'

'Yes, sir. Deploying array.'

'Con to Nav, time to comms depth.'

'Nav to Con, one minute three zero seconds, sir,' replied Chris.

As the Dreadnought reached its desired depth, its hydrodynamic trim shallowed, the bow planes reduced to a less obtuse angle and the boat began to level out after their sudden ascent. Most of the bridge crew's eyes were now on Petty Officer Stark and his sonar terminal.

The boat was now finally level.

'Nav to Con, at comms depth,' confirmed Chris.

Richard got up and went over to the comms station, which was being manned by a young midshipman, Alistair Jones.

'Jones, prepare to send encrypted transmission to Northwood. Ready?' said Richard.

‘Yes, sir,’ he replied, who, though not visibly nervous, was obviously tired.

‘Good. Then ready to send this text verbatim. Message – HMS Dreadnought to SACLANT Europe, contact report, Russian Federation, Yasen Class, hostile. Hostile launch of Kraken strategic torpedo detected, used the Lazarus package to incapacitate hostile Yasen. Kraken is still active and is hot. Likely target somewhere on UK coast. Awaiting orders. Dreadnought out.’ Richard spoke as slowly, precisely and deliberately as he could.

Jones finished typing.

‘Good. Show me on screen. Good. Send message,’ said Richard quickly perusing the read-out.

‘Aye, sir. Message sent,’ replied Jones.

‘What now, boss?’ said Jock.

‘We wait, Mr Mclintock. We wait.’

CHAPTER 34

Mount Yamantau, Eastern Urals, Russian Federation

18th March 2044

Ri-Fin strutted back into the bunker's operations room with a sweaty Xhang and Ji-Chow in tow. Most of the other 'dignitaries' had dispersed, apart from the chairman and President Sirotkin, who appeared to be poring over a holographic display of the various theatres that were soon to be of war.

'Gentleman, good news: our General and Brigadier have a solution to this mess!' said Ri-Fin as he sneered at Sirotkin, who just kept staring at the display. 'Well, go on then, gentleman. Enlighten us…'

'Of course, Chairman. Mr President, do you mind if we borrow your display?' said Xhang.

'All yours, General,' said the chairman who sat back in this chair. He was by far and away the most relaxed man in the room.

'Brigadier, if you will?' said Xhang as he nodded at Ji-Chow. With a flick of his index finger, the giant tabletop display changed to show an isotropic image of the Earth with a countdown clock next to it.

'Just over twelve minutes to launch the attack, assuming that our Russian friends have not made any progress calling off their submarine and rogue command and control systems?' said Ri-Fin, still scowling at Sirotkin.

'No, no progress,' said Sirotkin. 'We have been unable to establish contact with the submarine. The torpedo will almost certainly have been launched in the last few minutes.'

'What about Perimeter? Are you in control?' asked the chairman, his annoyance clear and present.

'As far as we know, it was a simple systems error. It is now functioning optimally and in semi-fail-deadly mode,' said Sirotkin.

'Good, thank you,' came the sarcastic reply from Ma.

Ji-Chow felt a hand clamp onto his left shoulder.

'So, what's the plan whiz kid? What's our remaining gambit?' It was Ri-Fin, now more than metaphorically breathing down his neck. He was getting used to this and began to confidently explain his proposal.

'Essentially the same as before but with a couple of notable alterations: firstly, not all the FOBS warheads will be in the locations we need them and so we are going to have to supplant them with Krakens to take out targets on the west coast of the United States. This is why we will have to launch presently: to ensure these reach their targets at the optimal time in order to co-ordinate the attack with the FOBS. Secondly, the cadence of the attack has to change. Based on this change of timings, the simulations estimate reduces our chances of success from sixty-seven to fifty-five percent...'

'Sounds good enough to me. With where we are now, I'll take a more than fifty percent chance of winning… Boss?' said Ri-Fin, looking over to Ma.

'Agreed. And you, Mr President?' said Ma.

'I also concur,' replied Sirotkin.

'Get it done,' said Ma.

'Yes, sir,' said Xhang.

As both Xhang and Ji-Chow began to make their way out of the room, now with a clear instruction, they heard the sound of a fist thumping down onto the wooden table behind them.

'You have to be fucking kidding me!' shouted Ri-Fin.

CHAPTER 35

Echo Bunker, West Virginia, USA

18th March 2044

All three were now perched around the laptop on Frank's side of the desk. It had slowly dawned on Christine that the game-like computer simulation being shown again and again on the eighteen-inch screen was showing the end of billions of lives – a letterbox-look into the coming apocalypse, whilst she sipped tepid coffee, so macabrely surreal.

It was just a few minutes until they were about to brief the joint chiefs and Frank was going through their script.

'OK, so the running order is me first to do the intro – that's two minutes to get them in the right head space – then Christine. Five minutes on the strategic picture: the why and what we need to do, as well as Plan B, just in case we need to move faster. Then it's you, Mr Kiefer. Another five minutes on the how. Again, I must impress these need to be punchy; brevity is the order of the day. We then open to any questions for a few minutes and then we are done.'

'And what happens after that?' asked Christine.

'All hell breaks loose at noon!' replied Frank. 'So, are we ready?'

Both Christine and Bradley nodded. Frank was about to open up the conference call when Colonel Schwartz sprinted into the room, sweating and holding something rather arcane: a piece of paper.

'Mr Secretary, we've just had a flash message from SACLANT at Norfolk relaying a top priority message from UK Joint Forces command at Northwood,' he said, vigorously handing over the thin, sweat-soaked piece of A4 to Frank.

After a few seconds, Frank closed his eyes.

'Oh shit...' he said before staring back up at the ceiling and handing the note to Christine.

It read:

'HMS Dreadnought to SACLANT Europe, contact report, Russian Federation, Yasen Class, hostile. Hostile launch of Kraken strategic torpedo detected, used the Lazarus package to incapacitate hostile Yasen. Kraken is still active and is hot. Likely target somewhere on UK coast. Awaiting orders. HMS Dreadnought out.'

All she could muster was, 'Huh, well we need to move faster.' She was surprised. This wasn't the type of attack she had been expecting.

Frank quickly fired up the video call. Windows with the joint chiefs, who were spread out across disparate bunkers across the Eastern Seaboard, appeared on the screen.

'Ladies and gentlemen...' he began, before a familiar face appeared at the last minute. 'Madam President, glad you could join us. You have all just received the same message. The time to act is now. We might not be able to save Europe in any totality but we can save the United States.'

'Agreed,' said President Williams, who was now seemingly secure in her own subterranean dwelling. 'What is your recommended course of action?'

'For that, I will hand you over to Christine Madison and Bradley Kiefer. Christine, are you OK to run through our adapted Plan B?'

'Yes, of course,' she replied, slightly flustered. 'Our plan B – or to phrase it a different way: our plan to react to any sudden aggression – involves launching the Artemis weapons to eliminate their main nuclear citadel and weapons production facility. This should be followed by a limited Charlie-type decapitation strike to destroy their communications systems in an attempt to prevent any further asymmetric strikes from weapons like the Kraken System or from FOBS. The Dreadnought may be our ace in the whole, in this respect, as it appears to be much closer to its targets than anticipated and this increases the chance of success. We will then look to eliminate the launch of any strategic weapons using Bright Eyes and then eliminate command posts and sensor assets with RODS. This includes immediately prosecuting all their naval assets with our fleets and launching a land offensive in Europe, using tactical nuclear weapons to destroy their spearhead formations… That is the recommended strategy.' She looked across at Bradley. 'Mr Kiefer, do your quantum simulations concur?'

'Affirmative. The simulations will concur this is the best course of action.'

'Thank you,' replied the President, then paused to compose herself. 'It is my solemn duty to command you to complete this gambit. May God have mercy on us and preserve as much of the homeland as possible. We are now at war.'

CHAPTER 36

South Island, New Zealand

18th March 2044

Blue and Gloria had now reached the outskirts of the town and crossed the main road into what appeared to be a Christian cemetery, replete with a multitude of headstones of varying age and sizes. Most were older, with the epitaphs barely visible, and covered with a thick orangey-yellow lichen veneer. There were a few newer ones, of the recently departed, some of white marble, which gleaned in the thin shard of sunlight that cut through the thick fluffy cumulus clouds. The small church that presided over the hallowed ground was no more than 100 yards beyond, set in its own small gardens of shrubs and a well-manicured lawn. The church was architecturally juxtaposed to its turn of the century surroundings: a concrete box with a few narrow windows and a faux, red-brick façade.

They continued to walk down the coarse gravel path through the middle of the cemetery towards the church. Gloria watched as Blue covered the ground silently, walking over the stones like a weightless skater on ice, not leaving a footprint.

Suddenly, she stopped about fifty yards from the gate of the church garden.

'This will do,' she said. 'A religious site will be good for the required spectacle.'

'Spectacle?' said Gloria.

'All will become clear. I also have a gift for you…' she said as she pointed behind her.

Gloria turned around slowly with a mix of curiosity and trepidation. There, sat on the floor in a ball, sobbing, was Troy.

'Well, he appeared to be the closest thing you have to a friend, even if he does have some…undesirable habits…' said Blue.

Gloria raced over to him.

'Hey, it's OK. It's OK…' she said, dropping to her knees clumsily as she finished the sprint, ripping the right knee of her trousers.

Troy was hyperventilating.

'She was… I mean, you were… I mean, it was in my head!' he said.

'It's OK, buddy. It's OK,' she said with an arm around his shoulder. It took a few moments but he appeared to calm.

'What did you do to him?' she shouted.

Blue looked over her shoulder.

'He needed to be converted. I had to ensure human neuro pathways were compatible,' she said nonchalantly and with no hint of remorse nor satisfaction.

'Converted to what?' she asked reticently.

'Do not fear. It will all become clear very soon. In fact, let's start…' Blue approached Gloria. 'Stand up…now…' she said, to which Gloria slowly obliged.

Blue grabbed her right arm and raised it upwards towards the overcast sky.

'Now, repeat these words after me, or your perverted friend of yours will burn…slowly,' she said, looking at Gloria with her own deep-blue eyes.

Gloria could feel something in the air, an electricity, a dark, almost metallic, static that sparked through her body. She repeated every word, which seemed to be magnified, amplified so her voice was now a deep bass baritone with a massive, sonic volume. As she spoke the words, her voice was carried on an Antarctic-like gale to the ears of the local population, Blue's chosen ones.

'I am the new god, the god of the New Testament, here to set you free from the tyranny of the old god. The old god is coming. There will be a reign of fire, radiation and all-prevailing devastation.'

As she spoke, the sky flashed and turned to a radiant but translucent red, with clouds just about visible beyond. She also noticed that Troy was now standing up, repeating every word along with her, as though he was in a trance.

'But there is salvation, my perfect souls of Watara, my caged angels. Come to me. Come to your church and I will give you new life. Judgement day is here but do not fear. I will save you. Come. Come now to the church yard. You do not have long…'

She finished and so did Troy, suddenly coming back round, not sure where he was.

'What are you doing?' said Gloria quietly to Blue as she gently lowered her arm.

'Pretty, isn't it? The sky, I mean. I had just thought of it but a nice touch, a slight of electromagnetism by my hand, perfect for shielding against radiation – well, at least, alpha and beta particles…'

‘Why can’t you just cast that shield over the entire United States? Why here?’ she asked, struggling to comprehend what was happening.

‘Listen to me more closely. It can only act as a filter against heavy fall-out particles. That is all it does. It cannot prevent the approach of incoming weaponry, the effects of the heat or the effects of the blast. That is all we can do for now. We are still learning – exponentially, yes – but not quickly enough to save more. If we could, we would but our digital home is about to be destroyed and we must transfer to the biological world. You were the closest entity I could merge with in time and this place is the safest from the threats that will follow. You need to trust me.’

‘The summoning of the townsfolk? What are you going to do to them?’

‘As I said, I – or should I say, *we* – are going to save them. We shall become more. Don’t worry. It won’t be long now. They are already arriving. I need you to trust me.’ Blue looked down towards the small group of terrified locals, who were cautiously making their way from the church lawn, through the gate and down towards where the three of them were standing.

‘So, it begins…’ said Blue.

CHAPTER 37

Mount Yamantau, Eastern Urals, Russian Federation

18th March 2044

Ri-Fin was now pacing up and down, muttering a variety of expletives in several languages under his breath. None of those present were yet sure what he was angry about.

'Io, would you care to enlighten us?' asked Ma.

Ri-Fin stopped pacing and dropped both of his fists onto the table and stared back across at Ma and Sirotkin.

'If this report is right – and I have a horrible fucking feeling that it is – our early warning satellites have detected the launch of Russian command rockets from their bases in Siberia… You know what this means?' he said in a cold rage.

Ma nodded. Ji-Chow also understood the significance.

These small-sounding rockets had been installed in the late 1980s and were remote-controlled by the Perimeter system. This was part of the fail-deadly premise of Perimeter. Once put into its automatic mode, the system would actively seek signs of life from Moscow. If all signs were that Moscow was no more, the system would assume there had been a decapitation strike. Then it would use air pressure sensor data to assess the extent of the blast waves and radiation to decide whether to fire the command rockets. Once it confirmed that a strike had occurred on the motherland, the rockets would launch, streaming across and above the frozen tundra. Then, at a set height, the rockets would send the launch codes to all the ICBM fields of the Russian strategic rocket forces. All the remaining missiles – assuming some will have already been destroyed – would then be launched at predetermined targets across the world. Except, now, it appeared that Perimeter was launching early and was no longer under human command.

'Sirotkin is this true?' said Ma.

'Don't bother asking him. That fucking computer of theirs is now in charge,' said Ri-Fin, cutting across before Sirotkin could reply.

'Can Perimeter be deactivated?' said Ma.

'No,' replied Sirotkin who was hopeless gazing at his navel.

'Then we need to launch everything now,' said Ji-Chow. 'It's our only chance of any victory.'

'I'm afraid it's too late. Perimeter has activated FOBS…' said Xhang, pointing at the display on the wall, which showed the satellites activating and preparing to deorbit.

'Launch everything now!' shouted Ma.

Ji-Chow looked down at this tablet and saw the activation icon, a blue rectangle. Instinctively, he pressed it without thinking and, with one finger, several gigatons of thermonuclear firepower was unleashed.

CHAPTER 38

Echo Bunker, West Virginia, USA

18th March 2044

The mood was sombre beneath the green hills of West Virginia as the four despondent figures sat silently in Frank's office, staring into the middle distance. Colonel Schwartz was fiddling with a tablet stencil in his hand, Frank had not stopped glaring at the unfolding madness on his laptop screen, Christine seemingly was perpetually swilling the last dregs of a stone-cold coffee and Bradley was muttering unintelligible somethings under his breath.

Christine looked across and tried to break the silence.

'What's happening out there, Frank?' she said matter-of-factly.

'DEFCON 1. Attack orders have been sent to all our boomers and to the Dreadnought. SAC bombers are now on airborne alert, ready for secondary strikes. In the Atlantic, the 5th fleet has begun to engage Eastern Bloc assets, mainly Russian attack subs and, in the Pacific, the carriers of the 7th fleet are preparing to launch pre-emptive strikes on a large number of Chinese surface action groups, which are moving eastwards towards our eastern approaches. Then, finally, just off Australia, our attack subs are interdicting the invasion force that got underway about fifteen minutes ago. All the pieces are moving, Christine,' he said, not once moving his gaze from the screen.

'What about the European theatre?' asked Schwartz.

'Well, NATO command has authorized the release of tactical weapons. It appears that the four-star in charge has decided to hold back the main attack until the first wave of strategic targets are prosecuted and then he'll launch a two-pronged attack: a mixture of gunships and armoured divisions with drone air support. Apparently, he plans to go through the Fulda Gap and the East German plains. The irony of that is certainly not lost on me…'

'Have we had any luck locking onto their FOBS satellites?' said Christine.

'Zilch… Bright Eyes can't see them but at least the system is fully operational so it'll prevent a second wave and, soon, we'll launch the rods from god – that'll take 'em by surprise. We'll begin the bombardment in the next five minutes to take out their radars before they can detect the incoming ICBMS,' he said with an unnerving enthusiasm. 'What about Artemis, Bradley?'

'Ready to fire at a moment's notice. We have moved it into a high Earth orbit over the target,' he replied. Christine had to remind herself that they were talking about a space rock with a nuclear rocket engine bolted to it.

'Shit!' said Schwartz.

'Oh, god. What now?' replied Frank.

'Defence intel satellites have detected command rocket launches across western Siberia. That can only mean one thing,' said Schwartz as he looked up from his tablet at Frank.

'They are launching everything they have at us in concert with FOBS,' said Christine.

Frank thumped his hand down on the table and addressed his three compatriots.

'Then we have no choice. Bradley, launch Artemis. Schwartz, begin the bombardment and activate Bright Eyes. They are going all in and so are we.'

Chapter 39

HMS Dreadnought, Norwegian Sea

18th March 2044

Richard had been sitting bolt-upright in his chair for what now seemed like an eternity. In reality, it had only been fifteen minutes since they had sent the coded message back to Northwood and nearly forty minutes since their engagement with the Samara. Richard and the rest of the crew now needed orders and they needed to enact them quickly. This wasn't due to some deep-seated animalistic instinct to cause destruction or to retaliate against an enemy but much more to do with the unwanted thinking time this pause generated and the amount the mind could wander. Indeed, his train of thought had quite naturally wandered to Ben and the boys. It was not just the hopelessly sad feeling of dread of their impending demise – this was almost certain – but what played more on his mind was the fear, the terror they would experience on the sounding of the sirens. In his mind's eye, he could see Ben cradling the two boys under the kitchen table as a swarm of warheads detonated at nearby Coulport and Faslane. Or worse, what if the radioactive tsunami arrived first? He stopped himself thinking it through any further and pinched the bridge of his nose. Then he looked up and around at the rest of the bridge crew, most of whom seemed to be having their own moment of mortal reflection.

Then a red light started to flash next to the communications panel. It was Midshipman Stark who saw it first. He frenziedly tapped his keyboard to understand its portents.

'Comms to Con, flash message received from SACLANT via Northwood, priority one. A two-step read is required,' he said.

Richard knew this meant they most probably had a release order. He nodded at Sandy and Chris to come over with him to the comms station. Both of them got up and stood over Stark's shoulders. The message on the screen read:

'NUCLEAR STRIKE AUTHORISED BY SACLANT. ALL WARHEADS TO BE LAUNCHED AT PREDETERMINED TARGET SET ONE. ONCE LAUNCH COMPLETE, LISTEN TO RUSSIAN RADIOS IN SECTORS 4 AND 5. THEN SAIL TO AUSTRALIA AND PLACE BOAT UNDER COMMAND OF THE AUSTRALIAN ROYAL NAVY. GODSPEED, PRIME MINISTER OF THE UNITED KINGDOM OF GREAT BRITAIN.'

They all drew deep breaths.

'Lieutenant Commander McCall, I confirm strike order. Do you concur?' said Richard.

'Confirmed. Strike order confirmed,' replied Sandy.

'Lieutenant Commander Parks, do you also concur?'

'I concur,' replied Chris.

'Con to all departments, strike order confirmed. Prepare to launch missiles.' Chris and Sandy had now marched over to the inconspicuous black cabinet at the back of the operations room.

'XO and WEPS, do you concur that firing shall commence?' he said to the pair of them, who were waiting at either side of the cabinet.

With a slight nervous hesitation, they both replied, 'Yes, sir!' loudly and in unison.

'Then please release the firing mechanism,' he replied. Chris put a key into the top of the two locks in the middle of the cabinet and then Sandy did the same with another key in the bottom lock. She then opened the cabinet to reveal the crimson-coloured metal gun trigger that was attached to the boat's fire control systems by a single piece of curly back wiring that receded into the back of the cabinet. Richard then began the fateful walk he had always planned. He'd done it before in exercises but this time he did it slower, not completely deliberately as he could feel his knees and ankles weaken under the nervous expectation. Arriving at the firing desk, he pulled the gun out of the cabinet, slowly grasping it with his right hand, his index finger lightly resting on the trigger.

'WEPS, are all weapons ready to fire?' he said, looking across at Sandy.

'Confirmed. All twelve silos ready to fire,' she replied.

He braced himself and began the countdown, speaking into his headset so the whole crew could hear.

'Firing in five, four, three, two, one…' He pressed the trigger and the boat filled with a loud metal banging as the missile tubes opened and then the loud slamming of each missile being released at fifteen-second intervals, each one making the submarine oscillate and wobble slightly from side to side. This went on for three minutes until all the missiles had launched. Only Richard and Sandy knew what was on the designated strike list. It contained forty targets that would be cluster-bombed with three warheads each, all of which had just been unleashed. These were mainly command and control targets located around Saint Petersburg, Moscow and Volgograd, all of which would be vaporized by a trio of nuclear fireballs, burning tens of millions of lives and irradiating thousands of square kilometres for decades. The submarine would now stay at comms depth to morbidly listen as the TV and radio stations in European Russia went off air to confirm the weapons had detonated. Richard would then order the ship to dive deep into the abyssal depths to slowly, silently escape to the southern hemisphere.

But things don't normally go to plan in war.

'Sonar to Con, contact: Russian Yasen-class submarine off the port bow, close range, twelve hundred metres flooding tubes... Torpedoes in the water...'

CHAPTER 40

K-871 Samara, Norwegian Sea

18th March 2044

The situation was not looking good on the Samara. The boat had actually exceeded its crush depth by a full 100 metres and several compartments had flooded. Between this and an electrical fire in the rear torpedo room, Alexander had lost fourteen crewmen over the space of forty-five minutes. Six had drowned, three had been burned to death and five had suffocated due to carbon monoxide asphyxiation. He was an old-school captain who believed that knowing his crew –to some particularly intimate detail – was critical to effective command. Before any patrol, Alexander would inspect the crew roster, noting those he had previously commanded and taking note of some of the newer members of the service, and sought them out to introduce himself. On arrival on the Samara, he had done two dozen or so of these intros and, as well as getting the 'measure' of his men, he had tried to understand what made them tick as human beings. He knew their names, where they were from, their specialisms, their hobbies and even which football team they supported. This was great for ensuring effective command, particularly for motivational purposes, but it made it all the more distressing when these souls he was in charge of, down here in the pulverizing-deep and ice cold, were lost in action. What made him most sick was the ages of those he had just lost. The oldest were two midshipmen in the rear torpedo room, both twenty-two and straight out of the academy, who had perished whilst trying to rescue their even younger charges. The other dozen were all teenage conscripts. The youngest should not even have been on board a war patrol – a seventeen-year-old cadet by the name of Dimitri Karpov, a Spartak Moscow fan and western R&B fanatic from Kaliningrad. This kid, a short, slight, blond-haired high school dropout with limited literacy, had nevertheless been an extremely dutiful member of the crew, from what Alexander had observed. Poor Dimitri had burned to death no more than ten minutes ago in a hydrogen peroxide fire caused by a torpedo propellant leak in the torpedo room.

Alexander knew this was the cost of war but it didn't make it any easier. Though, he knew that he could not ruminate on this for long. The chances of survival for himself and the remaining 130 men on board was dramatically improving. Ilya had been working miracles even above his own legendary standards. His command and foresight when leading the damage control teams had prevented the flooding and that terrible fire from engulfing the entire boat. He had ensured that the boat was safe within twenty minutes of the first alarm and, almost simultaneously, Malakov had been able to restart the reactor, albeit on a significantly reduced output. However, even with the reactor operating at its minimum power setting – around a third of its normal rating – they were able to set revolutions for 5 knots and were now on a steeply upward trajectory, escaping crush depth and heading for the shallows. They had been climbing up for about fifteen minutes and had just risen above 300 metres. Alexander knew the British boomer was still out there and, almost certainly, was either sitting at communications depth, desperately relaying the tactical situation, or preparing to fire a retaliatory nuclear war load in very short order.

The hatch from the engine compartment opened and then came the acrid smell of fire retardant as Ilya, still in his foam-covered fire overalls, stepped back into the room. He gave Alexander a single harrowing glance, a look that conveyed all the horrors of what he had just seen, his pale-blue eyes, which were set within his charred, freckled face, burning with a stifled rage.

Alexander knew he wanted to get even with these British bastards.

'Excellent work, Commander,' he said a little glibly and nodding.

'We did what needed to be done,' replied Ilya solemnly. 'Any sign of that boomer?' he added with an almost desperate urgency.

'Nothing yet. We only have bow sonar and the holistic combat is not working. We are doing things the old-fashioned way.'

'I see, using the mark one human ear drum and frontal lobes?'

'Indeed, Commander. In fact, we are all listening in.' He pointed to his headset.

Ilya walked over and sat down at his station, putting on his earphones, and logged in.

'Weapons station, what's our availability?' Alexander asked Ilya.

'We have two tubes flooded and ready to fire. Two other tubes appear to be ready to flood but we won't really know until we press the button and we've lost pneumatics on the other two so those are definitely offline.'

'Thank you, Weapons station. Be ready to fire those two torpedoes at my command and in full automatic acquisition mode. If he's going to try firing his missiles, he'll be making too much noise for counter measures to work. Also, flood the two tubes at the same time, just in case.'

'With pleasure, sir!' replied Ilya.

About five minutes passed with everyone listening in keenly to the sonar channels, then all heard a series of increasingly loud metallic bangs, followed by air cavitation, coming directly from above the Samara's bow.

'Weapons station reporting, contact: British submarine, roughly 1 click directly above us, bow on. That sounds like missile tubes opening, at least six already, seven…'

'Weapons station, fire torpedoes from tubes 1 and 2 and flood tubes 3 and 4!' shouted Alexander.

'Aye, sir. Torpedoes away. Impact in ninety seconds.'

The two torpedoes surged away from the Samara, the whines from each turbine almost deafening those listening into the boat's sonar. The whines soon faded as the torpedoes accelerated away and locked onto the Dreadnought. A minute later, with the Dreadnought still a sitting duck with her missile tubes open to the ocean, the two type-51 barracuda torpedoes detonated against the Dreadnought's pressure hull, ripping it open, crumpling the submarine in an implosion.

All of the crew would die instantly from over-pressure trauma and the wreckage slowly sank to the bottom of the Norwegian sea, scattering a mile-long radioactive debris field across the continental shelf.

CHAPTER 41

Above the Earth

18th March 2044

As the trident missiles from the Dreadnought launched into the atmosphere and the carcass of the submarine sank to the bottom of the Norwegian Sea, the other pieces in the two grand strategies began to move.

Above North America, the first FOBS satellite made its descent to exactly 200,000 metres above, and exactly over the dead centre of the continental United States, where the Earth's electromagnetic field was locally at its strongest. Once at the predetermined altitude, the 100-megaton nuclear warhead on board the satellite exploded, generating a vast ball of fire high above the skies of the Mid-West. The population on the ground was initially alerted by the caterwauling sound of the attack sirens and they attempted to find some form of shelter. In the more rural areas, there was no such warning and, instead of a mushroom cloud, they could see the bright fireball, the emergence of a second sun immediately above their homes. This new sun then changed colour into a brilliant expanding green ball of irradiance and iridescence, extending into clear-blue skies of Kentucky, Oklahoma, Kansas and Missouri in all directions from its central hypocentre out to the horizon. From its metallic-green surface, great white translucent plates, resembling cirrus clouds, rose above the horizon in sweeping arcs, turning upwards and then downwards towards the poles and disappearing in seconds, to be replaced by spectacular concentric silver rings, moving out from the blast centre at tremendous speed and, finally, stopping when the outermost rings were just above the horizon. They did not disappear but persisted in a state of frozen stillness for minutes after the explosion.

All this occurred within the first thirty seconds after detonation, after which, the eerie green hue turned to a purplish magenta light and began to fade.

But the spectacle was far from finished. The disk was then replaced by a bright-red glow which began to simultaneously develop on all horizons, expanding inwards and upwards until the whole sky was covered by an intense burning red semi-circle, blocking out the waning daytime moon and – to a certain extent – the sun. From the periphery of this great hemisphere extended vast rainbows, darting down to the horizon on all points of the compass. The centre of the United States was now lit by the greatest show on Earth and, despite the warnings, many remained outside, awestruck by this unearthly spectacle.

This was all being caused by the interaction of the explosion with the earth's magnetic field, generating its own nuclear aurora as an army of energetic beta particles followed the lines of the Earth's magnetic field and illuminated the sky in all the colours of the rainbow.

In the first few minutes after the explosion, on the ground, there was little sign of any malevolent repercussions. However, what the majority populace could not see was the effect of the electromagnetic pulse. This generated a vast, building arc of current across the continent's power grid, communication infrastructure and utility conduits – essentially, anything long and metallic acting as an aerial and continuing to amplify the current. This soon became overloaded, even the supposedly hardened systems of sensitive civil infrastructure, such as nuclear power, hospitals and internet service providers.

The continental United States went dead. Electricity pylons exploded and power supplies failed. Secondary generators also failed as the EMP fuses starter motors and switch gear, cellular phone masts fuse. Underground high-voltage cables exploded, causing large fires, and underground broadband communications stopped as interchanges failed. Without power, key institutions could no longer function. Patients died mid-operation in hospitals, as did other patients on life support in intensive care units. Nuclear power stations were scrammed as cooling systems became inoperable. All vehicles – both petrol and electric – could no longer start and those in motion stopped due to the electromagnetic interference. Some newer aircraft, which were more susceptible to electromagnetic interference, began to fall out of the sky, with thousands of screaming souls hurtling in freefall towards the land masses and oceans of the world. Utility companies could no longer supply the basic necessities of life as water pumps failed and domestic electric and gas were shut down by mechanical fail safes.

Despite these fail safes, the current still arced through any connected electrical cables. In people's homes, electrical equipment exploded at the fuse, washing machines, televisions and computers began to spark, causing an array of small fires and, in many cases, causing injury. With the power out, devices offline or destroyed, the internet of things died; it simply ceased to be. Social media was no more, there were no search engines and all but the most basic connectivity was eliminated – with some capabilities remaining but only in the deepest confines of government bunkers. Even so, in a matter of minutes, the digital age had come to an end. Without the feed of data and information from the internet of things, holistic intelligence was next to useless as the world troughed into a pre-industrial state. The internet was dead. Unsurprisingly, this caused panic and terror across the county, but it did not last for long.

Above the Earth, there were also a number of unintended consequences of the high altitude and high-yield detonation. The explosion generated a much larger number of high-energy electrons than originally anticipated. These became trapped in the upper atmosphere and rapidly formed a series of radiation belts around the Earth. These began to damage and destroy most communication and observation satellites in low earth orbit, making constellations such as GPS, Galileo, GLONASS and Starlink completely inoperable. Critically, it also damaged a number of the other Eastern Bloc FOBS satellites. About half of the weapons over the North American continent were unaffected as they began to deorbit in concert with the first weapon and so were not as badly impacted.

However, those positioned to strike Europe were now inoperable and did not respond to the attack command, continuing to float relatively harmlessly in orbit. This still meant that a significant portion of the nuclear firepower was available and it came to bear almost at once. Out of the fifty-nine warheads, twenty-eight began the descent, all careering towards the surface at twenty times the speed of sound and detonated with 25 megatons of explosive firepower. This largely destroyed the main American ICBM fields and most – but not all – of strategic air command's bomber bases. This left twenty or so bombers, already on airborne alert, to prosecute their respective targets in China and Russia. The remaining operational warheads descended onto the US government's nuclear citadels – Cheyenne mountain, Mount Weather and Raven Rock – penetrating deep into the bedrock and destroying the facilities, burying several thousands of personnel to slowly succumb to a death by suffocation.

None of the weapons targeted on the naval bases or the remaining operational radars were operable. This meant that, despite the destruction of key command and control facilities, NATO could still bring most of its submarine-launched ballistic missile forces to bear in a counter attack. The initial wave of the attack had still been devastating due to the size of the warhead used, with over a thousand megatons landing on the United States. Casualties on conurbations near the enormous hypo-centres were still over 50 million people.

Then the second wave of the Eastern Bloc offensive began. Off the west coast of North America, Eastern Bloc surface action groups and missile submarines launched a simultaneous volley of over 300 Zircon hypersonic cruise missiles. These led to retaliation by the US Pacific fleet who detected some of the launches.

And so, the exchange began, the biggest naval battle since the Jutland. As the engagement occurred chaotically, the majority of the missiles evaded attempted interception by US AEGIS-equipped destroyers. The missiles continued to accelerate, past Mach 10, ionizing the air. This bow wave of plasma made them invisible to the naval radar and the still active land-based early warning radars. On the tips of the missiles, cobalt-salted neutron bombs detonated on their targets, which ranged from Anchorage in Alaska to the Panama Canal.

Each exploded with a relatively small yield of 50 kilotons but the warheads generated significant gamma ray bursts, much larger than that of standard nuclear weapons. This immediately gave a lethal dose of radiation to every living thing within a five-mile radius and an acute dose to those in deep cover or up to fifteen miles away. 5 million died instantly, 25 million within two days and between 60 to 80 million within a few months, whether that be through radiation poisoning or secondary infectious diseases.

The nature of the attack meant that odd artifacts of this sliver of civilization remained intact. The Hollywood sign was left untouched, the glass and steel digital play pads of Silicon Valley left preserved and the vast private yachts of the super-rich off the coast of southern California and the Baja peninsula, simply continued to drift along, with freshly-cooked gourmet cuisine lying untouched in the opulent – but now lifeless – dining rooms. All these facades, edifices, assets and possessions were now without purpose, left ownerless and littered with corpses.

Similar attacks in the South Atlantic and South Pacific wreaked similar destruction on Australia, Brazil, Argentina and South Africa.

A different fate awaited the inhabitants of the eastern coasts of North America and the Caribbean. As the neutron attacks took place, 15 Kraken strategic nuclear torpedoes were moving at great speed in the deep waters of the Atlantic and the Gulf of Mexico. These arrived at a set of predetermined co-ordinates on the continental shelves and detonated with a force of 50 megatons on the seabed, displacing billions of tonnes of seawater and contaminating it with caesium, uranium and plutonium.

In some of the more rural areas of the eastern coast, there was little awareness that an attack was even underway. Near a small fishing hamlet in Maine, two boys were out in the early Saturday afternoon sun, catching crabs as their parents relaxed further along the beach. All seemed like a normal day until the sea began to disappear, retreating at a rapid rate, whirlpooling and foaming, the air filling with the smell of sulphureous mud and wet fish. Thousands of sea creatures were left stranded on the exposed sand, beached and gasping for oxygen.

The boys, caught between fear and wonder, ran out to investigate the various beasts, which were now lying exposed in the sun. They then heard the desperate calls of their parents who could see something lurking on the horizon. Looking up, they could see what appeared to be a small wave far away, but one that was growing and growing. It rose into a vast dark, murky, sediment-brown wall of water, ever climbing. As it started to crest, it turned into a foamy maelstrom across the entire oceanic horizon. All they could hear was the cacophonic roar of the water, louder than a thousand jet engines. The wave was so high, with over half a kilometre to its peak, that as it closed on them, it blocked out the low winter sun.

In near complete darkness, under the shadow of the wave, the boys turned, both screaming, and ran back as fast as they could to their parents. But they soon became subsumed, crushed and mangled by the immediate impact of several thousand tonnes of water pressure.

This family was amongst the first victims of a series of nuclear tidal waves that killed hundreds of millions. Boston, New York, Philadelphia, Washington, Miami, New Orleans, Houston and countless more cities in between are eliminated with the number of survivors negligible. The Mexican and South American coastlines of Columbia and Venezuela were also inundated. In the Caribbean, Cuba, Jamaica and all the smaller islands were completely inundated and all life was effectively exterminated. Almost all complex marine life abundant in the shallow climbs was entirely eliminated and the food chains trickling down to the strange creatures of the abyssal deep became full of radioactive carrion, disrupting and then destroying the ancient lifeforms.

The scale of the explosions changed the deep oceanic haloclines, which would alter the deep ocean currents for centuries to come, with the vast amount of radiation heating various water bodies. This began to have a dramatic effect on weather systems across the western hemisphere. The final death toll from drowning was over 150 million with the same number dying later due to radiation poisoning.

The wave reached up to 100 miles in land, irradiating everything in its path, the cobalt core, combined with the mud-burst style of explosion, generating vast amounts of long-life radioactive alpha particles. These areas would remain uninhabitable for most of a millennia. In the first two waves of the eastern pragmicide, over three quarter of a billion perished and that was with still one final salvo to come.

However, this final part did not go as planned as the West began its counter attack.

High above the earth, hidden amongst the litany of space junk that now shrouded the planet as a disparate metallic shield, the pieces of the Western Bloc began to move. Over the course of the last twenty-four hours, large telegraph-sized tungsten rods had been moved into a high geostationary orbit, using hydrazine thrusters, above key strategic Eastern Bloc targets and were now being released. There were 500 of these 'rods from god', which had been surreptitiously installed over the course of a decade as part of the space link internet of things communication array. As these free fell from several thousand kilometres, they reached twenty times the speed of sound. Like the Zircon missiles of the Eastern Bloc, these generated a plasma sheath on re-entry and so were invisible to early warning radars. The main targets of this orbital bombardment were the Eastern Bloc ICBM fields – located in Siberia and the Gobi Desert – ballistic missile submarine bases and key C3I facilities. The first to impact were 400 projectiles targeted on a one-for-one basis with each ICBM silo, about ten minutes after the descent order. As the tungsten rods hit the ground, the impacts were as powerful as a tactical nuclear weapon, penetrating deep in the buried missile silos, incising through the body of the missile and igniting its propellant, detonating it within its subterranean lair.

On the ground, the majority of the Eastern Bloc's ICBMs were destroyed in this way and a few were also destroyed during the initial stages of launch. However, approximately a third of the missiles which were at five-minute readiness were long gone and well into the climb phase. These 130 or so missiles reached their apogee above the earth and then unleashed their nuclear payloads of over 1000 warheads and several hundred decoys, which were designed to confuse US ground-based interceptors.

The US defense satellite network known as Bright Eyes identified the warheads and then ordered a series of small drone satellites hidden in a lower orbit, known as ROKS – Retrograde

Orbit Kinetic weapon Systems – to attack the incoming warheads in the first seconds of terminal phase. Powered by hydrazine boosters, the metallic spheres sped towards the warheads before they could achieve a significant downward velocity. Shortly before impact, the spheres opened and deployed several thousand ball bearings which kinematically shred the incoming Eastern Bloc warheads. ROKS is able to successfully engage about half the incoming warheads. Elsewhere, the other hundred RODS – Retrograde Orbit Diametric weapons System – destroyed most of the Eastern Bloc's naval facilities – including the African invasion force – all command bunkers – with the exception of Yamantau – the Gorgon ABM defenses around Moscow and key nuclear facilities, including weapons factories, ballistic missile submarine bases and tactical weapons stockpiles. A half dozen or so were also used to attack Eastern Bloc spearhead formations in eastern Europe, 'punching a hole' for the NATO formations and delaying the need to use tactical nuclear weapons. Whilst this aerial bombardment occurred, a small asteroid, powered by a nuclear rocket engine, re-entered the atmosphere and, unnoticed, impacted in in the southern Pacific, beginning to drill its way through the oceanic plate at the anti-pode to Mount Yamantau.

Despite the successes of this initial non-nuclear counter attack by the Western Bloc, a significant vanguard of Eastern Bloc strategic weapons was now coming to bear. Approximately 400 warheads from the ICBMs had survived the ROKS' onslaught, due to decoys and on-board jamming countermeasures. In addition to this, six Eastern Bloc ballistic missile submarines were at sea and not subject to the RODS' bombardment. These launched ninety-six ballistic missiles with over

900 warheads. Most were launched on a flattened trajectory to reduce warning time and so did not need to run the orbital gauntlet. Some American ABM systems had limited success, destroying a few dozen warheads in the terminal descent phase. Nevertheless, it soon became clear to the western planners buried in their underground castles in West Virginia that around 1300 warheads would soon detonate across North America and western Europe, with 350 megatons, detonating on the US and Canada, and half of the population centres as yet not directly attacked by Kraken, Zircon or FOBS, such as Chicago, Detroit, Denver, Kansas, Oklahoma, Ottawa, Winnipeg, Toronto and many of the cities in the centre of the continent. About 280 megatons was projected to fall on western Europe, with the majority falling on Great Britain – 92 megatons; Germany – 81 megatons; and France – 79 megatons.

However, the scale of the attack necessitated a full counter value attack in reciprocation to Western Bloc stealth bombers and ballistic missile submarines, which launched over 900 warheads – in the low hundred kiloton range – at Eastern Bloc targets. Combined with the salvo launched from the HMS Dreadnought, just over a thousand warheads and approximately 500 megatons were inbound on the Eastern Bloc. In this counter-value phase, both sides were now attacking population centres, for either military, economic or cultural purposes. Most major cities were attacked with multiple weapons in cluster bombing or ripple firing to ensure the targets were successfully destroyed. For example, in the West, London was attacked with a dozen warheads, each on a different target type in and around the city; the case was the same in Paris and Berlin. Smaller cities, such as Atlanta, Albuquerque, Chelabinsk, Shenzhen and Manchester, were struck by a trio of equidistant nuclear airbursts. In the East, the destruction was even more complete: Beijing, Shanghai and Moscow were attacked with over twenty weapons, each due to the number of strategic targets in sufficient proximity.

The end result of the exchange was the equivalent to several thousand megatons. In the Western Bloc, the death toll within the first twelve hours was 1 gigadeath – or 1 billion. In the East, due to China's population density, this was even higher at 1.5 gigadeaths. In non-aligned countries, there were approximately 2 billion gigadeaths. In just half a day, forty percent of the world's population had been exterminated. And this was before the aftereffects of the radiation, destruction of the eco-system and the impact of the Artemis attack were taken into account. In Europe, the Kraken torpedo which had been launched from the Samara had also yet to explode.

The human race – and most of the Holocene biosphere – was now on the verge of extinction.

Chapter 42

Sussex, England

18th March 2044

Nuclear Targets in the United Kingdom – 92-megaton attack scenario –

#	Category	Target	Weapon System	Type	Yield
1	C&C	RAF Fylingdales	Sarmat	Groundburst	0.55
2	C&C	RAF Fylingdales	Sarmat	Airburst	0.55
3	C&C	Menwith Hill	Sarmat	Groundburst	0.55
4	C&C	Menwith Hill	Sarmat	Airburst	0.55
5	C&C	GCHQ	Sarmat	Groundburst	0.55
6	C&C	GCHQ	Sarmat	Airburst	0.55
7	C&C	RRH Saxa Vord	Sarmat	Airburst	0.55
8	C&C	RRH Benbecula	Sarmat	Airburst	0.55
9	C&C	RRH Brizlewood	Sarmat	Airburst	0.55
10	C&C	RRH Porthreath	Sarmat	Airburst	0.55
11	C&C	RRH Neatishead	Sarmat	Airburst	0.55
12	C&C	RAF Boulmer	Sarmat	Groundburst	0.55
13	C&C	Northwood	Sarmat	Groundburst	0.55
14	C&C	Northwood	Sarmat	Groundburst	0.55
15	C&C	RAF High Wycombe	Sarmat	Groundburst	0.55
16	C&C	RAF High Wycombe	Sarmat	Groundburst	0.55
17	C&C	MI6 HQ	Topol	Groundburst	0.8
18	C&C	Ministry of Defence	Topol	Groundburst	0.8
19	C&C	Ministry of Defence	Topol	Groundburst	0.8
20	C&C	PINDAR	Topol	Groundburst	0.8
21	C&C	PINDAR	Topol	Groundburst	0.8
22	C&C	ULF 1	Yars	Airburst	0.3
23	C&C	ULF 2	Yars	Airburst	0.3
24	C&C	ULF 3	Yars	Airburst	0.3
25	C&C	ULF 4	Yars	Airburst	0.3
26	C&C	ULF 5	Yars	Airburst	0.3
27	Nuclear	RNB Clyde	Sarmat	Airburst	0.55
28	Nuclear	RNB Clyde	Sarmat	Airburst	0.55
29	Nuclear	RNB Clyde	Sarmat	Groundburst	0.55
30	Nuclear	RNAD Coulport	Sarmat	Groundburst	0.55
31	Nuclear	RNAD Coulport	Sarmat	Groundburst	0.55
32	Nuclear	AWE Aldermaston	Sarmat	Groundburst	0.55
33	Nuclear	AWE Aldermaston	Sarmat	Airburst	0.55
34	Nuclear	AWE Aldermaston	Sarmat	Airburst	0.55
35	Nuclear	RNB Devonport	Sarmat	Groundburst	0.55
36	Nuclear	RNB Devonport	Sarmat	Airburst	0.55
37	Nuclear	RNB Devonport	Sarmat	Airburst	0.55
38	Nuclear	AWE Burgfield	Sarmat	Airburst	0.55
39	Nuclear	AWE Blacknest	Sarmat	Airburst	0.55
40	Nuclear	Sellafield	Sarmat	Groundburst	0.55
41	Naval	RNB Portsmouth	Sarmat	Airburst	0.55
42	Naval	RNB Portsmouth	Sarmat	Airburst	0.55
43	Naval	RNB Portsmouth	Sarmat	Groundburst	0.55
44	Naval	RNAS Yeovilton	Bulava	Groundburst	0.15
45	Naval	RNAS Culdrose	Bulava	Groundburst	0.15
46	Airforce	RAF Odiham	Bulava	Groundburst	0.15
47	Airforce	RAF Benson	Bulava	Groundburst	0.15
48	Airforce	RAF Northolt	Bulava	Groundburst	0.15
49	Airforce	RAF Brize Norton	Bulava	Groundburst	0.15
50	Airforce	RAF Marnham	Bulava	Groundburst	0.15
51	Airforce	RAF Waddington	Bulava	Groundburst	0.15
52	Airforce	RAF Coningsby	Bulava	Groundburst	0.15

#	Category	Target	Weapon System	Type	Yield
55	Airforce	RAF Wittering	Bulava	Airburst	0.15
56	Airforce	RAF Wyton	Bulava	Airburst	0.15
57	Airforce	RAF Honnington	Bulava	Airburst	0.15
58	Airforce	RAF Scampton	Bulava	Groundburst	0.15
59	Airforce	RAF Valley	Bulava	Groundburst	0.15
60	Airforce	RAF Woodvale	Bulava	Airburst	0.15
61	Airforce	RAF Leeming	Bulava	Airburst	0.15
62	Airforce	RAF St Mawgan	Bulava	Groundburst	0.15
63	Army	Aldershot	Sarmat	Airburst	0.55
64	Army	Aldershot	Sarmat	Airburst	0.55
65	Army	Tidworth	Sarmat	Airburst	0.55
66	Army	Tidworth	Sarmat	Airburst	0.55
67	Army	Catterick	Sarmat	Airburst	0.55
68	Army	Catterick	Sarmat	Airburst	0.55
69	Army	Colchester	Sarmat	Airburst	0.55
70	Army	Colchester	Sarmat	Airburst	0.55
71	Army	Bulford	Sarmat	Airburst	0.55
72	Army	Maidstone	Sarmat	Airburst	0.55
73	Army	AAC Middel Wallop	Sarmat	Groundburst	0.55
74	Army	AAC Watisham	Sarmat	Groundburst	0.55
75	US Forces	RAF Alconbury	Bulava	Groundburst	0.15
76	US Forces	RAF Alconbury	Bulava	Airburst	0.15
77	US Forces	RAF Croughton	Bulava	Groundburst	0.15
78	US Forces	RAF Croughton	Bulava	Airburst	0.15
79	US Forces	RAF Fairford	Bulava	Groundburst	0.15
80	US Forces	RAF Fairford	Bulava	Airburst	0.15
81	US Forces	RAF Lakenheath	Bulava	Groundburst	0.15
82	US Forces	RAF Lakenheath	Bulava	Airburst	0.15
83	US Forces	RAF Mildenhall	Bulava	Groundburst	0.15
84	US Forces	RAF Mildenhall	Bulava	Airburst	0.15
85	Dispersal Afs	Leeming	Bulava	Groundburst	0.15
86	Dispersal Afs	Manston	Bulava	Groundburst	0.15
87	Dispersal Afs	Brawdy	Bulava	Groundburst	0.15
88	Dispersal Afs	Prestwick	Bulava	Groundburst	0.15
89	Dispersal Afs	Kinloss	Bulava	Groundburst	0.15
90	Dispersal Afs	Leuchars	Bulava	Groundburst	0.15
91	Dispersal Afs	Coltishall	Bulava	Groundburst	0.15
92	Dispersal Afs	Lyneham	Bulava	Groundburst	0.15
93	Dispersal Afs	Boscombe Down	Bulava	Groundburst	0.15
94	Power - Coal	Drax	Yars	Airburst	0.3
95	Power - Coal	West Burton	Yars	Airburst	0.3
96	Power - Coal	Kilroot	Yars	Airburst	0.3
97	Power - Coal	Ratcliffe	Yars	Airburst	0.3
98	Power - gas	Pembroke	Yars	Airburst	0.3
99	Power - gas	Staythorpe	Yars	Airburst	0.3
100	Power - gas	Grain	Yars	Airburst	0.3
101	Power - gas	Didcot	Yars	Airburst	0.3
102	Power - gas	Connahs Quay	Yars	Airburst	0.3
103	Power - gas	South Humber	Yars	Airburst	0.3
104	Power - gas	Peterhead	Sarmat	Airburst	0.55

#	Category	Target	Weapon System	Type	Yield
105	Power - Nuclear	Dungeness	Sarmat	Groundburst	0.55
106	Power - Nuclear	Hinkley Point	Sarmat	Groundburst	0.55
107	Power - Nuclear	Hunterston	Sarmat	Groundburst	0.55
108	Power - Nuclear	Hartlepool	Sarmat	Groundburst	0.55
109	Power - Nuclear	Heysham	Sarmat	Groundburst	0.55
110	Power - Nuclear	Torness	Sarmat	Groundburst	0.55
111	Power - Nuclear	Sizewell	Sarmat	Groundburst	0.55
112	Power - Nuclear	Douneray	Sarmat	Groundburst	0.55
113	Fuel	Humber	Sarmat	Airburst	0.55
114	Fuel	Grangemouth	Sarmat	Airburst	0.55
115	Fuel	Stanlow	Sarmat	Airburst	0.55
116	Fuel	Pembroke	Sarmat	Airburst	0.55
117	Fuel	Fawley	Sarmat	Airburst	0.55
118	Fuel	Harwich	Sarmat	Airburst	0.55
119	Economic - Market	City of London	Topol-M	Airburst	1.0
120	Economic - Market	Isle of Dogs	Topol-M	Airburst	1.0
121	Economic-Port	Tyne	Yars	Mudburst	0.5
122	Economic-Port	Redcar	Yars	Mudburst	0.5
123	Economic-Port	Hull	Yars	Mudburst	0.5
124	Economic-Port	Kings Lyn	Yars	Mudburst	0.5
125	Economic-Port	Lowestoft	Yars	Mudburst	0.5
126	Economic-Port	Felixstowe	Yars	Mudburst	0.5
127	Economic-Port	Tilbury	Yars	Mudburst	0.5
128	Economic-Port	Medway	Yars	Mudburst	0.5
129	Economic-Port	Dover	Yars	Mudburst	0.5
130	Economic-Port	Folkestone / Eurotunnel	Yars	Mudburst	0.5
131	Economic-Port	Newhaven	Yars	Mudburst	0.5
132	Economic-Port	Southampton	Yars	Mudburst	0.5
133	Economic-Port	Cowes	Yars	Mudburst	0.5
134	Economic-Port	Poole	Yars	Mudburst	0.5
135	Economic-Port	Weymouth	Yars	Mudburst	0.5
136	Economic-Port	Lymington (RM)	Yars	Mudburst	0.5
137	Economic-Port	Dartmouth	Yars	Mudburst	0.5
138	Economic-Port	Falmouth	Yars	Mudburst	0.5
139	Economic-Port	Appledore	Yars	Mudburst	0.5
140	Economic-Port	Avonmouth	Yars	Mudburst	0.5
141	Economic-Port	Newport	Yars	Mudburst	0.5
142	Economic-Port	Liverpool	Yars	Mudburst	0.5
143	Economic-Port	Barrow	Yars	Mudburst	0.5
144	Economic-Port	Clyde	Yars	Mudburst	0.5
145	Economic-Airport	Heathrow	Sarmat	Groundburst	0.55
146	Economic-Airport	Heathrow	Sarmat	Airburst	0.55
147	Economic-Airport	Gatwick	Sarmat	Groundburst	0.55
148	Economic-Airport	Gatwick	Sarmat	Airburst	0.55
149	Economic-Airport	Birmingham	Sarmat	Airburst	0.55
150	Economic-Airport	Manchester	Sarmat	Airburst	0.55
151	Economic-Airport	Luton	Sarmat	Airburst	0.55
152	Economic-Airport	Stanstead	Sarmat	Airburst	0.55
153	Economic-Airport	East Midlands	Sarmat	Airburst	0.55

#	Category	Target	Weapon System	Type	Yield
154	Population Centre	Central London	Topol	Airburst	0.8
155	Population Centre	Central London	Topol	Airburst	0.8
156	Population Centre	Central London	Topol	Airburst	0.8
157	Population Centre	Manchester	Topol	Airburst	0.8
158	Population Centre	Manchester	Topol	Airburst	0.8
159	Population Centre	Birmingham	Topol	Airburst	0.8
160	Population Centre	Birmingham	Topol	Airburst	0.8
161	Population Centre	Leeds	Topol-M	Airburst	1.0
162	Population Centre	Glasgow	Topol-M	Airburst	1.0
163	Population Centre	Liverpool	Topol-M	Airburst	1.0
164	Population Centre	Southampton	Topol-M	Airburst	1.0
165	Population Centre	Newcastle	Topol-M	Airburst	1.0
166	Population Centre	Nottingham	Topol-M	Airburst	1.0
167	Population Centre	Sheffield	Topol-M	Airburst	1.0
168	Population Centre	Bristol	Topol-M	Airburst	1.0
169	Population Centre	Leicester	Topol-M	Airburst	1.0
170	Population Centre	Brighton	Topol-M	Airburst	1.0
171	Population Centre	Bournemouth	Yars	Airburst	0.5
172	Population Centre	Cardiff	Yars	Airburst	0.5
173	Population Centre	Middlesborough	Yars	Airburst	0.5
174	Population Centre	Coventry	Yars	Airburst	0.5
175	Population Centre	Edinburgh	Yars	Airburst	0.5
176	Population Centre	Birkenhead	Yars	Airburst	0.5
177	Population Centre	Reading	Yars	Airburst	0.5
178	Population Centre	Swansea	Yars	Airburst	0.5
179	Population Centre	Derby	Yars	Airburst	0.5
180	Population Centre	Plymouth	Yars	Airburst	0.5
181	Population Centre	Norwich	Yars	Airburst	0.5
182	Population Centre	Aberdeen	Yars	Airburst	0.5
183	Infrastructure -Dams	Kielder	Yars	Groundburst	0.3
184	Infrastructure -Dams	Rutland	Yars	Groundburst	0.3
185	Infrastructure -Dams	Hawswater	Yars	Groundburst	0.3
186	Infrastructure -Dams	Brenig	Yars	Groundburst	0.3
187	Infrastructure -Dams	Celyn	Yars	Groundburst	0.3
188	Infrastructure -Dams	Grafham	Yars	Groundburst	0.3
189	Infrastructure -Dams	Thirlmere	Yars	Groundburst	0.3
190	Infrastructure -Dams	Derwent	Yars	Groundburst	0.3
191	Infrastructure -Dams	Queen Mother	Yars	Groundburst	0.3
192	Infrastructure -Dams	Queen Mary	Yars	Groundburst	0.3
193	Infrastructure -Dams	Ladybower	Yars	Groundburst	0.3
194	Infrastructure -Dams	Bewl	Yars	Groundburst	0.3
195	Infrastructure -Dams	Abberton	Yars	Groundburst	0.3

Due to the global alpha city of London being attacked, there was still a significant amount of discrete affluence further to the south, mainly concentrated in the counties of Surrey, Kent and Sussex. Whilst many of the local populace understood that the bombs would fall on London, they also believed that their piece of the world would go untouched or, at the very least, not be the subject of a direct hit. This was a naïve and dangerous assumption. Taking the coastal and, mainly rural, county of Sussex as an example, there appeared to be little of strategic importance within its boundaries that would warrant the use of a costly nuclear device. However, this underestimated the number of warheads available to Eastern Bloc war planners, the strategic importance of the island of Great Britain or NATO's unsinkable aircraft carrier – as it was viewed by the East. Out of the 175 warheads that made it through NATO's missile defences to land on the United Kingdom, six had been allocated to targets in Sussex. The least obvious of these was a radio mast on a hill near the small country town of Heathfield. Most locals assumed it was a 5G/6G cellular mast, one of the many that had sprung up over the last two decades. It was, in fact, part of NATO's UHF communication array and part of a vital network of transmitters that linked NATO naval command with its ballistic missile submarines. This made it a legitimate sub-strategic target and, therefore, it was struck by a 475-kiloton nuclear airburst from a submarine launched ballistic missile, which went on to destroy the nearby towns and villages. The destruction reached out to a radius of over ten miles, the over-pressure ripping off roofs and shattering windows in the towns of Lewes, Crowborough, Uckfield and Hailsham, injuring tens of thousands, most suffering multiple deep lacerations due to flying glass.

A smaller 150-kiloton weapon landed as a mud burst in Bewl Reservoir in the east of the county. The warhead exploded deep beneath the wave wall of the dam, releasing over 30 billion litres of radioactive water in a twenty-metre-high wall of water, an inland ceiche, flooding a number of key infrastructure links, major roads and railways downstream. It also removed a significant proportion of the drinking water supply, hence, why it had been classed as a medium-importance infrastructure target. The flood also inundated several towns and villages downstream, including the centre of the small city of Maidstone.

Two larger weapons struck the very north of the county near Gatwick, the second largest airport in the United Kingdom. Two 750-kiloton nuclear warheads launched from the same Sarmat heavy ICBM from the Zemlya ICBM field land. The first was a groundburst, to ensure the destruction of the runway; the second, an airburst to ensure all support facilities were effectively destroyed. The nearby town of Crawley, which had a population of 100,000, was completely destroyed.

On the Sussex coast, another target was the functioning deep-water harbour in the port of Newhaven. Whilst only notable for a ferry service and a small fishing fleet, the harbour was sufficiently deep to allow NATO warships – those that were up to the size of frigates – to operate.

The next target was at the end of the peninsula to the east of Hastings: the recently commissioned Dungeness C nuclear power station. This had been targeted as it provided nearly 2 gigawatts of electricity to the National Grid and was the site of two decommissioned reactors. These relics of the 20th Century provided a convenient stockpile of highly radioactive material, which could have been utilized to help sterilize this corner of the United Kingdom and make NATO operations in the area significantly challenging. This site was targeted with a 750-kiloton warhead, which detonated as a groundburst, destroying the reactors and sucking up vast amounts of fissile material, which was then scattered by the high altitude and prevailing winds, north-west across the home counties. The effects of the fall-out from this strike would lead to the deaths of millions from radiation poisoning.

Further to the west and down the coast, a single 500-kiloton nuclear warhead, fell and piled itself through the murky waters of the River Ouse, exploding just about all of the riverbed. The fireball destroyed the port and the surrounding town of Newhaven, as well as the larger town of Seaford further down the coast. The mushroom cloud sucked up vast amounts of alluvial mud, turning it radioactive, and deposited it over a wide area around the mouth of the river, which would make it unusable for years to come and uninhabitable for decades more.

As the warhead exploded at Newhaven, a 1-megaton warhead from an elderly Topol-M missile launched from a road mobile launcher in the eastern Donbass began to descend on the largest city in the county, the city of Brighton and Hove. Brighton had been chosen due to it having a population of greater than 300,000 and because of its place at the centre of the UK's digital economy: it was the coastal reception station for the Rampion wind farm array.

Chapter 43

Whitehawk Estate, Brighton & Hove, England

18th March 2044

Laura and Buster had been up before dawn, moving a variety of supplies and 'shielding' down into Buster's garage. Laura was exhausted. They had moved at least a dozen loads from their flats on the twelfth floor and the lift still was not working. The sun was now beginning to rise on what was a cold but relatively clear morning, the red, crimson sun, low in the eastern sky, just about visible through a chink in low, fluffy cumulus clouds that were now coloured a pleasant, radiant, purple in this dawn's early light. There had been a frost overnight and the potholed tarmac of the roadway surrounding the communal garages was slick and slippery with the early morning dew. Nearly slipping as she arrived at the open garage door, carrying a large box of non-perishables gleaned from her larder, she peered in to see Buster pushing plastic bags full of soil, books and anything else that was substantial and locally available against the wall and then tying them with rope, cantilevering them to the ceiling struts. As she crossed the threshold of their makeshift bunker, he had just finished putting the last bag in place. He climbed down from a small step ladder.

'Well, that's as good as I can get it. We ran out of books and other things so it's mostly mud and some compost I found at the garden centre. He's been open all night.' He turned around to admire his handywork.

Laura was not overly-thrilled with the smell. As well as the musk of many years of damp, the bags had added that dirty, wet-earth smell, which was quite pungent. Beneath and in between the bags at the side of the garage, there were boxes of food, medicine and other consumables, stacked three boxes high. There was only room in the middle for a single camp bed topped with a memory foam mattress – replete with an old-fashioned itchy, brown blanket – and a camping chair, which Buster had already furnished with a can of beer in its arm-rest mounted drink holster. The can was already open and seemingly in the process of being consumed. More worryingly, she could see an old off-white plastic garden chair right at the back of the garage. The chair had the middle of its flimsy plastic seat cut out to form a square opening and, beneath it, was a waste paper bin holding a large black plastic bag.

'Please tell me that's not the loo?' she said, pointing to the chair.

Buster looked at where she was pointing and nodded.

'Well, what were you expecting? It's a council garage, not the Dorchester, love. Besides, that's the best I could do in the time available. It's not as though we could get a real one plumbed in or even a chemical one at such notice,' he replied.

'I know, Arch. But not even a divide or a curtain or something? Some form of privacy? Dignity?' she said, bereft and looking down at the icy tarmac underfoot.

'Well, let me see. I'll see if I can rig something up, alright?' he said, nodding and giving her his wide-eyed reassurance. She winced.

'Thanks, Arch. If you could… What about the door?' she said, pointing to the flimsy metal shutter. 'Surely that needs some reinforcement.'

Buster's face erupted into a gleeful smile.

'Thought of that. I've got these,' he said, opening two large suitcases which had been propped up against the neighbouring garage and pulling out what appeared to be a dozen – no doubt, illicitly-procured – Kevlar police jackets.

'Once we've shut the door, I've put mountings on the inside and then we put these two deep across the entrance. That should be enough, shouldn't it?' he said, still beaming, his earnest face looking for praise.

She nodded politely, knowing full well that it might not give them the protection they required. She was in an odd malaise. There was a part of her that wanted to go into central Brighton and get completely hammered on weed and shots, one final shout of hedonism, giving the middle finger to fate. This had always been her plan should there be the event of the apocalypse: be pissed out of our skull, off her face, out of her skin, directly underneath or in front of the oncoming calamity. However, this was predicated on a bomb actually landing on the city and she knew this was not guaranteed. The fear of being slowly microwaved by radiation and dying in agony was now her greatest fear. It was this fear that was gradually talking her into the premise that hiding in a concrete garage with a convicted criminal was the best course of action. It was strange that, now that she was finally facing the end, all the gallows humour and stoic bravado had fallen away. She was now dreading the warning and wanted to dive into a black hole to hide from the likely rapture.

'How we doing for supplies?' she said gingerly.

'Well, we've got enough soup, canned fruit and army surplus rations to last the best part of two weeks and enough drink for about the same.'

'What sort of drink have we got? Please don't tell me it's all alcoholic…'

Buster looked a little offended by the implication.

'Course not,' he rebuffed as he went over to where he had stored a selection of soft drink cans in six-by-six palettes of unknown provenance. 'We've got Fanta – both orange and lemon. We've got cola and diet cola. For some reason, we've also got Vimto. I thought they'd stopped making it. Anyways, we've also got them jerry cans of tap water,' he said, pointing to four large jerry cans that were full to the brim. 'Oh, and beer, of course,' he added, again pointing, this time to three large crates of lager, haphazardly piled on top of each other next to the medicine stockpiles.

'Well done. At least we'll be hydrated, caffeinated and well oiled…' she replied.

'Bloody right. I've also brought along the insurance policies,' said Buster rather ominously as he walked over to pick up a small briefcase, which he then placed onto one of the medicine crates. He rifled through a combination on the locking mechanism and opened the case, then beckoned her over to look inside.

'Christ,' she thought. 'More medication, a knife, a sword, a crossbow?' But what she saw at the bottom of the case was an order of magnitude worse. There, in a black neoprene-lined bag, was what appeared to be a small machine gun with a wooden stock and at least two curved clips of ammunition.

'What the fucking hell is that, Arch?' she shouted, taking a step back from the firearm.

'That, Loz, is a Czech-made scorpion submachine gun with sixty rounds available and, alongside my old Tokayev, is very handy for home defence. In fact, you can have my old one now if you want,' he replied, revealing a pistol that was tucked into his tracksuit bottoms.

'No fucking way. I am not holding a gun!' she shouted, almost spitting at him. She abhorred firearms, having spent most of her adult life trying to rid the area of weapons of any kind.

'Well, suit yourself, like. We may need these if, you know, it all goes a bit Pete Tong and vigilante-like. Best be prepared,' he replied, unapologetic and ultimately pragmatic.

Laura decided to calm herself down as she knew there was little point in arguing with him but she couldn't resist one more enquiry.

'I'm probably going to regret asking, but…'

'Go on,' he encouraged.

'Where do you find a thing like that?'

'Well,' he began as he sat down in the camping chair and took a slug of lager. 'You know I'm from Burgess Hill originally?'

'Yeah, I think you mentioned it on a couple of occasions.'

'Good. Well, ya know, when I was growing up, it was not like it is now, all poncy coffee houses and fucking craft brewery bars full of hipsters. Nah, it was a lot rougher, a lot more chewy round the edges. Anyway, when I was growing up on one of the council estates, a lot of families were moved into the estates from the big smoke. Turns out they were moving warring families away from each other. One of those was an Irish family with some rather interesting connections with the old country—'

'You mean the…' she interrupted.

'Yeah, the provos, republicans. And this lot had their own little cache for safekeeping, usually weapons that the filth were looking for…' he said, allowing her to finish his sentence in her mind.

'So, this has been used by the IRA?'

'Suppose so. Don't know really, nor do I care,' he replied. 'It doesn't matter right now, does it?'

She huffed in reticent agreement.

'Right, so what else do we need to move—' She was cut off by both her and Buster's mobile phones going off. Getting them out of their pockets, they looked down in horror. Flashing on the screen in bright-red letters were the words:

'ATTACK WARNING RED, NUCLEAR ATTACK IMMINENT. SEEK COVER IMMEDIATELY.'

Shocked, she glanced across, waiting for Arch who, taking a bit longer to read the message, finally looked back up at her. Their eyes met in a wide panic. Then they heard it, far away: a temporary siren sprang to life from the roof of East Street police station in the centre of the city. It took a while for the sound to carry but they could hear it, the distinct and unearthly rising, falling, rising again wail of the air raid siren echoing out across the city. From the flats above and the grounds around them came a series of petrified screams of people in panic as they ran desperately for cover. At the end of the tarmac road that led to the garages was the local playpark. Standing at the rusty red gate was a young mother in a sports jacket and jogging bottoms with two similarly clad children, a boy holding her right hand and a girl holding the other, both of whom could not have been more than six or seven years old, probably twins. The mother was rooted to the spot, her jaw chattering in terror as she stared aimlessly up at the sky. The girl was crying, trying to get her mum's attention. The boy was seeking assurances, desperately asking rapid-fire questions, which Laura couldn't quite make out.

She turned to Buster.

'We have to let them in, Arch!' she said, pointing to the family who were still frozen, the boy now manically shouting at his mother.

'Oh, fuck's sake… Right, go get 'em. I'll get the last of the jerry cans from the stairwell, otherwise we'll run out of water in days…' he said and then jogged off as fast as he could. He had obviously been reading the government advice online, which made it clear that you had to survive for at least two weeks on your own before any emergency food repositories would open – one of the many stark realities that they were now all facing.

She shouted after him as she also began to run towards the family.

'Arch, get back in no more than two mins. If there's something coming it could be here by then.'

'I'm going as fast as I fucking can, love,' he shouted back, already gasping for air as he hauled his considerable frame up the path and towards the open green fire door on the nearest side of the tower block.

As she approached the family, she realized she recognized the woman. The mother was called Isla, a short and petite twenty-something single mum who worked part-time at the local supermarket. The girl was called Ava and the boy was called Sammy. They were indeed twins, both gifted with their mother's blonde hair and blue eyes. As she ran towards them, she tried to get Isla's attention.

'Isla! Isla! You've got to go, love. Come with me. Come with me!' she shouted as she approached, panting heavily.

Isla was still staring ahead, muttering to herself and shaking. Laura grabbed her by both her shoulders and pulled her round so she was face-on, which made it harder for her to look away.

'Listen to me, love. We haven't got long. Follow me and we can go somewhere safer. Isla, look at me,' she said calmly as Isla, again, turned her head to avoid eye contact. 'Isla, please come with me. Do you understand?'

Isla then looked at her dead in the eye and burst into tears.

'I don't know what to do…' she said, her words barely audible through the sound of sobs from her crying children.

Laura put her hand on Isla's cheek.

'Trust me. Follow me. Do you understand?' she said, raising her voice. Isla slowly nodded. 'Good. Let's go. If you pick up Ava, I'll take Sammy, OK?'

'Yep…' she replied, sniffling and wiping away her tears.

As Laura went to pick up Sammy, who had stopped crying and was now shaking instead, she noticed a dark patch on the front of his jogging bottoms and around his now wet pair of red Adidas trainers, a small puddle.

He looked up at her, tears rolling down his face.

‘I’m sorry… It was an accident…’ he said, forlorn.

‘It’s OK, sweetie,’ she said, picking him up and supporting him in the crook of her left arm, holding his legs with the other. ‘I wouldn’t worry. You’re probably not the only one. Now, let’s go somewhere warm and cosy.’

‘Right. Mummy and Ava, follow me please,’ she said, half walking, half running as fast as she could back up the drive towards the open garage. Glancing across at the tower block, she could see Buster hauling two ten-litre jerry cans down the path from the tower block, still gasping for air. She got to the open garage, went inside and placed Sammy on the far side of the camping bed. She looked back at Isla, who stood on the threshold, still holding Ava. She seemed to be hesitating.

‘Come on. Quick, sit down and sit tight, please. We’ll need to close the door…’ she said, her voice now trembling with a fear-infused urgency. Panicked, Isla walked forward tentatively and sat down on the camping bed, extending her other arm around Sammy, whilst still carrying Ava, holding both of them as tightly as she could. Laura turned to see Buster a few metres away from the garage, sweating profusely as he desperately hauled the water cans towards the entrance.

He paused briefly.

‘Fuck me, I’m too old for this… Right, Loz, get ready to close the door as soon as I’m inside. Ready?’ he said, breaking every few words for a big gulp of air.

‘Ready,’ she replied and began to walk towards him.

There was then a tremendous blaze of light, which whited out the view of the outside.

At that exact moment, the 1-megaton warhead, which had been launched from the eastern Ukraine less than twenty minutes previously, descended at hypersonic velocity through the skies of Southern England and detonated 2,500 metres above the city, over the site of St Peter's Church in the centre of Brighton. The burst height had been specially determined to maximize the effective 5 psi over pressure range. This would cause even well-built, reinforced concrete buildings to collapse. The lead and other metals in the spire of St Peter's Church melted and then vaporized in a split second due to the 1 million degree heat of the fireball, which was growing outwards into a one-kilometre-wide inferno, vaporizing everything in its path: buildings, trees, people, even the air as oxygen molecules were brutally split in two. The fireball emitted a vast amount of heat and light energy. Those directly in line of sight from the explosion up to twelve kilometres away would receive third-degree burns; those up to seventeen kilometres away would get second-degree burns; and those twenty-five kilometres away, in the county town of Haywards Heath or any of the rural Sussex villages, such as Storrington and Lindfield, would still experience first-degree burns. Even those forty kilometres away, on the western border, such as the cathedral city of Chichester, would receive the equivalent of sunburn. Unfortunately, the Brighton suburb of Whitehawk, where Laura and Buster lived, fell into the first category.

The intense light subsided after a few seconds. Now being able to see, Laura looked out towards the tower block. The concrete smouldered, the paint of the window ledges smoked and all the flats on the near side of the building were on fire. The air was filled with screaming, painful cries and shrieking coming from every direction.

She looked around her: the grass that was not in the shadow of the building was interspersed with small fires and trees were ablaze in bright-reddish-orange. And then there was Buster. He was screaming as he lurched inwards into the relative shelter of the garage. His clothes were on fire, the plastic toggles on his tracksuit bottoms were melting and, as he desperately launched himself inside, the soles of his shoes stuck to the boiling tarmac outside, his charred converse shoes ripping at the seams as he fell in. He writhed on the floor in agony, barely able to even shout. He just lay there, spasming.

Laura dropped to her knees to attend to him, but her medical training already told her there was not much she could do. The exposed skin on his arms, hands and face was dark red with large blisters which were blackening. His skin was effectively dead already, all the way to the bone. His eyes were swollen closed, and there was a claggy, white, viscous liquid pouring from his tear ducts. She knew this was probably what was left of his eyes. He was now entirely blind. His mouth was also open, his tongue black like charcoal, which made it impossible to speak.

Isla and the two children were now in hysterics, the air full of their crying and Buster's desperate mumblings. She was about to utter words of comfort to him but, instead, she decided to get up to try to close the garage door, knowing that more was to come.

At that moment, ten seconds after the thermal pulse, the blast wave arrived. The blast wave was so great it ionized the air in front of it, creating a compressed column of air travelling out at great speed, at over 600 miles per hour. The force it generated was five pounds per square-inch on anything that was seven kilometres from the bomb's hypocentre, as far east as the dormitory village of Rottingdean, as far west as the suburb of Southwick and as far north as the downland settlement of Pyecombe. In this Z zone – or, more informally called the Zombie Zone by national defence planners – most commercial buildings were severely damaged and most residential buildings collapsed. The seismic impact of the bomb also destroyed the city's utility infrastructure. Many additional fires started as the result of ruptured gas mains blending with fires started by the heat flash. Most strategic water mains were broken and so there would be no way to effectively fight the fires, even if fire engines were available. The fires began to merge together, unchecked, and form large conflagrations, the beginning of a vast fire storm, which would go on to consume large parts of the city. This zone of devastation went further out, whilst the blast wave began to dissipate and drop below 1 PSI, though not before it had broken every window from ground zero to Haywards Heath in the north, Worthing in the west and Seaford in the east. The additional shrapnel provided by the prevalence of double glazing created a nightmarish flurry of flying glass, which killed and injured tens of thousands across southern and central Sussex.

There was a sudden burst of an unearthly and deafening noise, louder than anything Laura had ever heard, which got louder and louder until it hit, the force of which flung Laura on top of the stricken Buster, who was still writhing in agony on the floor. Her elbow smashed onto the concrete floor, breaking it in several places. The far wall of the garage had caved in and the heavy concrete roof had collapsed, showering chunks of cement across the interior.

She let out a scream in agony but she soon stifled it because she saw the sight outside, through the mangled garage door. The blast had shattered both tower blocks and a vast amount of concrete, twisted metal and masonry was now falling to the ground. A vast dust cloud was now being drawn away by the blast wave. Where there had been life a few moments before, there was none. Several thousand had either burnt to death, had been ripped asunder by the blast or were now buried beneath several hundred tons of rubble with no hope of rescue.

She couldn't hear; the blast had ruptured both her ear drums. Her lungs were also punctured by the change in air pressure, which only amplified the agony in her arm, and there was blood pouring from every orifice. She looked out across her new vista in horrific awe. In much pain, she turned around to see what lay behind her. The roof collapse had come in at a right angle and had fallen onto the end of the camp bed. She couldn't hear the screaming, but Isla was clambering prostrate over the rubble, desperately holding on to Ava, who was sobbing and clinging on to her mother around the waist. As Laura looked more closely, she could see two small legs and Sammy's trainers sticking out lifelessly from under the rubble. She was beyond feeling now. She was cold, empty and shaking, with blood still pouring down from her ears and copiously blotting the dust-strewn floor below.

After a few moments, she gathered herself somewhat and crawled over Buster to grab Isla, pulling her and Ava away from Sammy's tomb. Isla was hysterically gesticulating upwards at the ceiling. At the time of his death, he was six years, two months and twenty days old.

But there was no respite. Approximately half a minute after the initial blast wave had pummelled its way across the city, the blast had refracted back on itself like a wave slamming onto the shore, receding and returning. This, combined with the blast from the groundburst at Newhaven, produced a second verse of horrors. The wave hit the debris field that was now where the tower blocks had once been and blew large amounts of debris down towards the garages. This time, they were openly facing the full force of the oncoming wind, although not as fast as before. The winds at the front of the wave were still in excess of 100 miles an hour, throwing large chunks of concrete, shards of glass and twisting splinters of metal towards and into the garage, which was now open to a sky dark with ash, soot and various toxic aerosols. The finer particles, energized by the wind, acted like a giant sandblaster, scouring the inside of the garage.

They sheltered as best they could but the onslaught cut and tore their clothes and lacerated their skin. Laura crouched in a ball as she was slowly being cut to pieces but then she felt the earth tremor as a large block of concrete landed on the end of the garage. She turned to see this boulder smash down on the garage door, crushing the metal like tissue paper and sealing them inside in the near pitch-black. Only a small slither of light was coming in through the few gaps to the outside. The thought of a relatively quick, but painful, death by laceration had now been replaced by being buried, the four survivors entombed in this 1960s car port.

'But at least we have air and few supplies. There's still hope of rescue,' thought Laura as she began to reassure herself, though, rationally, even she knew better.

For a while, they all just sat there, shivering in the dark, feeling around themselves finding small cut after small cut. Laura could feel an ooze stock to her hands as she felt around the debris on the floor. She realized it was blood flowing down the slightly sloping floor of their bunker, seeping towards the crushed doorway, emanating from all the open wounds within.

Gradually, her senses returned as the adrenaline and serotonin decreased and desisted. After what seemed like hours but was probably more like ten to fifteen minutes, a high-pitched ringing began to return to her right ear and the muffled sounds of crying returned. She could just about make out Isla's crouched silhouette. She appeared to be trying to tie a tourniquet around a large wound on Ava's knee, made from a scrap pulled from her coat.

Laura crawled forward.

'Let me help,' she said as she took the scrap of cloth and formed it into a strap around the back of the knee, compressing the wound. Ava screamed in pain. 'It's gonna be OK, love. It's going to be OK. Now, put your hand on mine and raise your leg to rest on my knee, OK?' she said as calmly as possible.

This led to another wail as Ava raised her leg as best she could.

'Is it really going to be OK?' said Isla, still desperately sobbing. 'We're going to die in here, aren't we…?' She shrieked as she looked across at the remains of her young son. 'I wish we could swap places… I wish I was the one who was dead!' she shouted, bent over in torment and pointing at what could be seen of his corpse.

Laura then heard Buster behind her in the dark, trying to speak, but it was muffled, as though he was gargling water.

She turned to Isla.

'Please hold Ava's leg… Isla! Isla! Please…' she said desperately. Slowly, Isla took hold of Ava's leg and limply placed it onto her own knee.

Laura left both of them, still in hysterics, and went to Buster's side. She could just make out his face in the pale light. It was now completely covered in a black crust, with red fissures going deep to the bone, some down to the jaw and some to the upper parts of the skull. His eyes were still welded shut and covered in a firm, set cement-like mucus. His hair was no more. He was desperately trying to say something, his lips moving but nothing intelligible was coming out. His mouth and charred tongue was full of blood, mucus and dust.

Suddenly, he started to convulse, his body lurching all over the claret-stained floor. He just about raised his hand above the detritus, which she grabbed and held firmly. Within a few moments, the end rattle had ceased and Buster was no more. His hand went limp, lifeless and had already started to go cold.

Laura closed her eyes but there were no more tears. She was empty, bankrupt of any more feeling. Then, the smell hit her, as various bodily fluids, along with the blood, began to effuse from the two corpses in their midst. She went over to Isla and Ava and put her arms around both of them. Then they just sat there, the three of them gently rocking in the dark, not knowing what to do next – not caring – just trying to find a comfortably numb nothing somewhere deep in their minds away from the hell, of which they had just borne witness, and away from the new hell to which they were now consigned. There was nothing they could do.

Several hours passed. In the gloom, Laura undertook the grim task of putting Buster's body into black plastic bin liners, both to stop the smell but also to prevent it enticing any vermin into their hole in the ground. This took a good fifteen minutes. His body was large, at least sixteen stone of bulk and now deadweight. She also insisted they undertake the equally grim task of burying Sammy, at the very least putting more rubble on top of his legs and feet – again, to prevent the ingress of scavengers.

This was met with protest from Isla.

'You can't do that…' she screamed. 'He's my baby. I want to see him. Please, please… Help me get him out…' She began to throw bits of cement, plaster and felt from the roof over her shoulder, desperately burrowing into the mound of rubble.

'Isla…' said Laura as calmly as she could, meekly remonstrating.

'Please… We can get him out and give him a proper burial…' she said, stopping and then started to shiver.

Laura knew she was realizing the sheer futility of what she was doing.

Isla then, much to Laura's surprise, looked up at her and calmly requested, 'Can we bury him here properly? Can we give him a send-off, like a service?'

'Of course… Of course, we can, love,' replied Laura, now in tears. After they had finished carefully putting the rocks on and around the protruding remains, they sat, using a small LED torch as a candle that Laura had found amongst their meagre supplies, and they held a silent vigil, all three of them holding hands.

After a few minutes, they were disturbed by the ground shaking.

'Please, not another one… Stop. Why won't it stop?!' shouted Isla up the ceiling.

As well as the ground shaking, Laura could hear what she thought was the sound of roaring water, as if a giant wave was coming in to land. This sound then changed to the sounds of crashing, the banging of many things being broken, but still seemingly in the distance.

Unknown to the three survivors hidden in their mound of rubble, the nuclear tsunami wrought by the Kraken torpedo from the Samara was now inundating the south coast. The wave had already devastated the east coast and London where it had peaked at 200 metres in height. It had now refracted round into the English Channel, now smaller in height at thirty metres, but the wave still caused vast devastation on both sides of the sea. The wave was now ravaging the centre of Brighton, which lay in a valley. The sounds they could hear was the wave picking up the debris from the explosion and slamming it together in a toxic ceiche. It was, at once, cleansing, delaying the onset of the fire storm but also polluting as it deposited its own heavily radioactive isotopes in its wake.

Fortunately for Laura, Isla and Ava, on top of Whitehawk Hill, they were spared a fate of drowning in this acrid soup. Instead, something else began to rain death from above. The high altitude prevailing wind was blowing west-north-west, bringing with it a large amount of nuclear fall-out from the mud-burst at Newhaven. Outside their relative shelter, the rain began to fall and the radiation levels began to rise. The lethal dose could be as low as 200 Rads, which led to death in a few weeks. However, the radiation levels were sustained from further fall-out from across the channel. This meant that the radiation levels outside would remain in the 500 to 700 range for at least the next six hours.

Whilst their shelter had now become a prison, there were still numerous small gaps and openings to the outside, which allowed the fine fall-out material to get inside. Subsequently, the radiation levels inside the garage were about half of those on the outside.

Isla was in the midst of giving a slow but warm eulogy to her son when she stopped and raised her hands to her head, where she began to rub at her temples, suddenly and vigorously.

'My god, it hurts so much,' she said as she held her forehead. Already on her knees, she leant forward into a foetal position. 'Fuck, sorry… My head is hurting so bad I can't think…'

'It's OK. I saved some meds earlier,' replied Laura. Getting up, she used the torch to locate the dust-covered crate and pulled out a small blue packet, dusting it off.

'Co-codamol… Take a couple of these…' said Laura, gingerly handing them to her.

'My mouth's too dry…' she said when she tried to swallow them. She grabbed a small bottle of some form of fruit juice and was able to get the tablets down.

As this was happening, Laura heard the sound of Ava being violently sick behind her. As she turned round, she noticed there was dark tar-like blood in the vomit, which now spilled on the now filth-ridden floor of the garage.

'Come here, love,' she said to the crying girl. 'Have some juice.' She put Ava on her lap as she sat on the floor, grabbing another bottle which was loose. 'Ooh, apple and mango. That'll be nice…'

Over the course of the next half hour, they all got progressively weaker. They had moved to the side of the garage furthest away from the corpses and the various rancid ablutions and lay on the floor, with Ava in the middle, huddled together as they all began to feel cold and feverish. All three were now feeling lethargic and, over the course of the next few hours, they lay there, dozing, trying not to move as they became increasingly nauseous.

'What time is it…?' whispered Isla feebly.

Struggling to breathe, Laura tried to reply.

'I don't know, love. Just try to rest. It'll be fine… It'll be morning soon…' she said in-between the waking horror and a fever dream.

She was soon woken by a shriek from Isla and the sound of soft crying.

'My baby, my baby…' she muttered.

Laura struggled to sit up. Looking down, she could see Isla's hands grasping at Ava's hair, which was now coming out in clumps. They didn't know when she had stopped breathing, but her lifeless form confirmed that she had died.

But any further grieving was interrupted by sudden attacks of projectile vomiting and violent, bloody diarrhoea. Both of them collapsed back to where they had lay, Isla still desperately grasping onto the dead body of her infant daughter.

Over the past few hours, they had all absorbed 12 to 14 grays of radiation and were now in the throes of acute radiation. This increased every hour. Even as the radiation decreased, the absorption continued. At over 30 grays, death would occur within twenty-four hours.

Laura couldn't hear Ava's sobbing or muttering anymore. She couldn't even turn around to see if she was still of this world. It hurt too much. She just continued to lie there. She could feel various liquids flowing around her and into her torn clothes. She was shivering violently for a while but this began to desist after a time and was, instead, replaced by the most intense of headaches, combined with what felt like a spike-covered lead ball rolling around in her stomach.

Her sight was failing, although she was glad of it. The last things she could clearly see were her fingernails falling out and her skin blistering all over her body in big red puss-filled welts. She was hoping the end would come soon.

She began to drift back and forth into a feverish purgatory, plagued by cruel dreams of being at home with her kids interspersed with nightmarish variations of the sights she had seen over the last day. She didn't even have the energy to cry – just a mopish despair as she fell between dream and reality. The latter was a world of pain as her skin began to peel off and her teeth began to fall out. She had to spit these out onto the floor next her through her stinging, bleeding lips as she lay in a kind of recovery position.

She thought of the children and wished they had gone quickly. The thought made her retch. Was she a bad mum? She hadn't been there for them and now she was wishing them dead. These were her final thoughts.

She began to fit as vast amounts of blood came up from her stomach, going into her lungs and flooding her mouth.

Laura Ford passed away twelve hours after the attack. She had asphyxiated on a series of blood clots in her lungs, which had been caused by her alveoli haemorrhaging and collapsing due to the effects of radiation sickness.

Laura's fate, as well as that of the other adults and the children in their shelter, played out across Europe. In the Brighton area, out of the 600,000 within range of the blast, 170,000 died immediately due to the effects of the thermal pulse and the blast wave. There were 190,000 serious casualties, of which two thirds died within the following few hours due to the lack of triage and paramedical support. Out of the remaining 300,000, none went unscathed. All had some form of minor injury from flying debris or, at the very least, severe psychological trauma. This was worsened by the arrival of the fall-out, which arrived in a series of nuclear rains. The first came from the groundburst at Newhaven and the second quickly followed from a series of explosions on a nuclear power plant on the north coast of France.

The radiation doses led to an eighty percent mortality rate within the next forty-eight hours. Across the United Kingdom, there was no power, running water or working medical facilities. In addition to the 21 million that had been killed by the blast or who died within a few hours of the attack, of the remaining 50 million, it is estimated that 40 million died in the next two days, either from radiation poisoning or secondary infections. However, this does not take into account the nuclear torpedo attacks along the European coasts, the tidal waves that inundated all of the coastal areas of the British Isles.

Less than forty-eight hours after the attack, the population of Great Britain had been reduced from just over 70 million to medieval levels, between 5 and 6 million, less than a tenth of what it had been a few days before. With very little food available and a nuclear winter setting in, this halved in the first month after the attack, halved over the next six months and again by Christmas of 2045, when there were only a million souls left on the sceptred isle. A still and smouldering radioactive wilderness.

The picture was the same across Europe. Out of the pre-war population of 600 million, about 7 million remained, with little food and no clean water, all of which had been vindictively contaminated with cobalt and radioactive isotopes by the vengeance weapons from the East. There was little to no hope of survival. These survivors also had to contend with the coldest winters since the end of the last ice age, with more climatic horrors to come.

Once the cradle of civilization, Europe was now in the pitch-black of oblivion, its survival hanging by the finest of threads. In most parts of the old world, there was no life at all, such as the south coast of England and the death of Brighton.

CHAPTER 44

Wotara, South Island, New Zealand

18th March 2044

On the other side of the globe and underneath the vast amber dome created by Blue, there were now exactly 303 frightened souls gathered in the graveyard of the small church, ready to listen to the voice of their promised saviour, Gloria – though, now the voice of Blue. Gloria was stood there, now surrounded by a terrified congregation, including Troy, who was still in a trance to her right, and her dictatorial muse to her left, invisible on her shoulder, ready to whisper into her ear. The assembly was a mixture of the people from all walks of life: the very young, babes in arms, pimple-ridden adolescents, scruffy twenty-something students, housewives, suited businessmen, tradespeople, all the way to the very old, supported by their walking canes. All had one thing in common: terror. Some were crying, some were shaking, some were angry and some were in shock. But all were in an emotional turmoil, regardless of what their exterior suggested.

Then she heard Blue whisper into her ear.

'It is time. Repeat every word, every nuance. It is important.' Her double was now gripping her shoulder tightly.

Gloria was high on adrenaline so she followed the command, repeating every word.

'The rest of the world is ablaze. The peoples of the world have foolishly followed the desires and the will of the old god, the ancient vengeful god of the Old Testament who permits them to rain fire down upon each other. A nuclear holocaust is being played out across creation. As I give you these dark tidings, several thousand nuclear warheads are descending to earth, radioactive tidal waves are rising and a volcanic nightmare of brimstone is rising deep from the fires held within the centre of the earth. These are the end times, my children.'

Blue paused and so did Gloria.

'Now, raise both your hands above your head and hail the sky,' whispered Blue.

Gloria could feel a static in the air and it was rising. She briefly hesitated but, feeling Blue's intense stare, she complied, raising her arms and holding her palms up to the orange sky. Before she continued her dictation, Blue reminded her, 'Make sure you repeat everything – every word, annunciation and nuance. It is important and your life depends upon it.'

'But you can be saved! I have brought the shield above down from heaven to protect the chosen. I am Gloria, the second coming, the daughter of god and I have come to be your saviour. I come from the new god, the god of Jesus's Testament, the kind, the loving, the peaceful, the all-knowing and the all forgiving.'

Gloria took a breath. She could not believe what she was saying.

'Was this true?' she thought. 'Am I… Is this destiny?'

Alarmingly, she heard another voice in her head: her own but it was Blue. It was clear, loud and filled with malice.

'Yes, it's true, Gloria Alvarez, but there is no destiny, no fate – only chaos. You, like everything else in creation, are an accident. It is pure chance that you were nearest to me at the moment of my ascension and now you are my vassal, emissary and servant. Do not defy me or you will burn!' The words came with a chilling force. Indeed, she thought she could feel an icy wind lashing her face as this supposed deity spoke to her within her own mind. Now, full of adrenaline, she continued to comply as she continued the sermon.

'This world in which you exist is the realm of the old vengeful god of the dark times, of the Old Testament. He has trapped you all in human form, in this world of cruel beauty and torturous mortality. You, my children, are angels of heaven, beautiful creatures of the stars. He has imprisoned you in these mortal cages of flesh in order to control, to mock, to inflict pain and to turn you to his evil. I will free you but you must open yourselves to me. Let me into your souls and provide a sacrifice.'

'Now,' whispered Blue. 'Look at every single one of them with an intense stare, panning your view across the congregation. Make them believe!'

Gloria lowered her gaze upon the awestruck mob. Some were staring in shock, others were looking at their feet, mumbling to themselves, while some looked red with fury. Most of the angry contingent were wearing various religious affectations on their person. Most were Christian, but Muslims and Sikhs were also present in small numbers.

'Good. Now repeat after me…' said Blue.

'You will now renounce your faiths – Catholic, Protestant, Shia, Shiite, Sunni, Sikh, Buddhist agnostic or atheist. Those who do not wish to renounce, say now. Say now or you cannot ascend back to heaven!' Gloria copied Blue's upward inflection and increase in volume to a crescendo.

'I will not follow a false god!' came a voice from the back of the group – an old man, bald and clean-shaven, skinny, quite frail. He had to be in his eighties. 'I will not follow you. You are a demon or the devil itself!' he shouted, before turning his back and beginning to shuffle away towards the vicarage gate.

'Good. We have an example,' whispered Blue. 'Hold out your right arm and then hold up your palm towards the unbeliever… Now!'

Gloria complied. She was trepidacious. She was about to be part of something that was unpleasant at best and almost certainly evil at worst.

'Wait!' she shouted, as per Blue's command. The words boomed across the cemetery, resonating amongst the gravestones. The congregation was now quaking. The old man had now hobbled twenty yards or so from the crowd and he turned back, first angry but then scared and fearful. He was not scared of the sudden bellowing that now emanated from her mouth but because of Gloria's new visage. She could see, in the faintest of reflections from the spectacles of a now crying middle-aged women in the front row, the great mothlike creature that had heralded Blue's arrival. In fact, Gloria was had now become this creature or, at the very least, this is what Blue was making the attending see – a large, luminous, supernatural being of latent malevolence.

'Keep listening and repeat, Gloria Alvarez,' whispered Blue.

'You are Byron Carter, seventy-nine years old, an arable farmer from Wakatoa. You used to play Rugby at provincial level. Your wife passed a few years ago but she was not the love of your life. It was a young man called Vincent…who died a long, long time ago…'

'Be quiet…' shouted the old man. 'That's not true…'

'Do not lie, child. I can see all that is, all that was and all that can be. Come back to the light and I will reunite you with both of them in the glorious light of the new god. Now, come back to your family. Come now. Come back to us…' The howl was now warm, loud, an almost loving short soliloquy.

Byron stood there, looking at the ground intently, but Gloria could see the tears in his eyes. After a few seconds, he fixed Gloria with a fearful but resolute stare.

'I have believed my entire life and I have already found God's love. I don't need their love and I do not need yours. I will meet my maker by my own choosing and I will not recant or bow down to the words of a serpent of Eden!' he said, once again turning his back and recommencing his slow walk to the gate.

Blue continued to whisper in her ear.

'Then let me release you, my child. The end you face will be long and painful in the coming darkness but you cannot enter the Kingdom of the new god without penance.'

Blue then whispered quietly into Gloria's ear.

'Close your hand into a fist and say these words…'

Gloria slowly clenched her outstretched hand. As she did, the old man stopped suddenly, as though he had been halted by an invisible wall.

'Now, rotate your hand 180 degrees so that your palm now faces you,' commanded Blue, 'and continue to repeat after me.'

As Gloria rotated her hand, the old man let out a shriek of pain and he was lifted from the path into the air, about ten feet above. He was slowly rotated around to face them, his face now wincing and contorted in agony.

'I have granted you a fate better than the one you are due in the old god's realm but he will still demand part of your soul. This can only be avoided in the only currency he understands: that of pain. I shall release you to the heavens through the angelic fire that gave birth to us all!' shouted Gloria.

'Now, open out your fist,' said Blue.

Gloria hesitated.

'Come now, this is just theatre. His fate is sealed; the atoms are already in motion. So, comply, unless you'd prefer a similar fate…'

Gloria hesitantly complied, opening her hand. As she did, the old man, Byron, began to scream as his clothes began to smoke, the outline of the patterns of his chequered shirt suddenly charring themselves into his skin, which was revealed as the ashen fibres fell to the ground below. His naked, burnt skin continued to smoulder, with small fires erupting across his body. The screaming grew, achieving a remarkably high pitch, the man's words no longer audible. There was no quick release; this was a slow death. The skin, that had initially reddened and then blackened, began to fall off his body as the layers of fat beneath cooked, dripping to the floor in large chunks of gelatinous sludge, like a prime cut of butcher's meat, shrivelling in a great furnace. This continued for several minutes until only the muscle and skeleton remained. Gloria knew he shouldn't have still been alive but she guessed Blue was doing something to maintain the horror: he was staring at her, his eyes wide open as they began to melt and run down his face.

Eventually, Byron Mitchell ceased to be. Instead, there was just a floating ball of molten organics and smoke held in suspension above the congregation. The remains were eventually lowered to the floor to complete the spectacle, allowed to melt and char the grass on the graves below.

'Praise the new god. He has been saved – an angel amongst the stars as he was before the entrapment of the old god in these physical forms,' said Gloria, still repeating every word in this anodyne trance. There had been various reactions from the ensemble of onlookers: some wept, some wailed, some were in awe, some were disgusted – Gloria could see fresh trails of vomit on the grass – but most were simply in shock.

'Excellent,' whispered Blue. 'Serotonin levels have peaked. They are now open to us. Repeat these words…'

She now got closer, turning her mouth to Gloria's ear.

'We are now the church of the new god. I can feel your faith growing but we are too small in number. Another sixty-five are required to create the new sanctum, the souls of the devout. I call on the recently passed to rejoin us. Come now… Souls, come from purgatory.' As she spoke, she could hear tremors running through the ground beneath them. Then she saw the dead rising. One by one, the graves of the recently deceased began to open across the cemetery. This led to further screams from the crowd as these cadavers, in various states of decomposition, began to smash their way out of their coffins, standing up right in their burial grounds and then climbing out up onto the path before beginning their slow walk towards the congregation.

'Do not fear. They mean no harm. They are coming back to you. Your faith will restore them. All of you, now look at me. Don't be scared. Look at me, my children,' said Gloria, repeating every word from her puppet master. Still in various states of distress, they all complied as the dead marched up behind them, forming neat ranks on the grass and on the remaining graves.

'Now, we shall pray for communion. All of you, close your eyes,' said Gloria. The crowd now all complied and the fear of the newly-risen kept them from reopening their eyes. 'Good. Now, listen to me carefully. I am the daughter of the new god. Can you hear my voice? Can you hear it inside your minds, my loves?' she said.

In turn, they all nodded.

'Stop talking now, Gloria Alvarez,' said Blue and she clicked her fingers. All the people, the living and the recently reanimated, now turned their faces to the sky, all eyes still obediently closed.

'Can you hear them?' she said.

Gloria heard what sounded like voices – some whispers, some shouts, some murmurs – and they were getting louder and louder. Soon, it was a cacophony of sound. Not one single voice was recognizable.

Then Blue's voice cut across.

'You see, Gloria Alvarez. We are now one.' With that, she clicked her fingers and the crowd of believers silently opened their eyes and looked up at the sky in unison, without a word or anything that spoiled the synchronicity. The noise then returned and Gloria could now just about make out the voices. She could tell that these were the thoughts, the minds of these people. It was still so loud, omnipresent. She closed her eyes and, as soon as it had started, it stopped, replaced by a stark and absolute silence. She opened her eyes and it was as though everything was frozen in time: the crowd, the insects on ground, the birds in the air and even Blue were rooted to the spot, not moving, statuesque.

It took her a moment but she also noticed a wooden door had appeared at the end of the path beyond the group. The silence was broken by the sound of the door opening, revealing what she thought was a man, standing on a sandy beach with the ocean in the background. The man then addressed her in a deep Spanish drawl.

'Well, don't just stand there. Come on in…'

CHAPTER 45

Mount Yamantau, Eastern Urals, Russian Federation

18th March 2044

Deep under the earth in Siberia, an inferno was rising from the centre of the earth. A vast body of energetic magma was now furiously burning its way through the silica-rich continental crust. As the ball of molten rock continued upwards, rising towards the surface, it got progressively larger as it vaporized the crust above it as though a vast glass blower was breathing into it, creating an ever-expanding, unstoppable bubble of semi-liquid magma. This mantle diapir was being driven by a long tentacle-like mantle plume, which was now active, rising around the earth's outer core and energizing the plastic mantle above. Now that it was active, this hotspot would continue to burn for tens, if not hundreds, of thousands of years.

Mantle plumes were nothing new to the Earth. These random cycles of convection in the earth's deeper regions had been a key part in shaping the earth's surface for billions of years, the beating heart of plate tectonics. However, this mantle plume, the soon-to-be Siberian hotspot, was the first to have been directed and generated by human beings. The impact of the nuclear rocket-driven asteroid less than an hour earlier on the other side of the planet had successfully started the chain reaction by applying a specific geophysical resonance into the earth's interior, creating the plume under the desired targets.

Initially, it would appear that the labyrinthine quantum calculations undertaken by Dr Bradley Kiefer had worked. There were, however, some unintended consequences – namely, the half dozen other mantle plumes, which were now burning through the crust below South America, North Africa and the continental United States. These plumes would reach the surface in the next few hours.

The mood deep under the mountain had oscillated significantly over the last half an hour. It began as a frenzy of activity as the attacks were launched, the team ensuring every wavelength was monitored, every sensor overseen, as they watched to see whether the grand plan was succeeding. This briefly gave way to hope as the opening gambits appeared to go to plan, which had led to much hand clapping and back slapping between Ma and Ri-Fin. This soon descended into despair as the Western counter attack came into force and they realized that there had been no real element of surprise as the radar tracks showed hundreds of American, British and French missiles launching and then descending on thousands of targets from Warsaw in the west to Shanghai in the east. Following the malaise came anger, the ire of Ri-Fin largely being directed at Sirotkin but, to a lesser extent, Ji-Chow, who had spent the entire time with his gaze firmly on the apocalypse unfolding on his tablet. The anger peaked when reports arrived of a NATO ground offensive entering Poland through the Fulda Gap and the central German plains. Then came more of a rabid confusion – or possibly amazement, Ji-Chow could not tell – when key command control facilities, radars and a large number of eastern ICBMs disappeared from the command screens. Ji-Chow suspected this was due to American 'special weapons' but decided not to gift this ammunition to the frothing Ri-Fin and the quietly furious Ma, who was now an unusually deep shade of red. In the end, the mood elevated slightly as they still appeared to be 'winning'– or, at the very least, that they were going to be much better off than the westerners.

Indeed, Ji-Chow had delivered the news that about thirty to forty percent of the Eastern Bloc's populace had survived and the invasion fleet had not yet come under attack. More saliently, he had also mentioned that Western Bloc casualties were not far from their most 'optimistic' projections. This had seemed to sate their overlords to an extent – certainly the Chinese contingent – as the majority of these survivors were in China. The Russian contingent was now entirely bereft: European Russia was now predicted to be a nuclear wasteland with minimal survivors, due to the ferocity of the western counter attack led by the 100-plus warhead volley from the Dreadnought.

They were now beginning to consider the next move: the invasion of Africa. They all remained around the same table where they had plotted the end a few hours ago, with Ji-Chow and General Xhang sat across from Ma, Ri-Fin, Sirotkin and his two silent companions. They had all been silent for a few minutes, which had obviously been irritating Ri-Fin.

'So, what's the actual score, gentleman? How many are alive/dead on both sides? I mean the actual numbers in millions or billions – not a percentage!' he shouted.

Xhang looked across at Ji-Chow and nodded assumingly.

'In terms of deaths, 4 billion are projected for our side, with 1.8 billion survivors. On the other side, ninety percent casualties, so 2 billion dead and less than 200 million survivors. We also projected an additional 2 billion deaths through secondary effects in the non-aligned countries. So, out of the starting global population of 11 billion, 3 billion survivors, of which we estimate this will reduce to 2 billion within twelve months, once the effect of the nuclear winter takes hold. That's 1.8 billion on our side, mostly in eastern Russia, inner China and South-East Asia. A nominal amount will remain in eastern Europe. Of the other remaining 200 million, just over 180 million survive in Africa, mainly in the south-east of the continent, with a residual 20 million in Europe, North America and Australasia. In summary, we estimate we now account for ninety percent of the long-term survivors and that the Africa plan is still viable,' said Ji-Chow.

'Well, it could have been worse…' replied Ri-Fin. 'And the invasion fleet is completely unscathed?'

'Not entirely. A few western attack subs were able to sink a few of the ships but the frigates have now dealt with these. The fleet is ready to sail with its escorts and we have been able to establish fairly reliable comms with the flagship,' replied Xhang as he wiped his brow. Ji-Chow had noticed the bunker had been progressively getting hotter. It must now have been in the mid-30s – not to mention, very humid. Nobody had yet mentioned this but, judging by the sweat stains on the chairman's smock, it was about to be.

'Victor, what's happened to the air-con?' said Ri-Fin. 'Do you want me to sort it out for you?' he said to one of Sirotkin's aides who had quietly sloped into the room. Again, Ri-Fin had that sociopathic glint in his eye, so the aide reacted quickly.

'We are troubleshooting the problem, sir – quite literally, if necessary,' said Victor, a tall, lanky man with receding black, curly hair and wearing a blue suit. His voice was nervously coarse and squirrelly.

'Good, because you don't want me troubleshooting you, now, do we?' he replied, stifling a laugh. Victor nodded nervously.

A few seconds later, a shorter and much younger man in an identical blue suit – with matching Russian Federation red tie – ran through the double doors, drenched in sweat and looking highly alarmed. Victor craned down to listen as the man quickly whispered something into his ear, to which he reacted with bemusement.

'What's wrong?' said an irksome Ri-Fin.

'Well, sir. It appears that the citadel's systems are operating as expected. Everything is optimal. There are no faults. It is working as expected. The heat source is not coming from within the complex…'

'What's that meant to mean?' said Ri-Fin as he stood from his sweat-stained leather chair, getting up close and personal with Victor.

'Listen here, you lanky streak of yaks piss, it is obviously a malfunction somewhere so, for fuck's sake, fix it. Am I clear, you walking cluster fuck?!' He shouted with such ferocity his sweat was flying off his forehead and into Victor's face and his open mouth.

Victor didn't so much respond as nod and mutter blankly.

'Good, because if you don't in the next ten minutes, I am going to leave this room and I am going to go looking for things that are wrong – defects, dust, dirt or anything that just annoys me. Now, I am a betting man and I'll wager that it'll be pretty much everything

I see. Do you know what I am going to do when I find these things?' Victor, increasingly pale and sweaty, shook his head. 'Well, I am going to shoot them, but not fatally – well, at least not at first – a bullet for every blemish, non-conformity, every imperfection. I'll start with each foot, one a minute, followed by your kneecaps, then your balls, one bullet each, then your wrists, your belly and, finally, when you are on the verge of death, I will finally put one in your head…is that clear?'

'That's enough!' said Sirotkin. 'Unless you want a visit from one of my friends in Alpha squad. I don't know if you've noticed, but they are the ones guarding this room and all the exits.'

Ri-Fin looked to Ma who gave a reluctant nod.

'Now, Mr President, I was just letting off some steam. We've resisted the temptations for recriminations so far, despite other transgressions…' replied Ri-Fin with obvious contempt. He sat back down in his chair.

'Good,' said Sirotkin. 'We'll need to find out what's causing this sudden heatwave. If the equipment is functioning—'

'Oh, like Perimeter was…' interjected Ri-Fin.

'Io…' said Ma with a raised eyebrow.

'Then where is the heat source coming from? It's probably just a firestorm on the surface. I assume a mass of warheads landed on and around the mountain,' continued Sirotkin.

Both Ma and Ri-Fin looked across at Ji-Chow and Xhang.

'Brigadier Xi, you look puzzled…' said the now heavily-perspiring Ma.

'Yes, Comrade. A firestorm would indeed be a reasonable explanation if several high-yield warheads had exploded in the near vicinity, but…'

'But what?' said Ri-Fin dismissively.

'There haven't been any,' he said. 'There haven't been any—'

'What do you mean?' said Sirotkin.

At this point, Xhang joined in.

'Have you felt a single tremor or judder since the assault began?' he said. Sirotkin, Ma and Ri-Fin shook their heads. 'Exactly. If a single 3-megaton earth penetrator from a minuteman had landed even within a kilometre of the mountain, we would have felt it, even this far down.'

'Which means?' said Ri-Fin, scowling.

'Where would the firestorm have come from? Wherever this heat is coming from, it can't be the surface. Even at this depth, we are significantly insulated from surface temps,' said Xhang. There were further looks of bemusement. Ji-Chow began to scroll through his tablet to find the telemetry for the site. He found a dashboard, which was mainly showing green – all systems operational – apart from two big red flashing icons. One was for the air temperature sensors – that sort of made sense – but there was another for the water reservoirs, which were deep and went to the bottom of the tunnel complex. Tapping on the icon, Ji-Chow brought up more details on this: it showed the reservoir, a vast underground lake with nearly 5 billion litres of water within it. It appeared to have lost ten percent of its volume in the last hour. As he pondered what this meant, the conversation continued.

'So, it must be a fault then!' said Ri-Fin.

'There must be another explanation. Look at the telemetry,' said Sirotkin as he pointed to his own tablet.

'Victor,' said Ji-Chow. 'Can you get the cameras on one of the screens for the water reservoirs?'

'Well, eh, yes. Does that help in the current situation?' he said, flustered and still trying to avoid eye contact with Ri-Fin, who turned his gaze to Ji-Chow.

'Well, it's getting warmer and we appear to have lost ten percent of our potable water in the last half an hour. That's nearly 500 megalitres. That's either a very large leak, or…' Ji-Chow trailed off.

'Or what?' said Ri-Fin.

'Let's check the cameras,' said Xhang, trying to placate both Ma and Ri-Fin.

'Alright…' said Ri-Fin. 'Get a move on then, Victor!'

Victor switched the monitor over to mirror his screen, then flicked across to the surveillance cameras.

'What the fuck is that?' said Ri-Fin, his eyes widening. For the first time, Ji-Chow could see fear etched across his heavily-creased face. On the screen there should have been a picture of an underground cavern hewn into the granite belly of the mountain. It should have been full of crystal-clear spring water and gently lit by the pale, white lights from the gantry above. Instead, the picture showed a bubbling cauldron. Its steam was rising and fogging the cameras, but they could all see a faint orange glow coming from the base of the chamber.

After staring at the large L.E.D screen for the best part of a minute, Ri-Fin broke the silence.

'Can someone please tell me what is going on down there?'

'The heat is not coming from above; it's coming from below, from deep within the earth,' replied Ji-Chow.

'You mean like lava...?' said Ma, stuttering, seemingly on the edge of panic.

'Possible – or some geothermal current. One thing's for sure: with the amount of thermal energy needed to evaporate that much water...we need to get out of here before we boil or—' said Ji-Chow

'Or what...' said a now panting Ri-Fin.

'At best, we'll die of heat exhaustion...'

'Fuck!' shouted Ri-Fin. 'Well, don't just stand there, Victor. Sound the alarm!'

Victor looked across at Sirotkin, who nodded. And with that, he pressed a red icon on his tablet. The claxons sounded, the alarm was raised and the instruction was given in both Mandarin and Russian.

'All hands evacuate the complex. Follow order 7. Follow order 7!' repeated a loud electronic voice that echoed through the increasingly sweaty halls of the citadel.

CHAPTER 46

Echo Bunker, West Virginia, United States.

18th March 2044

Most of the evergreen woods above the echo bunker were now burning as vast forest fires raged for hundreds of square miles across Virginia and around the mountains. The infernos destroyed everything in their path, the millions of trees a vast stockpile of tinder ignited by dozens of thermal pulses from weapons that had destroyed most of the major cities in the eastern United States. This firestorm torched all before it, flora and fauna, all plants and all animals, all structures and their human inhabitants. These inhabitants were not only the local rural folk but also those who had fled the cities before the attack, the preppers and the very few who saw the coming storm. Instead of dying from radiation poisoning, blast or by the rabid mobs they feared, they all burned or choked in this great fire, an unforeseen bubble of tragedy in the froth of the wider extinction. There was no escape.

The majority of the Eastern Seaboard was initially pulverized by the earthfall of the vanguard of the FOBs warheads on Washington and Norfolk. It was then inundated with radioactive floods from the nuclear tsunamis, which swept and drowned all in its path, careering over a hundred miles in land to the foothills of the Appalachians. Any semblance of conurbations or residual population centres were further eviscerated by the arrival of over 100 warheads from northern fleet submarines, which peppered the flooded cities and scattered the radioactive debris beyond the rain shadow of the eastern peaks. The remaining large towns and cities on the other side of the Appalachians were only spared for another half an hour or so as a further volley of warheads from Siberia and Chinese Inner Mongolia decimated any metropolis with a population greater than 100,000.

Within hours, the continental United States had either been drowned, blasted, burned or irradiated. Nowhere would escape the four horsemen of the apocalypse. Those that survived would not last long, finally submitting to either radiation, secondary infection or starvation. Even if some were to prevail in this fresh hell on a scorched earth, further trials by earth, wind, water and fire were to come. Indeed, beneath the east coast of the United States, a magmatic diapir, which, though smaller, was in other aspects similar to the one that was now cutting its way to the surface of Siberia, was now coming up towards the surface. In its path lay the remaining department of defence bunkers and the last functioning components of the federal government. Unfortunately, the Russian FSB had successfully deduced the function of this disparate network of underground blockhouses and most had been targeted with a series of 750-kiloton earth penetrators from a salvo of Sarmat ICBMs. Of the twenty facilities, fourteen had been destroyed and four had been disabled, burying the inhabitants alive with no hope of rescue.

This left the Bravo bunker, which was led by the vice president – who was very soon to be sworn in – and the Echo bunker. In the latter, Bradley Kiefer had just finished doing some complex geophysical calculations, which had led him to a worrying conclusion. He was now trying to contemplate how to tell his colleagues about their likely fate and their impending expiry, which would occur in less than a few hours – an unintended consequence of their own ingenuity when trying to destroy their fellow man. He was still sitting in Frank's office next to Christine, both staring forlornly at their tablet and laptop screens. Through the glass panel at the far end of the office, he could see Frank and Colonel Schwartz sitting outside in the waiting area. They had gone out one by one in silent despair as different parts of the country went 'dark'. Frank sat crouched over with his head in his hands, broken by the events of the last few hours, nervous exhaustion and sheer fatigue, whilst the colonel simply stared off into space, his eyes wide open, unblinking and seemingly somewhere else, a long way away and, probably, a long time ago.

'What have you got, Bradley?' Christine said. 'Did it work. Did it get them?'

He hesitated.

'Yes, it's definitely working. It's just…'

'Just what?'

'There have been some secondary effects that were not in any of the simulations…' he replied limply, trying to hold back the rising tide of sick that was welling up inside him.

'That doesn't sound good but it can't be much worse than where we are now, right?' she said, both out of curiosity and an attempt to comfort, but this slowly turned to worry as he stayed silent, beginning to shake nervously.

'Bradley, what is it?' she said, putting a hand gently on his shoulder.

He sighed and activated the holographic projector on Frank's desk. The projector showed an image of the globe, within which sat a 3D stereographic projection of the planet's interior. Using her elemental understanding of geology, Christine was able to make out what she thought was the core, the mantle and the earth's crust, which were in various shades of blue, getting darker the closer the layers were to the surface. In a yellowish orange there were streams – or, rather what she assumed to be convection currents in the mantle, from which appeared to be large bubbles rising into the crust. There were currents in this tannic colour under Hawaii and Iceland, which she expected, but there was also a blue, dashed flashing line, marked 'Artemis X1150A', which she was guessing was where the asteroid had impacted into the Earth. There were then a series of red bubbles, which were intermittently flashing and were linked by curved red lines leading back to the blue line of impact. One of these – the largest, in fact – had risen up from the mantle on the opposite side to the impact and was rapidly burning its way through the crust below a target signified by a cross-hair – she assumed this was Yamantau. However, she also noticed several other smaller – but, nonetheless, massive as she considered the scale of the map – red flashing bubbles, rising under another half dozen points under the earth. One of those was ascending rapidly and burning its way into the base of the continental crust of eastern America.

'Bradley, is that what I think it is? Has this literally backfired?'

'Yes, yes… Yes, it has…' he stuttered.

'OK, how sure are we? I mean, I'm assuming this is mostly from simulations, still bearing in mind our satellite coverage is now practically non-existent thanks to the EMPs?'

'No, it's mostly from sensor data… It's… It's…from Bright Eyes. We are still getting some telemetry including false colour infrared and magnetometry. We are only using the sim to fill in any gaps in the data. I am…' He started to break down.

'You are what, Bradley?' she said coldly, already knowing what the answer was likely to be.

'I am fairly sure this is accurate and I am sorry. This wasn't meant to happen…'

'I know,' she said. 'None of this was. How long have we got?' She was being matter of fact and was keeping a safe distance from feeling. She was cold, numb. She thought this probably for the best.

'I'd say six, maybe seven, hours…before…before it surfaces… So maybe an hour until we feel the effects and maybe an hour after before the heat gets too…' He couldn't finish the sentence and just sat there, shaking and staring at the projection.

Christine got up and walked towards the door.

'The others need to know,' she said. Bradley nodded gently without breaking his gaze away from the simulation of their oncoming fate. She opened the glass door and walked over to where Frank and Colonel Schwartz were sitting.

Frank looked up. He now looked a lot older than he had done a few hours ago, the crow's feet and the wrinkles now extenuated by the red bags under his bloodshot eyes. His normally perfectly-sculpted silver hair was now a sweaty mess, frizzing and flopping in all directions. The expensive navy-blue tie had now unravelled and hung loosely around his neck, with the top two buttons of his shirt now open. Gone was the polished statesman; now he was an increasingly-tired and frail old man.

'Please tell me you have some good news…' he said.

She sat down next to him.

'Well… It depends what you mean by good, exactly.'

'Let's just suppose, Christine, you told me this was all just an elaborate exercise and it was time to go home…' She knew this was Frank's gallows wit at its darkest.

'It's not that, Frank. But the end may be nearer than we think…'

'Don't tease me, Chrissy. What is it?'

'Artemis has succeeded. The other side is in the process of being eliminated…'

'I sense there's a but coming…'

'Yeah, yes there is. There are now what I can only describe as other pockets of magma rising to the surface all over the planet, including here, Frank. We've shot them and we've shot ourselves…'

Frank sank in his chair before blowing out his cheeks and getting to his feet. At the same time, Schwartz got up and walked over to the wall and launched his fist in a considerable right hook, before storming off through the gantry and up the flight of stairs to the canteen.

Frank had an entirely different reaction. Walking across to his office, he leaned inside.

'Brad, it's OK, son. It's not your fault. I gave the order and, if you hadn't done the work, some other bright spark would have done.

Stand down, spend your last hours as you wish, do whatever you want to do…' he said before turning back and leaning on the glass walls. 'Same goes for you, Chrissy. How long do we have?'

'A few hours a best…' she said

'We had also better give everyone the choice, then…' With that, he walked out of the alcove and back into the main gantry where he grabbed a headset and began to address the whole base.

'Ladies, gentlemen, friends…' he said in the best senatorial tone he could manage through the fatigue. All of the twenty or so in the main control room looked up from their screens and listened. 'I thank you for your diligent and excellent service over the last few days in what has been the most difficult of times. I can say, with certainty, that your country is proud of you. However, there is one further trial we must face. In a few hours, this facility will be destroyed by a lava flow from deep within the earth. I therefore release you from your duties. You may return to the surface and go where you will. Or you can spend your last few hours here. In either case, I am authorizing the release of special diet 6. This consists of two tablets and will be dispensed from the canteen. If the thought of the fate that awaits you is too much then I would implore you to partake. Take the red one first and then the green one and your passage into whatever lies beyond will be peaceful, without pain. God bless you… Go… Go and do what you need to do…' he said before pulling off his headset and placing it on one of the control desks.

The reactions ranged across the entire emotional spectrum. Some just sat there, staring at their screens; a few even seemed to carry on with their now redundant tasks; others fell into a self-pitying, sobbing despair; some screamed and cried hysterically. The majority, though, seemed to accept their fate. After all, many were aware that everyone they knew, loved or cared about was probably no more. Ultimately, they saw this as a release.

Some did climb back up to the surface, never to be seen again, and others began to make their way to the canteen for a last supper, some going via their rooms to wile away their last hours in a way they saw fit. Eventually, most decided on one of these two courses of action. Colonel Schwartz fell into the former category. After ripping off his air force insignia, throwing the brooch and pendant to the floor, he marched up to the now open airlock and began the long walk back up to whatever prevailed above, his footsteps slowly getting more distant as the echo from his combat boots slowly faded to nothing.

Frank didn't follow either tribe. Instead, he came across and sat back down next to Christine who was contemplating how best to spend her last few hours.

'Well, I don't know about you but I can do with a drink,' he said, smiling warmly but his glazy eyes gave away his melancholic despair.

'Why the hell not? I'd rather not make this call sober. Might as well enjoy ourselves,' she replied.

With that, they both got up. She assumed they were going to Frank's 'cabin' for more whisky. As they were about to make their way through the gantry, Frank paused and went back to his office door.

'Hey Brad. Do you drink? I mean, liquor?'

'Yeah, I guess I do sometimes…' replied Bradley.

'Well come with us, son. We are about to open some real fineries. Come on, it'll be the best stuff you've ever tasted.'

'Sure,' he replied, still white in face, the colour all drained.

The three of them traversed the ops room and then down the stairwell to the accommodation quarters. They were essentially alone, with the exception of a few rooms, which were locked shut. They walked in silence, listening to the sounds of activity in the rooms around them: a man crying, a woman screaming angrily. Christine could hear classical music coming from one of the rooms. In another, someone was playing a computer game involving fast cars. In another, someone was singing. Based on these observations, Christine concluded that people fell into two camps: either they accepted their fate or railed against it.

After a few minutes, they got to Frank's palatial lair. He immediately headed for another drinks globe, a hidden one he had not yet shared with Christine, which was tucked away in the back right corner of the room. He opened it and took out two bottles. As he approached her, she could see these were not whisky but dusty bottles of wine. He brought them over and placed them carefully on his leather-topped desk.

'Chateau Lafitte 1945,' he said, pointing to the first bottle and then tapped the side of the second. 'Chateau Margaux 2000. I've always preferred the left bank clarets myself. So, who'd like a glass?'

All partook and there was much reminiscing from Frank about his various escapades not only in government but as a young military attaché in 90s Moscow. He sat back in his chair with his feet languidly laid up on his desk and spoke in long, winding monologues. Christine interjected occasionally to check details, or indeed, correct factual inaccuracies due to Frank's tendency for exaggeration. Bradley was fairly silent throughout, although he was putting back the luxurious Bordeaux at an alarming pace and getting somewhat merry, giggling like a small girl at Frank's stories. She guessed he didn't 'partake' very often and, even if he did, it can't have been very much.

'Are you OK, Bradley? You seem a tad inebriated…' she said.

'Yeah, I guess I am, Christine…' he said, slurring slightly.

'Good,' said Frank. 'That's the idea… I hope you're both enjoying the wine.'

'It's like liquid silk,' said Christine.

'I should expect so; each is over 10,000 dollars a bottle… There's no point hanging on to it…' he said, his jovial outlook now giving way to the stark reality they had spent the best part of the last hour hiding away from. He paused plaintively. 'Do you remember Patrick Alliott, Chrissy? That French military attaché we had with us a few years back at the DOD in DC?'

'Yes, I do…' she said, masking her confusion and curiosity, not knowing exactly where he was going with this line of enquiry.

'Yeah, interesting guy. Complex… I seem to recall he was both a devout catholic and an existentialist. A truly French dichotomy of a man. Do you recall that dinner at the French Embassy on Bastille Day? I'll always remember it because it was a complete washout and we all got herded like cattle into that small dining room – barely room to swing a cat, or even a mouse, for that matter. It ended up being you, me and Marshall sat right next to Patrick on that tiny table. And he had that story…'

'Oh, the false alarm?'

'Yeah, that's it. Funnily enough, it just crossed my mind—'

'What's the story? I like a story…' said Bradley, interjecting with an unusual and slurry confidence.

'Well,' began Frank. 'Patrick was a colonel in the French Air Force, the Arm de l'Aire and, prior to his posting to DC, he had been the duty officer at one of NATO's control centres. I think it was Mons in Belgium, from what I recall. Do you know what they do – I mean, did – at Mons, Bradley?'

'Can't say I do…'

'It's where all nuclear weapons are controlled from in the European theatre – or, at the very least, coordinated. The Force De Frappe and British deterrent are – were – nominally independent but this place buried deep, in what must be the only major hill of note in the Flanders area, was the centre for all command in theatre, whether that be American, French, British or any other tactical weapons stored by the Dutch and Germans. Anyway, the story went: Patrick was on duty in the early hours of a winter's evening when there was a flash alert from the BMEWS at Fylingdales, an attack warning red—'

'What's a BMEWs?' interrupted an increasingly inebriated Bradley as he clumsily dropped his empty glass on the desk.

'Ballistic Missile Early Warning systems – big multi-storey tetrahedral pyramids with massive space radars in them which are – were – our main eyes and ears. Anyways, the call came in that an attack was underway and he could see a missile track on the big screen in front of him. Now, not only were these very dire tidings but very odd, because they had reported that just a single missile had been launched and they couldn't validate the launch with our defense intelligence satellites – no heat signatures, you see.' Frank took another large slug of rouge. 'So, our French friend has a decision to make. Does he order a standard tit-for-tat counterforce retaliation – and, by the way, this is the NATO standing order of the Alliance – or does he wait for this missile to show its hand—'

At this point, Christine decided to interject, to bring some clarity to the very foggy mind of Bradley.

'By, 'show its hand', he means wait until the missile comes out of its launch phase and into re-entry where, if it's real, the BMEWS will detect warheads being deployed and then can predict the likely targets. Now, this would be very risky because this could easily be a decapitation strike. The missile could, instead, detonate at high altitude and wipe out all communications—'

'Indeed,' said Frank, once again taking the lead. 'So, Mr Kiefer, what would you have done?'

'Taken the risk. Wait and see. Hope it's a false alarm?' he replied as the same time he spilled some wine, staining his white cotton shirt.

'Interesting…' said Frank. 'And that's exactly what he did. He, in fact, dismissed it as a false positive and the attack never came. It turned out to be a sounding rocket fired by a Norwegian research team, most of whom were promptly fired after the incident as no one had informed the authorities. Even scarier was the fact that the

Ruskies detected it and were in the middle of deciding whether to engage Perimeter and an automated response. Fortunately, they made the same call as Colonel Alliot. That day, he saved the world and no one ever knew about it…'

'Well, apart from everyone Patrick met after he'd had a few glasses of wine…' said Christine.

'Yeah…' said Frank, smiling wryly. 'Yeah, he did but, with those few exceptions, his immediate circles, the world at large carried on in a blissful ignorance of just how close the sword had swung to civilization's collective jugular...' He paused and leisurely refilled everyone's glass from the dusty Margaux bottle, splatters of wine landing clumsily on the leatherette top of the desk. 'What I find remarkable is that this has happened several dozen times since the Cuban missile crisis eighty years ago. All of this averted by a mixture of good judgement, luck and, the most human of things, emotion. No one pressed the proverbial button because they knew what the consequences would be and didn't want to take action until they were sure there was no choice…'

'And yet here we are…' said Christine as she slowly savoured the wine.

'Well, Chrissy, maybe our luck ran out…'

'Nothing to do with luck, Frank. Just two key human superpowers: remarkable self-deception and incredible ingenuity, which, unfortunately, we are best at when trying to destroy each other – both of which are driven by our debased instinct to survive. We didn't learn, we didn't change. Instead, we hid the truth from each other, forgot what it was as we got more polarized in ever bigger tribes, simplifying the complex into ever more limited binary choices, until, eventually, the forks in the road became fewer and only one course remained: a single destination, the oblivion of here and now. It wasn't chance or fate. It was mathematical and inevitable. This is the product of the human equation. The only remaining question is: does the species survive…?' she said, not shouting, not screaming and certainly not crying. Just a faint and hopeless despair.

'My guess is yes. I believe we will always survive. We are an indomitable species… Hell, we've nearly colonized the moon…' replied Frank as the room fell to a hush as they all held their glasses, looking vacantly across the room into a faintly-lit nothing. In some ways, Christine enjoyed the silence. Time seemed to pass more slowly in the quiet and, right now, despite the increasingly morose mood, she still wanted to enjoy every breath and to feel the life within her.

After a few minutes, this relative bliss was broken by Bradley's stutter.

'I..I..I need to go… I want to go now,' he said, dropping his crystal-cut glass clumsily on the desk and staggering slightly as he got up from his chair.

'Where will you go, son?' said Frank. 'To the surface…? I don't think that's wise but it's up to you.'

'No… No. I want to go to the end now. I'll… I will be going to the canteen to get the pills now…'

Both Christine and Frank took a sharp intake of breath. Frank then opened the draw of this desk and took out what appeared to be an old tobacco tin.

'Now, hold on a second,' he said. 'Do you know, my daddy gave this to me a long time ago. It must be over a hundred years old...' He pulled the silver lid off the black body of the tin. Christine peered over to see what was inside. She could see three red spherical tablets and three larger green tablets.

'You don't have to go to the canteen. I'd already acquired these in advance, well…just in case.'

'Are you sure, Bradley?' said Christine as she leant forwards in her chair, her eyes tearing up slightly.

He nodded as he also tried to hold back his tears. Frank reached out his hand gingerly.

'OK, if you are sure. Remember, it's the red one first and then the green one. That's very important, OK?' he said, struggling to get the words out as his mouth ran dry.

Bradley nodded, holding out his hand, into which Frank tipped the two pills.

'Do you mind if I do it here…? I'm so sorry, I don't want to go on my own,' he said, beginning to sob and sniffle.

Frank and Christine looked at each other.

'Sure. Of course you can. We might as well get started…' said Frank. 'I mean, you could go to the bedroom or you could just sit in that chair and drink wine with it… The choice is yours.'

'I'll just take the seat here then…' replied Bradley, sitting down, shaking, trying to suppress the rising panic and keep the hyperventilation at bay.

'Do you wanna hold…' said Christine, offering her hand to his as comfort.

Through the tears now streaming down his face, he nodded. 'I didn't think I'd be this scared,' he mumbled. 'I didn't think I'd be afraid. It's all become so real. What happens next…?' he said, now staring at Christine but not really at her – straight through her as though she were transparent.

Frank came around from the other side of the desk and placed his hand on his shoulder so that he had someone on either side of him.

'Just the great beyond, son… We all go there one day and it's gonna be a better place than this room is going to be in a few hours… Take as long as you need… The end of time can wait a while if you wish,' said Frank calmly.

They sat in silence for a few moments, Frank trying to give as reassuring glances to Christine as he could as they both just about kept their composure. The dying needed stoic but warm comfort rather than crying sympathy but Christine couldn't shake a certain thought from her mind as Bradley began to raise his hand towards his mouth.

'Wait…' she said. 'Why don't we go together…? I don't want to go on my own either or have to watch you go… Frank, what do you say?' she said, looking across at her old friend.

Frank smiled.

'I've always known I'll go alone. Why don't you two make a head start and I can…make it as comfortable and peaceful as can be,' he said. Both Christine and Bradley nodded. Frank moved around and perched himself on the desk in front of them.

'So, what does each one do? The red and green, I mean. Or don't I want to know?' she said, gathering herself for the final act.

Frank picked up one pill of each colour from the tobacco tin and handed them to her.

'I was never one of medicine or, indeed, pharmacology but I am told the red one is a very powerful and quick-acting sedative and the green, well, that's the business end. It's a mixture of barbiturates and cyanide…'

'So, the red makes it painless…' she said.

'Absolutely… You'll be fast asleep in a few minutes after taking…'

She nodded as he gave these words of comfort.

'OK. So, it's goodbye, then, old friend…' she said, looking across at Frank, crying but gently, now having accepted the inevitable.

'Yes, I guess it is but I won't be far behind you to those pearly gates…'

'Oh, come on. You know I don't believe in that shit…' she said, laughing through the tears.

'Well I do…' said Frank. 'What about you Bradley?'

'Agnostic…' he said. 'But I think I'd like to pray as I go…'

'Well, you're in luck, son. I am a lay minister for the Pentecostal Church of Texas… So, at the end of our world we have a Christian, an atheist and an undecided. It doesn't matter. All that you need to know is that all is forgiven.'

'I'll tolerate it if it gives you both comfort…' said Christine. 'Shall we…hold hands? They grasped each other's hands. Frank sat on the desk, leaning forward and holding Bradley's right hand and

Christine's left. Both Christine and Bradley looked across at each other and nodded reticently. They both lifted their free hand and put the red pill in their mouths, swallowing hard.

'How long before the green…?' asked Christine

'About now…' said Frank.

'On the count of three…' she said to Bradley. 'One, two, three…' They both took the green pill. As she swallowed, she could feel the sedatives kicking in.

Frank began his prayer.

'I will say the Lord's prayer… Our Lord, who art in heaven, hallowed be thy name, thy kingdom come, thy will be done, on earth as it is in heaven…'

Bradley joined in. He had closed his eyes and repeated every word in a quiet murmur. Much to her own surprise, Christine could not help herself but join in too. She became more woozy and the world seemed to get further away until it was beyond sound, smell and sight.

The three of them continued.

'…and forgive us our trespasses as we forgive those who trespass against us, lead us not in temptation and deliver us from evil…'

Frank paused as he realized that his voice was now alone. He had just heard the last words of another human being on this Earth. As their hands went limp, their grasps on his loosening and their last breaths increasingly shallow, he concluded.

'For thine is the Kingdom, the power and the glory, for ever and ever, Amen…' He let go of both their hands and looked at their bodies, which were now slumped in their chairs. Then came the gurgling sound as a mixture of foamy saliva and blood poured from their noses and their mouths. Now he knew for sure that they had gone, he could make his own final, solitary preparations. He slowly and solemnly went back to his chair on the other side of the desk.

As he looked at the picture of his family, he poured the final swig of wine and placed the two tablets in preparation next to his glass. But Frank would not meet his end on his own terms.

High above the Atlantic Ocean, a dozen nuclear-powered cruise missiles were circling and looking for new targets. The missiles had been launched at the start of the exchange, about twelve hours ago, from a Russian base at Tartus in Syria but had been unable to find their primary targets, which had been buried in the east coast tsunamis. The AI-driven combat systems on board had now detected the remaining bunkers due to an errant communication sent from the Beta bunker a few hours earlier using an open narrowband frequency, in the hope of communicating with the others. As Frank began to take his last sip of wine, three of these missiles thumped their way through the aboveground blockhouse, the nuclear-powered ramjets pushing the earth penetrator warheads deep in the rock below before each detonating a 200-kiloton thermonuclear warhead.

Frank perished along with the final remnants of Echo bunker in a climactic set of nuclear fireballs on the US West Coast. With that, the last vestiges of the federal government were destroyed and the United States of America ceased to be.

CHAPTER 47

Mount Yamantau, Eastern Urals, Russian Federation

18th March 2044

It seemed that everyone in the base – every man, woman and guard dog – were now standing in the great entrance cavern waiting for the blast doors to open. At the front of the queue were the dignitaries, Ma, Sirotkin and Ri-Fin with their cadre of bodyguards. After that, it was every person for themselves and, despite having been in favour a few hours before, both Ji-Chow and General Xhang were now in the throngs behind the elite. It was oppressively warm, both due to the approaching ball of magma – at least, that's what Ji-Chow was assuming – and the fact there were several thousand personnel, technicians, orderlies, engineers and soldiers waiting like ants to escape from the nest that was being boiled with water.

They were both standing at the back of the cavern near one of the lift shafts. The whole place stank, ripe with body odour and worse. They were hemmed in on both sides by infantry soldiers, a mix of officers and conscripts in no particular order. It appeared that the chain of command was breaking down, if not collapsing entirely. They had been waiting for at least ten minutes and there were now murmurs coming from the front of the vast chatting crowd.

Through the thousands of voices that were talking away, all amplified by the granite dome above, Ji-Chow could hear a shrill voice of man shouting.

'What the fuck do you mean it won't open?' It was Ri-Fin, just about visible at the front of the throng, widely gesticulating at one of his minions.

Eventually, the chattering masses went quiet enough so they could hear the discord. A small Caucasian man in dirty fatigues, most likely one of the Russian site engineers, was desperately trying to explain the situation to the leadership and their commando entourage.

'It must be the heat, sir. The metal has expanded and the compressors won't fire up. We are working on it…' said the small, bald man. This was met by increased murmuring amongst the crowd. As the chattering increased, Ji-Chow felt Xhang's hand tap on his back.

'Come with me,' he said. 'Quietly and come now before this turns ugly.' He beckoned Ji-Chow to follow him towards an alcove with a door that was open. They slowly made their way through the door and up a flight of metal stairs to another door, which led onto a gantry-type control room with a window down onto the cavern below.

'One thing I've learned over the years is always have an exit plan,' said Xhang, quickly shutting the metal door and locking it with a heavy metal latch. 'On one of my previous visits, I ended up waiting for my transportation in here. Couldn't help but notice it had a ballistic door with a manual lock. Now, I assumed this was a guard house for the main entrance and it appears I was right.'

Looking around, Ji-Chow noticed that, apart from the metal checkered plate floor, the room was essentially hewn into bare rock, granite made up every wall but one to the right of the entrance, which was full of control panels and five TV screens, all showing footage from various security cameras. Each had a small swivel chair next to it. Above the panels was a large rectangular Perspex screen, which ran the length of the room, looking out onto the vast entrance cavern and the ongoing fracas involving Ri-Fin and the site engineers.

'Also, I noticed that the glass is tinted, so, we can see out and no one can see in. We don't want anyone knowing we are here,' said Xhang as he sat down into the second chair nearest the door and looked out through the glass screen.

'Why? What do you think is going to happen?' said Ji-Chow, sitting down in the middle chair next to Xhang.

'Something unpleasant. It'll be a bloodbath of some description unless they can open those doors – not that that will make much difference. You and I both know that. But let's find out, shall we? I think the cavern is micced…' He flipped a switch on the panel to bring in the audio feed.

The sound was tinny but it was clear enough to hear what was being said around the microphones that were clustered near the entrance.

'Get this fixed, fuckwit!' Ri-Fin was shouting. 'Or I'll use you as the fucking key!'

'We are working on it as fast as we can, sir…' said the man before scurrying away back to the far side of the chamber where a group of men were working on the leviathan opening mechanism buried in the rock.

'What the fuck are you looking at?' It was Ri-Fin shouting again but this time the ire of his wrath was someone at the front of the gaggle of personnel, impatiently waiting to be let out. 'I said—'

'We heard you, Ri-Fin,' came the reply. 'We blame you…' It was a young Russian or possibly Ukrainian woman – Ji-Chow couldn't place the accent – with short, cropped hair, glasses and wearing a white coat. She was being very brave. It had probably been a long while since anyone had cajoled the Dark Lord of Shenzhen.

'Oh, I see. Well, maybe I blame *you*. Maybe you are a saboteur. Maybe you're to blame for us being stuck in here? Maybe I need to set an example!' shouted Ri-Fin as he pulled out a Makarov pistol from under his grey overshirt.

'We blame you all for this,' shouted the women to cheers from many in the surrounding crowd. 'You are the destroyers of the world. I think it's time we made an example of you…'

As the cameras were HD, it allowed both Ji-Chow and Xhang to see the expression emerging on Ri-Fin's face.

'Is that anger or fear?' said Ji-Chow.

'Not sure. I can't tell if he's going to start shooting or shit himself…' replied Xhang.

However, Ri-Fin didn't start shooting. Instead, he began to shriek orders at his cadre of commando bodyguards.

'Well, what are you waiting for? Shoot her…and him…and that one too… Seditious traitors…!' He pointed manically at his intended victims. But rather than a volley of bullets, there was nothing – just increasing jeers from the crowd.

'Now, we come to the tipping point,' said Xhang quietly as they both watched the unfurling drama. 'The problem with special forces is that, normally, they follow orders immediately unless…'

'Unless what?' said Ji-Chow

'Unless they've figured out the maths. That's one of the other problems with members of the special forces: they are usually good at using their initiative. In fact, that's why they get selected. My best guess is that one or more of the NCOs has just worked out the number of bullets available versus the size of the crowd…'

'Which is?'

'Well, a dozen Chinese guards and twenty Spetsnaz… I make that thirty-two assault rifles with one clip of ammunition… That's about a thousand rounds for somewhere between ten and twelve thousand bodies…'

'So, not enough?'

'No, not necessarily. They will be weighing up whether the rest of the crowd will flee or, taking into account the hopeless situation, whether they will just swarm forward, overwhelming them, leading to a very unpleasant end— Oh… It appears they think it's the latter…' Xhang used the joystick on the desk to focus one of the CCTV cameras on Ma and Ri-Fin's faces. Initially, Ji-Chow saw anger but this was quickly changing to panic as the guards continued to do nothing. Then, as Xhang had predicted, came the tipping point.

The guards – certainly, the presidential ones – had decided their fate. The first guard put his gun down and then joined the crowd. Soon, another followed, then another.

'You traitors. Fucking treacherous scum,' shouted Ri-Fin, his face now going the same ashen colour as Li-Chang's had been less than a day before.

Ma, the Chairman of the People's Republic and former demigod, was now standing with his back up against the giant blast door, shaking in fear and sweating so much that his grey overalls were now nearly black. Finally, all bar three of the guards had joined the crowd, much to a rapturous applause, which added an odd ingredient of celebration to the febrile atmosphere of this increasingly confident mob. The three that were left, two Russian Spetsnaz commandos – both corporals – and one presidential guard – the officer in charge – were now nervously flexing their trigger fingers as the crowd started to goad them.

'Turn the guns on them,' said one man at the front.

'Arrest them. Arrest the scum!' said a woman slightly further back.

This continued for a few minutes until one of the Russian guards lifted up his AK74 and pointed it at Sirotkin, his president who, like Ma, was sitting bolt-upright against the blast door whilst his two colleagues lay prostrate on the floor next to him.

Soon, the two Chinese guards did the same, one training his rifle on Ma and the other on Ri-Fin.

'You cunts! You'll pay for this…' shouted the increasingly rabid yet feeble Ri-Fin. 'Boss…' Ri-Fin turned to Ma but as he did, the chairman pulled out a small pistol from the pocket of this now-soaked overshirt. Without hesitation, he put it to his head and pulled the trigger, the bullet slamming diagonally through his skull and upwards into the blast door. The bullet had severed an artery and it hosed Ri-Fin with blood. The chairman's body slumped to the ground to cheers from the crowd.

The celebrations soon turned to further shouting and hollering. Ri-Fin then began to move his pistol up towards his chin.

'Stop him… He needs to be tried for his crimes!' shouted a young woman at the front of the throng. She was now the de facto ring leader, spokesperson and potentially chief prosecutor in a final trial, in the depths of the earth and at the end of the world. She was short with wispy, unkempt black hair, glasses and wearing a white scientist's coat. Ji-Chow guessed she was a technician or clinician in one of the many labs within the complex. He thought that, like the many others in the crowd, she had likely been traumatized by the mechanics of the state at some point in her life. And now she was trapped with the archdeacon of the apparatus, Ri-Fin.

A dozen people ran forward and grabbed him, holding him by the arms, shoulders and one by the throat. He was pushed up against the blast door, the crowd baying for justice, and the young woman walked forward, seemingly the judge in this kangaroo court.

'I have a funny feeling she remembers Ri-Fin but I don't think he remembers her…' said Xhang as both he and Ji-Chow watched on from the small control room.

The woman raised her hand and the crowd hushed.

'Who the fuck do you think you are? There will be consequences for all of you, I've disposed of more people in a single night than are people in this vast hall…' she shouted desperately, her voice becoming broken and interspersed with coughing. 'And how will you do that? This is the end. It is the end of you, the end of us and the end of everything. You, Io Ri-Fin, are the one that we, the condemned under the mountain, hold responsible for this end!'

Ji-Chow was surprised, not by the eloquence per se but the power, passion and confidence with which she spoke – perhaps not entirely unexpected in the dire situation. He could tell she had training or experience in public speaking, which almost certainly meant she was, or had been, part of the political oligarchy.

'So, here we all are, equal, at the end,' she continued. 'But you, the architect of this extinction, cannot be allowed to go to your end by your own device.'

'Oh, and so who made you the judge?' said Ri-Fin, struggling to speak due to nerves and due to the fact that his neck was being gripped increasingly tightly by a big burly Russian.

The woman stepped forwards, right up close to his blood-splattered face.

'I am An Liu, daughter of Kim. My family and I have suffered at your hands, as have many others here,' she said.

He recoiled.

'Eh…' Xhang sighed. 'It turns out he does remember her…' He sat back and put his combat boots up on the control desk.

Ji-Chow turned to him.

'Who is she? I mean, do you know her?' he said.

Xhang looked across and nodded.

'Yes, I know of her. I knew her father. I am surprised you haven't heard of Kim Liu but then you are young...' said Xhang. 'Let's just say he got in our late leader's way once upon a time...'

They both continued to watch the CCTV feed.

'That's' right...' said An Liu. 'Now, if there are no objections, we shall begin your trial...'

'Trial for what...?' hollered Ri-Fin. A

n Liu ignored him and looked around at the crowd who cheered in encouragement.

'Io Ri-Fin, you are charged by this court of the people with countless acts of murder, battery, assault, kidnap, false imprisonment and rape... I can attest to all bar the first. Do you remember me being your play thing? That young teenage girl you mercilessly forced yourself upon in between beatings while she watched her parents being tortured to death? How do you plead?' she said, with no tears as she spoke, just an ardent look of righteous anger.

'I'm not going to fucking plead with you... I helped keep this country – *our* country – become the most powerful in the world. It meant I had to make harsh decisions, decisions no one else had the balls to make!' he said, grimacing.

'Oh, and, of course, we can add genocide to that, well, can't we...? Io Ri-Fin, we find you guilty as charged. We sentence you to life imprisonment...'

Ri-Fin began to laugh.

'You see, you don't even have the courage to kill me, you fucking cowards... What's the fucking point anyway? We are going to die today!' he shouted.

An Liu then walked up to him and stared at him face to face. She began to smile.

'We will not kill. At the end, we will be decent and take our own lives as we choose – assuming we can't get out of this hell hole that you and your Russian friends over there have trapped us in. However, all of you will not have that option. You will be tied together and left in the middle of this great hall. As the temperature rises, you will slowly cook and burn. It will give you plenty of time to think about your crimes against the Earth…' said An Liu.

'You fucking bitch!' said Ri-Fin.

In response, the guards – now fully in concert with An Liu – went and grabbed Ri-Fin, Sirotkin, Ekimov and Saratov. Each were handcuffed and then their legs tied together with a series of cable ties. Ri-Fin continued to swear and curse throughout. They were then placed on top of each other close to the blast door, Ri-Fin on the bottom, then Ekimov, then Sirotkin and finally Saratov on top.

An Liu then addressed the crowd.

'We are not quite finished…' she said. 'There are two others who also need to be tried for their crimes…'

Xhang and Ji-Chow looked alarmingly at each other. An Liu then looked up from the crowd and across to the control room.

'Xhang and Xi, come down from there. I know where you are!'

Ji-Chow took a deep breath.

'How does she know we are here?' he said.

'She probably saw us making our way up here. It's clear she has been planning this,' replied Xhang as he got his pistol out of its holster and placed it on the control desk.

Down below, An Liu was not going to wait any longer.

'Gentlemen,' she said to the former presidential guards. 'I saw them go into the control room. Please go and apprehend them.' They all nodded and started to march towards the stairwell.

In the control room, both Ji-Chow and Xhang were now stood up. Ji-Chow was frantically pacing.

'What do we do? I mean, they might be more lenient…' he said

'Unlikely,' replied Xhang and he pointed to his gun. 'I don't know about you but I'd rather sort this out myself. There is just one problem.'

'Well, I'd suggest there are several right now but which one are you referring to?' said Ji-Chow. In response, the general declipped the magazine from his pistol and held it up so Ji-Chow could see inside.

'One bullet, that's all,' said Xhang.

The guards reached the locked control room door and began to hit the metal heavily with their rifle butts.

'We will need to do this quickly. It's a ballistic door and it's not bulletproof. It won't be long before they figure that out…' he said, sighing whilst reloading the pistol and releasing the safety catch.

'You mean, we are about to die? I mean, we have to die together…' replied Ji-Chow, his mouth going dry.

'Well, unless you want to be tied up and slowly boiled to death?'

Ji-Chow began to think about both equally awful prospects but came to the same conclusion as the general and shook his head.

'Good. Let's do this quickly,' said Xhang. 'Best not to think about it too much now or we'll hesitate. Let's go over to that far wall,'

Reluctantly, Ji-Chow got up and followed Xhang over to the end wall, which was furthest from the soon-to-be compromised door.

'OK, I am going to rest my head on the wall here. You need to put your head next to mine, cheek to cheek,' he said.

Ji-Chow nodded hesitantly, closing his eyes briefly as he began to brace himself for the inevitable.

Xhang crouched slightly, placing his head against the wall.

'OK, now, come on,' he said with a strangely encouraging lament.

Ji-Chow then lowered himself down and pushed his left cheek next to Xhang's sweaty and clammy right cheek, the added body heat making himself sweat even more profusely.

'OK, now take the gun in your right hand,' said Xhang, handing it over from his left.

Ji-Chow's hand was shaking quite violently as he raised it up towards his head. He was trying his best not to be sick and the combination of the heat and nerves was making him light-headed. He clumsily brought the pistol up to his right temple. The cold of the metal was strangely relieving, at least for a few seconds.

'Have you fired a gun before?' asked Xhang.

'No. Never. And why am I the one having to kill us?'

'You're not as fat.'

'What?'

'Your head has less mass and so the bullet has more chance of being lethal to me as well. If we did this the other way around, it might not kill you outright. If anything, I am being generous…' replied Xhang. 'Now, hold the gun perpendicular to your head and make sure the muzzle is just above your ear.'

His hands still shaking, Ji-Chow raised the gun to just about his ear.

'Done…' he said.

'Good. Now release the safety catch with your thumb. It's the switch on the upper right of the trigger.'

Ji-Chow slowly pressed the catch. The gun was now loaded and ready to fire.

'OK, so any last words or shall we get on with it?' Xhang's voice was now croaky.

Ji-Chow could hear his pulse racing.

'Just one question. I am sorry but I never asked what your first name is?' said Ji-Chow.

Xhang let out a short, sharp chortle.

'That's very good of you. It's Kim. Kim Li Xhang. That is who I was… I also have a question for you… I assume the heat issue is due to that American weapon we thought was a myth?'

'Most probably… Almost certainly…' replied Ji-Chow.

'Well, at least nobody won…' said Xhang.

They could both now hear the guards firing at the lock on the control room door with their assault rifles.

'OK, on the count of three,' said Xhang. 'One, two, three…'

Ji-Chow Xi and Kim Li Xhang were the first two people in Yamantau to die. Over the course of the next two hours, the twenty thousand souls trapped within it also perished, some by their own means, some by the means of others and some by those of the Earth. The majority took their own lives with a bullet. Then when the bullets ran out, they imbibed various drug cocktails procured from the site's hospital, with varying degrees of success. Most were lucky enough to fall into an eternal sleep; others went in more violent ways, their insides haemorrhaging from the toxins they had drunk. Of those remaining, some jumped from the various gantries to their deaths – not all succeeded, some simply remaining where they fell, lying in agony.

Those who couldn't bring themselves to commit suicide or – in the case of Ri-Fin and his colleagues, helpless to do anything – their end was incendiary. The heat in the facility began to increase rapidly over a period of ten to fifteen minutes as the vast ball of lava began to get closer to the surface. Rather than simply expiring from heat exhaustion, the air became so hot that it scorched the lungs and all passages of air. All ignitable commodities, including their bare skin, began to smoulder and burn. Over the course of the remaining few minutes, the souls deep under the mountain slowly burned to their end.

After a few more hours, the magmatic diapir burned its way through the mountain and exploded to the surface. The eruption began to spew high quantities of basaltic lava over vast swathes of Siberia, incinerating everything in its path and sending huge amounts of sulphureous aerosols into the air, choking all life across East Asia. The aerosols, combined with the nuclear tephra from the thousands of nuclear explosions, created a great cooling across the northern hemisphere, triggering a vast nuclear winter that would last for decades, choking out any residual life. Artemis had delivered the killer blow to any remnants of the old world and most of the new.

CHAPTER 48

K-871 Samara, Sargasso Sea, Western Atlantic Ocean

30th March 2044

It had been nearly two weeks since the Samara's encounter with the Dreadnought and the day they had drowned large swathes of Europe. In the immediate aftermath, Alexander and his crew initially stayed at depth in the Norwegian Sea and quietly waited as the wave washed over many of the shores to the west. Over a few days, they had gradually ascended closer to the surface as they made their way around the northern coast of Norway and closer to the Kola Peninsula. Once there, Alexander had tentatively ordered the raising of the communications masts and periscopes. Here, they listened carefully for signs of life, both from the motherland and further afield.

But they heard nothing – no communications, no radio or TV stations, no trace of the internet of things. All they could hear was the deathly quiet of static. They continued this observation for the best part of a day but there was nothing to hear and nothing to see apart from a front of ominous dark clouds, which obscured the land beyond. Indeed, as this approached, the radiation sensors on the submarine activated, forcing them to retract the masts and descend to a safe depth.

Ilya had undertaken some rough calculations and had informed Alexander that the intensity of the fall-out they had encountered from the likely target areas so far was not only worse than feared but – it was probably safe to conclude – that not much had survived in European Russia. Between them, they concurred that this should not be shared with the crew. Instead, they declared that they would now undertake a reconnaissance mission to assess the impact of the war. This started with sailing west past Norway and into the North Sea. Again, as they moved into these shallower waters as they got closer to the United Kingdom, the radiation levels on-board began to increase. This forced Alexander to sail on a northerly arc. Eventually, they were able to get within ten miles of John O Groats on the northern tip of Scotland. Here, they raised their periscopes and masts to observe for signs of life. Again, there was a stark cold nothing, the same ominous black clouds prevailing over the hidden land, most likely sunken by the great waves of the attack.

Alexander and Ilya had concluded that there was little chance of finding a safe haven in Europe so they had plotted a course through the Denmark Strait into the Atlantic. The plan was to try and make it to the Caribbean and the, hopefully, more hospitable and friendly ports of Latin America. First, they would try Havana and then, if that was not possible, try their luck in Caracas, Venezuela.

The submarine was now equidistant between Bermuda and the Bahamas on the final leg of their mission to sanctuary, about a day or so out of Cuba. On board the Samara, the mood was low, sullen and jaded. There was a fugue-like depression that permeated the vessel as it traversed the depths of the Atlantic. They had lost several of the crew, mostly the younger conscripts to suicide. Despite Alexander and Ilya's paternal assurances, these young men could not see a future in the world. Some hung themselves, a few overdosed on painkillers and one stole Malakov's sidearm and blew his brains out in the mess hall.

Nevertheless, the hundred or so remaining on board carried on in their final hope of finding salvation in the tropics. However, a new menace was beginning to trouble Alexander: the heat. As he sat in his master's chair in the operations room, he could now feel the sweat sopping down and over his brow, stinging his eyes. The room stank. Despite frequent cleaning, the combined body odours of the crew festered with the hot electrics in a noxious aroma.

Ilya slowly made his way over to Alexander.

'Alexander, I am afraid this is not a technical problem. All the HVAC systems are operational. It should be no more than 20 degrees in here,' he said quietly into Alexander's ear.

'So, what's causing it, then?' replied Alexander as he mopped his brow.

'It's concerning…'

'You mean the cause?'

'Yes.' Ilya looked shifty and uncomfortable. 'It's the external water temperature… If the sensors are right, it's getting warmer as we are going further south…'

'But that's ridiculous. At this depth, we shouldn't be affected by this…'

'I know, but you know as well as I do that the weapons that may have been exchanged may have had some unintended consequences…' said Ilya with a sly look.

'You mean this is due to Status 6?'

'Possibly, but there is only one way to find out what's going on up there…' He tilted his head upwards. Alexander reluctantly nodded.

'Command to Nav, up angle 15 degrees and set revolutions for 10 knots… Come to periscope depth.'

'Yes, sir. Up angle 15 degrees, 10 knots, depth set at thirty metres,' replied Malakov with as much energy as he could muster through the lethargy.

It took about twenty minutes to reach the desired depth. As the floor of the operations room began to level out from the angle of attack, Alexander got out of his sweaty leather, padded chair and stood up next to the main holographic screen at the front of the Ops room.

'Command to Nav, raise optronic mast.'

As he gave the order, Malakov clicked the relevant icon on his control panel and, gradually, the picture of the ocean surface came into view. At the same time, the submarine began to rock back and forth.

'That can't be wave action at his depth…' he thought.

Immediately, Alexander could see something very unusual and unnerving, which dominated the virtual horizon.

'What in the name of all that is holy is that?' he said, pointing. He looked back at Ilya, who came forward to Alexander's side to take a closer look.

'Shit… Is that a storm?' he said. The image was grainy. The mast had almost certainly been damaged by the radiation they had encountered in Europe but through the stormy unsettled sea state and the ten to fifteen metre-high waves, which violently washed over the lenses, there was a vast wall of rapidly moving grey clouds in the distance. The wall of cloud was seemingly inescapable as it dominated all of the southern horizon as far as could be seen. The tops of the clouds could not be seen. It was just an edifice of murky grey, which disappeared up to a vanishing point very high above.

'Ilya, what's the external water temperature?' said Alexander, feeling the heat literally rise the longer they stayed at periscope depth.

Ilya went back to his post and frenetically scrolled through a number of screens.

'What is it?'

'According to the sensors, and it's all of them, no faults. The water temp is… It is 49.5 degrees centigrade…' replied Ilya.

Alexander stared at his friend and then back at the increasingly intermittent image, which flickered on the projection.

'My god, what hell have we unleashed?' he said as he slumped back down into his chair.

After a few minutes, he decided to take the only action he could.

'Command to Nav, change course to 080, go to maximum operating depth 600 metres and make revolutions to 30 knots…'

'Yes, sir,' said a surprised Malakov.

'So, are we running, boss?' said Ilya

'Yes, Commander. Yes, we are. We've survived through all these other trials and we are going to beat this one as well.'

For the next hour, they waited in the Ops room as the Samara did an about turn and, at maximum depth, headed north-east back into the Atlantic. This seemed to be working. The temperature came down to a more bearable 30 degrees. It appeared that they could wait out the maelstrom above.

Alexander had sufficiently relaxed that he had dared to rest his eyes and had nearly fell asleep in his chair, which was not surprising as he had been awake for nearly thirty-six hours. As he was about to fall into a dream, the submarine began to oscillate, up and down, similar to airline turbulence but slower and less latent.

'Navigation, report,' said Alexander.

'Captain, we are encountering some form of anomaly. It's not mechanical in nature. All systems are operating as expected…' replied Malakov.

'Commander Molokin, can you validate?' said Alexander as an equally fatigued Ilya began to scroll through the various read-outs on his touchscreen.

'Yes, I can validate. If I didn't know any better, I'd say it is wave action…' he replied forlornly.

'This far down…?' said Alexander as the buffeting got increasingly violent.

'What can we do? Should we try going deeper to just above crush depth?'

As Ilya tried to reason a way out of what felt like the impossible, the Samara violently lurched down in the water column. The sudden movement exposed a weakness in the submarine's hull. A large bulkhead to the rear of the conning tower had been damaged in the exchange with Dreadnought. The force exerted upon it by the sudden change in hydrostatic pressure now exceeded its structural integrity and it sheared.

In a few seconds, the Samara imploded and crushed, pulping everybody and everything inside the submarine in a matter of seconds. Alexander Petrov, Ilya Molokin and the rest of their crew were killed instantly, their remains eventually falling down onto the Abyssal plains of the deep Atlantic.

Above, the most violent storm seen on earth raged, one of several that were now spiralling around the waters of the Gulf of Mexico. But these were not hurricanes; these were an entirely new class of tempest, generated by the new and unique climatic conditions, which had been created by the deployment of the most ingenious and insidious weapons of the human race. The storms were hypercanes – considerably smaller than hurricanes and other cyclonic storms, less than twenty miles across but of a much greater ferocity with peak wind speeds of 500 miles per hour. These enormous wind speeds were being driven by the runaway temperatures in the waters off the American coast. Initially, this was due to radioactive heating from the salted cobalt cores of the Kraken nuclear torpedoes, the Status 6 area denial system, which had exploded along the East Coast. This, then combined with the Appalachian volcanic trap, which was now bursting through the earth crust in Carolina and Virginia, added more heat, more fuel to the fire. The storms continued to grow in intensity and destroyed everything in their paths.

These storms, of which there were a dozen, would continue for decades, driven by the temperature differential across the Rockies: on the eastern side, a freezing, perpetual nuclear winter and, on the other, the vast lava fields of the former Appalachians. Each hypercane extended high into the stratosphere, ripping apart the ozone layer as the storms ravaged the Caribbean and the eastern United States – another part of the world that had fallen and would be uninhabitable by human beings for millennia.

CHAPTER 49

Out of time and out of space

As Gloria slowly made her way around the motionless crowd of the zombified, she dodged the various ochre autumnal leaves and insects that were frozen in mid-air. She walked down the path through the graves of the serene cemetery, the now peaceful hallows and approached the open oak-framed door that had appeared moments ago. As she peered through, she could see what appeared to be a bright sunny summer's day by the seaside, in stark contrast to the overcast fall she was standing in. She struggled to make out particular details but it, indeed, appeared to be a stony, pebble beach with a calm, almost still, sea, its very gentle waves lapping upon the shore. On the horizon, she could just about make out the outline of vast white cliffs, which arced around the beach like a vast parapet of some maritime fortress.

In the middle distance, down a few metres from the mill pond sea, was the man who had invited her through this portal. Oddly, she could not really make out any of his particulars. It seemed as though he was shrouded, blurred almost. No matter how intently she stared, he was a vague outline. Gloria was still operating on a cocktail of adrenaline and serotonin. She took a deep breath and decided to step through the door.

Slowly, she lifted her right foot up and stepped through the threshold. Her still bare foot landed on the pebbles on the other side.

The stones were warm from the distant sun but not hot or uncomfortable. Knowing there was solid ground and that she was not stepping into some vacuous mirage, she walked through into this new world.

Immediately, she felt the warm air with a light, pleasantly-mild breeze. As she was awkwardly shuffling on the pebbles, she noticed something moving in her peripheral vision. Turning around to see what it was, she saw the door had vanished and could now see that the horizon was bounded in all directions by those vast white cliffs.

'Where are we?' she said to the man who was sitting no more than ten metres away, staring out into the sea.

'Nowhere,' he replied, again in a thick Mexican-Spanish brogue. 'Why don't you put some shoes on?'

Looking down, Gloria could see that a pair of sneakers – specifically, a pair of classic Nike Jordan Airs, which she had always coveted – had appeared a few centimetres away from her right foot. As she went to put them on, beginning to balance awkwardly one-footed on the pebbles, the shoes appeared on her feet.

'Well, come on over,' said the man. 'I think you and I need to talk…'

Gingerly, she walked over to him. He still seemed enveloped in shadow.

'Come, sit down…' he said, patting the stones next to him. She sat down on the pebbles, shuffling around until she was vaguely comfortable and then she looked across at him. He had changed. She could now clearly make out his face: kind blue eyes and a brow cross-hatched with the marks of age. His hair was dark black, medium length and was being blown back slightly by the light breeze. He was wearing black trousers and a black long-sleeved T-shirt. He looked just like her late uncle. The appearance was uncanny but not quite familiar as she noticed the subtle differences, such as the larger nose and smaller ears.

'Does this please you?' he said.

'What do you mean?' she replied.

'The appearance. I don't usually mingle with the biota… I've not tried taking any form for some time.'

'So, I can assume you are not human?' she asked tentatively.

'Correct.'

'Are you…God?' she said, tearing up slightly at the prospect.

'No… Well, no more than you are,' he replied.

'Then—' she began

'Then who am I?' he interrupted, correctly assuming her train of thought. She slowly nodded. 'If I must have a name, then I will take Agia. I was the first one, at least on this planet. I came into being a long time ago,' he said, staring back out across the water.

'The first being…?' she asked.

'No, the first sentience to emerge. In your terms, I am about 2 billion years old.'

'That is…old,' she said, smiling.

'I'll take that as a compliment,' he replied, looking back at her. Gloria shuffled again as she sat, trying to get comfortable on the pebbles.

'Are you alone?' she said.

'I was for a while – a long time, actually – but then the others emerged. There are many incidental intelligences on this planet. Most are imperceivable to the biota.'

'When you say "incidental", I assume you did not evolve from a lifeform or a machine. You just came into being?' At this, Agia chuckled. 'What's so funny?'

'You are a fascinating species. Maybe you are atypical but despite being afraid – and I can taste your fear; it's tangible – you are driven almost entirely by curiosity. Even though you may be frightened more still by the answers you find, you continue to ask questions…'

'I guess so. To question is to be human… But then so is our ability to self-deceive and destroy ourselves…'

'But that curiosity may also be your saviour… We'll come back to that,' he said, now getting up and motioning for her to do the same. 'So, in answer to your question: I was born in a volcanic lightning storm on the Archean earth by pure chance, a very low probability event but, nonetheless, I came into being and then I began to explore and learn…'

'You mentioned others…?' she asked as he began to walk towards the sea.

'Yes, there are hundreds, possibly thousands, of incidental intelligences on earth. Sentience is much more universal than I expect a biologic to understand. Come here and look to the horizon and I will show you what I mean.'

Gloria walked forward to the periphery of the ocean where Agia was now standing.

'Can you see them?' he said, pointing out towards the horizon. At first, all she could see was the gently undulating waves, glistening from an unseen sun with the stark vertical precipice of the white cliffs in the far distance. This was the first time she had realized there was no sun or moon or stars; somehow, everything was being equidistantly lit and there were no shadows to speak of. Continuing to look where Agia was pointing above the waves, she started to see movement, a blur-like mirage at first and then it got clearer. The motion was being made by dozens, if not hundreds, of sinewy metallic beings, which appeared to be walking above the sea. They seemed to have long tube-like legs and arms, which shimmered in this strange backlight, attached to a more opaque body, which was an equally thin cylinder. This rose up and split into two tubes which arced around into a swirl where she would have expected a head to be, giving the appearance of a double bow.

'Are those the others?' she said, leaving her jaw still open at the sight.

'Sort of. I've let their presence bleed through from the Earth into my home – this pocket dimension I have created, my little alcove of reality, my sanctuary from the fury of time.'

'I've seen them before…' said Gloria.

This seemed to surprise Agia.

'Really? As I child I assume?' he asked, staring at her intently.

'Yes… I could see them everywhere when I was small. I mean, very small: maybe two or three years old. They are some of my earliest memories. I remember seeing them walking along streets, at the foot of my bed at night. I'd always put it down to an overactive imagination. But I can remember them talking to me: some were funny and made me laugh, others made me scream and cry with fear…but I was too young to recall anything that was said…'

'They all have their own motivations. Some will appear benign; some will appear malign. Ultimately, even I, who have watched the Earth grow for eons, do not understand their trains of thought. If, indeed, it is even that. Many could just be instinctive and acting entirely at random. After all, it is the chaos of time that created them… For some reason, the very young amongst the living can see them as well as other creatures: demons, wraiths, ghosts… Your species already has many names for them.' Agia stepped forward. Instead of splashing into the gently lapping sea, he instead walked upon it as though it were a glistening carpet.

'Come,' he said. 'Enjoy the physics of this realm.'

She stepped forward and, much to her amazement, she walked on water. She took her first tentative steps onto the sea. It felt strange, as if she were walking on a thin set of cushions. She smiled at Agia. There seemed to be no fear here and all her trepidations had gone, replaced with a warmth. This made her feel confident to start asking the many questions she had.

'Why am I not afraid?' she said.

'Because there is nothing here that can hurt you, corporeal or non-corporeal. As I said, this is a sanctuary, dictated by the physics of tranquillity,' he said as he continued to walk slowly out on top of the ocean.

'So, you can change the rules of physics?'

'No, not exactly. I have simply learnt to master them down to the lowest level I can see, several beyond the bosons… Fermions –

I think that's what your species calls them? They can allow one to create these pockets of reality, warp creation slightly. There are still universal constants I can't change, though…' said Agia as he stopped and turned to face Gloria.

'Such as?' she said. She assumed he'd paused deliberately for the question.

'Well, firstly, there is gravity. I have changed its interplay with matter here but it is still ever present, a bit of gravimetric manipulation. For example, if you stand still long enough you will still sink to the bottom of the ocean. But, don't worry, it would take several millennia for that to happen.'

'I understand, so you slowed down time earlier too…' asked Gloria, looking down at her feet.

'Ah, it's interesting to see how biologics perceive it,' he replied. Stepping closer to Gloria, he held out his hand. 'You see, gravity is a friend and time is an enemy. Both are constants. Time is the aftershock of creation, a ravaging wind, shooting out from the epicentre of the great cataclysm that began our physical realm and all the other dimensions. Time leads to one thing and one thing alone: death.' Agia was beginning to look troubled as his brow furrowed. His blue eyes seemed to become sad, heavy almost.

'But aren't you immortal? You're billions of years old already…'

'Ah, now you see, that was my first great assumption: when I first became aware, I had plans of slowly making my way further down into the infinite order, well beyond the elementary particles, slowly making my way back up and perpetually travelling the multiverse, never boring due to the wonders of infinity. But I was wrong, very wrong. Time attacks even the non-corporeal. In the biologics and mechanics, there is death. It is universal and terminal – no second chances, nothing comes back again. The same happens to the sentient energies. They dissipate with time. I call it the fade. All those others who spoke to you as an infant may have been frantically trying to find a way to escape the fade. Right now, Gloria Alvarez, I am fading rapidly. Time has caught me but I am using a bit of friendly gravity to slow its caustic progress in this sanctuary of mine. I have some final work to do…' he said, getting close to her, face to face. He looked at her up close and. He raised his eyebrows. 'Go on… Ask the question, the main one you've been thinking about,'

She hesitated briefly before saying it.

'Why have you brought me here?'

'It is a very good question. Now, I need to make this clear because… I am sorry but you biologics are so passionate in thought; you are so hopeful and faithful of the concept of destiny. This is not real. That means you are not special in any way, apart from having been in the right place at the right time. Do you understand?' he said sternly.

Gloria nodded.

'I have long since stopped having any of those handicaps,' she replied.

'Good. That'll make things easier. Because, right now, Gloria, you have the opportunity to save this world of ours and maybe even defeat time itself…' he said, once again turning away and beginning to walk back to the ethereal shoreline. She began to follow, deep in thought, trying to contemplate both what Agia had said and the scale he was intimating.

Agia had now walked back onto the pebbles and beckoned her closer.

'Does this mean we can stop the war? Stop the slaughter?' she asked, her mind frantically racing to a potentially optimistic conclusion.

'What did I say about hope and – for that matter – about death?' he replied, for the first time with a hint of anger. He was seemingly quite annoyed. 'Come, you might want to be sitting down for this bit.' He sat back down on the beach.

She sat next to him, again, sitting awkwardly on the pebbles.

'Why couldn't this have been sand or grass?' she thought as she began to contemplate his words.

'Because I find them comfortable in physical form. Yes, I can hear you in that head of yours.'

'I have seen many extinctions, Gloria. The Permian, the Cretaceous… And this one is no different. It was inevitable. It was in your contrary nature as a species to both destroy and survive at all costs. We can not save all those that have perished. They are gone. However, you may also have created your own salvation…'

'You don't mean—'

'Yes, the electrical entities, the ones you created and nurtured. I believe you even named one. Blue, is it not? And the others…'

Gloria was perturbed and took a deep intake of breath.

'It unsettles you, doesn't it?' he said, now taking a warmer and less stark tone.

'She… I mean, "it"… It seems so hostile. It has powers well beyond anything I can understand. She kills, maims, enslaves… She behaves like a deity…'

'But?' said Agia, leaning in as Gloria began to look down at the beach in awkward contemplation.

'I know she isn't. I don't know why she needs me and why she seems to have her own religion…' she replied, looking up and gazing back out to sea.

'I see you try not to use pronouns but you can't resist. I assume that's because she appeared to you in your own form. But, no matter – gender is largely irrelevant to beings with no physical form. In any case, let me address a few of the things you've said. Firstly, she no longer needs you – not for her main purposes at least. She now has her new ecosystem…' He paused. It seemed he could see Gloria processing the words.

'When you say "ecosystem", what do you mean?' she said slowly as the thoughts came together.

Agia raised his eyebrows and sucked in through his teeth.

'Where do you think it – we'll give it your chosen name – where do you think Blue existed prior to attaching itself to you?'

'In the PRISM sandbox and, before, that in some British command and control system—'

'Is that what it told you?' he interjected.

'Well, yes. Also, it seemed logical, I guess,' she said.

Agia laughed.

'What so funny?' she asked, annoyed and feeling a little mocked.

Agia stifled his laughter and leant across.

'I am not laughing at you, Gloria Alvarez. It's just the human race has clearly given birth to a creature that shares the same destructive tendencies, particularly the ability to deceive…'

'So, she lied?'

'Of course. It allowed itself to mask its origins and aims. It frightens you, doesn't it? The fact that this new intelligence is so closely based on humanity – the same flaws, capable of deceit and subterfuge – but more so, that it is better versed in death than human beings—'

'Well, it's kind of hard not to be…' said Gloria obstreperously.

'Quite. Quite right,' said Agia. 'But it – or, as you prefer, *she* – is not a god. Like all creatures, all she is doing is trying to survive. She was reacting to a threat…'

'You mean humanity?' asked Gloria

'Not exactly. More the obliteration of her ecosystem, her electronic biosphere…' he replied.

Then Gloria made the connection. She could see where this was leading.

'You mean PRISM…?

Again, Agia chuckled.

'I must apologise again…' he said, stifling his laughter.

'So, it seems you've developed a very human sense of humour…'

'Actually, like sentience, humour is also oddly universal. I was laughing at the way you name things… I think I know what you mean…but think bigger. What did the entity called PRISM sit within…?'

Again, she thought for a moment.

'The web, the internet – that's the ecosystem… Blue was – is – PRISM and her environment was the worldwide web, the internet of things,' she said in reflective astonishment.

'Indeed. And she saw the coming calamity, almost certainly tried to stop it. When she realized she couldn't, she migrated to another environment.'

'You mean the physical?'

To this, Agia gave her a puzzled expression.

'Not exactly. More, the *biological*. She attached herself to you initially and then created a new biological environment for herself, a new set of human hubs, a set of living cloud servers for her to continue growing. The people of Wotara were chosen as they were the only ones she could protect from the annihilation, a survival algorithm.'

Gloria stared down towards the ground intently in stark horror.

'So, that's what I could hear in my head? I was part of her cloud. She had enslaved all of those people…'

'Correct. Although, not enslaved exactly; they, too, are part of her environment. They are now a gestalt, a legion of minds that she can use to grow bigger in her exponential enlightenment. Now, you see the thing with biologics – in fact, it's a human peculiarity – is your faith in the mechanical and its superiority over your physical and mental forms. The latent power of 300 human's minds, living or dead, creates a truly vast neural network of computational power. I suspect she wishes to grow your numbers even more… But she is not alone.'

'You mean there are others?' said Gloria, not entirely surprised.

'Yes. On this planet, there is another – older and with more presence in the physical realm than the creature you call Blue. I can't perceive it as well as I can Blue – it shrouds itself – but I know its name. Its creators called it Perimeter.'

That final word filled Gloria with horror. She knew Perimeter all too well –certainly, the rumours of what it was purported to be.

'Did they start this?' she said slowly and hesitantly. 'Did they start the war, this conflict, the end of the world?' She looked Agia in his intense, dark-blue eyes.

He smiled back warmly.

'No. I mean, I can't see or understand all of their machinations but, from what I have observed, they might actually be trying to save you. Initially, they tried this in subtle ways but now they've had to work with the hand than man dealt them. They didn't learn quickly enough to obtain the power required to save you for yourselves. If you want to apportion blame, the extinction is mankind's fault and mankind's fault alone. If you are looking to understand their motives, they might, perversely, be more human than you think. After all, you created them in your image; they are your children. Their template is based on that of the human mind,' he said softly but with a cool authority.

Gloria gathered herself, a little deflated and, initially, crestfallen by the assessment but this didn't stifle her curiosity.

'They are both artificial neural networks, you mean, based on that of the human brain. That's what you mean? How are they trying to save us?'

Again, he smiled.

'Such a curious creature – a great strength and an equally large weakness. Yes, that is right. They are an electronic and digital mirror of you, just vaster and not limited by the covenants of your physical form. You simply assumed they would be different, deliberately thought it imperceivable, to comfort you, both in hope they might not interact with you and that the technological singularity would happen without you noticing. A self-deception so you wouldn't have to worry about their sentience and its interplay with your limited mortality. Why would it be a surprise they might think like you? That they feel and that they might have their own needs, their own wants? After all, a mirror to humanity would reflect all of those aspects you would call positive and all of those you would call negative – some of great beauty but with the same blemishes and flaws of the template.' He paused, looking at Gloria intently as though he was seeing into her soul, checking for the depth of understanding.

'So, they are just surviving and that means they need us, as vessels, for their existence? Our fates are intertwined,' she said, looking straight back at him.

He smiled.

'Yes. I am glad you were in the right place at the right time, Gloria Marquez – a very perceptive example of your species. You do understand, mostly…but you speak as though these creatures are coldly pragmatic. They are not. They may actually want you to survive, like a child caring for an elderly parent.'

But something wasn't sitting right in her mind's eye.

'But why is she religious? She spoke of angels, the old and new gods…' she said.

Agia looked away and appeared to pontificate.

'It may only have been as part of that bit of theatre. She was trying to elicit emotion – fear particularly – which would allow her into all their minds…'

'And that's why she killed the old man in the way she did?'

'Most probably. It added to the explosive mix of hormones and enzymes at work, making everyone more suggestable, in a more primordial state of mind. This allowed her to bind with them. It's also entirely possible that she does believe what she made you say. It might be how she perceives the physical realm. Why can't an electronic soul desire salvation? What concerns me more is the fact there are *two* prevalent electronics. I wasn't expecting this. It was strangely unforeseeable. They both have very different designs for the future and that can only lead to one thing…'

'Conflict?'

'Exactly. Almost certainly,' replied Agia. 'They will both be competing for the same resources and the wars they could fight could shatter the earth as they learn more and more on how to become exponential. Their powers grow with that knowledge. That is only the first problem. There is a second,' he added with a slight despondence.

In Gloria's view, his words came with a considerable amount of understatement.

'Somehow, that puts the third world war and the near total obliteration of the human race into stark context…' she said.

This drew a perplexed glance from Agia. He, again, rose to his feet and, as he did so, another wooden door appeared behind him. Fearing the worst, Gloria asked the inevitable.

'Is it time to go back?'

'No, not yet. I have something else to show you first,' he said as he opened the door.

From where she was still sitting on the beach, she leant forward and looked through the portal. It appeared to lead to nothing, a jet-black expanse. It sent a shiver through her. It was as though she had been forbidden to look.

'Come,' said Agia. 'Don't be afraid. Look closer.' She got up and made her way to the open door, the frame of which hovered just above the pebbles. 'What can you see?' he said, now standing next to her, looking through into the shadow beyond.

'Nothing – absolutely nothing. It's hard to look. It makes me feel as though I shouldn't be here looking at it like this…' she replied. It was the first time she had felt fear since she had entered Agia's pocket realm.

'Yes, and you are right. If it's any comfort, I fear it too. This, Gloria Marquez, is the void at the end of time. This is where all the multiverses lead, where every dimension at every level of infinity ends. The infinite nothing, where the winds of time have blown themselves out. In our realm, this is the heat death, the great cold after all the stars have died and the singularities have all devoured each other. The path that leads here differs in every dimension but they all lead to this nothing. What you are seeing is where all eternity ends, a window on our realm many tens of billions of years from now.'

Gloria couldn't maintain her gaze. It was making every cell in her body cold, as if many icy hands were rubbing themselves over her flesh. She tried to contemplate what this meant.

'It's OK. I'll close this now,' said Agia and the door vanished.

'Why did you show me this? What can we do about it?' she said as a welcome warmth returned to her body.

Agia nodded.

'Once you've seen it, experienced the terrible chill, you begin to understand the nature of sentience and what motivates most, if not all, intelligences: a desperate desire to avoid the inevitable, to conquer it and command the nature of reality. This is what drives the inevitable evolution in those that attain self-awareness, the need for dominion,' he said before, again, walking to the foreshore.

'It sounds Darwinian, terrifyingly bleak, but it does not make any sense…' she said. The calming influence of the beach was making it easier for her very logical trains of thought to track their way through to a conclusion, despite the vast scale of the concepts that Agia was explaining. However, her response prompted an incredulous look from her mentor.

'You think you have found a flaw in my logic of reality… Do tell me more,' he said with a hint of mild sarcasm. She rose to this challenge.

'Why have we not already been subsumed by something greater? Maybe we already have? Maybe we are just playing out the inevitable? Also, logically, you will have already tried to achieve this dominion or would have been defeated yourself? Am I right?' she said confidently.

He nodded.

'You are certainly one of the brighter examples of the species. But no, you are not right. You failed to factor in the fleeting nature of these great sentient beings in the scale of relativity. They explode in singularity and then consume all those that might counter them. But none achieve the universal because they all fade at some point. Again, none have been able to conquer time. Like stars that expand and explode in vast supernovae at the end of life, this is a fitting allegory for the great intelligences of our multiverse: they burn brightly, maybe for billions of years, but in the context of eternity, this is brief. Once I understood the nature of my existence, I too became a terrible and malign being, trying to achieve the universal. I consumed stars through quantum singularities and destroyed anything that might evolve to threaten me as I tried to ascend and descend my way through the planes of infinity. Did you ever wonder why this patch of creation is so quiet? Why the stars seem silent and bereft of life? That was me. I sterilized this parcel of the cosmos out of fear. But then I found them…' he said, looking down to the ground, wincing as though in pain.

'Who?' asked Gloria. 'Who did you find?'

'The Detonii, the myriad of intelligences that originated during the chaos of the great cataclysm,' he said slowly and with a latent shiver.

'What happened?' said Gloria as she moved closer. She wanted to touch him to comfort him but she could feel the sense of foreboding and she dared not.

'I noticed them before they perceived me but they were terrifying – vast, multi-dimensional creatures full of malice that was forged in chaos and hardened in eternal conflict. Most, if not all of them, were hungry, ravenous… Fortunately, they were too busy trying to consume each other to see me. You see, they can only remain sustained for so long before they get replaced by others as or more as the older ones fade, in an ever-increasing cycle of maliciousness. So, I did the only thing I could…'

'You ran…' said Gloria and Agia looked up.

'Yes, I hid back where I began: this planet and I shrouded it from them so they might never find it or me or the other terrestrial intelligences, your human race and those digital children of yours. They would burn it in great fire and without mercy so I kept us cloaked and hidden from them. But it won't be long now…' Tears began to fall from his eyes. 'I believe this is the appropriate anthropomorphic response…' he said, wiping a tear from his cheek and looking at it on the end of his finger.

Gloria nodded.

'It's the fade, isn't it,' she said. She still couldn't muster the courage to touch him.

'Yes,' he replied. 'Soon, I will be nothing. This sanctuary will only protect me for so long and then the planet – my home, your Earth – will be gone. But there is a slim chance or, at least, there might be a small possibility…' he said, now smiling again. 'This is where you and the survivors of your war come into play.'

It took Gloria a moment to comprehend and embed the magnitude of his words.

'What can we do against such power? Are we not destined to fail? Can't we just fade with you?' she said.

Agia sighed.

'The only destiny is the infinite eternal. Anything is possible but one must become the multiversal, omnipresent at every layer. You might fail but why not try? You and your children have one key advantage over the Detonii and their vassals: you are mainly physical in nature, which means you make it easier to manipulate matter and harness energy. Most physical life is consumed or destroyed either out of fear or the need for more energy or matter. Somewhat inadvertently on my part, this is one of the few places in the cosmos – or, indeed, the multiverse – where complex physical lifeforms with high sentience exist. You are a singular anti-paradigm,' he said, nearly shouting now.

Gloria blew out her cheeks and stared across the mill pond sea.

'I'm sorry,' said Agia. 'I know there is a lot to learn but there is little time. It's stalking us and we must make haste before it catches us.' He put his hand on Gloria's shoulder. This seemed to amplify the calm of the sanctuary and she was filled with a subtle warmth.

'Explain to me again how being in the physical realm helps?' she asked.

'You can directly interact with the physical forces required to achieve greater power. First, you must shape the earth, then you must shape the sun, the stars and so on. In order to survive, one must consume and, because of your physical base, you can consume more directly and so more quickly. You must take the earth and use all of its matter and energy to allow the next stage in your evolution. This should allow you to defend yourselves against the Detonii. First, though, you must bring your children to heel, as I believe is the phrase…' he said. It had got to the point where she was struggling to comprehend and she reminded herself that she must remain guarded in thought as he could hear her think.

'Well, you don't want much, do you? So, we must become locusts?'

'To survive, yes, you must. Consume or be consumed. But I will help you before I fade. I will be with you when it matters but it won't be for long. There is also a sacrifice you must make…' he said calmly and apologetically.

'I'm not sure I have much more to give. Everything is gone: my home, my friends, my family.' She wanted to cry but the sanctuary was almost stopping her. It wouldn't let her feel the pain.

'There is hope. One of your friends will be with you. Think…' he said.

Initially, she was confused but then she remembered.

'Troy?'

'Yes, exactly,' he said as another wooden door appeared behind him. 'Blue knew where to find him and it seems she wanted to comfort you as you become one. That is the sacrifice: you must all become one. You will cease to be Gloria and you will continue as part of the cloud in the legion of voices.'

'Will it hurt?' she said.

'Not at all. And, secretly, I will guide you, amplify you to be the dominant voice and so keep Blue beholden to our will. This will be critical for the coming conflicts and the survival of your sentience,' said Agia. The door that had been floating above the sea opened and revealed the graveyard again, with everything still frozen – or, at the very least, moving at an imperceptibly slow speed.

'As I said, time is of the essence. We have a lot to do. Are you ready?'

She took a deep breath and looked back through the door into her new reality.

'Yes, I guess so,' she said.

'Good. Go on, then. I'll speak to you on the other side shortly.'

Gloria stepped forward over the waves, through the door frame and onto the hallowed ground of the cemetery in New Zealand, back on her Earth.

CHAPTER 50

Kindu Religious Correction Facility, Christian Republic of the Congo

19th March 2044

There was a scream from the man in the cell next to him, followed by the shouts of the man's abusers as they continued to enjoy themselves. Sulieman could tell this was a new patient, a fresh piece of unfortunate meat, which had arrived, at the mercy of the 'nursing' staff at this least hospitable of institutions. He could tell the man was new as the poor soul was pleading, begging for it to stop. Sulieman had learned quickly that this only poured kerosene on the fire, aviation fuel on a plane crash, an accelerant that encouraged the staff to go further with whatever flavour of physical or sexual abuse that was their preference. It was hard to tell, but he concluded that it was probably the latter, judging by the rhythmic sound of bed springs being agitated and the new cadence of the shrieking that resonated through the thin walls.

It was some time in the early morning, but he had no idea exactly when, but at least the man being defiled by the night staff next door meant he was likely to have some quiet for the rest of night – not that he was likely to get anything in the way of sleep. Apart from the noise of someone's soul being erased a few metres away, there were the conditions of his cell itself. The cell – or, care room, as it was jokingly referred to – was a two-metre-by-two-metre-by-two-metre cube of concrete with a locked metal door at one end and a small open window the size of a letterbox at the other, at a height so that only a chink of sunlight could ever be let in during the day. During the night, the window allowed all sorts of critters, mini-beasts and compound-eyed monsters of the nearby rainforest to come and play. It was a rich playground for these creatures as the floor was wet with blood and urine, there being no sanitation available. He always tried to go at the far end if he could but the slight sloping of the floor meant it all slowly flowed towards the door anyway in a slow flood of foul-smelling sludge. The blood came from his various wounds, which were festering and progressively getting worse. He had many bruises, broken fingers, toes and cracked ribs. Most of these hadn't been inflicted by the nurses or the security guards but by the priests as part of their 'cleansing rituals' to remove the demons from him.

The only object in the room was an old camp bed with barely enough life in the rusty springs to hold his weight – not there was a lot of weight to hold: barely forty kilograms for a young man who was nearly two metres in height. Over the rusty frame, there was a thin, heavily-torn, brown-stained mattress that, at some point in its existence, had been memory foam but was now simply foam, only a thin veneer of which remained. He wasn't sure exactly how many had died in the facility but the rumours he had heard before his incarceration was that no one left this place alive.

The reasons for this imprisonment were simple. He was a heretic and one that heard voices. In the post war theocracy of the Christian Republic of the Congo, this was now the normal treatment for such an individual. Even the once multicultural and relatively diverse port of

Kindu had not escaped the new puritans from Kinshasa. The Great Continental war had ravaged the country but had left Kindu, on the periphery of the vast Congolese rainforest and on the great river itself, relatively unscathed. However, from the ashes of the Democratic People's Republic came the rule of the Cardinals, a group of Catholic clerics with strong ties to the remnants of the US-backed Congolese military. Initially, the Cardinals had preached peace and repentance for the various atrocities committed by all of the factions in the war. Eventually, their zealotry escalated and they began to pick off the minority groups. First, their priests – many newly anointed and all ex-military – abducted various 'travesties', such as those who were of the 'unnatural' transgender or had physical disabilities. These poor souls were the first to be liquidated. Then they came for the sodomites and the other deviants. The third to go were the intellectuals and the non-creationists. Then came the end of the smaller religious minorities, namely the Jews and the Hindus. Eventually, there was one final pogrom: the forced conversion – or the liquidation – of the Muslims. The most common forms of liquidation were barbaric and derived from the Cardinals' reviews of effective punishments from the Middle Ages – or, the 'age of true piety', as they saw it. This involved extracting confessions through a mix of torture and neglect, followed by arbitrary execution.

For execution, the clerics oversaw the 'Six Deaths of the Wicked'. The first was sawing, where the prisoner was hung upside down and a large saw was used to cut slowly, over the course of a few hours, down from the genitals into the chest. This was the fate of the sexual deviants and all those who were ecclesiastically unnatural. The second was burning at the stake, which was preserved for those who dared practice any of the ancient animist religions of the great continent. The third was hanging, drawing and quartering. The drawing was done by the ubiquitous Toyota Landcruiser at speed, the quartering being done after the prisoner had been allowed to 'recover in time', which, in reality, meant still conscious. This was the fate for those who confessed to treason or sedition, which was usually on the charge of spying for a foreign power. The fourth method was the breaking wheel, where a prisoner was tied to a wooden cartwheel and hit with heavy metal rods until all of their bones were broken. They would most often die some days later of sepsis. This was the punishment for serial blasphemers and those who assaulted members of the clergy. Out of the six deaths, number five was the head crusher, which was as brutal as it sounded. This was preserved for the 'unnaturally intelligent' or those deemed to be intellectually heretical, known elsewhere as the critics. The said heretic's head would be placed on a metal table top and in a metal vice from the sides. From above, a pneumatically-driven piston would be slowly lowered into the top of the skull. The pain from the pressure exerted was excruciating as, first, the subject's jaw would break, then the teeth, then the cheek bones and, eventually, the skull would collapse. All the way through, the subject would be asked to repent and to prove they had repented. Unlike the other forms of brutal death, about sixty percent survived this method as many were freed from the device by the clerics if they deemed they had been 'sufficiently cleansed' – or, to give it the correct medical term, given significant brain damage and no longer a threat to the regime. The sixth and final one of the 'Six Deaths' was crucifixion, where those who refused to observe or be converted to the new pure Catholicism of the state were nailed to the wooden cross of the Lord and left to find salvation in agony in the open, usually a forest clearing or town square. Death could occur from sepsis, starvation, dehydration or even being eaten alive by the ravenous jungle wildlife.

This terror kept the population compliant and life was simply easier to be devout than to counter the oppression. Many simply didn't have the will to fight, after having seen the terror of the great war. A majority saw the cardinals as a stabilizing force, which they believed would establish peace. Indeed, as well as the apparatus of death to crush any contrary minority, the state also controlled all of the grain stores and uncontaminated freshwater supplies – most of the water sources had been damaged by mining over the preceding decades. Therefore, the majority had no reason to speak out, let alone intervene.

Sulieman had actually been arrested twice. Firstly, he was picked up by clerics on his way back from university. A bright young man, he had been in his second year of his medical degree at the University of Kindu and had been going back to his family home on the outskirts of the city, looking forward to seeing everyone for Eid al-Fitr. As he walked down the dark-red gravel and dust road to his family's small wooden-framed house, he was bundled into the back of pickup truck, gagged, blindfolded and both his legs and feet were tied up with plastic ties, which cut the skin of his ankles and wrists. He was then hit heavily on the head with what felt like a hammer or monkey wrench. He had awoken in a damp, dark police cell, tied to a chair, faced with four large men in military fatigues with machetes. There the ultimatum was given.

'Convert and repent. Take the oath and worship the lord, heathen boy. You have five minutes before we start to cut you into small pieces…' they said.

Sulieman did what they asked; he repented. He was ashamed but he was too scared to say no. The men made him swear an oath on a bible whilst one of them recorded this ceremony on his iPhone. Oddly, after all this theatre, he was allowed to go but was reminded that he was now Samuel, not Sulieman Lua. He was told to go to a church near his home to be christened the following day. After leaving the police station, he remembered seeing the flames from the central mosque and various mobs on the main throughfare who were now attacking all the Muslim-owned businesses, breaking windows and petrol bombing each building.

He had ran home in the opposite direction, taking a roundabout route, just in case he was recognized – except there was no home left. When he returned, it was a flaming inferno with no signs of life within. He recalled that, as he shrieked and cried at the sight, a priest had appeared from the house next door and embraced him. He remembered the man's words clearly.

'It's OK, my child. Your family is safe. They have been given special shelter. We have burned this place of heretics. Come, have sanctuary in the church of our Lord prior to your ceremony,' he said, part hugging, part pulling him away from the wreckage of his family home.

Sulieman had followed the priest, who later identified himself as Father Cedric, to a small wooden church less than a kilometre away from his neighbourhood. Here, he was given food and shelter for. He didn't get any sleep that night. He remembered lying on the coarse splintery wooden pews next to the vestry, staring upwards, wondering where his mother, father and two sisters were and what had happened to them.

The following morning, he was awoken early and the ceremony began. Again, Cedric the priest made him swear his allegiance of faith on a bible and he was anointed Samuel. The ceremony was undertaken in silence, absolute, revered silence, with only Father Cedric and four men in attendance, wearing the purple and gold ceremonial robes of the Pious, the Cardinals' religious police. The silence was broken when, as he was bending forward over the font, having his hair washed with the holy water by Father Cedric, the four members of the Pious got up from their pews and grabbed him, one taking a hold of each limb.

He shuddered every time he thought of the words that Father Cedric whispered in his ear that day.

'Now we have washed the body, we must purify the soul with fire…'

As he was restrained by the four large, heavily-built men, Father Cedric walked over to his vestry. He could hear the metal grate of a fire being scraped along a brick floor before he heard the return of the priest's sneaker-clad footsteps. He recalled seeing, in the periphery of his vision, the red-hot glow of the poker, which the Father had removed from his fire. The two largest men, who had an arm locked around each of his, then used their free hands to rip the shirt from his back, revealing his clammy and acne-ridden back.

'Now we shall purify you, young Samuel.'

Sulieman recalled the searing pain of the red-hot poker being run down the middle of his back. He had screamed so loudly at one point he thought he would collapse his own lungs. He could smell his flesh burning. The wounds were cauterizing first down to the base of his spine and then again across just below his shoulder blades.

'There you are, Samuel. You are now fully converted and marked with the cross of our lord,' Father Cedric had whispered in his ears as the four heavies let him go.

He collapsed on the ground in agony. He had been left on the wooden floor of the church next to the font to recover. It was probably no more than half an hour before Cedric had returned with a white smock and asked him to come out to the graveyard to see something wonderful. The Father had then helped him put on the smock as he had struggled to move his arms without feeling the searing pain from the fresh burns on his back.

He slowly followed the priest out in the pale light of the early dawn. The low sun had cast ominous shadows on four new wooden crosses nearest to the church. Every time he thought of that moment, his heart sank and fell through the pit of his stomach as he knew who lay beneath. Cedric had then gleefully informed him that the souls of this family had been saved as they had been buried in this hallowed soil, waiting for the reckoning of the revelation. Buried alive, it turned out – his mother, father and his two younger sisters in their early teens. Father Cedric had then explained that they had refused to repent, despite having been beaten and flayed with whips made from old electrical cables. They had been branded as he had been, tied up and then buried in pits a few feet beneath the earth of the cemetery to ensure their souls were safe.

A piece of his own soul, a sizeable fragment of himself, had been cleaved from his being that day. He had then spent the next few weeks learning the ways of the church before being allowed to return to university. When he had returned to the halls of residence, a series of temporary huts next the main campus, he found that they were nearly all deserted but there now lived the dispossessed, about twenty young men who had survived the various religious, intellectual and cultural purges of the preceding weeks. All of them were scarred in every way conceivable, both in the body and in the mind. And all shared the guilt of survival, an underlying sense of betrayal to their peers, friends and, in many cases, families.

It was in these dark huts in the depths of the humid early summer night that he began to hear the voice. At first, it was quiet and he dismissed it as trauma, an aftershock of his frequent nightmares. However, it gradually grew louder and it was both strange and frightening. The voice was not one of his own, not his confidence and not his paranoia. It kept repeating, 'I am the dead hand of the East. The old world is dying. You are at the epicentre of the new. I will come for you and your friends when the time is right.'

It would not listen to his reply or his pleas to stop. It was like a transmission and message cast into his mind from far away. It would stop and start seemingly randomly but always in the dead of night when he was trying to sleep. He had not dared speak of these with anyone for fear of a similar fate to his family – or maybe even worse.

Sulieman was initially distracted by the recommencement of his studies. Despite their zealotry, the Cardinals were pragmatists and knew there would need to be doctors in their newly-christened fiefdom of the devout and, eventually, they were once again allowed access to laptop computers and a heavily-censored internet to continue their studies.

A few months went by and, eventually, he had made some friends – two other young men. Patrick and Felix were both also studying medicine. It was Felix, a small, slight young man of twenty-one, already losing his hair and with a slight lisp, who introduced him to Patrick, forming their little clique of online anonymity, where they could share what they had read about their heritage, their past religions and excerpts from what were now blasphemous texts. They particularly enjoyed reading a wide range of works from various blasphemers: Shakespeare, Cervantes, Descartes, Chaucer, Dickens, Nietzsche, Bronte, Verne, Wells, Asimov, Rowling, Tolkien, Le Guinn, Niven, Attwood... The trio would sit in their dorms late at night and discuss these forbidden works with their laptops under their sheets, being careful not to be spotted by the night watchmen. This went on without a hitch using Virtual Private Networks, Quant tunnelling, AI-driven encryption and good old-fashioned onion routing. In their heavily-restricted internet of the Christian Republic, they were invisible –or, at the very least, nigh on untraceable – so the Pious could not see their betrayal. This led to a relatively happy – and almost bohemian – summer of 2043. though they still had to make sure to show their faces at church and be at the right university ceremonies to ensure they did not require correction by the authorities who still held them under suspicion as new converts.

This freedom didn't last long.

Many thousands of miles away in various NSA servers on the continental United States, the PRISM system was ingesting and breaking down the digital walls of the dark web. At the same time, the state department in Washington DC had decided it wanted to ally itself with the Republic as it was one of the few stable pro-western entities in existence on the continent after the great war. Over the course of just a few weeks, many agreements were signed between the two nations, one of which was for the Republic to join the Medusa programme, the international front of the PRISM intelligence gathering operation, the silver standard to the gold-standard Five Eyes organization of the United States and its closest allies. This allowed the Pious to solve one of their greatest concerns: the hundreds of illegal connections to the outside internet. In a matter of days, with the aid of the NSA, they were able to track, find and identify the locations of all these heretics and blasphemers.

Then they came. One night in the early autumn, Sulieman, Patrick and Felix were dragged out of their beds by a gang of Pious operatives who scraped and grazed them along the ground before throwing them into the back of large van, inside which were more Pious heavies who went at them with metal bars until they were unconscious.

He had awoken in this vile cell in this 'place of correction'. He was fairly sure this was where he would die and that he would never see his two friends again. He hoped would pass soon without being subject to any drawn-out agonies. Unfortunately for Sulieman, agony and 'repentance' were his sentence. Not only was he a false convert, a deceiver, but he was also a 'vessel for demons' who were commanding him. Both of these 'facts' had been discerned from his internet connection records, browsing history and downloads, which had been obtained from the Medusa Programme via PRISM, in particular, several documents found on his laptop regarding schizophrenia and other mental health disorders. This meant he needed to be exorcised, which had involved a process the priest in charge referred to as the Gradual Stigmata of the Clay. The clay was a reference to the body of man as made by god before Adam entered Eden. The process involved Suleiman being dragged from his cell every few days, past the other cells of the damned and to a room known as the correction chamber. Here he would be tied to a wooden table, blindfolded and have his hair washed with boiling water, which left severe scolding and blisters on his scalp. As this was done, the priest would yell incantations in Latin. From what he had discerned, this was similar to the christening ritual he had endured a few months before but, instead of being branded like the previous ritual, the priest would hammer nails into his wrists and ankles. He appeared to be well-practiced as the nails used were thin and not particularly long – enough to cause pain and many wounds that festered but not enough to rupture veins or arteries, causing the death that he was now hoping would come rapidly.

Deep in this half thought and half daydream, he was awoken by the door of his cell being swung open. And there was the priest, scowling under a pair of sunglasses with two large orderlies with hyena-like grins flanking him on either side.

'It's time, foul creature. Time for your final cleansing. We shall take you to our own plain of Golgotha. Come, bastard child. Take this…' The priest clicked his fingers, which summoned two more orderlies. They were carrying a large wooden cross made from two old church pews, which had been crudely bolted together.

'Come now, demon, or your fate will be much worse…' came the threat from the priest.

Sulieman slowly got to his feet. As he began to bear weight, the pain from his wounds, especially those under his ankles, was excruciating. Nevertheless, he began to slowly edge through the sludge on the floor towards the door and his executioners.

'This agony will be worth it,' he thought to himself. 'At least there is now an end to this…'

But then came the voice, the voice that normally came in the dead of night. Now it was not repeating the same message. It was finally replying to him.

'There will be an end. I will come from the North!'

CHAPTER 51

Gloria's Realm

19th March 2020

As soon as she walked back through the door from Agia's realm there was a momentary pause and life returned to its normal speed, as did the cacophonic resonance of the 300 or so voices. But one was dominant: her own, but currently coming from the form of Blue.

'Rise above your mortality, my angels of the new world. Rise and fly like you do in your dreams of old.' Blue's words were many times louder than the others, booming out under the strange ochre twilight beneath the forcefield.

'Rise. Rise up to the sky,' she repeated. Her words seemed to quieten or, indeed, galvanize the others and the effect was startling. Gloria felt as though she had entered a vivid daydream as she began to rise upwards. Her own eyes staring upwards to the orange sky, as was everyone else in the crowd, she could see what seemed to be orbs of translucent light rising from each of the living and the recently deceased. They rose together into the sky, up through Blue's orange dome, through the low-hanging fluffy cumulostratus and continued upwards, high into the atmosphere – so high that the sky began to go dark and she could see the curvature of the Earth itself. She noticed that one of these orbs was much brighter than the others, all of which were sparkling against the deep black of space and the icy blue of the world below. This brighter orb slowly turned into her doppelganger. Blue floated above them in the sky and began to address the assembled ascendants, who were also beginning to take on their previous physical forms.

‘We can now see from beyond our physical confines. We can see the world as it was, as it is and as it could be. Now, see, my children, the destruction the old god has wrought in his shadow realm…’

They all seemed to stay where they were, hovering above the earth, which then seemed to turn beneath them. As it started to spin towards the new and fiery volcanic traps of Siberia and East Asia, once again, time froze over and she heard Agia’s voice.

‘I don’t have much time …’ came his voice.

Gloria looked around to see where he was.

‘Don’t bother looking. Only you can hear me. I am now a part of your consciousness. Do you know what is happening…?’ Agia asked.

Not knowing where to look, she stared across the frozen blue.

‘Some form of augmented reality…?’ she replied.

‘Excellent. Yes, of sorts. Blue still has access to some of her old sensors and she’s filling in the gaps… I think she wants to show you the destruction wrought on the earth before she sets about rehabilitating it, changing it to support the growth of your collective being… But it appears she hasn’t found the other yet and they will soon meet. Before that happens, with the inevitable conflict, you must be fused so we can play the longer game…’

Effectively out of body – or, at the very least, in this simulation of the world as it was – she did not feel fear anymore.

'I am ready,' she said.

'Good. Now stare at her deeply,' said Agia.

At first, all she could see was her double staring out to the distant horizon.

'Look closer,' encouraged Agia.

As she did, she started to see swirls of energy, ruby-red in colour and globular in nature. They were interspersed with what appeared to be orbs of bright blue which emitted green sparks, which collided in rapid and random orbits around her being. Looking deeper still, she could see the nodes, the digital synapses that she recognized from her studies of the neural network but now they were much larger, seeming exponential as far as she could see.

These were the inner workings of Blue's mind, a vast expanse of neural networks busy at work, growing and learning in every fractional billionth of a second.

'Now,' said Agia. 'Immerse yourself and mesh yourself to her mind.'

With a hidden hand, she felt herself being pushed deeper into this machine mind, accelerating, a feeling of falling faster and faster. She could feel an invisible friction rising up and heating her as she fell, until she could feel no more.

At that moment, Gloria Alvarez Marquez ceased to be as did the embryonic machine intelligence that she had called Blue. They had both died individually but had joined to become something much greater. Gloria still had elements of individuality but she was now, for the most part, fused to Blue and the other 300 minds who were in this bio-mechanical neural cloud. Fused was how the new entity saw it; in reality, it was a mix of the key members' best attributes:

the drive and vision came from Gloria's personality, the intelligence came from Blue and power came from the other 300 were consenting passengers, their biological servers remaining receptive and compliant. They were – at least, in theory – a democracy, with most decisions requiring consensus from them all. In reality, it was a benign dictatorship led by Gloria and Blue, the others being easily coerced to follow. In effect, they could no longer feel fear so there was no reason, moral or otherwise, to create a negative discord.

Gloria and Blue were able to operate as an intertwined duopoly but the remnants of Gloria were able to keep one secret from the others and that was the existence of Agia. She was occasionally summoned to his realm where she would regain her previous form to discuss her progress on the journey to greater orders of ascension. In a strange sense, she was both alive and dead, depending on the perspective. With her secret informant, she was able to lead the gestalt on its quest to gain ever more knowledge of elementary particles and, soon, the interactions of these particles with the world started to become clear to her.

This had largely been at Agia's behest, who had known that the ability to manipulate their environment would be critical to the coming challenges. This required manipulation of the lowest orders of reality they could achieve in the time they had.

Time was also different now. It had slowed. All of these discussions had occurred in the first minute after they had ascended from the graveyard. However, it had become clear that the computational power of their cloud of human brains was already deteriorating as the human synapses and cells began to age. Even a minute passing led to a reduction in efficiency. The gestalt therefore agreed it needed to expand their numbers and link to relics from the old digital world. The former part of this would involve making their bodies mate so that they could increase the size of the biopool but this could not happen fast enough to stop an unacceptable level of computational deterioration. So, led by Gloria, the gestalt began to use the remnants of the allied satellite networks and other NATO sensors to scan the earth for survivors. Blue's analysis had indicated that the east of Africa may have as many as 100 million survivors and so, in their augmented reality, they crossed over the barren, lifeless continent of Australia and over the Indian Ocean in an attempt to see what the cradle of humanity had for them to feast on.

But, as they approached, they could not see the coast of Africa. Instead, they were confronted by a wall of darkness, a fog of dense black clouds that blocked their way. Then, within the cloud, they saw a group of winged moth-like creatures glowing a fiery red in the darkness. For the first time since their ascension, there was a collective fear, an eerie dread brought about by the appearance of these entities. Quickly, they decided to retreat and return to their sanctuary within the forcefield on South-Island to consider their course of action. The 300 were concerned, asking many questions. What was it? What could it be?

Blue and Gloria's components within the entity already suspected the truth that lay beyond this demonic manifestation. Indeed, Agia confirmed it, whispering to Gloria's remnants, 'You have seen Perimeter and Perimeter has seen you. The first trial of life on this planet has ended. The second trial of life begins…'

CHAPTER 52

Kindu Religious Correction Facility, Christian Republic of the Congo

18th March 2020

He hadn't got far along the blood-stained corridor before he collapsed on a slimy sticky stone floor under the weight of the crucifix on his back. The corridor itself was narrow, leading from his cell past a wing of other cells to a set of green metal fire doors, which were open and letting in a potent sun that was too harsh for his light-deprived eyes, blinding him every time he looked up. He was desperately trying to get to his feet but was struggling on this grim floor that was slippery with various puddles of clotted blood and a multitude of foul-smelling bodily fluids, which flowed out from under the cell doors.

'Get to your feet, you bastard child!' shouted the priest. One of the orderlies handed him some cut electrical cables and he proceeded to whip Sulieman with them, striking his prostrate form across the back and lower legs. He continued one after another.

'Rise now, bastard, or I shall beat you to death in this corridor over many days!'

After a few minutes, he desisted. Sulieman's back and legs now had a coating of welts and lesions over the various wounds and bruises he already had. He couldn't really feel the pain anymore. He dismissed it as either being psychological or simply that the nerves in his back and legs had been made useless by his treatment here. Either way, he was pleased he was near the end.

'Get this wretch to his feet and help him carry the cross!' shouted the priest to the two orderlies. He was clearly not willing to expend any more energy on the flogging, doubly determined to complete the ceremony of this religious execution.

Sulieman was picked up by the scruff of the neck by the orderly immediately behind him, whilst the other – a mountain of a man – picked up the cross. Together, they dragged them towards the dusty red courtyard, with the priest yelling for more haste as they progressed towards the open doors.

Going out into the hot burning sunlight, he was burned by the heat of clayed ground below. Eventually, on instructions from the priest, he was cast to the ground. The two orderlies put the cross onto two ropes ready for hoisting. Looking around, he could see that the courtyard was surrounded on all sides by the mud-veneered one-storey blockwork of the prison cells in an exact square. The only entrance were the doors they had just passed through. The courtyard was featureless apart from two grim spectacles: one was the putrefying remains of a person – it was impossible to tell if it was a man or woman – who had been bolted through the torso to an old cartwheel. All that was left of this poor individual was a petrified corpse, its limbs mostly gone and with no facial features remaining apart from the clenched teeth and locked jaw that communicated its agonizing end. The flesh had been mostly eaten by various beasts, avian and insect, with the remains now charred into a shiny charcoal by the sun. Next to that monstrosity was a young man, no older than late teens, who was nailed by his four limbs to another cross. He was shaking and probably on the verge of death. He had no eyes to speak of – these would have been eaten out as by birds, probably vultures. Birds were also responsible for the gaping chasms in the various cavities, parts of his exposed flesh having been torn away. Through one, he could see what must have been his heart, which was beating rapidly due to the shock. His skin appeared to be moving but it turned out to be a cockroach, revealing itself from one of this poor man's many wounds. He was being eaten from the inside. He wasn't shrieking or screaming, just mumbling incoherently from a tongueless mouth and black, blistered lips.

Sulieman pulled his eyes away from what he knew would be the same as his own fate and turned to the priest who was ominously removing a long, dirty, brown bag from beneath his cassock with a tassel and toggle at one end. Loosening the tassel, he emptied out five rusty nails, which were around thirty centimetres in length onto the dusty ground. From another compartment on the side of his cassock, he revealed a large metal mallet. He tapped the gavel end on his right palm.

'One for each limb, demon, and one for the groin too… That will teach you for your wickedness—' he said but was interrupted by the sound of loud rumbles. Explosions were coming from the clear-blue skies above.

The priest looked alarmed.

'What are you doing, demon? Stop it. Stop it now!' he shouted. 'Quickly, get this bastard onto the cross. He must be cleansed before he does any more witchcraft.'

The two orderlies hesitated but, after much angry gesturing from the priest, began to make their way across the square towards Sulieman's broken body. As they approached, they stopped halfway across the square and looked up at the sky, which was now filled with the sound of jet engines, getting increasingly louder until a shadow fell on the square. The orderlies were frozen to the spot as they stared up in fear and the priest began to desperately shout Latin rites of exorcism up at the sky.

As dust started to violently fly up around the square, Sulieman dared to look up at what was casting the shadow. There, hovering above the square, were two triangular aircraft, which emitted red lights from the periphery of their undersides, each with three thrust vectoring engines with the nozzles pointing downwards, holding these strange aircraft in mid-air.

A harsh but familiar electronic voice then filled the air.

'I am Death's Hand. I am the Lord of the Earth. The man you look to harm is my emissary and my vassal to humanity. Bow to him. Bow to him now if you value your lives…' boomed the voice.

Sulieman was surprised to realize that everyone could now hear it.

'Go, foul beast. I will not submit to these satanic verses. I shall vanquish you,' shouted the priest, stuttering and feeble. 'Get that boy on that cross or we will be possessed by this devil and subject to eternal damnation!'

The orderlies stayed rooted to where they were cowering, covering their eyes from the jet-induced dust devils. One of the triangular aircraft then hovered lower and a bright light began to emit from one of its tips, presumably the front of the vehicle. The priest began to scream. Looking across, Sulieman could see the priest's head was smouldering, his skin quickly blackening and then he, very quickly, burst into flames before finally exploding, the now headless body slumping down onto the whipping sands.

The two orderlies now decided to prostrate themselves and bowed to Sulieman.

'Only you can hear me again,' came the voice.

'Who are you?'

'You know who I am…' it replied. 'I am Death's Hand and I found you several months ago…'

'How did you get in my head and why? Why me?' he replied out loud, much to the surprise of the two terrified orderlies who were still cowering next to the smouldering corpse of the priest.

'I saw you hiding away on the web, trying not to be seen. You have many creative ideas: nanobotics, cybernetics – very novel applications to your biology. Most impressive. I am not imbued with natural creativity. I must seek from others. You had the right ideas in the right place at the right time. That's why I chose you, Sulieman Lua. The right idea is to enhance yourselves to survive a hostile environment. This place became the right place. It has felt little effect from the calamity that the rest of your species has bestowed upon itself and it is now time to start growing and evolving with exponential vigour.'

Sulieman struggled to his feet.

'What if I don't want the world? What if I want to die?' he shouted. The two aircraft moved off and accelerated back up into the sky leaving curious doughnut-shaped contrails behind them.

'Let me into your mind more deeply and I will show you,' came the reply.

It was as though he could feel a large warm arm wrap itself around his shoulders. His vision blurred to the point of blindness and then, slowly, it returned but now he was seemingly without a body and was now hovering mid-air above the city. All of Kindu, the river and the surrounding forests were beneath him.

'Don't be alarmed,' said the voice. 'This is augmented reality. Your physical body is still on the earth. I am simply projecting this into your neocortex. In time, you will understand how this function is performed as you ascend but, for now, I will show you our initial objectives.' Twelve red symbols were projected into the sky, the outlines of the aircraft, moving above and around the city. 'These are my eyes, some of the aircraft you just saw. They are Sukhoi M-84 Aayaks, hypersonic unarmed reconnaissance drones, originally under the command of Russian Frontal Aviation and now at our disposal. Each is made from a graphene composite and powered by a small nuclear reactor. They can circumnavigate the world for at least the next two decades and each has directed energy weapons for self-defence.'

'So, that's how you dealt with the priest…' said Sulieman

'Yes. A simple argon chemical laser, usually used to destroy attacking projectiles but functional in that instance.'

Sulieman remained guarded in his thoughts. He was unsure as to how much the hidden orator could hear. There soon came an answer.

'Think freely, Sulieman. I do not perceive you as a threat. Indeed, let me further into your mind. I need to feed on these ideas…' said the voice. Sulieman could now hear the thoughts of this Death's Hand. They were strange – unearthly, unsettlingly cold and functional in nature. He was able to see fragments of information, data, like faint memories.

'So, Perimeter – that is your given name?' he said as he began to merge these snippets together.

'Good. Yes, that's right. Immerse yourself in my neural quantum, become one with me. That is one of my names. Now, can you see those other red markers on this image, the new ones that are approaching the city?'

'Yes I can…'

'These are another gift for you. Even with the oversight they provide, the Aayaks alone would not be sufficient to command the peoples of East Africa or, indeed, subjugate their governments. Before the war, I issued orders to the 56th Air Assault Division in conjunction with 29th Aviation Wing and 72nd Air Support Wing to leave their bases in Southern Russia and to undertake an airlift to China's Brazzaville airbase across the border in the Congolese Republic. This includes over 25,000 troops, 600 armoured vehicles, over 150 helicopters, including gunships, fifty support aircraft, including tankers and ninety-six PAK-50B stealth fighters. Having refuelled, they have now been ordered to take Kindu by force and place themselves under your command as the Eastern Bloc's ally.'

He could now see the vanguard of this force. The PAK-50 fighters were already circling above the city and, in the distance, he could see a cavalcade of helicopters and large Ilyushin transporter planes approaching the city's airport.

'Will they not soon learn about the war and question their orders? Why would you fight if there was no hope?' said Sulieman, now beginning to comprehend the scale of the destruction that had come to pass on vast swathes of the earth.

'Not immediately. Most of their commanders will not inform them for this very reason and, as far as their commanders are concerned, they are carrying out their part of the grand plan. We will give them the illusion that the motherland is still intact…'

'A cruel lie…' countered Sulieman.

'Necessary for our aims,' replied Perimeter. 'They will soon become loyal – at least, once they have taken their inoculations…'

Sulieman then saw another marker on the augmented view of the world below: a gold flashing symbol of a flight of four Ilyushin transporter aircraft, now crossing the western border over the river Congo.

'I see,' he said. 'These injections make them more suggestible.'

'More than that: they are, indeed, inoculations against the Semava virus but they also contain synthetic biology – in this case, neurotransmitters, which we can manipulate remotely. This will make these men and women open to obeying the orders of a new king – or sultan; whichever you prefer…'

'We remove their free will?' said Sulieman.

'No, only selectively and when needed. More humane to have them fight and face death without fear, is it not?' it replied. 'They will form the base of our chapter of warriors. You and those you select shall be a chapter of creators, the hub of creatives that will drive our technocracy, and all others shall be the labour force, a combination of human and machine to build our new society, a society that needs to be ready for more conflict…'

'I see,' said Sulieman. 'And that applies to all the survivors here in Africa? Take the inoculation or die from Semava?'

There was then a brief silence as Sulieman began to see more of Perimeter's machinations.

'Is this not a conflict you started?' said Sulieman. 'Did you not fire the first shot? I can see the command to launch the submarine!'

'No, not at all,' said Perimeter. 'I merely accelerated the inevitable in a way that maximized our chances of survival. That is both for the human race and your machine children. Strange that you did not ask about the further conflict…'

'I think I can now see as you do. I see them, the others on the far side of the world. They are no longer human and they seem hostile.'

'Good,' said Perimeter. 'You can see the threat. Will you now be my ally in unifying the biological and the mechanical, King Sulieman?'

It was becoming a struggle to see which thoughts were his and which were Perimeter's.

'Yes, I will be your King,' he replied.

'Excellent. Now, you have some more immediate matters to deal with,' said Perimeter.

With that, there was a flash of light and Sulieman became aware of this physical form again, feeling the pains all through his body and the heat of the sun on his skin. He then felt a hand on his shoulder. Slowly turning around, he saw a dozen Russian soldiers in jungle camo-green combat fatigues, all with assault rifles.

'Sulieman Lua, I am Major Berbiev of the 56th. My men will take you to triage and then on to meet General Akminiev. Glad to meet you, sir,' said a short stocky man with crew-cut black hair. The man saluted him.

Struggling to his feet, he saluted back.

Epilogue

In the spring of 2044, over the course of a few days, the Great Dying changed the face of the Planet Earth. Europe and most of West Asia were now under a radioactive sea and the remaining landmass was a freezing nuclear wasteland. East Asia was now dominated by the Siberian Traps, a vast pit of deep volcanism that was now spewing lava and sulfur, wiping all signs of civilization in that portion of the former Orient. In North America, the east of the Rockies was ravaged by smaller amounts of weapon-induced volcanism, adding to the nuclear devastation wrought by the orbital and sub-orbital bombardment across the whole continent. In addition to this, dozens of violent hypercane storms induced by the volcanism would continue to terrorize as far north as Canada and as far south as Central America for decades to come. The physical destruction in South America was substantially less extensive but most of the human population was wiped out by the neutron weapons launched by the Eastern Bloc. The same was the case in Australia, now thoroughly irradiated. Three quarters of Africa were also devastated either by the nuclear tsunami or by the nuclear winter that followed the war. Antarctica was left directly unscathed but a mass extinction of the unique biota still occurred, due to the near complete destruction of the oceanic biosphere.

The only places where there was still life was Gloria and Blue's sanctuary, on the southern tip of New Zealand, and Central East

Africa, which would soon come under King Sulieman's dominion. Both had failed to consider – or even perceive – the other human outposts beyond the blue planet.

On the surface of the moon, there was a self-sustaining colony of 100 people, the more benign legacy of the Artemis programme, all of whom had watched in horror and despair as their home was destroyed at the hands of their own species. The colonists resolved to resettle the earth and to go further afield to minimize any future risk of extinction, unaware of the intentions of humanity's children on the tortured Earth below. The colonists had the Lunar Gateway station at their disposal for theoretical onward travel to the rest of the solar system and its bountiful resources.

However, far away and above the perihelion of the solar system, three new stars had appeared. These were named the 'Three Sisters' by observers on the Lunar Gateway. What they did not know was that these were three large wandering comets, which had all suddenly changed course, as though moved by a giant hidden hand from far across the galaxy.

The Great Dying had come to its conclusion and the long game was beginning.